Necessary Ends

Necessary Ends

A Tai Randolph Mystery

Tina Whittle

Poisoned Pen Press

First Edition 2018

10 9 8 7 6 5 4 3 2 1

Library of Congress Control Number: 2017951353

ISBN: 9781464209833   Hardcover
      9781464209857   Trade Paperback

Poisoned Pen Press
4014 N. Goldwater Boulevard, #201
Scottsdale, Arizona 85251
www.poisonedpenpress.com
info@poisonedpenpress.com

Printed in the United States of America

To my writerly sisters in the Mojito Literary Society—
Annie Hogsett, Susan Newman, Katrina Murphy,
and Laura Valeri.
May the words always be sweet to you.

Acknowledgments

Every time I sit down to the page, I am reminded of the enormous debt of gratitude I owe to so many. And even though I am supposedly a woman of words, I know that words can never truly demonstrate how much the people in my life support and encourage me.

If you've ever answered a weird question about Civil War history, concussions, French grammar, legal procedure, the dirt in North Georgia, animal husbandry, police ten codes or the annual upkeep costs of a Ferrari…then you are my hero. Thank you.

Special thanks to my fellow Sisters in Crime, especially the members of my home chapter, the Low Country Sisters in Crime, which wouldn't exist without our officers Donna Kortes, Maggie Toussaint, and Rebecca Butler; my *Lowcountry Crime* co-authors Jonathan M. Bryant, Polly Iyer, and James M. Jackson (who is also our esteemed publisher); my patient friends Toni Deal, Sharon Hudson, Theresa Booker, and Robin White; the Friday Night Board Game crew—Lisa Abbott, Sean Devine, and Karen Sanders; and my fence neighbors, Danielle and Andy Walden and Sean Clarke.

The debt of gratitude to my excellent and forbearing family just keeps getting greater: my parents, Dinah and Archie; my parents-in-law, Yvonne and Gene; my brother and three siblings-in-law, Tim and Lisa, and Patty and Rich; plus my ever-awesome niece and nephews—Connor, Sydney, Drew, and Hayden.

They say it takes a village to publish a book, and my village is full of geniuses. Many thanks to the fine folks at Poisoned Pen Press—Barbara Peters, Annette Rogers, Diane DiBiase, Robert Rosenwald, Raj Dayal, Suzan Baroni, Beth Deveny, Holli Roach, and Kacie Blackburn. I am also grateful to my fellow PPPers— the Posse—for their warm camaraderie and generous smarts, and my agent Paige Wheeler, for her can-do encouragement and unfailing support.

And—as always and forever—much love to my husband, James, and daughter, Kaley. Y'all provide the spin that keeps my world in motion.

Chapter One

The closet was narrow and dusty, with barely enough room for me to stand. Dead insects crunched under my sneakers, and spider webs glued themselves to my ponytail. Though empty of appliances and devoid of air conditioning, the foreclosed duplex was crammed with beat-up sofas and ratty mattresses, and it smelled like sawdust and old shoes. Faux suburban meth-dealer chic.

Trey handed me a weapon. "Do you remember the plan?"

I wrapped my hands around the gun, a semi-auto designed to shoot projectiles, not bullets. My palms were slick with sweat, and I had to concentrate to keep the thing from thudding to the floor.

"Surrender," I said.

"Because?"

"This scenario is designed to practice surrender protocol."

"And you are not to…?"

"Fight. Not even a little bit." I wiped my hands on my jeans one at a time. "What are their chances of getting past you?"

"Not very good. These particular trainees haven't yet grasped the concept of three-sixty periphery."

"But they will, after they tangle with you."

A ghost of a smile flickered at the edge of Trey's mouth. "Yes."

He knelt and adjusted my protective vest. He was dressed for special ops—his black BDU pants paired with a long-sleeved tee, also black, plus his old service boots, the ones he'd shoved into storage almost four years ago. His orange-tipped training weapon was a ridiculous contrast, but it was the only thing keeping me in the moment. Otherwise, it would have been easy to get pulled back in time into his SWAT days, and to believe that the Trey on his knees in front of me was the Trey I'd never met, the man who'd existed before the car accident, before the frontal lobe damage, the Trey who really was a cop and not just volunteering at a training session.

I brushed a stray cobweb from his dark hair. "If any of them do make it past you, I'm going to get pocked with paintballs."

Trey stood and double-checked my body camera, wiped a smudge from my eye protection with his sleeve. "If you surrender and drop your weapon, you're supposed to come out unharmed. That's the protocol."

I sneezed. He produced a bottle of allergy medicine from some hidden pocket, and I swallowed two tablets dry.

"Does this really help?" I said.

"For the dust, yes. The pigeons, however…"

"Not the pills, these scenarios. Deliberately wading into a simulation where people come after you. Does it really make the nightmares better?"

Trey stopped messing with my gear, his blue eyes serious in the slanted light. "Yes. It does."

When my brother the psychologist had suggested moving Trey back into simulations training, I hadn't been convinced. I still wasn't. But I knew he needed something, some way to work out the part of him that sometimes sizzled like an overloaded circuit. There was only so much aggression he could exorcise through running, after all, and smothering it with routine and structure hadn't worked either. He needed an outlet, and this one—one without actual bullets and bad guys—seemed a safe alternative.

I adjusted my goggles and felt for the spare ammo on my belt. Training rounds, the SWAT version of paintballs. Each pellet contained a harmless green dye, though for actual combat, they came as capsaicin-filled pepperballs. Trey had assured me that the hot shots were banned for this scenario. Only green boxes on the training ground, only orange-marked weapons. It was an elaborately structured game of cops and robbers, and I was a robber. So was Trey.

He gave me a searching evaluation. "Are you sure you're okay?"

"I'm sure."

He watched my mouth to make sure I was telling the truth. I was. Mostly.

"Okay," he said. "But remember, you can leave at any time. Tell the sentry you're vacating the scenario." He lowered his head to look me in the eye. "You're not trapped here, Tai. Not at all."

It was the right thing to say. "Ten-four. I'm good. Let's go."

Trey gave me one final looking-over. Then he closed the closet door, and I was alone in the darkness. I listened to his retreating footsteps, the sudden silence of his absence. Despite my best efforts, the first prickle of panic rose, and with it, the memories. The suffocating heat of the trunk. The gators bellowing on the banks. The green dot of the laser sight centered on my heart.

I tilted my head back and closed my eyes. *It's just a simulation*, I told myself. *Nothing but fake guns and fake bad guys.* The chemicals surging in my veins were real, though, and my body responded as if the threat were real too. That was the point, I knew, to stir up the adrenaline spike and then deconstruct it. *Rewire the experience*, my brother had explained, *rewire the response.*

I wasn't sure I was buying his theory.

I heard it then, the light susurration of combat gear sliding against ripstop fabric, the unmistakable thump of police boots on the wooden floor. Not from the back, though, where the team was supposed to enter, but from the front. The sentry abandoning his post.

I frowned. This wasn't how things were supposed to play out.

I could feel the slosh of my pulse, and as I wrapped my hands around the butt of the weapon, the nervousness peaked and swelled into…something else. Something darker. I recognized that sharp clean jolt, red at the edges. Red, like my nightmares, like kill or be killed. And in my dreams, I killed. I slashed and screamed and bit and…

I pushed out of the closet, unable to take the confinement a second longer.

The trainee stood in the door, fully turned out in riot gear, his eyes wide and bright behind the plastic visor. He switched his gun my way. "Hands up! Weapon down!"

My vision narrowed to the barrel of the weapon, pointed straight at me, and I remembered in a flash all of the other times I'd stared down the wrong end of a firearm. My hands shook, and my finger itched to squeeze the trigger, but I forced myself to place the gun on the counter, orange muzzle pointing at the wall.

I raised my hands to shoulder height. "I surrender."

The trainee came around the counter, rifle aimed at my heart, and the fight instinct sang in hot spiked surges. He tried to grab my arm, but I snatched it away. He cursed and popped two paintballs into my chest.

The thud against the vest hurt like hell at that close proximity, and I gasped, partly from pain and partly from astonishment. "I just surrendered, you moron!"

"You're down. So get down."

"Screw you."

"I said—"

"Touch me again, and I will rip your arm off!"

I heard the opening of the back door at the other end of the house, the boots, the hushed voices. The covert entry team. And I could feel the panic rising. I was trapped, again, with a man with a gun, again. And I remembered what I was supposed to do—breathe and ground—but suddenly all I wanted to do was get out of there before I lost it, and in my mind, losing it looked like kicking the trainee's kneecaps into jelly.

Behind him, I saw movement at the door. Not Trey. This man wore the same clothes but was shorter, with red hair. Garrity. I was surprised to see him—as the supervisor of this particular training, he was supposed to be evaluating, not participating. He stayed in the threshold, orange-tipped carbine rifle in hand.

The trainee was sharper than I'd expected, though, and he caught the motion too. He whirled around and aimed his weapon at Garrity, a satisfied smirk on his face. "Got you, sir. Nice try, sir."

Garrity pointed to the green splotches on my vest, the gun on the counter. "You shot an unarmed suspect."

The recruit had the decency to color red. "She was noncompliant, sir."

"Like hell. I watched the whole thing through her camera."

"But—"

"There are no buts here. You had your orders. What were they?"

The recruit swallowed hard. "Post up outside, guard the secondary entry point. Sir."

"Right. Which you did not do. You waited for sixty seconds and then started clearing rooms, alone. I could ambush your team right now, and they wouldn't know what hit them because they think you've got the door."

The recruit clenched his teeth. He was wrong, and he knew it, and he blamed me. I could feel him wanting to shoot me again.

"And then you fire on an unarmed subject!" Garrity said. "How will your wife feel when she sees that on the news?"

The recruit straightened his spine. "Husband. Sir."

Garrity stared at him for two seconds. "Let me rephrase. How will it feel when your *husband* is visiting you in prison because you shot and killed an unarmed *surrendering* suspect with her goddamn hands in the air, and so help me, that's where I would send you if you pulled such a fuck-up on my watch."

Then all hell broke loose in the back room. A cacophony of voices, a scuffle, a volley of gunfire.

Garrity leaned backward slightly and stuck his head into the hallway "Seaver!"

"Yes, sir!"

"The count, please."

"Three down and one...make that four down, sir."

Garrity sighed. "They never look up." He returned his attention to the trainee. "And there goes the rest of your team. Y'all some sad-ass police today. Now get outta here before I really lose my temper."

The trainee filed past Garrity, not even brushing shoulders, and Garrity focused his attention on me. Suddenly he wasn't Special Agent in Charge anymore. He was my friend, his eyes tight with concern.

He stepped closer. "Hey? You okay?"

I nodded, but my hands were trembling. Not from fear. From pure thwarted anger. I wanted to hurt somebody, preferably the somebody who'd shot me in the chest, and I wanted it so bad I couldn't stop shaking. Garrity knew the difference. He saw it clearly.

"Ride it out, Tai. Breathe it down." He folded his arms. "Whose idea was it to bring you here today, Trey's?"

I put my elbows to my knees and breathed, trying to get the blood back to my head. "Mine. I read it in one of those books my brother gave him. He said it worked for him. I thought it might work for me."

"Did it?"

I unclenched my fists. There were half-moon indentions where my nails had cut into my skin, and my vision was still red at the edges. "I don't think so."

Chapter Two

I spent the rest of my Saturday at the gun shop, cursing the decrepit air conditioner. It had one job—keep the temperature below eighty degrees in the dinky one-room floor area—and it was failing. But that was early September in the South: good-bye summer, hello more summer.

I untucked my shirt, rolled up my sleeves. Only one customer remained in the shop, a young woman with cut-off denim shorts and brittle blond hair. She wore a tee shirt with the word *Moonshine* emblazoned across the front. Ever since the TV series had started filming in Kennesaw, fans of the Prohibition-era werewolf drama had been showing up at my door in packs, desperate for *Moonshine*-themed hats and posters. I'd pegged her as one of those. But then I'd watched her leave and come back twice, both times visiting the black F150 with the tinted windows parked in front of my door, and I'd known exactly what she was up to.

She was only my fourth customer of the afternoon. Except for my reenactor clientele and their steady appetite for black powder, business had been slow for months. The Civil War's sesquicentennial was over. All the tourists wanted was *Moonshine* merchandise. All the locals wanted was guns and ammo and cheap Confederate flags, the larger the better, which they could get on almost any street corner since every Tom, Dick, and Bubba in town sold them from the back of his pickup truck.

I checked the clock. Five-fifty. I locked the front counter and strolled up next to her. "Can I help you with something?"

She pointed to a Smith and Wesson .45 in the display case. "I need that one."

"You sure? That thing's heavy, with a trigger pull of eight pounds and a kick like a mule."

She twisted her mouth. "I can handle it."

I started to argue some more, but then I heard the unmistakable growl of Trey's Ferrari. Sunshine glinted off the black metal as he pulled into his preferred parking spot next to the empty flower boxes.

The woman's eyes jerked toward the door as Trey came inside. He'd changed out of his special ops outfit into workout pants and a tee, his staying-in clothes. He paused in the threshold, curious, wary. I shook my head. After a second's hesitation, he nodded and went behind the counter. This was his Saturday night routine, running the register while I closed up, and I was always happy to hand off the task. But this time he didn't start sorting receipts. This time he watched the woman, who was getting antsy.

"You gonna give me my gun or what?" she said.

I hooked my thumbs into my pockets. "Nope."

"What?"

"You don't like it, call the cops. I suspect they'll be keen to know why you came in here claiming to want to buy a gun for yourself when in reality you're buying it for your boyfriend in the parking lot."

She blanched. "He's helping me pick it out, that's all."

"From inside his truck?"

"He didn't want to come in."

I tsk-tsked. "Don't blame him there. He's probably got a felony or two under his belt, which means he can't buy a firearm. So he sends you in here to buy it for him, which is illegal, but since I didn't actually sell you a gun, you might only get a few years in prison."

She directed a furious, fearful glare out the window. That was when she noticed the camera above the door. She turned her head abruptly, but then she saw the camera over the other door.

I smiled. "Yeah, your face is on the video instead of his. Every spook in Washington D.C. is running down your record as we speak. You got any secrets? Guess what? They're not secrets anymore."

She made like a jackrabbit for the parking lot. Her boyfriend had the truck started, so she barely had time to shut the door behind her before he was peeling out, kicking up gravel on the sidewalk. Trey watched them drive off. He now had my flashlight in hand, the giant Maglight he'd bought me for my birthday. He was holding it like a police baton.

"Did you get the license plate?" I said.

"I did."

Not a word I'd said to her was true, of course. Well, the cameras *had* caught her face. And I *would* be downloading a still shot into my Do Not Ever Under Any Circumstances Sell A Gun To This Person file for my assistant Kenny.

I switched off the display lights. "I am sick to death of them, all of them. Cheaters. Liars. And I swear if one more person asks me if I have anything with a werewolf on it, I'm gonna commit bloody murder."

Trey held up one hand, and I tossed him the keys. He put away the flashlight and opened the cash register. While he ran the day's tally, I went around pulling the shades and double-checking the burglar bars. The air conditioner coughed and wheezed, like an asthmatic alien on its last legs.

"You didn't stay for lunch," he said, counting bills into neat stacks. "After the scenario."

"I had to get back here."

"You left before I could talk to you."

"You were busy yelling at the entry team."

Trey raised his head. He knew I wasn't telling the whole truth, and I knew there was no use trying to lie—his overly sensitive brain would register the deception before the words left my mouth. The best I could do was throw a bone in some other direction. But it was only him and me in the shop, and I was fresh out of bones.

"Garrity told me what happened," he said.

I joined him behind the counter. "I'm fine. Paint-splattered, but fine. I still have some in my hair, I think."

"Did it hurt?"

"Not much."

"Let me see."

I unbuttoned my shirt to reveal the reddish splotch above my breastbone—it would be a lovely purple bruise in a few days. Trey ran his fingers lightly across the skin. His touch was delicate, but his expression was sharp and annoyed.

"I recommended that individual be dropped from the training program."

"You're just mad because he was mean to me."

"Garrity said the same thing. Nonetheless." He dropped his hands, let them rest hesitantly on my hips. The bloodhound in him could smell something wrong even if he couldn't dig it up easily. "Come back tomorrow. Tomorrow is mantracking at Doll's Head Trail."

"I thought you sucked at mantracking."

"I do. That's why Price is leading it. I'll be the target, which I do not suck at."

Keesha Price. His partner back when he'd been a SWAT sniper with the Atlanta PD. I'd never met her, but I'd heard stories. Suddenly the training held a spark of interest. But then I remembered the sore spot on my chest and the marrow-melting rage that seethed millimeters beneath it.

I shook my head. "I don't know. I mean, I'm happy that reenactment therapy works for you. That's a good thing. But for me? I still got angry. Super angry. Practically homicidal."

"That's to be expected."

"I almost kicked his knees in."

"But you didn't."

"But I wanted to. Real bad."

"And yet you didn't. That's progress."

I looked up at him—so earnest, so wanting to help—and sighed. "I'll think about it. That's the best I can offer."

"Okay. Good. Thank you." He regarded me seriously, his hands still on my hips. "Tai?"

"Yes?"

"I saw the envelope from the lab. Under the drawer in the register." He hesitated again. "Is it the paternity results?"

I kept the curse under my tongue. Damn it, I'd meant to hide the letter before he'd arrived. He knew I'd been waiting to find out whether or not the disreputable bootlegging felon I'd always thought of as my uncle was actually my biological father. He also knew the emotional gut-wrench I'd been going through, so I understood his concern. Still…

"I'm not messing with that right now," I said.

"But—"

"You were the one who told me—and I quote—that I get to make these decisions, nobody else. Not even you, you said."

"Yes. That is true. But sometimes—"

"I know Boone calls you. I know you talk to him."

Trey's eyes narrowed in puzzlement. "Of course you know. I've never hidden—"

"What does he want? To get you on his side? Convince you to give him a chance?"

"No. He simply asks how you're doing. He knows you don't want to talk to him, so—"

"Of course I don't. I don't trust him!" I could feel my heart rate going up again. "You can't trust him either, Trey. Not one bit."

"I don't." His expression remained calm, but his voice was laced with worry. "Do you want me to stop taking his calls? I will if you—"

"I don't know!"

Trey didn't say anything. Six months since that night on the dock, since Boone's revelation, and I still woke up in a cold sweat, remembering. Three people died that night, including his son, who deserved every lick of hellfire he was surely suffering. Boone himself was dying too, though not by the sword. Idiopathic pulmonary fibrosis would be his eventual nemesis. It would be a slow, hard death, robbing him of breath long before it robbed him of life. A different kind of hell, especially for a man as vital as he'd once been.

That night he'd told me he was my father. Which would never be true, no matter what the envelope said. My father was Bennett Randolph, a man of hangdog hazel eyes and a tall, lanky frame, an academic who drank himself into a heart attack when I was twenty. Boone was raw-boned and rough, a former KKK Grand Dragon reformed of any race-hating, though two stints behind bars had not broken him of smuggling and gun-running. He'd married my mother's sister, who had abandoned him with two small boys and fled to parts unknown, probably dying young, as the fast-living and loose-moraled tended to do. That was the story I'd been told, one of them anyway. My mother had edited the family history with a ruthless eye for sanitation, and she hadn't been afraid to revise.

My mother. Lillian Randolph, a poor redneck who'd made good and who was always trying to make better. Always with her eye on a finer horizon, my mother. Whatever had happened between her and Boone, she'd taken it to the grave. I wished Boone had made the same decision.

"It's more than I can deal with right now," I said.

"Okay. It's just that…" Trey stared at the register, his forehead creased in deliberation. "I know Garrity has told you that after the accident, I was…difficult."

"He said you were a pain in the ass."

Trey considered, then nodded. "Not an unfair assessment. But he engaged me, nonetheless. Gabriella too, and your brother, and the PTs. They couldn't make decisions for me, but they reminded me over and over that I had to decide, even if my decision was no. Because no is a choice. Does that make sense?"

I sighed. "It means you're gonna keep bugging me about that envelope, that's what it means."

He winced almost imperceptibly. To an untrained eye, his expression never wavered—he usually seemed to be a combination of annoyed and bored. But there were subtleties, shadings, like quick clouds scudding before the sun.

"I don't like bugging you," he said. "You think I do, but I don't."

I felt myself soften. We bugged each other something awful at times. I stepped closer and slid my arms around his neck, ran my fingers under his collar. His skin was warm, fresh from the shower, his hair still damp.

He moved his hands to the small of my back. "You're doing it again."

"Doing what?"

"Trying to distract me."

"You always say it like I'm laying some trap. Like you're just standing there and then, whoops, suddenly we're making out and you have no idea how it happened."

He pulled me closer, gently, but with definite intent. "I'm not complaining."

My bedroom was upstairs, only a few steps away, but I contemplated taking him right where we stood, with all three security cameras still rolling and the OPEN sign still out. And I could forget the envelope in the drawer. And the bruise on my chest. And the cash register with very little cash in it. I stood on tiptoe, the better to reach his mouth.

The front door jingled. A familiar female voice said, "Uh oh, I'm interrupting something, aren't I?"

I glanced over Trey's shoulder. He turned toward the door as his right hand instinctively reached for the gun he didn't carry anymore.

"Finn," I said.

Chapter Three

Finn Hudson let the door jingle shut behind her. I hadn't seen her in months, not since Savannah. Now she'd materialized in my shop like some Goth fairy, her tawny hair pixie-cut, her slight frame decked head-to-toe in black—black mini, black tights, black stack-heel boots.

Trey stepped away from me, facing her. He kept his body at an angle, his left foot slightly behind, a fighting stance. He didn't trust Finn as far as he could throw her, and I'd seen him throw people quite a ways.

Of course, I didn't trust her either. She was a private investigator who occasionally worked for one of Atlanta's best known defense attorneys, although whether you'd call him infamous or celebrated depended on your frame of mind. For ex-cops like Trey? Definitely infamous. I tended to agree, especially since his firm had represented the racist sociopath who'd tried to kill me not once, but twice.

"What are you doing here?" I said.

She looked around the shop. "Nice place."

"You didn't answer the question."

"Not yet." She smiled. "How have you been, both of you? I've been thinking about you."

"That makes me nervous."

She laughed. She had a lovely bright laugh that rang as false as tinsel. Back during my tour guide days in Savannah, I'd told stories about the glamour, a sheen of magic that disguised a person's true nature. If any human being could conjure such a thing, it was Finn.

"Have a second?" she said.

"For what?"

She flipped the door sign to CLOSED. "It's complicated."

Trey remained silent and taut, like a trip wire. Finn spooked him. He could read most people, separate lies from truth with ease, but Finn was a blank. During the most recent troubles in Savannah, however, she'd been instrumental in our success, dropping us hints and pointing us toward clues that she herself could not investigate. She'd claimed it served her larger moral purpose. I doubted that, though it had served something, that was for sure, and it had served Trey and me well enough.

"Make it simple," I said. "And quick."

"Okay." She kept her expression business-like. "I'm investigating a possible assassination attempt."

"That sounds like a situation for the cops."

"My client wishes to avoid the PR nightmare that would result from filing a police report." She turned her attention to Trey. "Which is why I'm here. I need your help."

It was at this point I realized Finn hadn't come to my shop for me—she'd come for Trey. He realized it too, and immediately went into "absolutely not" mode.

"I don't contract independently," he said. "I'm bound by a strict noncompete clause at Phoenix."

"Yes, yes, I know. Marisa keeps you on a short leash. Not that I blame her—if I were your boss, I would too—so let me rephrase. By help, I mean off the books. Unofficial."

Trey crossed his arms. "I don't—"

"What if I told you that the target of this alleged assassination was Nicholas Talbot?"

Trey's head snapped back. His expression hardened, and I was grateful at that moment he didn't have a gun on him.

"Nicholas Talbot?" I said. "Wasn't he that hotshot Hollywood import who got charged with his wife's murder a few years back? The case is still unsolved, isn't it?"

Trey's voice was level, but his eyes burned. "No. It was solved. But the evidence that solved it was thrown out of court, and Talbot went free."

Uh oh, I thought. Trey was holding a grudge. A big, nasty, deeply embedded grudge, one that he'd cradled and nurtured for a long time. And Finn knew it.

She kept her voice low and calm. "Of course the evidence was thrown out, it was compromised."

Trey glared. "What I saw was not compromised. What I recorded was not compromised. My testimony should have gone into evidence, and it would have gone into evidence if…if…"

He shook his head, frustrated. The words weren't happening. He'd lost them, a casualty of the brain damage exerting itself again, as it did during times of high emotional stress. I placed my hand on his back, which was a rigid sheet of muscle, full lockdown. He looked my way, then back to Finn.

"The evidence demonstrated that the scene was staged to look like a burglary gone wrong. I documented this evidence and turned it over to the crime scene techs, following all the proper protocols. But because the first responding…because he was…"

"Dirty," Finn supplied softly.

Trey didn't reply, but I saw it clear on his face. Finn was right. A dirty cop was the bottom of the barrel as far as Trey was concerned, the worst kind of criminal, and what I was seeing now was a mixture of hatred, disgust, and violation.

"What happened?" I said.

Finn gave Trey a second to fill in the blanks. When he didn't, she started explaining. "The day Jessica Talbot was killed, Trey was second responding to the scene. The first responding, an Atlanta PD patrol officer named Joe Macklin, took an opportunity to stuff his pockets with some of the victim's jewelry. He also altered the scene to hide the theft."

"That did not change the other evidence," Trey said.

"The judge thought it did. Fruit of the poisonous tree."

"The judge was wrong. It was murder. And the murderer went free."

Trey was on high seethe. He was certain where he could not be certain. Where he normally would have hedged with an "approximately," he was now doubling down on wrongness and guilt.

"What does this have to do with us?" I said.

Finn's expression turned businesslike. "I've been contracted by the Talbot Creative Group to investigate—discreetly—whether or not someone tried to kill Nick Talbot last night."

Trey was not biting. "None of this concerns me."

"It should. Your hatred of the man is well-established. There's paperwork on it. And considering how the assassination attempt occurred…"

She trailed off, but I got the gist.

"Let me guess," I said. "Somebody took a shot at him."

She pointed a finger in my direction. "Bingo."

"Is that why you're here?" Trey said. "To accuse me of trying to kill Nicholas Talbot?"

"Of course not. Mr. Talbot is still alive, and if it had been your finger on that trigger, he wouldn't be. Dead simple, that. But if the authorities come, and if they ask Mr. Talbot who in the area might have a reason to want to kill him, your name would go to the top of the list. With a bullet." She smiled tightly. "You might want to be figuring out your alibi."

Trey stared. His hands, normally open, had been clenched into tight fists. I waited for him to speak, but he didn't. Whatever words he had remained locked inside. But he didn't need to say anything. I had this one covered.

"In that case, Ms. Hudson, you're dogging the wrong bush," I said. "Trey was with me last night. At his place. I can vouch for his presence."

"All night?"

"All night."

Trey shook his head. "Most of the night. You were asleep some of the night. So you can't verify that I was there the entire night." He looked back at Finn. "When did the shooting take place?"

"Around ten p.m."

Trey had been asleep then. So had I, which was a sad commentary on my evening.

"This is ridiculous," I said. "You think Trey snuck out of bed, snuck out of his apartment, got in his freaking Ferrari, which has a decibel level of ninety-five, then drove—"

"Two point two miles via Piedmont and Powers Ferry, which at that time of night should have taken less than ten minutes. But no, I'm not suggesting Trey drove that supremely loud car anywhere near Mr. Talbot's home. With his background, he would have left the car in Chastain Park, jogged three blocks, set up in Mr. Talbot's backyard, then took a ping at his head before vanishing once again into the night. Round trip less than thirty minutes."

I was incredulous. "You can't possibly believe he did that."

"I don't believe it, no. But I do believe that if Mr. Talbot goes to the police, things are going to turn out badly. For me. For him. And for Trey."

Trey closed his eyes, counted to three, and then opened them. "What do you want?"

An eminently sensible question. Finn had been waiting for it.

"Mr. Talbot wants to call the police. The Talbot Creative Group, headed by his brother Quint, does not. They want to handle it privately. I proposed a compromise."

"Which is?"

"Mr. Talbot agreed to let me investigate instead of the police in return for an interview with you."

Trey stared at her. "What?"

"One hour. Off the books. No recording devices. Just the two of you."

Trey folded his arms. "And what does he think that will accomplish?"

"Perhaps he thinks you'll confess all, I don't know, but it makes my problem go away and it keeps you from getting dragged downtown and—"

Trey didn't let her finish the sentence. He marched out the front door and climbed into the Ferrari. Then, as Finn and I watched, he ripped it into a three-point turn and rocketed out of the parking lot.

"Well," I said. "So we have Trey's opinion on that."

Chapter Four

Finn watched the Ferrari's taillights vanish around the corner. "I didn't see that coming."

I threw a hand in the air. "What did you think was going to happen? You come in here, accuse him of trying to kill someone—"

"I did not."

"—and then you offer to take it all back if only he'll sit down face-to-face with this man he's convinced is a killer."

Finn chewed her bottom lip, weighing her options. She had them, I was sure. She carried options like spare ammo, and she wasn't sweating at all, not even in the humidity-thick confines of my shop.

"What are you really up to?" I said.

"Up to?"

"Right. This is just like Savannah. You take a job that's got a lot of moral compromise in it, and for reasons I don't get, pursue it with one hand and undermine it with the other."

"I'm not undermining anything."

"Then tell Nicholas Talbot to go to the authorities."

"That would not be in his best interest. Trey's either, and not just because he'll get dragged downtown." Her expression grew serious. "Savannah was hard on him."

That was an understatement—Savannah had almost cracked him open. He'd followed me there against Marisa's orders, and on the sly, an action which had gotten him suspended and almost fired. I'd been kidnapped and almost killed, and it had taken a lot of hard psychological work before Trey had let me out of his sight again. Decompensation, my brother called it. A psychological regression partly from PTSD, partly from the cognitive damage from the accident, and partly from whatever drove Trey toward protecting people, especially me.

I went behind the counter and poured the last of the cold coffee into a mug. I held the pot Finn's way, but she shook her head.

"How much do you know about Jessica Talbot's murder?"

I stuck the mug in the microwave. "That was before I moved here, but it was big news everywhere. Anytime a pretty rich white woman is killed, the whole country goes nuts. She was an actress, right?"

"A model with acting aspirations."

Atlanta ran heavy with those. Small-town sweethearts arrived every day with stars in their eyes and Pinewood Studios in their sights. I pulled my coffee out of the microwave, spooned some sugar in. Finn stayed near the door, one eye on the parking lot.

"Nick Talbot was a producer," she said, "back in Los Angeles. He and his brother Quint founded Talbot Creative with fair to middling success in the indie film market. Then Nick derailed himself with a very unglamorous drug arrest and tried to get a fresh start out here with a modeling agency. That flopped, but he met and married Jessica, a gorgeous wannabe who proceeded to spend every penny she could get her hands on. And sleep with every available man, if you believe the tabloids."

"Do you?"

"I do. Nick was spreading himself around too, including an affair with the woman who is now his fiancée, and who also alibied him for Jessica's murder, not that anyone believed her. Anyway, Nick and Jessica had a train wreck of a marriage. They were two steps from divorce court when someone broke into their Buckhead home one lovely morning and murdered her. Nick was charged in the crime, but during the preliminary hearing, evidence surfaced that Macklin, the first responding officer, had pocketed some of the victim's jewelry. Macklin's fence gets hauled in, and he lays the finger down."

"The cop had a fence?"

"Oh, yeah. This was not his first larceny, as it turned out. He was also hip-deep in illegal gambling and prostitutes and maybe even extortion for some of Atlanta's seedier loan sharks."

"And Trey?"

"He was second responding. The Office of Professional Standards worked him over good too. He was pronounced clean, but Macklin was charged with felony theft by taking. He committed suicide before they could arrest him. But his crime tainted the evidence, and the grand jury didn't indict." She leaned back against the counter, folded her arms. "Nick Talbot's life fell apart, though. He filed for bankruptcy, quit his fancy job. Now he works as a makeup artist on *Moonshine*."

I almost choked on my coffee. "*Moonshine* the TV series?"

"Yeah. Talbot Creative produces it. A dark horse hit, they tell me, maybe their biggest."

That was an understatement. The show filmed all over Kennesaw, especially in the outlying rural areas and around Kennesaw Mountain, lots of secret base camps, very hush hush. Deciphering the bright yellow directional signs emblazoned with code words was the hot thing to do, with star-spotting Twitter feeds and celebrity-finder apps flourishing. I'd looked into the vendor licenses for the show and abandoned that idea. Too rich for my humble blood.

"Nick Talbot lived the opposite of a Cinderella story," Finn said, "and you can bet the entire Atlanta PD was happy to see him fall. So even if somebody took a shot at him, not a single cop in Zone 2 will care."

"Wait a second, you said *if* somebody took a shot. Is there some doubt?"

She gave me a crafty look. "His brother Quint was there when it happened. He insists there was no shooting. He says what Nick thought was a gunshot was actually kids messing around in Chastain Park with some firecrackers."

"His own brother doesn't believe him?"

Finn drummed her fingers along the countertop. "Nick has suffered from a destabilizing mental illness for most of his adult life. Paranoid delusional disorder. He's been involuntarily committed twice in addition to his stints in alcohol and drug rehab. After the grand jury trial, he was almost admitted a third time, but was released under the conservatory care of his brother."

"What does that mean?"

"It means Quint is in charge of Nick's life, everything from whether or not he takes his meds to his financial arrangements. Well, that used to be the case. A few years ago, a judge granted Nick's fiancée custodial care, so Quint only controls the financial now. The fiancée wants that too, but Quint is arguing that she's not doing a great job, that Nick is relapsing."

"Exhibit A being the shooting that may or may not have happened?"

"Yep. Quint says he can find no evidence of a gunshot—no bullet, no nothing. He thinks Nick's delusions are returning."

"Are they?"

"That would be the simplest explanation."

"But is it the right one?"

"It's the one Nick's brother believes."

"What do you believe?"

She smiled. "I haven't decided. But you understand now why nobody at Talbot Creative wants to get the police involved. And why I need Trey."

And suddenly, I did. "You know, don't you?"

"About Trey's lie-detecting ability? Sure. Your brother wrote an article in last month's *Psychology Today*. Trey is obviously Subject J."

My brother's fascination with Trey's brain parlayed into another professional publication. Trey himself kept this particular function disguised and turned down to low. Truthfully, it was more of a handicap. In a world where people lied with every other breath, the cognitive overload could be overwhelming.

I smacked my coffee mug on the counter. "You want Trey to be your own personal lie detector."

She winced delicately. "You make that sound so cold-blooded."

"It is."

"Not if I have something to offer in return, and I do—Trey has the chance to look Nick Talbot in the eye and find out once and for all if he is guilty of Jessica's murder."

She was right. That should have been bait enough to capture Trey's interest.

"Trey can only pick out lies," I said. "If Nick is suffering from delusions, if he believes what he's saying, Trey won't read it as deception."

"I know. But I don't think he's delusional. I think something really happened. And I'd like to figure out what it was." She looked straight at me. "Convince Trey to do this."

"Finn—"

"Three and a half years ago, somebody shot Jessica Talbot twice in the back and then point-blank in the chest as she lay paralyzed at the foot of her staircase. If Trey tells me Nick Talbot is guilty of *that*, I'm cutting the Talbots loose, all of them. But if he tells me Nick Talbot is innocent…" She shrugged. "Then I have work to do."

"And money to make."

"That too." She headed for the door. "Because I'm an optimist, I've gone ahead and scheduled the interview with Nick. It's Monday at five."

"That's two days from now!"

"Which should give you plenty of time. So work your wiles. Remind him how good closure feels. Also remind him that if Nick does end up calling the police, he's gonna be in the thick of another investigation. I am certain Marisa will not like that."

Finn had that correct. Marisa didn't like any publicity she didn't create herself. She'd be annoyed if Trey's name ended up in the papers again, but if she found out he was meeting with Nick Talbot, she'd go full tornado and drop a trailer on him.

"I'll talk to him," I said. "That's all I'm promising."

"That's all I'm asking." Finn pulled open the door. "I'll let you get on with it. Because you and I both know he drove that Ferrari around back and is sitting there right now waiting for you." She smiled. "Call me."

Chapter Five

I closed the door after her and locked it, unplugged the coffee-pot, and switched off the lights. Then I got two cold Pellegrinos from the fridge and took them to the back lot, where I found the Ferrari parked next to my Camaro.

Trey didn't look at me when I got in. He kept his eyes straight ahead, backbone rigid, index finger tapping against the steering wheel. The sun burned low behind us, thick and heavy as syrup.

I handed him a Pellegrino. "All right. One of two things has happened. Either you got overwhelmed and came out here to recuperate. Or you got fired up and came out here to marshal your resources for a full frontal assault. Which is it?"

He turned his face toward me. I didn't see an ounce of back-down in him.

"Okay," I said. "The latter. Good to know. You wanna start by telling me what's really going on? Because you didn't say a lot in there, but the one thing you especially didn't say was 'fine, call the authorities.' And that, boyfriend of mine, is not like you."

He twisted open the Pellegrino and took a long swallow. Part of me wanted to poke harder, but I knew that would only make him lock down. Whatever this was, it was tender. I had to go slow and easy.

I leaned back in the seat. "Finn said taking her offer was in your best interest. She reminded me that this would not go over well with the boss lady, which is true, but…there's something else going on, isn't there?"

He flexed his fingers, rested his hand once again on the steering wheel. "Yes."

"Care to explain?"

He considered. "The murder happened approximately three and a half years ago, in January. Right before the accident."

So there was my first clue. That time had been a tumultuous one in his life, a harbinger of even more tumult to come. A rainy night, a tractor-trailer crossing into his lane, no place to go but headfirst into a concrete embankment, no time for even a skilled driver like Trey to avoid a collision. His mother had died in the crash, his most wrenching and tangible loss, but there were other losses, some of them only becoming clear when he'd blinked back into consciousness after five days in a coma.

Frontal lobe damage, the doctors said, cognitive impairments in language processing and executive function, the control center of the personality. His IQ stayed the same, but his ability to think peripherally or abstractly took a hit. His long-term memory improved, however, as did his ability to tell when others were lying—surprising new strengths that came with their own challenges. Unable to effectively filter the stream of memories and deception coming at him, he grew more easily overwhelmed, less willing to engage. So he took the money from his legal settlement and bought a high-rise apartment and a fast car and a wardrobe straight out of the Italian-style issue of *GQ*, shoving his former life into storage.

And now he was telling me a new story from that time. One that had hit him hard.

He stared at the dashboard as he spoke. "I was second on the scene. I got the call for backup when I was less than a mile away, so I arrived within approximately two minutes. I was met in the living room by Macklin, weapon drawn, saying that he was in pursuit of the suspect. There was what appeared to be blood on his shirt, and he had his hand pressed over his forehead. Multiple contusions there and on his right cheek."

"Macklin was hurt?"

"Yes. He said that he'd surprised the suspect, who then bludgeoned him with a handgun and fled. He told me there was one victim at the foot of the stairs, female. Deceased. He told me to finish clearing the house, and then he ran into the backyard. The patio doors were already open. I called in backup and EMTs."

"And then?"

He took a deep breath, then let it out slow. "Macklin returned. He said he'd lost the intruder in the park."

"What park?"

"Chastain Park. Across the street from the Talbots' backyard. Macklin said he'd found the presumptive murder weapon, however, a nine-millimeter semi-auto that turned out to belong to Nicholas Talbot. Macklin said it had been dropped at the edge of the property."

"He picked it up? Aren't cops supposed to leave things as they found them?"

"Yes, usually. But his justification, a valid one, was that he didn't want the suspect to return for the weapon. And he didn't want to leave me alone at the crime scene."

This was a bare-bones description, even for Trey, who did not tend toward the flowery. He was speaking cop talk, the spare, just-the-facts-ma'am language of law enforcement reports everywhere. Who, where, and when sprinkled with the appropriate wiggle words when necessary. An "alleged" here, a "presumptive" there.

I kept my tone nonchalant. "Finn said he took some of Jessica's jewelry."

"He did, along with cash from the master bedroom upstairs. He may have taken other items, but there was no proof."

"But they didn't think you stole anything, did they?"

"I was never accused of theft, only of aiding and abetting the contamination of the scene to cover up Macklin's crime. OPS investigated, and I was absolved. Regardless, the chain of custody was tainted. The evidence was ruled inadmissible. The charges against Talbot were dropped."

"But you're convinced he did it."

"I am. Regardless of what Macklin did, the evidence implicated Talbot beyond a reasonable doubt. That scene was staged to look like one of the recent burglaries, which I am certain was the reason Macklin decided to take the jewelry. But he didn't stage it. Someone else did. Before he arrived. He simply took advantage of that for his own purposes."

"And you think that someone was Nick Talbot."

"I do."

"Finn said he had an alibi."

"The woman he was having an affair with. Addison Canright. Her testimony was always suspect, and we could have broken it in court. If he'd been indicted."

I looked at him. Underneath the clipped, no-nonsense diction, he was haunted. Not once had his index finger stopped its relentless tap-tap-tapping.

"Why?" I said.

"Why what?"

"Why is this hitting you so hard?"

He shook his head, stared down at his lap. "It's complicated."

"Because there's something you're not telling me."

He hesitated, then nodded. I got a sinking feeling in the pit of my stomach.

"Something serious?"

Two seconds' consideration, then another nod.

"What is it?"

He didn't reply, not at first. He was doing some complicated emotional algebra, I could tell. I could almost see the flowchart in his head, decisions branching into choices, choices stagnating into dead ends. Finally, he found his answer.

He motioned for me to put on my seat belt. "It will be easier if I show you."

Chapter Six

Before Westview was a neighborhood, it was a battleground. In 1864, over three thousand soldiers died in what would be memorialized as the Battle of Ezra Church, a defeat for the Confederacy. This was how I knew Westview, as a piece of Civil War trivia. Trey knew it as home.

He'd grown up here in the eighties, in a sturdy square house with thick porch posts and a low sloping roof. The neighborhood was in decline then, hit hard with the rising drug crime of that era and devastated further as its residents abandoned it for the suburbs. Now in the uncertain first lurches of revitalization, it felt scrappy and optimistic, its citizens not yet priced out of their own history. Trey still owned the basement of his former residence, but the ground floor served as the parish house for St. Anthony's Catholic Church, an arrangement his mother had specified in her will.

He pulled around back next to the basement door as the first twilight settled around us, dampening and softening the world beyond. He had recently unlocked his whole past for me, literally. He'd given me the key to this basement where he'd stored all the artifacts of his life before the accident. Too much for him to go through at once, he'd said. And, as it had turned out, too much for me too. It felt like occupied territory in that basement, a psychological terrain with no map, only myths and rumors and veiled legends. I'd been taking it slowly.

"Why are we here?" I said.

"To find my files from the Talbot case."

"Atlanta PD let you keep them?"

Trey tapped his finger on the steering wheel. "Not exactly."

"Oh. I see."

He got out of the car, keys in hand. I followed him inside. He clicked on a floor lamp, and it cast a dim glow around the room. What had once been an efficiency apartment was now storage space: a bar table with two wooden stools upended on top, a hunter green velour sofa, a bookshelf filled with photo albums, and *many* paper boxes stacked against the walls.

I closed the door behind me, shutting out the last of the sunlight. Above us I could hear footsteps—the church's secretary, going about her duties.

"Are you going to explain why you have contraband files in your basement?" I said.

"They're not contraband."

"So they're public?"

"Not technically. They're…complicated."

I thought about that one for a second. "Fine. Any idea where to start looking?"

He pointed. A filing cabinet stood in the corner, slate gray and thick with dust. It was an exact match of the one Trey had in his present apartment, the one I knew to be fireproof, waterproof, impact proof, and ridiculously expensive.

He looked around the room. "I need to find the globe."

"Globe?"

"Yes. That's where the keys to the cabinet are." He held up his hands and measured an imaginary circle. "About this big. If I remember correctly. It's been a long time."

We gave the room another once-over. Trey seemed hesitant about wading in. Going through the things from his life before the accident was like performing an archaeological dig on his own existence. There would be surprises. I sympathized. Given the state of my own personal history, I completely understood.

I started with a box helpfully labeled DESK STUFF. Garrity's handiwork, no doubt. He'd been the one who packed up most of Trey's things while he was in the hospital. I ignored the dust and pulled off the lid, revealing Trey's personal effects from the police station: a stapler with his name written on top in permanent marker, APD coffee cups filled with ballpoint pens, business cards. Another box labeled JOB STUFF contained employment records, which we set aside to take back to his apartment, along with another box filled with newspaper clippings and photocopied reports.

"Nonclassified," he said.

Eventually he found a plastic tub buried under old CD cases. He wrenched the top off and dug into the contents with both hands. After a minute's searching, he pulled out a globe, an old-school faded and dinged model, probably with the USSR still on it. He turned it upside down and twisted the base. A tiny compartment opened, and a silver key the size of his little finger tumbled out.

"That's a lot of precautions," I said.

Trey went to the file cabinet. "They're warranted."

I watched as he twisted the lock and the cabinet creaked open. He did a quick search of both drawers, looked confused, then performed a more thorough examination of the files, one by one.

He straightened. "They're not here."

"What's not there?"

"The files. But they have to be here. These locks are UL-listed high-security. Pick- and drill-resistant, with keys that cannot be duplicated without my permission. All the other files are here, but not those. I don't…this doesn't…"

He started pacing the narrow width of the apartment, six steps, pivot, six steps, pivot. I shoved my hair from my face. Even the normally cool basement was hot.

I tried to keep my voice calm. "Okay. Let's stop and think for a second. Did anybody else have keys to that cabinet?"

"No."

"What about to the basement?"

Trey pulled out his phone and hit speed dial. He spoke

quickly, without preamble. "The Talbot files are missing. What did you do with them?"

I could hear Garrity on the other end of the line, sounding baffled. Of course he was. Trey had started mid-story with zero explanation. I felt the first twist in my gut. Finn was wrong. Getting involved in this case was not going to be for his own good. There were depths here, cold murky ones.

Trey pressed his thumb to the middle of his forehead. "Yes, yes, I know. Regardless, they're missing, and I need to know... Oh. Right. Of course."

He hung up, stared at the phone.

"Well?"

"It wasn't Garrity."

"Who was it?"

Trey closed the cabinet, locked the door, slipped the key into his pocket. "Gabriella."

Chapter Seven

Despite its location in the heart of Buckhead, Gabriella's cottage was fairy-tale cozy, with weathered plank siding the color of ripe plums and exuberantly overgrown flower beds. Late summer roses scented the evening air, and a single lantern illuminated the porch. Trey marched right up the path to the front door with me right behind.

"You should try calling her again," I said.

"She's not answering."

"Then at least text her."

He ignored me. He was reaching for the doorknob when he caught himself. Straightening his shoulders, he took a step back and knocked three times. On the other side of the beveled glass, I saw the blur of movement, heard the patter of bare feet against muted jazz. The door swung open.

Gabriella snatched a sash around a white satin robe that barely reached the top of her thighs. She'd cut her hair since I'd last seen her, razoring the red ringlets into an angled bob. With her pale skin and cat-green eyes, she looked straight out of a 1920s speakeasy. And—something else new—she had large black dog at her side. A greyhound.

She pointed to the ground. "Sit. *Assis*!"

The dog remained standing, its eyes large and doe-like. I held my hand out, fingers curled down in a loose fist. The dog gave me a polite sniff.

Gabriella's frown vanished when she saw the expression on Trey's face. "What is wrong?"

"Where are the Talbot files?" he said.

"The what?"

"The files from the Jessica Talbot case."

Comprehension washed over her features. "Oh, *those*. I don't know why you think I—"

"Garrity said he didn't move the things from my personal office. He says it was you."

"Yes, but Garrity packed everything first." She ran a hand through her hair, thinking back. "I simply picked up the boxes and the furniture and took them to the basement. That is all."

"And the file cabinet?"

"If it was in your apartment, yes."

"Did you open it?"

"Of course not." She looked my way. "Tai, what is happening here?"

I shrugged. "You're getting the story as coherently as I am."

She sighed and put the back of her hand to her forehead. Somewhere inside the house a clock chimed the hour.

"I don't have your files," she said.

He fixed his gaze on her. "Say it again."

Her eyes flashed. "Trey Seaver! You are not standing on my own front porch and accusing me of lying!"

"You've lied before. You took my gun once. And then there was that time—"

"Enough!" She belted her robe tighter. "These files, they are that important?"

"They are."

She opened the door all the way and waved us in. I noticed then the wisp of a chemise under the robe, the whisper of scent about her, the artful tousling of her hair. A bottle of Viogner sat on the coffee table, open, with two crystal goblets side by side. The lights were low, and candles burned on the side table.

We hadn't woken her up. She was expecting company.

Once we were inside, Gabriella turned down the music and switched on the overhead light. She folded her arms and glared at Trey. "Quickly."

And so he explained. As he did, I watched her expression grown less stern. She glanced at the clock. Sighed.

"I don't have any files," she said. "I didn't open the file cabinet. I simply had it placed in the basement."

"By yourself?"

She looked at him as if he were deranged. "Of course not. I hired Peter from the shop. Very trustworthy."

Trey opened his mouth, but she held up a single finger.

"And, no, I never left him alone with anything. No one has opened that file cabinet since you went into the hospital, not to my knowledge. Does anybody else have a key to the basement?"

"No," he said. "Except for…but that's not…"

"Who?"

"The church secretary. Mary Elaine. The basement is technically my property, but the rest of the house belongs to the church, so I thought it prudent to…" He pulled out his phone. "Excuse me for a second."

He went back to the porch, shutting the door behind him. Gabriella dropped onto the sofa and tilted her head back to stare at the ceiling. We'd had a long talk, she and I, about the proper dynamics a former lover should maintain around her ex's current girlfriend. Also about how said girlfriend had nothing to fear from said former lover, regardless, and should probably stop being so suspicious. After all, I knew that Trey's heart beat with an intensely singular focus. I imagined two women would short-circuit him. Indeed, Gabriella and I almost had. Hence his insistence that we work things out.

She patted the sofa, and the dog jumped up beside her, resting its head next to her knee. I'd had the idea that greyhounds were hyperactive creatures, always bouncing around as if their veins ran with espresso. This one, however, had the poise of an Art Deco sculpture.

"What's his name?"

"Trois. He is a rescue from the local greyhound group. The woman at the adoption center told me his final racing number was three, hence Trois."

Outside, Trey continued talking on his cell. His voice was low, clipped. I could see him through the windows as he paced back and forth, half in shadow, half in the opalescent glow of the porch light.

Gabriella shook her head. "I cannot believe he is ripping open this case again."

"You're familiar with it?"

"Very. Is he perseverating?"

The clinical term for what happened when Trey locked onto an idea and wouldn't—couldn't, Eric reminded me—let go. Breaking his laser lock was almost impossible at those times.

"I don't know," I said.

She narrowed her eyes at me. "This is not your doing, is it?"

"This is all Trey, I promise you."

"But you are involved?"

I felt the first prickle of annoyance. "I just told you that I wasn't."

"I am not suggesting that you are at fault. It is simply that where you are concerned, Trey tends to..." She rubbed her temple with her forefinger. "I am sorry. *Mon Dieu*, this is difficult."

"It's not easy at this end either."

She flung a hand toward the porch. "It does not help when he comes stomping in here as if he were still...as if..."

"I know. He and I are going to have a talk about this."

"Good."

She stood up and crossed the room. Ignoring the wine, she pulled down a crystal decanter, held it in my direction. I shook my head, and she sloshed a cocktail glass half full. She took a long sip, then swirled the liquor as she spoke.

"He became obsessed, you must understand. He had always been very boundaried about his work. But this case, the Talbot case, was different."

"Because his testimony was thrown out?"

"Yes. But there was something else." Another sip, her eyes assessing and sharp. "He was not supposed to be in Buckhead that morning. It was not his assigned beat at the time."

"Then what was he doing there?"

She kept the edge of the glass pressed against her bottom lip. "He was here. At this house."

"With you?"

"No. Trey and I had…" She pursed her lips. "I do not like the phrase 'broken up.' But we had decided that we could no longer be together, and I had gone back to Provence to clear my head. And my heart. I was not in Atlanta during this time."

I folded my hands in my lap. The clock chimed the quarter hour. "But Trey was here?"

"He was. Out front. Watching the house, he said. Thinking. The Talbots lived less than a mile away, right across Chastain Park. When the request for backup came, he was the closest officer on duty. So he responded, even though he knew he would be reprimanded." She tilted her head, focused on the fireplace across the room. "It was a very difficult time for me. Trey too, I think, even though he knew our uncoupling was the right thing to do. He felt as if he'd failed. As if he'd been unable to save our relationship. I told him I would come back, and that we would talk. But he had the accident before I could."

Uncoupling, she called it. And it hit me hard again, right in the gut, the whole history of these two people, years that I was not a part of. I could not deny him his past—I had quite the colorful one myself—but his backstory occasionally pole-axed me.

Outside, Trey walked back and forth on the porch, phone at his ear. The gauzy curtains blurred his features, but his posture was rigid.

Gabriella regarded me over the liquor. "I saw you in the cards before I ever met you. The Queen of Wands. And I am grateful for you in his life. I know that you and I do not always agree on what is best for him, but we have agreed to respect each other's opinions, yes?"

"Yes."

"Then, please, be careful here. You and I both know Trey is a man of rules. That is his primary method of recovery. But if there is one case that could cause him to break every rule in his book, it is this one."

Before I could say anything, Trey came back inside. He stood in the threshold, determined and frustrated and confused all at the same time.

I stood up. "Well?"

He put his phone back in his pocket. "I know who has the files."

"And?"

He exhaled in a burst. "And now I really don't know what to do."

Chapter Eight

Trey stared out the passenger seat window as I drove us back to Kennesaw. He did this when he had to think or calm down, and both were on his agenda now. He'd decided to stay with me for the night, which surprised me. His apartment was usually a refuge during times of stress. He'd click the triple locks in place, close the shades, and recompose himself in stillness and silence. But tonight he wanted to stay at my place, where the hot water ran out in five minutes and the mattress was uneven.

"I don't want to be in the city," he'd said, and I hadn't argued.

We left the cloistered tidiness of Gabriella's neighborhood, down through Buckhead proper, where the glass and steel gleamed even more brightly at night. I waited until we were on the interstate to speak.

"So are you gonna tell me?"

"Yes." He kept his face toward the window. "When I can."

"When will that be?"

"I don't know."

"But you do know who has the files, right?"

"Yes. That only complicates matters, however."

"Why?"

"I can't explain."

"Can't or won't?"

He thought about that. "Both. I'm very tired. And I need more information. I need things to be more…something. Multi-syllabic, starts with…starts with…" He let his head fall back against the seat. "I can't even think of what it starts with."

He seemed unusually vexed by his vocabulary hiccups. It was late, and his gears ground when he got tired, but he typically dealt with it matter-of-factly. Unlike tonight.

"D," he finally said, his eyes closed. "It starts with D."

"Detailed?"

He shook his head.

"Definite?"

"No." He opened his eyes. "Wait. Yes. Definitive. I need more definitive information before I can make a decision." Now he did look at me. "It's for your own—"

"Don't even say it."

"But—"

"Do you remember what you made me promise? That I would always tell you the truth, even if it made you angry?"

"Of course I remember. But—"

"But nothing. I'm holding you to the same deal. You're not behaving like yourself. You're unwilling to get the police involved, which is exactly the opposite of your normal response. You were rude to Gabriella. Garrity too. And now you're refusing to explain things to me, which I hate."

He turned back to the window. "Tomorrow. I'll explain what I can tomorrow. Once I've had some sleep."

"Trey—"

"Please."

I took the exit for Kennesaw. "All right. Sleep it is. But then you and I are having a long discussion."

The nightmare started as it always did—with me bound and gagged in the trunk. I writhed and twisted, desperate to get free, but my body moved too slowly, like I was swimming in molasses. And then the darkness collapsed, and I strangled on my own tongue, and—

The hand on my shoulder was strong. I pulled away from it. "No!"

"Tai—"

"No!" I bolted upright. A light flared to my left, and I kicked myself away, feet tangling in the sheets.

The voice was steady and familiar. "Tai. Look at me."

I looked. Trey sat beside me. I was panting and delirious, but I knew that Trey wasn't in the trunk of the car, which meant that I wasn't in the trunk of the car. Reality crept back like a slow-drip IV. I was numb, stuck with one foot in dreamscape, one in flesh and blood. I breathed heavily. The air was clean, not the hot rubbery stink of the trunk. Trey sat on my side of the bed, but did not touch me again.

"Are you okay?"

"Yeah." I raked my hand through my hair. "I'm good now."

His touch had brought me back, but he'd known better than to get too close. I'd have kicked and flailed, maybe hurting him, or myself, or both of us. Distance was the protocol. I knew this from all the times I'd roused him from some nocturnal horror. During the waking up, I couldn't get too close. He sometimes swung out in panicked self-defense, and his punches were deadly. Mine were just punchy, but dangerous enough in close quarters.

Suddenly the bed felt too small, the room too close. I shoved the sheets aside and sat up. "Do you have any of those little herbal pills, the calming ones?"

"I do. Let me—"

"I know where they are."

I pushed myself up and went to his overnight bag, rummaged around until I found the bottle. Chamomile and *Avena sativa* and other exotic pharmaceuticals. Then I went to the kitchen and came back with the Jack Daniels.

Trey shook his head. "That's not—"

"—a good idea. I know." I tipped two fingers into a glass. "But it's an idea whose time has come."

He frowned. "I was going to say that while alcohol isn't contraindicated with that particular herbal combination, it won't help the problem."

"It's helping well enough."

What I really wanted was a cigarette. I suspected that I always would, that during any time of stress, the craving would kick up. There was no cigarette like a relapse cigarette, sweet as candy, soothing as cool fingers stroking my forehead. But I didn't have any. So whiskey it was.

I plopped down next to him. "It's always the trunk. The dock was where I thought I was going to die, but when I dream, it's the trunk."

"The trunk is where you were confined. You had choices on the dock. Not in the trunk."

I sipped the liquor, feeling the warmth spread as I washed down the pills. He was right. Confinement pushed my panic button. I didn't need my brother's psychology degree to figure out the symbolic connections. I didn't like being deprived of my own volition. And I didn't like being kept in the dark.

Trey slid closer and put his hand between my shoulder blades, tender and tentative. I let it rest there. He'd come for me that night. I'd been practically catatonic on the deck, Jasper's body only a few feet away, a steel-tipped arrow through his heart. Trey had been unable to pry the bloody rifle out of my hands, so he'd sat behind me and held me against his chest until the ambulance arrived. My official statement was that I didn't know who'd killed Jasper. Trey knew better. And yet he'd said not one word about it. He'd let my lie stand.

Now I centered on his hand, solid and reassuring. I relaxed a little, leaned my head on his shoulder. I noticed then that he wore a tee shirt, and that he didn't have the slightly fuzzy expression and sleep-mussed hair of a man snatched from slumber. I slid my hand to his side of the bed. It was cold.

"You were awake," I said.

He nodded. This was unusual. Trey usually hit the sack at nine sharp. He needed sleep, lots of it, and when he slept, he slept deeply and completely, so thick in slumber that an earthquake could tumble him out of bed and he wouldn't wake up until he'd hit the floor.

"You're worried. And not normal worried, either. Can't-sleep worried." I lifted my head and looked him in the eye. "You said you wanted to talk about this in the morning. But I think we need to talk now. I think—"

"You're right. I need to tell you. What I can."

I held out the medicine bottle. He opened his hand, and I shook two tablets in his palm. I offered the bourbon, but he swallowed them dry.

"Talk," I said.

He kept his eyes down. "Someone gave me the files. I wasn't supposed to have them. Neither of us were."

I was beginning to understand. It was odd to think of this past Trey breaking rules and sneaking home forbidden files. Current Trey would be positively apoplectic at the thought.

I shrugged. "So you have files you shouldn't have? Big deal. You're not a cop anymore, they can't—"

"It's a crime, Tai. A violation of Georgia code 50-18-72. Section 4. This isn't simply a violation of procedure. It's illegal. For me, and for the person who gave them to me. But that's not the problem. Not exactly."

"What is the problem?"

"I can't tell you."

"I swear to God, if you say that one more time, the top of my head is gonna come off."

Trey kept his eyes on his folded hands. "I have to find the files before I can tell you anything. I have to talk to her."

"Who?

"The person who gave them to me. The person I suspect took them back."

"And who is this person?"

He hesitated. Then he told me. I pondered the information for a second, threw back the rest of the whiskey. Trey watched me like maybe he'd changed his mind, like maybe getting hammered on Jack was a fine idea after all.

I wiped my mouth with the back of my hand and handed him the bottle. "Here. You need this more than I do."

Chapter Nine

The noonday sun beat at Garrity's car like a deranged hitchhiker. Even in the mottled shade, we had to keep the air conditioner running. He'd already started on his sandwich—the rest remained in the box in the backseat along with a cooler full of soft drinks and water bottles. The car smelled strongly of pulled pork and grande sauce, this ominous concoction involving ghost pepper and Vidalia onion jam.

He pulled out another wad of napkins. "I never thought I'd hear the name Nick Talbot on Trey's lips again, and now you tell me he's going face-to-face with the guy?"

"Once he gets the files back."

"And he thinks Price has them?"

"Yep."

"That's gonna be hard country there. She's still active SWAT." Garrity licked sauce from his fingers "Why'd she give him those files in the first place? And what possessed him to keep them?"

"He hasn't explained. I was hoping you could."

The parking lot at Constitution Lakes was packed. As usual, Trey had parked his Ferrari far away from the rest of the vehicles, some Dekalb County sheriff, others civilian. The park was closed to the public for the day. The water oaks beyond the rutty dirt lot were tall and slender and close, textbook bottomland. This was a young forest, reclaimed from the degradation of a former brickworks factory. It filled me with homesickness, this spot of boggy wildness in a sea of concrete and asphalt.

Garrity shook his head. "I'd moved on to Major Crimes when all this happened, so we weren't partners anymore. I got the off-duty vent and fume from him, of course, but Price was by his side during the investigation and the OPS interviews. If anybody knows what's going on, it's her." Garrity shoved three tortilla chips in his mouth and talked around them. "Still, it's been what, almost four years ago? Nobody's going to retroactively prosecute him for having those files. Confidentiality only applies to current investigations or pending cases, and the Talbot case isn't either of those things. That case is cold as old stone."

"He seems to think otherwise."

"So I'm learning." Garrity reached in the backseat and pulled a Coke from the cooler, shook the ice water from his hand. "Every cop's got that quicksand case, you know, and I think the murder of Jessica Talbot is Trey's. One dirty cop fouled the works, and the bad guy got away with it."

Got away with it. Every cop's sticking point. Revenge is a dish best served cold, they say, and Trey could do ice-blooded with the best of them. But when he'd told me about the case, what I'd seen flashing in his eyes had been the opposite of cold.

Garrity took another bite of his sandwich, a *torta cubana* with hot pickle relish falling out the sides. "That was the angriest I've ever see him. I'm talking spitting, cursing, foaming-at-the-mouth furious."

"I'd be mad too, if my testimony got thrown out."

"It was more than that. I mean, testimony gets thrown out all the time. You get used to cases going south."

"This one seemed to go south very quickly."

"This case had no brakes from the get-go. No matter how meticulously Trey documented that scene, it was already tainted when he got there. The prosecutor knew any half-decent defense attorney would have destroyed it in court." He dropped mustard on his jeans, cursed and dabbed at it with the napkin. "You know the story of how Price got tangled up in all this?"

"I know nothing, Garrity. That's why I'm sitting here with you."

He eyed me over the sandwich. He had this way of looking at me like I was on the witness stand, but he was my go-to source if any blanks needed filling in about Trey. He wasn't training today, so he was in jeans and a tee shirt. My brain kept superimposing images of him from the day before, tactical gear over denim, ballistic helmet over Atlanta Braves ball cap.

He finished chewing and wiped his mouth. "Price had ridden with Macklin herself, back when she was a rookie. He already had a shady rep, one of those cops you get saddled with if you're being punished for something. In her case, it was for refusing to play good old boy games. Stupid detrimental shit, but it happens. She sicced OPS on Macklin, and it almost ruined her career."

"For doing the right thing?"

"For not handling it in-house. For calling in OPS."

As if the Office of Professional Standards wasn't made of cops. But the attitude was common, I'd discovered. Good cops hated dirty cops, but a lot of good cops wanted to deal with the situation "in the family." Bad cops had many ways to get back at a pushy rabble-rouser, and sticking them with a partner they couldn't trust was top of the list. Few things chilled a cop's nerve faster.

"Anyway, they moved her to a new zone, did zippo to Macklin. She and Trey started working together on SWAT. When she learned about the Talbot murder, and how Trey was getting implicated in Macklin's dirt, she made it her personal mission to take Macklin down. So she got one of her confidential informants to cough up some pertinent leads, including the guy who was his fence, and bam. Macklin's done."

"But when Macklin went down, the case against Talbot went with him."

"Yep. Sank like the *Titanic*." Garrity squinched up his eyes. "That could be why the files are so problematic, if they revealed the identity of Price's CI. Documents that do that are not protected by sunshine laws, pending investigation or otherwise. All kinda illegal there."

I popped the top on my Coke. I had my own theory, and it had nothing to do with Keesha Price's confidential informant and everything to do with Keesha Price herself. And if I was right, Trey wasn't overreacting. But I didn't dare spill any of this to Garrity, not yet.

He grabbed more chips. "Here's the thing—CI identities are redacted and coded in any case files. There shouldn't be a single speck of compromising data in there. So this still doesn't make sense."

"Trey said he'd explain."

"Well, he'd better. He likes to play close to the vest, especially with information that could potentially hurt people. But if those files have CI information, they're a hot potato, and he needs to relieve himself of them, and fast."

At the edge of the woods, a trio of crows descended on a piece of trash, squabbling, wings beating. It was the only activity in the lot. The hubbub of highway traffic lay just a few hundred feet away, but in this separate place, the city seemed a distant memory.

"Trey mentioned they suspected a robbery gone bad?"

"Burglary. Yeah." Garrity chewed thoughtfully. "There was a thief active in the fancier neighborhoods then. They called him the Buckhead Burglar. Always struck during the morning when people were at work or yoga or whatever—get in, go straight for the good stuff, get out, empty house, no violence. The theory was the thief finally screwed up and broke into the house with Jessica still there. She ran, he panicked, and in the heat of the moment, he picked up the handgun lying on the nightstand and shot her dead."

"This is where Macklin came in?"

"Supposedly. The physical evidence backed up that part of the story—the nine-millimeter Macklin claimed to have found at the edge of the property, the one belonging to Nicholas Talbot, was the murder weapon. Talbot admitted it was his, said he kept it in the nightstand because of the thefts. And after that, the Buckhead Burglar was never heard from again. We figured the guy realized he was suddenly looking at a felony murder rap, so he dropped Atlanta like it was on fire and vanished."

"But Trey didn't buy that theory."

"About the burglar making himself scarce after the killing? Sure. But he always liked Nick Talbot for the murder. Said the scene was obviously faked to make it look like a burglary."

"And Price?"

"Same theory, different suspect. She was convinced Macklin was the guilty party. He had a gambling habit, a prostitute habit too, plus a temper. He was lazy and sleazy and bad police."

"If he was such a bad cop, why was he still on the force?"

Garrity shrugged. "Back then, it wasn't as easy to get rid of a bad apple. OPS had problems. They've cleaned their act up. Mostly. But even if Macklin was a skeeze, Price's theory that he killed Jessica Talbot had one big problem—Macklin was at a traffic stop on the other side of Chastain Park when she died. His dash cam was his alibi. Trey was convinced that video eliminated Macklin as a suspect. Price was convinced he faked the videos somehow, and I gotta admit, it does seem hella convenient that he just happened to have a tailor-made alibi ready to go. Like he knew he'd get suspected."

"And there was Trey parked suspiciously down the road at Gabriella's."

Garrity paused, sandwich halfway to his mouth. "You heard about that?"

"Gabriella told me."

"Oh. You two are talking?"

"Sort of."

"Good." He sank his teeth into the sandwich, chewed heartily. "I mean, Trey wasn't doing anything but sitting at the curb. But the GPS in his cruiser had him in that same spot for an hour, not patrolling, like he was supposed to be."

I could see it like a news reel. Gabriella gone. The house empty. Trey sitting there, watching. Stewing. Regretting. And then the call coming in right down the street.

"Did they ever suspect Trey of wrongdoing?"

"It was looking bad for a little while. But then Price went ballistic on his behalf." Garrity chewed, stared over the dash at the trail head entrance. "Price blamed herself, I think, for the way everything fell apart at the end. Taking down Macklin protected Trey from any taint, for sure, and it nailed shut Macklin's coffin—literally, as it turned out—but that destroyed the case against Talbot."

"So case closed," I said.

"Case inactive. There's still a warrant out for the Buckhead Burglar, still a profile up for him in the LINX network, but there hasn't been any movement on it for years."

LINX. The Law Enforcement Information Exchange, a multi-jurisdictional database for security personnel of all stripes. If anyone matching the Burglar's MO surfaced, the Atlanta PD would hear about it.

Garrity shook his head. "That case still has its claws in Price too. She's primary contact on it." He hesitated. "You know things didn't end well for them, right? After the accident?"

"Trey told me he cut ties with almost everyone on the force."

"Yeah. He did. And Price took that harder than most. So now, after all these years, she's best approached as a hostile witness." He looked toward the edge of the woods, where the rutty parking lot met the trail head, jabbed his chin in that direction. "Speaking of the devil."

Chapter Ten

I spotted Trey first, emerging from the treeline. A woman walked beside him. She was tall, almost as tall as Trey, lean-hipped and lithe. Her skin was ashy underneath the layer of dust except where sweat sheened it obsidian, and she had bits of dead leaves in her hair, neat cornrow braids tight against her scalp. Despite the heat, she and Trey were dressed in long-sleeved black tees, with heavy boots and...

I did a double take. "Is Trey wearing camo pants?"

Garrity laughed. "That's ATACS, my friend. Advanced Tactical Concealment System. Tonal microstructures. Mimetic patterns. Very useful for mixed-terrain ops."

It looked like ordinary camo to me, splotches of dark green mixed with slate gray, but I was stunned to see it on Trey. His wardrobe consisted of black Italian suits and white shirts and workout clothes in the same colors. Price spotted us in the car, turned her head to Trey. Her lips moved, and he nodded. She looked our way again, assessing. Then Trey stopped suddenly and said something that made Keesha Price turn on her heel. She put her hands on her hips while Trey spoke, her face a mask.

I smacked my forehead with an open palm. "Now he decides to accuse her of taking his files? Now?"

Trey continued talking. She stared at him like he was sprouting horns. She said something abruptly, and Trey's eyes narrowed. He spread his feet hip-width and folded his arms across his chest.

"Uh oh," I said. "I know that look."

"You and me both." Garrity shook his head. "Even a bulldozer couldn't budge him now."

She was arguing in full force, one hand gesturing violently, chopping motions like she was decapitating someone, most likely Trey. And then he said a single word. I was no lip reader, but I knew that word, knew how much it meant when he dropped it. *Please.*

I saw her exhale sharply. Shake her head at him, but not in denial this time. She looked over her shoulder to where Garrity and I sat, then strode our way, pushing up her sleeves. Trey followed, silent and subdued. Garrity rolled down the window, and she leaned inside.

"Are you a part of this half-assed ambush, Dan Garrity?"

"Nope. I just brought the sandwiches." He jerked his chin in my direction. "This is Tai."

I sat up straighter. "Good to meet you, Sergeant Price."

She examined me with those sniper eyes. "It's Keesha. Seaver here says you will be joining our little lunch hour. If it's okay with me."

"Is it?"

She straightened. "Come to the table and find out."

• • ● • •

Trey and I followed her down the trail away from the rest of the trainees, two fewer than the day before. I was pleased to see that the guy who'd paintballed me was not among them. Trey carried the cooler; I took the box of sandwiches. Keesha took her time, not looking back. Once we got to the lakes, the sky opened above us, pastel blue with skeins of white clouds. Handmade signs proclaimed that only trash found in the park could be repurposed as community art. No outside garbage allowed.

Keesha led us across the boardwalk over muddy, flat pond water, hanging a left at Doll's Head Trail. The entrance was marked by—what else?—a grinning baby doll's face displayed in a broken TV set. It was a particularly creepy specimen, one bright blue eye open, fishing lures dangling from its rodent-chewed ears. I wondered why so much of the park's trash was disembodied doll parts. Plastic heads mounted on billiard pins, legs strung up on wires, torsos crowning stacks of bricks like strange altars.

"Did you know this training was in the woods when you signed up?" I said.

Trey switched the cooler to his left hand. "I did."

"And you came anyway?"

"Yes."

We continued to the picnic area, the only sounds the rustle of leaves, the hum of insects, police boots on wooden boards. Keesha led us to a rickety table in the shade. At the roots of the tree, four plastic doll arms sprouted from the ground, hoisting a toy dump truck high. The placard proclaimed: Giving Daddy a Hand.

Whatever. I sat, unwrapped one of the sandwiches, and dug in.

Trey got his food and sat next to me. I snuck a glance at Keesha. I'd met her mother once, the head of special collections at the Atlanta Public Library. Her daughter had her sharp eyes and her straightforward, no-nonsense demeanor. Definitely her intellect too. Snipers were the Beta Club of SWAT. Trey told me that he and Keesha had both carried a tiny book of equations in a compartment on their rifles—minute of angle calculations, temperature and wind resistance algorithms.

She sent a scathing look Trey's way. "Fucking Nicholas Talbot. Seriously, Seaver, why are you still carrying a hard-on for this guy?"

"I'm not." Trey pulled a bottled water from the cooler. "I haven't looked at the case in years."

"Then why now?"

"I told you why."

"No. You told me the circumstances. You have not explained why you feel it necessary to drag me into this." She pointed a potato chip at him. "Now that I'm up for promotion. Now that I got a microscope on my life."

He shook his head more firmly. "I am not asking you—"

"The hell you're not. You know all this gets dragged up, I get dragged into it. No way to do this clean."

"I simply want the files."

"You assume I have them."

"The secretary at the church reported a woman matching your description—"

"A black woman in Westview?" She laughed and attacked her sandwich. "You gotta do better that that, Seaver."

He folded his hands on the table. "A black woman in Westview who knew where I kept the key to my file cabinet."

She didn't argue the point. I heard the splash of a fish. Or perhaps a snake. I chewed and kept quiet.

Trey unwrapped his sandwich. "You won't be involved."

"You don't know that. And unlike you, the walking talking poster child for white boy privilege, it will cost me. So don't even start."

"I need them for the information, not for any official action. Your name is redacted."

"You know that doesn't matter." She stabbed the chip in punctuation. "If I took those files—not that I'm saying I did—it was for your own good. And if I had them—not that I'm saying I do—I would keep them for the same damn reason."

He exhaled and pulled his sandwich apart, removed the pickles and put them on my plate. Then he started scraping the mayonnaise off with a plastic knife.

She flicked her eyes at me, hard like onyx, but kept talking to Trey. "And what about her? What's she got to do with this?"

Trey reached for his water. "She's my partner."

"In what?"

"In everything."

He said it matter-of-factly, but Keesha caught the weight of the word as much as I did. Yes, I was his partner in life, partner in bed, partner in crime. And he was mine. Equal and always.

"Justice was not served," he said. "You know this."

"You intend to serve some? You think that'll help you sleep better?"

"I sleep well already."

She examined him steadily. "What's in those files you don't already know?"

"My OPS transcripts. My preliminary reports. My testimony before the grand jury. I can remember what happened. Mostly. But I can't put it into any context. And I need to do that before I meet with Nicholas Talbot."

"Which you are set on doing, come hell or high water."

"Maybe. Depending on what I find in those files."

"I'm not sticking my head out again, and you shouldn't either. You need to drop this thing." She picked up her trash, nodded my way. "Nice to meet you, Tai. See you in field, Seaver."

She balled up the wax paper and chucked it into the can from twenty feet, a slam dunk. She headed off into the woods without looking back.

I sighed. "Well, that went peachy."

Trey watched her go. "Yes, it did."

"I was being sarcastic."

"I'm not."

Keesha vanished into the trees. Soon he'd be out there with her, hiding. He had a balaclava and a jacket in the same camouflage pattern, concealment from head to toe, but his most effective weapon was patience. Trey was the most steadfast, unwavering man I knew.

"You seriously think that went well?" I said.

"I do. Considering what I'm asking of her."

I examined his expression. This was an old pattern with them. Whatever was in those files, she didn't want it out of her control. But she did want it resolved. I could see the tension. The question was, did she trust Trey to resolve it? And me?

"So now what?"

He finished chewing the last bite of his sandwich. "Now I wait."

He gathered his things—the jacket, the water bottle, a compass. He looked like he wanted to say something. I felt a stirring, not entirely uncomfortable, tingly like the leading edge of a thunderstorm. It was what I felt every time I found a mystery that needed solving, a puzzle that needed unpuzzling. Finn had delivered one to my doorstep. But another was standing right in front of me.

I ran a finger along the patterned fabric of his pants. "I gotta say, you have surprised me in many ways, but I never thought I'd see you in camo."

He looked a little offended. "It's ATACS."

"Whatever." I stood up, plucked a piece of pine straw out of his hair. "I always knew you had a little redneck in you."

Chapter Eleven

I spent the rest of the afternoon updating my ATF records and filing paperwork, which took longer than I expected. By the time I got inside Trey's apartment, it was almost dark, but the place was empty. Every sound echoed against the black hardwood floor and blank white walls.

I dropped my bag beside his desk and opened the French doors to the terrace. On the horizon I could see the skyline of Midtown and Downtown, the jagged line of the skyscrapers. Below me lay the heart of Buckhead with its exclusive clubs and organic spas and high-end boutiques. I couldn't see Chastain Park, but I knew it was close, which meant the Talbot mansion was nearby. Two miles away, Finn had said, at the juncture where Tuxedo Road dead-ended into Powers Ferry.

Trey hadn't lived in Buckhead when Jessica Talbot was murdered. He'd had an apartment in Edgewood, in a complex that was neither high end nor exclusive. Tuxedo Road was the ancestral home of the oldest of the old money, practically prehistoric money. But new money, Hollywood money, was buying its way into the club. Even Tuxedo Road couldn't resist all those fresh green millions.

I left the door open and went back inside. Took off my shoes. Got a cold beer and a clean glass. Then I settled in on the couch with my computer in my lap. Files or no files, I was betting I'd find a goldmine of information just a few clicks away.

I was right.

My first search on Jessica Talbot brought up a vast image library, and I felt a stab of...I couldn't even identify the emotion. She looked like Gabriella's dissolute baby sister. Same red hair, same green cat eyes, same milky complexion. But she was raw where Gabriella was refined, and she lapped up the camera's attentions, hungry for more.

Nick was on her arm in a couple of the photographs, the standard "fancy people arriving at the club" shots. He was good-looking in an over-ripened way, like a soft peach. His hair was his best feature, mahogany brown, long and curly and rakishly dipping over one eye. But his eyes were unfocused and his clothes rumpled, as if someone had pulled him out of the back of a limo and propped him upright.

Jessica Talbot. The one modeling success of Talbot Talent, which otherwise was a year of chaos and false starts. Nick had quickly assembled a client list, virtually all unknowns, then mismanaged it into bankruptcy, which, if I were to believe the gossip blogs, had mostly gone up his nose and straight to his liver. But before the crash and burn, they'd been living the life. *Architecture Today* featured the Talbot home in a slick, worshipful spread. Unlike most new-to-the-city moguls, they hadn't built an estate. Instead they'd renovated one of the older homes, doubling the square footage with two soaring, sprawling additions. Then they'd painted everything stark white, including the barn-like guest house. With dogwoods blooming out front, it had a contrived arctic charm. But there was nothing welcoming about the place.

I couldn't help making the comparison between the Talbot home and Trey's dichromatic apartment. The sophisticated black-and-white palette soothed him, but without his presence, it felt lifeless and blank. What would the Trey of the past—the emotionally scorched Trey parked outside Gabriella's empty bungalow, about to be called to a murder—think of this place? Of me? Of coming face-to-face with Nick Talbot again?

I took a deep breath and added the name Trey Seaver to the search box.

As I expected, the first hits came from newspapers all around the state. As the second responding officer, he'd testified about what he'd found at the scene. I clicked on the first link, an article in the *Atlanta Journal-Constitution*. It described him as "stoic" and his answers as "brief and plainspoken." I clicked the image search button and held my breath.

And there he was, the Trey I'd never met. He wore his uniform, the long-sleeved navy serge with the APD seal on his bicep, the phoenix rising over the single word *Resurgens*. He was being sworn in, his right hand raised, fingers stiff and straight. He was huskier, his features less honed. No silver scars on his chin or at his temple—those would come later, artifacts of the accident. His eyes were still as blue as the top of the sky, though, and as serious as a heart attack.

Yes, he'd been the second responding. No, he'd seen nothing suspicious in Macklin's behavior, not at the scene. Yes, the scene appeared to be consistent with a burglary at first glance, but upon further examination, it was clearly staged. I skimmed the articles, printed them out for deeper reading later. I did the same with the *AJC* articles about police misconduct. Trey was mentioned at the beginning of the coverage, but then disappeared as Macklin became the epicenter of the scandal. Not once was Keesha Price mentioned. Not even a hint of her involvement.

But Macklin? He was crucified.

They'd used the same photo of him over and over, his official APD ID, probably because he looked like a villain. Light brown hair buzz cut, small mean eyes. An aquiline nose too big for his face. Tanned skin with white patches around his eyes from wearing sunglasses all the time. He was stocky, muscled. He was the kind of cop that civilians dreaded seeing in their rearview mirror.

I pulled his image from the printer, held it up so that I could look him in the eye. I had no problem seeing him shoot Jessica Talbot in cold blood. No problem seeing him shoot himself rather than face disgrace.

I heard the sounds of the first deadbolt flipping, and then the second, and then the keyswitch lock. I heard footsteps next, though not the quiet ones of leather lace-ups or running shoes. Heavy, trying not to be, the thump of boots. And then Trey's silhouette in the door, duffel bag on shoulder.

I smiled. "Hey, you."

Trey paused in the door frame. "Hey. I'm sorry I'm late."

"It's all right. I've been working." I scooched to one end of the sofa. "Come sit with me."

He hesitated. "I need a shower."

"In a second. Talk to me first."

He had that wary look he got when he was worried he'd done something wrong, but he took off his boots and socks and came over barefoot, perching on the very edge of the sofa. Up close, he smelled like gunpowder and sweat and dirt. He had a fresh bandage across his knuckles and a blood blister in the webbing between his thumb and forefinger that looked like he'd snagged it in the recoil of a semi-auto. It was a beginner's injury, which meant he'd been caught off guard.

"Late day, huh?"

He nodded. "Price told me that if I could hide where she couldn't find me, she'd consider giving me the files."

"She admitted she had them."

"She did."

"Did she find you?"

"No." Satisfaction laced his voice. He dropped his head forward and showed me the back of his neck, covered in a thick layer of calamine. "But I got into some poison oak. And mosquitoes."

"Ouch."

He raised his head. He still had black grease shadows under his eyes, like a football player.

"So where are the files?" I said.

"I don't have them."

"But you said—"

"Price said she would *consider* giving them to me. She said she'd let me know as soon as she decided."

He noticed my printouts on the coffee table. He picked up the image of himself on the witness stand and examined it, his expression guarded. This wasn't about rules and regulations. This was deeper. There was injustice here, a seeping festering wound of it, and he was prepared to cauterize it. It was what he did. There was a victim, that much he was sure of, which meant there was a guilty party. Which meant there needed to be punishment.

I brushed his hair from his forehead and felt grit. Normally he came home from work as fresh and clean as he'd left, not with dirt under his fingernails and streaks of grime along his cheek. He was right. He had no business sitting on such a nice leather sofa as grungy as he was. But he was wearing that grunge as easily as he wore Armani.

He laid the photo back on the table, shaking his head. "It's strange. I can remember the events, but I can't remember...me. I was me, of course, but not. Does that make sense?"

And the thing was, it did. I understood completely and utterly.

Trey's phone buzzed with an incoming text. He looked at the readout. "It's Price. She said she's bringing the files."

"When?"

"Right now."

I laughed a little. "Well, that was fast."

Trey was thinking hard. He didn't look settled.

"Why are you making that face? She's giving you the files."

"She didn't say she was giving them to me. She said she was *bringing* them." He closed his eyes wearily. "And that is an entirely different matter."

Chapter Twelve

Thirty minutes later, Keesha met Trey at the front door with her sidearm on her hip. It was camouflaged by a flowing block-dyed vest the color of the ocean, but even in a sleeveless tank and frayed-hem jeans, she carried smackdown the way other women carried mace. Her only adornment was a tattoo on her bicep, a Latin phrase underneath a stylized square labyrinth. I recognized the image—Trey's SWAT uniform bore a patch just like it—but not the Latin.

She kept one fist wrapped around the strap of the messenger bag on her shoulder. "You got sunburned."

Trey touched his cheekbone, freshly scrubbed. "A little."

I watched from the kitchen as she held the bag close and came inside. She made straight for the armchair, sat with her legs tucked under her. Then she pulled a deck of cards from her pocket, bright green and worn at the edges, and smacked them in the middle of the coffee table.

"You want those files, Seaver, you gotta earn them."

Trey sat down on the sofa opposite her. "The game?"

"Slapjack."

He picked up the cards and started shuffling. Whatever was going down, it was old and familiar and strictly between the two of them. Trey dealt. Keesha looked at him, not the cards. The expression on her face reminded me of someone watching old home movies, seeing long-dead relatives talking and walking around.

She draped one arm along the back of the sofa. "You remember the last time we played? We didn't get to finish because we got that call to the Botanical Garden about the shooter on top of the greenhouse, and it turned out to be some naked drunk girl with a dildo?"

The corner of his mouth twitched, but he remained focused on the cards, one to him, one to her. "I remember. You called that one before we'd even set up."

"I know how to tell a sex toy from a firearm." She narrowed her eyes in a mock glare. "You made me go up there and get her all by myself. Said you wanted no part of trying to wrestle a rubber penis from a crazy woman twenty feet off the ground."

He dealt out the last card, the deck now split evenly between them. "You handled the situation."

"Of course I did."

"Of course." He looked up. "Are you ready?"

She nodded, placed one hand on top of her stack. On some signal I couldn't see, she flipped the top card face-up in the middle. Trey did the same on his turn. Back and forth they went until a jack appeared, and they both slapped a hand on top of it, Trey first. She cursed as he collected the cards.

"Damn, you got faster in your old age."

He shuffled the cards into his deck. "Perhaps you've gotten slower."

"Like hell."

Then back to flipping cards. She claimed the second jack, Trey the third. He didn't take his eyes off the table, didn't even look at the messenger bag.

She slid closer until she was on the edge of the chair. "You still think Nick Talbot did it?"

"I do." Trey turned over another card. "Do you still think Macklin did it?"

"Yep."

Trey snagged the fourth jack, and Keesha cursed. He gathered the last of the deck to himself.

"Macklin had no motive," he said.

"Greed not good enough for you? The man was up to his eyeballs in debt. Gambling debt, hooker debt, God knows what other kind of debt."

"He also had an alibi. His dash cam."

"His first visit is at 8:45, lasts approximately five minutes. Then he's there again an hour later, talking about some gut feeling. Gut feeling, my ass. He killed that woman somewhere in that hour between and then pretended to find her body, pretended to catch her killer in the act, hit his own self upside his own head and pretended to find that weapon on the edge of the property. And then everybody eats this story up like it was a damn doughnut."

She slapped her hand on the jack and dragged the stack of cards toward her. Trey took his stack and sat back. They regarded each other over the coffee table like gunslingers at the OK Corral.

Trey put his cards down. "Talbot bought that gun the month before."

"Because of the burglaries. Hundreds of Buckhead residents bought new guns."

"Still, Macklin knew better than to go back to the house. He knew Jessica was there. He'd spoken with her at 8:45."

"In gym clothes. He thought she was about to leave the house and go for a run." Keesha put her cards down, flipped the top one over. "So he parks the cruiser and sneaks back, thinks she's gone, she's not, she walks in on him stealing her jewelry and makes a break for it, he grabs the gun from the side table... pow pow. Twice in the back as she's running down the stairs, once in the chest when she falls. He makes the scene look like a burglary gone bad, goes back to his car, starts driving around again. Goes back to the house to pretend to find her body. At which point you show up."

They flipped cards the entire time she talked. I could picture them in some neighborhood bar with a beer-sticky floor, slapping down cards after a shift, surrounded by laughter. I was watching history, this moment added to a daisy chain of other moments going back years.

Keesha claimed the next jack. "But since you're all about alibis, you know your boy Nick Talbot has a solid one."

"The woman he was having an affair with. We could have broken her testimony in court."

"That sweet thing with the batty-bat eyelashes and heart full of love?" She scoffed. "Please. Nobody was breaking that child."

"Regardless, no connection was ever found between Macklin and the Talbots."

"That's because people stopped looking for it when he blew his brains out. But there's a big hole in that case, and it's shaped like Joe Macklin."

Garrity was right—she and Trey had matching grudges. As much as Trey wanted to take down Nicholas Talbot, Keesha wanted to take down Joe Macklin.

Trey flipped a card. "If Macklin had staged the scene, he would have done a better job. He knew the details that would make it look authentic. But Talbot didn't. Talbot only knew what he'd read about in the newspapers."

"Macklin was working fast. He made mistakes."

"Those mistakes weren't cop mistakes, they were civilian mistakes, and you know it."

Her eyes flashed as she flipped her card, an ace. "You know what I know? I know that when you got there you were supposed to secure the scene. But you didn't. Instead, you rendered aid to the victim. The dead victim. *Before* you cleared the house."

Trey flipped his card. The Jack of Clubs. But he didn't move to claim it. Neither did Keesha. It lay between them on the table, untouched.

"Now why would you do a fool-ass thing like that?" she said.

He stared at the jack. "I don't know. I remember feeling as if I were watching from somewhere else in the room. Watching somebody else count off the compressions and clear the airway."

My heart felt light in my chest. Disassociation. A psychological reaction to overwhelming stress.

He shrugged, eyes still on the table. "And then I was myself again. And I had her blood on my hands. On my knees. On my mouth. So I stood up. I secured the scene. And then I went back to my cruiser for the first aid kit for Macklin."

"I know what happened," Keesha said, her voice tightening. "I found out when I read the OPS report. Not because you told me. You never said a word to me."

He looked puzzled. "How could I tell you that I'd made that kind of fundamental mistake?"

"Just like that. That's how."

He shook his head. "You did not tolerate failure, not in yourself, certainly not in your partner."

"I don't give a good goddamn about what you did wrong! I care that you could have been killed!"

"But I wasn't. There was no suspect on premises." His expression stayed calm, but it was a manufactured calm. "Is that why you took the files without telling me? Because I wasn't honest with you?"

"I took them because I couldn't trust you."

Trey froze. Then he reached forward and claimed the jack, started shuffling it into his deck. "Okay."

Keesha arched an eyebrow. "That's all you got to say to that?"

"What do you want me to say?"

"I want you to say that you're sorry. Because I came to the hospital that night, after the accident. I came the next morning. I came over and over and over again. But all I got was the wall." Her voice shook, old pain rising to the surface. "And now you show up at my training. But not for me. Because you want those damn files."

He stopped shuffling. "You don't think...that's not why I signed up to help with the training. In the woods. With the mosquitoes and the poison oak and the...things in the trees."

Her brow creased. "Squirrels?"

"Right. Squirrels. I don't like squirrels. But I volunteered anyway because I wanted to see you. I wanted to...I was trying to...I can't find the word. Three syllables, starts with R."

I knew the word. But I wasn't about to interfere.

"Reconnect," Keesha said.

"Yes. That's it. I was trying to reconnect. But I'm very bad at it."

Keesha's expression didn't change. "You suck at it."

"Yes. But I *am* sorry. For all of it."

She didn't say anything for an entire minute. Then she switched her dark luminous gaze on me. "Seaver says you're his partner now. You know what that means?"

I was startled, but I'd been expecting the question. Trey and I had gone over this before she'd arrived. He had not used that word casually, he'd explained. It meant something to her, and to him. *Did I understand?* he'd asked.

"Yes," I said.

Keesha shoved the deck his way and stood, leaving the messenger bag on the sofa. "The files are yours now. For as long as you need them, or until I need them back, or until I tell you to burn 'em to fucking ash. We clear on that?"

He stood up too. "Very clear."

"And if you really want to reconnect, next time let me know that's what you're doing, all right?"

"All right."

"We'll find a squirrel-free zone."

She let a smile flicker around her mouth. She started walking toward the door, Trey right behind. She paused in the threshold.

"I'm still a better shot," she said.

Trey shrugged. "I still run faster."

"Maybe. But I'm gaining on you, Seaver."

She held out her fist, knuckles first. He tapped it lightly with his own. Then she left without looking back. Trey closed the door behind her. He didn't even hesitate, went right to the sofa and started removing files from the bag.

I came out of the kitchen. "You digging into all this right now?"

"Yes."

He stacked several folders on the coffee table. There were dozens more in the bag, hundreds of pages. I checked the time. Nine o'clock. I opened the cabinet and pulled down the coffee and a box of lapsang souchong tea, both highly caffeinated.

"Trey?"

"Yes?"

"Keesha's tattoo. I recognized the labyrinth, but not the Latin."

"*Alea iacta est.*" He spread another sheaf of folders on the table. "She told me it was a quote from Julius Caesar as he prepared to cross the Rubicon."

"What does it mean?"

Trey placed the empty bag on the floor. "It means, the die is cast."

Chapter Thirteen

Trey sat cross-legged on the floor, surrounded by yellow pads, mechanical pencils, and sticky notes. He understood information best if he could process it spatially—flowcharts and bubble maps, lists and graphs—and he liked it hard copy. Every now and then he'd take a sip of tea. The caffeine would buy him an extra hour or so before he finally crashed, but he'd pay at the end. His sleep would be jittery, restless, no matter how many valerian root capsules he took.

I propped my chin in my hand and watched him. Yes, tomorrow would suck for him, but he was crisp and utterly capable at the moment. First, he'd sorted Keesha's files into stacks. Then he'd hauled in the boxes we'd collected from his basement, now dusted and organized. I'd added my own research, the scattered online articles and magazine spreads, the lurid and the tacky all mixed up with the objective and professional.

He held his mug with both hands, his expression serious. "Tai—"

"I already know."

"Know what?"

"Why the files are so secret." I sat my coffee on the floor. "See, Garrity said the only reason you needed to be worried about breaching confidentiality was if those files revealed the identify of Keesha's CI. But your worries felt bigger than that." I tapped one folder, resting now on his knee. "I think Keesha *is* the CI. I think she's working undercover for OPS."

Trey didn't say anything; he simply extended the file my way. I skimmed the interview transcripts. Every single time the CI's name was mentioned, the name had been redacted. Not one mention of Keesha Price. Macklin, Talbot, lots of Trey Seaver in there too. But not a single CI.

And then I saw it. The same name, repeated, only not in the reports themselves. In the administrative section at the top of the page.

I pointed. "This is the OPS officer who investigated Macklin. And you."

Trey nodded. But I was still puzzled. Why would Keesha make copies of these files? To protect Trey, certainly, in case the incident came up again. But the official record still existed. It was still accessible. Unless…

I gave the papers a satisfying thump. "She's a double agent! An undercover OPS officer covertly investigating the OPS itself. She kept these copies because she worried the records might be altered, and then you'd have only your word to protect you."

"She suspected that might be the case, yes."

"But don't they video OPS interviews?"

"Yes. But the division is moving its video evidence to cloud storage. They hired an outside company to do this. Occasionally a recording becomes corrupted. Or misfiled. Or lost."

"Sometimes on purpose."

"Price is certain of it. Gathering the evidence, however, is proving…challenging."

I wasn't surprised. At every intersection of the investigation process, there was a chance for someone to interfere. Involve an outside firm in such a crucial process, give its people discretionary oversight, and bam: major fox and henhouse situation.

I placed the file in its proper stack. "Did she catch the guilty party?"

"Parties. And no, not yet. The investigation is ongoing."

"Four years ongoing?"

He nodded.

"So we have to treat these files like nuclear bombs?"

"Yes. But if I'm going to engage with Nicholas Talbot again, I needed to see the evidence again."

"*If* you're going to?"

"Correct." He scrutinized the semi-circle of information fanned around him like a rainbow. "I haven't decided yet."

I drained the last of my coffee, rubbed my hands together. "In that case, we'd best get on with it."

• ● ● ● •

The next hours were a parade of blood and betrayal and bad ends. The crime scene photos were few and horrific, but it was Trey's field sketches that hit me hardest. Drawn from an overhead perspective, they were bare and precise—blood spatter detailed as objectively as room measurements. He'd rendered the body of Jessica Talbot as a faceless figure, plain, a piece of evidence like the footprints or the shell casings…except for the waves of hair trailing across her face and the open palm of one hand. It was a painstaking detail, wrenching and human, and it revealed as much about Trey as it did about the body.

I closed the folder. "You told Keesha that Macklin would have done a better job of staging the scene. How?"

"The broken glass at the alleged entry site, for one." He pointed to the map of the garage. "The Buckhead Burglar came in quietly, usually through a door after disarming the security system. He wouldn't have shattered a side window. He never broke into an occupied home, and yet Jessica's car was in the garage, a clear indication that she was still on premises, as was the fact that the security system was not armed."

Trey had assembled the official crime scene sketches like a map of the home, each room a separate piece of paper. These were computer rendered, two-dimensional and bloodless. He pointed to the bank of doors overlooking the backyard patio.

"This would have been the entry site he would have most likely used. Hidden from the street, close to the main security box for easy disarming. The suspect fled through these doors, through the backyard and into a wooded area adjacent to Powers Ferry Road, and then, presumably, into Chastain Park where Macklin lost him. There was no hesitation, no wrong turns or backtracking."

"You're saying the killer knew where he was going?"

"Yes."

Trey put out the mug shot. Nick Talbot in a dark golf shirt, his eyes wide, like a startled nocturnal animal. I tried to imagine him shooting his wife in the back, but the image wouldn't take.

"Talbot had been having an affair for months," Trey said. "That morning, he told family and friends that he was going golfing. And he did park at the golf club, at the north end of the park. But he didn't stay there."

"His lover picked him up."

"That's what she testified to, yes. Addison Canright, a volunteer he'd met at his most recent rehab facility, now a writer on something called *Moonshine*. She said that she drove him to her apartment, where he stayed for two hours before she returned him to his car."

He pulled out her photo, a newspaper shot snapped as she was leaving the courthouse. A small, neat woman, she wore her black hair in a shoulder-length blunt cut, her features hidden behind sunglasses too big for her face. I remembered Keesha's words: *that sweet thing with the batty-bat eyelashes and heart full of love.* But in this photo, Addison Canfield's slate gray dress and sensible shoes spoke of restraint, not come-hither high jinks.

"But you think she's lying. You think he came back to his house and killed Jessica, that he was never at Addison's apartment."

"I do." Trey pointed to the map of Chastain Park. The tree-lined trail to the golf course ran along the edge of Powers Ferry, the street that bordered the backyard of the Talbots' home. "Talbot had no way of knowing that Macklin would return. He expected to have more time staging the scene before the body was discovered. He hadn't planned on using the murder weapon on Macklin, but he had planned on fleeing through the backyard back to the golf course clubhouse, where his car was parked. That was always a part of the plan."

"Did anybody see him?"

"We received several reports of a man matching his description crossing Powers Ferry that morning."

"A white man in golf clothes headed for the golf course."

Trey exhaled. "You see why this was not a conclusive ID."

He stretched his legs out and rolled his head in a slow circle. I crawled over and sat behind him. He bowed his head forward and let me massage the corded tendons of his neck.

"What about other people in Jessica's life?" I said. "Finn said she'd had multiple affairs. Surely there were some jilted lovers? Jealous wives?"

"We never found any with both motive and opportunity."

"Any other suspects?"

"Not that we discovered. We checked out the other members of the family—Talbot's brother and his wife, both of whom were verified at the Talbot Creative offices when Macklin called in the murder. We checked out the other employees of Talbot Creative. Also alibied. We ran background on all the service workers with access to the house. All of them came back clean and—"

"Let me guess. Alibied."

"Yes. And without motive. No matter where we looked, the evidence pointed to Nick Talbot."

"Except for his alibi."

"His highly suspect alibi."

His index finger tapped erratically against his thigh, his caffeine level reaching critical mass. What could I tell him? Let the dead lie? Let the past go to dust and sweep it away? I wasn't the one to make that case. I knew how hard it was to pull your roots out of the dirt that had made you, leave that ground behind, no matter how poisoned it had become. All our regrets and mistakes and hauntings, they were always ours, always. We hauled our own private graveyards with us everywhere we went.

I rested my chin on his shoulder. "Trey?"

"Yes?"

"Say you decide to do this. What if you learn that you were right all along, that Nick Talbot really is a cold-blooded killer?"

He kept his head bent forward. "Then I gather the evidence and take it in."

"It wasn't enough to get an indictment then, and it certainly won't be now, four years after the fact. And I don't think the APD is going to take your word on it, either, no matter how awesome your lie-detecting ability is."

He didn't answer. I pressed the heel of my hand into one particularly stubborn knot, and he inhaled sharply, but didn't complain. The night outside the window was complete, as complete as it ever got in the city.

I held the pressure, but the knot refused to yield. "You're going to see him regardless, aren't you?"

Trey exhaled, emptying his lungs. "Yes."

Chapter Fourteen

As I'd predicted, Trey slept terribly, tossing and turning most of the night. Despite that, he went to work an hour early so that he could leave in time for his meeting with Nick Talbot. I usually slept in on Mondays, the last day of my weekend. This Monday, however, after reading even more about the crime committed against the unsuspecting Jessica Talbot, I went to the gun range to practice my defensive skills.

I had new hearing protection earmuffs to try out, the electronic kind that blocked gunfire while still allowing conversation to come through. Trey had given them to me, and they did the job perfectly, which on this particular afternoon was a good news-bad news situation. They deadened the heart-stoppingly loud .357 Sig rounds from the lane next to me, but they amplified the conversation of the two guys shooting them off. Each whoop and holler barreled straight into my ear canal.

I turned the volume way down, blocking their voices as much as possible. Practicing with speedloaders meant I needed to concentrate. I didn't enjoy the process, though. Speedloaders were speedy, yes, and from a tactical perspective, necessary, but there was something satisfying about thumbing bullets one by one into the chamber, slow and purposeful. I'd shot many guns since I'd opened the shop, from the bulky Magnums to the sleek Heckler and Koch semi-autos, but the snub-nose Smith and Wesson 640 was my weapon of choice.

The guys next to me did a rapid-fire session and my earmuffs kicked in, dampening the booms into a white electronic hum punctuated with soft poofs. I adjusted my goggles, sighted and fired. Five rounds fast at ten yards, defensive distance. I placed the gun on the counter and stretched my fingers out as the target fluttered my way. Four ragged holes at center mass, one in the shoulder. I cursed. If a shot went wrong, it was always that first one, which was not the one I wanted to go wrong.

I sent the target back to the mark. I'd briefly considered bringing Trey's nine-millimeter. A matte black P7M8, it was the smoothest handgun I'd ever shot, too heavy to haul around in a carry purse, however. He still practiced with it, still cleaned and maintained it, but ever since he'd pulled it on his boss in a moment of spectacularly bad judgment, he'd relegated it to the personal gun safe next to his bed. Whenever I asked when he might carry it again, he shook his head and changed the subject.

The men next to me high-fived each other. I felt a tap on my shoulder—Patrick, the range guy. I turned up the amplification as he pointed to my tote bag in the corner. "Your phone's going off."

"Sorry about that! Thank you!"

He tossed off a little salute and continued down the line. I placed the gun on the counter and knelt beside my bag. Seven missed calls in the last three minutes. All from Trey.

I felt a wash of nervousness. Something had gone wrong, bad wrong. I had my thumb poised to call him back when it started ringing again. Trey. I pushed through the first set of doors, then the second, yanking off the headset.

I put the phone to my ear. "What's happened?"

"You have to go."

"Go where?"

"To the meeting with Nicholas Talbot. There's an accident. I can't get off the interstate."

"Call and reschedule."

"I can't. I…hold on." Horns sounded at his end, woven with the wail of an ambulance. Police sirens too. His voice was tight with frustration. "There's no way out. I'm blocked. If I can get to the next exit, I'll be there, but I'll be late. You have to go."

"Trey—"

"He's on set at Kennesaw Mountain. Go to the parking lot at the summit, next to the trail entrance."

I pulled off my goggles. "And what am I supposed to do when I get there? They're not going to let me in. You're on the security list, not me."

"I'll call and get your name added."

"But—"

"There's no time. He could change his mind. The Talbot board could reconsider. There may not be another chance."

His voice held an edge of panic. I heard another horn, this time from the Ferrari. I felt a larger stab of worry. Trey was not a lay-on-the-horn kind of driver.

"Are you okay?" I said.

"I'm fine. But this is the second time the truck beside me has swerved into my lane. He's not paying attention, he's texting. Nobody is paying attention, and the wrecking crew hasn't even...hold on."

He hit the horn again. I was suddenly relieved he didn't have his gun, because if some unfortunate soul tapped that car, Trey would go ballistic, and nobody wanted actual ballistics in his vicinity if that happened.

I steadied my voice. "Trey. Listen to me. You need to calm down."

"I am calm."

"No, you are not."

"Go to the meeting."

"But I have no clue what to—"

"Please. I think it's a fair request. Considering."

He didn't have to explain what needed considering. All the times he'd stood by me as I dug some hole deeper and deeper. All the times he'd helped me out of those very same holes.

"Are you seriously playing the 'you owe me one' card?"

"I am."

I checked the clock above the coffee bar. 5:45. I could just make it.

"Fine. I'll go."

"Thank you. Thank you very much. Remember, only Talbot and his brother know why we're there, so be discreet. I'll be there in…" Another honk of the horn, and what sounded like a muttered curse. "As soon as I can."

Chapter Fifteen

Both peaks of Kennesaw Mountain belonged to the National Park Service, as did the almost three thousand acres of fields and woods at its base. The park itself didn't allow camping, but the surrounding pastureland was in private hands and popular with local reenactment groups. On certain nights, when the fog rolled thick through the knee-high grass, and the only sound was the low talk of men around a campfire...on those nights it felt as if I'd slipped into a crack in time and found myself a hundred and fifty years in the past.

This afternoon the past was truly past, though, and Hollywood had conquered where even General Sherman had failed. I found the base camp by following the yellow directional markers with the word "redbird" on them until I reached the second parking lot, closed now to tourists. The coded signs were necessary to keep the lookie-loos from finding the set, but the *Moonshine* folks had put in extra protections, including portable chain-link fencing, roving security guards, and a check-in station.

I had to park on the grass because the paved portion of the lot housed a collection of silver trailers and utility vans. At the entrance to the trail head, a cherry-picker hoisted a camera crew three stories high. Men and women in jeans spoke into handheld radios, while other people schlepped screens and umbrellas and reels of cable back and forth. In the center of this bustling mechanical chaos, in a circle all by herself, stood Mad Luna Malone.

Not Luna, I reminded myself. *Portia Ray. An actress.*

But all I saw was Luna.

She wore clothes typical of her 1920s moonshiner character, a homespun sleeveless tank and men's trousers held up with suspenders, but the low afternoon light highlighted her other-worldly presence. Her pale skin gleamed, her hair tumbled in white-hot tangles, and her biceps looked cut from marble. In one thirteen-episode binge, I'd watched Luna defeat both crafty revenuers and rival bootleggers, battling her way to the top of her werewolf clan only to be left for dead in a cliffhanger season finale. And now here she was, three-dimensional flesh and blood, emphasis on the blood—a rusty blotch on her chest, a smear along her forehead, a clotted bite on her shoulder.

She held a machine gun in one hand and a LeMat revolver in the other as a photographer circled her with a light meter. I knew diddly about the automatic weapon, but I'd sold the film crew the LeMat. In the lore of the series, it had belonged to Luna's grandfather, a backwoods wild man who refused to fight for any side but his own.

I heard footsteps and turned. The makeup guy stood behind me, eyes on Portia. He carried a plastic crafter case filled with spray bottles and paint palettes and rubbery pretend wounds. Spare-framed and friendly-looking, he had a wispy beard trimmed to disguise a soft chin. It was the hair that cinched the identification—dark brown, curly, pulled back in a ponytail. I peeked at the ID clipped to the hem of his tee.

Nick Talbot.

I suppressed a shudder. I couldn't look at him without remembering the newspaper photos, the mug shot, Jessica Talbot's body on the floor. I couldn't look at his hands without thinking of them holding a gun, pulling the trigger three times.

Before I could say anything, a woman scooted up in a club cart, her cinnamon hair blowsy around her face. Three men got out of the cart. They wore deep charcoal business suits, almost identical, with ivory shirts open at the throat. White guys, nondescript, one of them obviously the alpha of the pack—the other two flanked him, mirroring his movements and never interrupting. They were smiling, easy with each other and with whatever privilege they were wielding. And they had some, that was for sure—they wore no IDs, yet they walked right up to Portia as if they were old friends. A khaki-clad security officer shot a quizzical look toward the woman in the cart, but she shook her head, and he backed down.

The woman climbed out and hurried toward Nick. Her jeans hugged her with painted-on efficiency, and her V-neck tee displayed an abundance of cleavage. She'd laid the perfume on a little thick, probably to cover the mosquito repellent, but her makeup was flawless.

"Where's Mr. Talbot?" she said.

Nick didn't take his eyes off Portia. "Quint's in my trailer. Who are these people and why are they being allowed to disturb a photo shoot?"

"They're investors. Big ones. They insisted on seeing her, said Mr. Talbot had promised to let them through."

"And you believed that?"

"After I called him and verified, yes, but now he's gone, and he's not answering his phone. The guard post says he checked out thirty minutes ago."

"Crap. He's probably gone to the house and left me to deal with Portia's wrath. He knows how much she hates sucking up to the money."

That part was obvious. I watched her slip a look of extreme malice at the newcomers, a look she wiped from her face the second they got close to her. She glowed then, as if she'd been waiting for them all day. The one in charge shook her hand, obviously dazzled. The other two men waited politely behind him, didn't say a word to her. Portia held his hand warmly between hers. The second he turned his back, she glared at Nick, who shrugged apologetically.

The woman beside us gathered her hair into a loose bun and clipped it into place. "Great. She's gonna eat me for dinner."

"Not if you get those people away from her ASAP."

"But Mr. Talbot said—"

"Investors start to devalue the asset if they get too much access. Haul them down to props, let them play with the fake guns. I'll run interference with Quint."

Relief flared in her eyes. "God, thank you. You're the best."

"Least I can do. Did you bring her shake?"

"Freshly made and waiting in her trailer. Lots of weird herbs and a scoop of that nasty protein powder."

"The kind that smells like sardines?"

The woman laughed and nodded. She was very pretty in a calculated way, perhaps a bit strong in the jaw, but she'd make a fine werewolf. Assuming she got the attention of someone with the power to cast her. And from the way she was looking at Nick, I was betting she thought she had. She had cunning in her eyes. Hunger, too, though not for a protein shake.

Nick waved a hand toward the men. "Go get 'em, Bree. Quick quick."

Bree scurried over. She expertly corralled the men, murmured an apology to Portia, who waved it off even as she glared at Nick, who didn't seem the least bit concerned. Having one's brother as executive producer provided a certain shield, I decided, even from celebrity anger.

"You've got a fan," I said.

He shook his head. "Bree? Hardly. Every runner around here thinks I've got the gold ticket to stardom."

"Do you?"

His smile turned wry. "I'm toting around silicone scars and bins of latex. What do you think?"

Portia rolled her shoulders, adjusted her grip on her weapons again. Beads of sweat marked her forehead and chest. The photographer said something, and she twisted around to examine her shoulder.

"Uh oh," Nick said. "Time for a touch-up."

He jogged over. After a quick confab, he lifted the prosthetic scar on her shoulder, then gave it a little squirt from a tube and smoothed it back. Portia tilted her head, and he spritzed her neck with water, patted it with a towel. She said something that made her mouth curl at the edge. Nick shook his head, his expression pleasant and unperturbed. He returned to my side as the photographer moved in again.

He examined me curiously. "Who did you say you were?"

I held up my visitor pass. "Tai Randolph. Mr. Seaver sent me. He's been detained."

"Mr. Seaver, huh?" Sharp amusement laced his voice. "Is he your boss? Because you don't say that like he is. You say that like someone who never calls him Mr. Seaver."

"He's my partner."

"Partner." Nick smiled knowingly. "I see." He knelt and screwed the cap on a bottle of viscous red liquid. "Did Mr. Seaver tell you why I asked him here?"

"He did."

"And you're cool with being his stunt double?"

"I am."

One of the photographers pulled his camera from around his neck. At that cue, a young man hurried up with a fresh bottle of water for Portia. She favored him with a smile, and I watched him melt. I'd never seen someone with such control over her charisma. She could deploy it like a smart bomb.

"Does Luna make it to next season?" I said.

Nick didn't look up from his kit. "So you're a fan."

"Just curious."

He laughed. "Everybody is. But I'm the makeup guy. They tell me nothing."

"Your fiancée not telling?"

"Addison doesn't know either."

"I thought she was the show's writer."

Nick wiped his hand on his jeans, leaving a streak of foundation. "She's *one* of the writers. There's a stable of them. Addison wrote one version of the season two debut, but somebody else wrote the other. They haven't said which one is legit. They're running counter-intelligence big-time now."

"They?"

"The producers."

"Meaning your brother?"

"He's one. But there's a whole board of them, not just Quint." He shook his head. "Addison's the biggest talent on this lot. Without her, *Moonshine* would be just another supernatural bloodbath. But producers think like producers, not artists, so they're not telling her crap."

"You were a producer too. Back in California."

Nick busied himself with a jar of brushes, sorting and examining. "I was."

"Do you miss it?"

"Backstabbing and mind games? No. I leave that to my power-junkie brother."

"Who abandoned a group of high-level investors, it seems. Is that typical?"

Nick propped an elbow on his knee. "You'll have to ask him. I'm sure he'll give you a big important earful. Just don't let Portia see you getting too close. My sister-in-law is a suspicious woman, and I haven't told her about Friday night, so—"

"Did you say sister-in-law?"

His eyebrows knit in puzzlement. "Portia is Quint's wife. Didn't you know?"

A club cart zipped next to Portia. She hopped in, and it hauled her down the twisty paved road toward her next shoot. A battalion of techs and runners and other second-tier crew jogged in her wake.

I shook my head. "I knew your brother was married. I didn't know it was to the star of the show."

Nick laughed as he stood. "Mr. Seaver didn't prep you very well. You should complain. Of course Portia went by Patsy during the trial, when she was a nobody, so I understand how he could miss the connection." Nick hoisted his kit, then started walking toward a cluster of tiny trailers, less sleek and silver than the massive ones I'd first seen. He looked over his shoulder at me. "You coming or what?"

Chapter Sixteen

The inside of the makeup trailer was empty except for the two of us, and it was still close quarters. Nick plopped his kit on a table crammed with cans of hairspray and rows of makeup brushes. It smelled like a cross between a nail salon and my high school chemistry lab, bright with marquee lights surrounding a wall of mirrors. He went to a table in the corner where an electric kettle perked next to an assortment of tea boxes. I recognized all of Trey's favorites—Darjeeling, green, rooibos.

Nick spooned loose leaves into an infusion ball. "Would you like some?"

I wrinkled my nose. It smelled like wet hay and mushrooms.

"No, thank you," I said.

He laughed as he dropped the ball into a mug and poured hot water over it. "Pu-erh. It's an acquired taste. I haven't actually acquired it yet, but Addison says it's got electrolytes and lipo-somethings, so I drink it. I have regular flavors too. You like vanilla?"

"I'm fine. Really."

As the tea steeped, Nick flung himself into a salon chair. I sat on a red velvet stool, the only other seating in the room, my feet inches from his. Images of the crime scene photos kept flashing in my head.

Nick swiveled in the chair. "You're wondering why, aren't you?"

"Why what?"

"Why I set up this interview."

I tried to get comfortable on the stool. "It has crossed my mind."

"I did it because somebody tried to kill me. I need to know if Officer Seaver is that somebody." He laced his fingers over his stomach. "Why did he say yes?"

"Because you threatened him."

Nick scoffed. "He was a SWAT bad-ass then and he's some kind of private security bad-ass now. He's not afraid of me. So why did he agree to this?"

Just then I heard footsteps coming up the rickety metal stairs, quick, followed by three solid knocks. Impatient knocks.

"Ask him yourself," I said.

Nick stopped spinning in the chair and pulled a medicine bottle from his pocket. Herbal relaxants, the same kind Trey carried. He grabbed for the still-steeping tea, cursing under his breath.

"You okay, Mr. Talbot?"

"Call me Nick. Maybe not. Too late for that now." He washed the pills down and cleared his throat. "Door's open."

Trey yanked the door with more force than necessary, and the trailer rattled. He was still in his suit, though the trek through the parking lot had deposited a few stray grass clippings around the hem of his trousers. Nick stood up and slipped the pills back in his pocket, putting the chair between himself and Trey.

I smiled. "You made it."

Trey looked my way. "I did." Then he fastened his gaze back on Nick Talbot. "You have fifty-nine minutes."

Nick gave him a ghost of a smile. "You haven't changed a bit."

Trey didn't reply. He wasn't going to play this game. He was willing to let Nick reminisce, though, because he was watching him talk, concentrating on his mouth. Nick didn't even know he was hooked up to a cranial lie detector.

He shook his head at Trey. "Finn told me you'd never agree to this."

"Finn was wrong."

"So I see." His hands were shaking, but his voice was stronger. "I knew you would, though. You made my life hell back then. I told her you'd jump at the chance to make it hell again."

Trey's jaw clenched. "Fifty-eight minutes."

"Fine." Nick sat back in the chair, balancing his mug on his stomach. "You think I'm a murderer. Fair enough. I think you tried to put a bullet in my head."

Trey's expression remained bland. "I did not."

"Really? Well, damn. Guess I have it all wrong. Glad you straightened that out for me."

He kept both hands wrapped around his mug as he talked, tried to look casual and calm. But his pupils were dilated, and one foot tapped the floor in manic rhythm. He acted as if he wanted to get right up in Trey's face. But there was a deep instinct that kept him from doing that, the same way it kept him from picking up a rattlesnake.

"I started to call the police," he said. "Show you what it felt like to be unjustly accused. But my brother reminded me of what happened last time. He reminded me that the APD still carries a grudge for me. And he was right. Because here you are, vindictive as ever."

"I'm here to see that justice is served."

"Really? Me too. How coincidental." He blinked rapidly, but he didn't break eye contact. "So. About that. What were you doing at ten o'clock on Friday night?"

Trey's voice was monotone. "I was asleep."

"Let me guess. Not alone." Nick said this with a knowing look in my direction. "The irony of it all, you telling me you couldn't have done it because the woman you were sleeping with says you were with her. What did you call it four years ago, when I said the exact same thing?"

"A soft alibi."

Nick's smile twitched, but did not fade. "Right."

It suddenly occurred to me that perhaps Finn had misinterpreted this entire setup and that I'd let Trey get drawn into a booby trap. I stood up and went to his side, but he didn't look at me. He kept his attention on Nick, and I knew this was the moment he'd been waiting for.

"Mr. Talbot," he said. "Did you kill your wife?"

Nick sighed. "Seriously? After everything that came out, you still think I did it?"

"I do."

"You're wrong."

"Then say it."

"Say what?"

Trey's expression never wavered. "Say you didn't kill her."

Nick returned the stare. "I didn't kill Jessica."

Trey froze. "Say it again."

"Why?"

"Just do it."

Nick's voice grew more adamant. "I did not kill my wife. And I don't know who did."

Trey went pale. Before I could speak, he turned and pushed open the door. He took the steps two at a time, then hit the ground and started pacing. Not the thoughtful kind of pacing. The kind that happened when he was trying to bleed off a bunch of frustration before he exploded and took out a few square miles of humanity.

I quick-stepped down the stairs after him. "Trey—"

"He's telling the truth."

"I guessed as much."

He pressed his thumb between his eyebrows, still pacing. This was not what he'd expected. He'd expected that Nick Talbot would lie, and then he'd catch it, and then the march toward justice and retribution would begin. Except for the inconvenient fact that Nick was innocent.

"Trey—"

"All the evidence. Every piece of it. I'm not...I can't..."

I put myself into his path. "Stop pacing and look at me."

He did both, and I breathed a silent sigh of relief. Good. He was listening and following instructions. I could work with that.

I placed one hand against his stomach. "Deep breath. All the way in."

He inhaled, and I felt his diaphragm expand. I placed my other hand against the center of his chest, and his heart galloped against my palm. People came and went in streams around us, talking on cell phones, eyes on clipboards.

"Now count with me," I said. "You know the drill."

He swallowed, drew in a shaky breath. "One."

He'd talked me down in exactly this same manner many, many times, his hands grounding and calming, his voice like a clear white light I could follow out of the dark. I took him by the hand and led him to a folding chair next to the steps. He sat, elbows to knees, still counting on the inhales and exhales.

I knelt in front of him. "Look. You came here with an idea. It was an idea based on evidence and experience, but it was an idea you made a long time ago."

Trey was breathing more steadily now. "Go on."

"Things have changed. You now know he didn't do it. Which means you gotta let go of the idea that this is the day you finally bring Nick Talbot to justice."

He drew in a deep breath, let it halfway out, a sniper's trick. "Yes. You're right, of course." Then he squared his shoulders, stood, and started back into the trailer.

I grabbed his elbow. "Whoa, whoa! What are you doing?"

He had one foot on the ground and one on the step. "I need to talk to him some more."

"Why?"

Trey looked perplexed. "Because he didn't kill his wife."

I should have seen it coming. We'd discovered that the man he'd decided was guilty beyond a shadow of a doubt, the man whose freedom irritated him like a splinter, was, in fact, innocent. Trey was still in the justice game, only now he had a different goal.

I didn't let go of his arm. "You sure this is a good idea?"

"No. Do you have a better one?"

"Not right this second."

"Okay then." He disengaged himself from my grasp. "We'll continue with this one."

Chapter Seventeen

So we went back in the trailer. Nick had a cigarette going, and the air inside was bluish with tobacco smoke. My throat caught at the scent, and my fingertips itched. Nick jumped when he saw us, then blew a narrow stream of smoke in our direction.

"You're back."

Trey cocked his head. "You didn't kill her."

"Of course I didn't! That's the whole point!" He tapped ash into an empty coffee mug and returned to the stylist chair. "Look, I sat through your testimony at the indictment, and I know what it looked like. Hell, if I hadn't had Addison keeping me straight, I might have started thinking I did it too. But I didn't kill Jessica. I loved her."

"Then why were you having an affair?"

"Because Jessica didn't love me." He sucked at the cigarette, let the smoke wallow in his mouth. "She wanted a divorce."

"But you didn't," I said.

"No, I was fine with a divorce. Not so fine with the money she wanted." He examined the smoldering tip of the cigarette, and behind the softness I saw calculation. "How would you feel if you learned that someone you loved had been using you as a meal ticket?"

"I'd feel pretty damn bad," I said. "Bad enough to kill said someone, I'm sure."

"Yeah, but I'm sure you wouldn't. I didn't either." He ground out the butt in the mug. "Have you ever done something you regretted? Because if you say you haven't, you're a liar. And if you say you have, and your life didn't go to hell because of it, then you are one lucky human being."

I couldn't argue with him there. He had a point. Life could go sideways in the blink of an eye, and playing it safe was no guarantee against tragedy. I glanced at Trey. He was listening, calmer now.

"Tell me what happened that morning," he said.

"You know what happened."

"I want to hear it from you."

Nick sighed, patting down his pockets for a fresh cigarette. He fished one out and lit it, then told the story of his wife's murder, starting from the top. It was a recitation, dispassionate, like he'd memorized the sequence of events.

"And then I got the call. I went home and the police intercepted me." He pointed the cigarette toward Trey. "The police being you. And then you handed me over to somebody in a suit, and he told me that Jessica was dead. And I don't remember much else except the dawning realization that no matter what I did or said from that moment on, my life was ruined."

His life. He'd just learned that someone had murdered his wife, and all he could think about was himself. Not his dead brutalized wife. Not even his surely panicked lover. Himself.

"They wouldn't let me see her," he said. "But that's SOP, isn't it? And then they asked me the same questions over and over."

"And you lied."

"At first. But only to protect Addison."

Bullshit, I thought. *You lied because you worried that if the cops knew you'd been off banging your hot sidepiece, you would look like Guilty Party Numero Uno. You were trying to keep that secret in your back pocket.*

"And then you realized you needed her alibi," Trey said.

"Addison insisted. And she wasn't lying, if that's what you're implying."

Trey remained unmoved. "I'm establishing the facts. And the fact is, you had no solid alibi except for her testimony."

"I didn't know I'd need one."

Nick took one final drag on the cigarette, then dropped it into the mug. He reached for the pack as if he were about to fire up a third, but changed his mind. He folded his hands on his stomach instead, interlaced his fingers. His foot did not stop bouncing, and he continuously swiveled in the salon chair, back and forth, back and forth.

Trey assessed his every move. Not once had his expression flared with that gotcha look, which meant that every word Nick had spoken had been the truth. So far.

"Tell me about Friday night," Trey said.

"It was late, around ten, I guess. I didn't look at the clock, but that's what Quint said. Anyway, just when I got on the patio, I heard the shot."

"Only one?"

"Yes."

"What did you do?"

"I ran back inside."

I was itching to jump in, literally itching with the fierce desire to pull apart his story layer by layer and see what twitched underneath. But I wasn't a part of this. This had nothing to do with me, at all.

Trey didn't move from his position in the corner. "Did you see anyone?"

"No."

"Anything suspicious?"

"No."

"Do you live there alone?"

"Nobody *lives* there. Addison and I have a place closer to the studio—that's where she was when all this happened, at home working. The house technically belongs to Talbot Creative now, but Quint has it on the market. There's a staging team coming tomorrow to get it ready. That's why Quint was there Friday night, supervising the real estate crew. The *Buckwild* people left it in a big mess."

Trey looked confused. "The what people?"

"*Buckwild in Buckhead.* You know."

Now Trey looked utterly baffled. But I knew exactly what Nick was talking about.

"It's a reality show," I said. "Lasted three seasons before it was canceled this year. They imported twelve rural Southerners into a fancy Buckhead mansion and tried to teach them to function in the upper echelons of Atlanta society. Hilarity ensued." I looked at Nick. "That was your place they used?"

"'Used' is the right word. We tried to sell it after the grand jury hearing—no luck—so Quint leased it to the *Buckwild* production company. But now that's canceled, and he's trying to get it ready to show again. Anyway, he needed me to fill out some paperwork, so I went. But he told me I couldn't smoke in the house, so I went outside."

"Where outside?" Trey said.

"By the pool. Next to the diving board."

"Were the lights on?"

"Outside? No."

"What about in the pool?"

He frowned. "Now that you mention it, yeah. Why is that important?"

"I don't know if it is."

Trey had his arms folded, his expression curious, calm. Some part of his brain was assembling a blueprint and a timeline, and every detail Nick shared went into its proper position.

"Continue," he said.

Nick shrugged. "That's it. I was standing there, cigarette in my mouth. I dug in my pocket for my lighter, heard this crack, high-pitched. And then this whistling hiss like something straight outta *Gunsmoke.*"

Trey slid a look my way. Nick was describing a sonic wave. Suddenly, his story seemed much more plausible.

"And you recognized that as a gunshot?" Trey said.

"Oh yeah. I hear them all the time on the set. This one was far away though, not close. Not like right beside me. Which is why I thought sniper." He pointed at Trey. "Which is why I thought you."

Trey ignored the implication. "What did you do next?"

"I ran back inside, what do you think I did?"

Trey knew the rest of the story from Finn. Nick's brother had searched for the bullet, found nothing. Trey didn't have any further questions, but I sure did, and I couldn't keep them inside any longer.

"If you don't live there anymore, why were you there Friday night?" I said.

"I told you. Paperwork."

"You can do paperwork anywhere. Why do it at the house where your wife was murdered?"

He reached for his lukewarm tea. "Because I haven't been there since she died. It had become a monster, in my mind anyway. On Monday, it will be a different place. The staging crew will have it stuffed with carefully curated art and knick-knacks." He shrugged. "I wanted to prove to myself that it had no more power over me."

"Is that why you wanted Trey to come? To prove he had no power over you either?"

Nick gave me a hard look, defensive and accusing at the same time. "Look, I can't move forward until I deal with the past. I thought I'd done that, but apparently my past is not done with me because it showed up the other night and tried to put a bullet in my head. I want it to be over. Over and done and finally, for the love of God, past. That's why I went out there."

Trey raised an eyebrow. "And did that work for you?"

"It did not." Nick looked Trey up and down. He wore the same expression Trey did when he was evaluating the veracity of a statement—gaze focused on the lips, eyes narrowed. "You know what? Go see for yourself."

"See what?"

"The house. You're a premises liability expert—I know, because I looked you up. Quint's probably there. I'll tell him you're on your way." He leaned over and pulled a key ring from the makeup table drawer. "But here. Just in case."

He tossed the key to Trey, who caught it one-handed. He examined it carefully, as if it were a trap, but Nick waved him toward the door.

"Go on. Investigate the scene. Only this time do it on your own terms and not some dirty cop's."

Trey hesitated for only one second before closing his fingers around the key.

Chapter Eighteen

Once we were out of the trailer, Trey made straight for the parking lot like some well-dressed homing pigeon. I had to hustle to keep up. "What are you doing?"

"Going to the Talbot house."

"I know that. I mean, why?"

"Nick Talbot didn't kill his wife. And now someone may be trying to kill him."

"Yes, but why does that mean you have to go over there?"

Trey didn't answer. Which didn't matter because I knew why he was doing it. It was the same reason why at least once a week, he drove past the concrete embankment he'd plowed into almost four years ago. Why I kept that envelope in the cash register right where I could see it. Keep your enemies close, and your demons closer.

I inserted myself between him and the Ferrari. His eyes were dark in the late light, his hair tipped with sunset flame, and I could feel the metal door behind me, hot through my jeans.

"I don't think you should go," I said.

"Really?"

"Yes, really. And I know what you're going to say next."

"Do you?"

"I do." I licked my lips. "I will admit, I do not always make the most cautious decisions. But you do. And your argument has always been that complicated criminal matters are best left to professionals."

His eyes flashed. "Yes. And then you ignore me, or lie to me, or distract me, or involve me without my knowledge, or—"

"Your point?"

He took a deep calming breath. "My point is that it would be…problematic for you to ask me to cease and desist now."

"Problematic? You know what's problematic?" I flung a finger back toward Nick's trailer. "Thirty minutes ago, you were two seconds away from a hyperventilating panic attack—"

"I was not."

"—and now you wanna go barge into—"

"Not barge."

"—the same damn house where you had such a traumatic emotional reaction that you broke protocol, you, the crown prince of procedure." I examined him closely. "Except that you aren't, are you? Not anymore. Maybe not then, either."

He slipped his hand into his pocket, and the door unlocked with an obedient snick. "Maybe not. That's something I intend to find out."

I didn't budge. "Fine. But there's no way in hell you're going without me."

He reached behind me and opened the door, the inside of his wrist brushing my hip. "I never expected that I would."

Sometimes I missed the old Buckhead, the one Rico had introduced to me back when it had been the last of the great American bar crawls. Dozens of clubs with pulsing lights and bass-heavy dance music so rich and deep you could practically ride it. That Buckhead had vanished, zoned into oblivion. Now it was upscale again, all the clubs genteel and leather-chaired, with craft cocktails and lithographs. More Rodeo Drive than Bourbon Street. Of course, a lot fewer people got stabbed or shot or run over or beaten about the head and face. But I missed its wilder, more raucous vibe.

The Talbot estate lay west of the North Fulton Golf Course. The undulating Bermuda grass fairway was mostly empty this late in the day, but Powers Ferry was heavy with traffic. Down-range I heard the metallic thwack of a golf ball taking flight, and I could see why Nick had chosen this place as the cover for his lover's tryst. It was close and casual. Nobody would have noticed or missed him, which also made it a fine place to flee a murder.

Trey parked at the clubhouse so that we could walk across the street, following in reverse the burglar/killer's alleged escape route. He slowed his normally brisk pace so that he could take in details, construct a map in his head. The houses in this neighbor-hood secluded themselves behind landscaped islands and security system warning signs. Trey stopped at the mouth of a river slate driveway. He didn't need to double-check the directions.

"Here," he said.

I followed him up the driveway. Eventually the house mate-rialized like a three-story iceberg on the horizon—white bricks, white roof tiles, silvery-white shutters. The shrubs and trees had once been well-groomed, but were now blowsy and overgrown, and there were ruts on the lawn from a large truck. Moving van, I decided. The *Buckwild* production team clearing out.

"How much are the Talbots asking?"

"Two point four million."

I whistled. "Wow. Damn proud of this place, those Talbots."

We walked under a trellised rosebush to the front door, but Trey didn't knock. This was familiar territory for him, rolling up in some civilian's yard with a list of pointed questions and a suspicious eye.

I leaned closer. "What are we—?"

"Shhh."

I heard it then, from inside. Footsteps. Trey adjusted his pos-ture into a neutral stance, ready to react should the door open and some unexpected assailant take a swing at us. Luckily, that didn't happen. The man who opened up was dressed for busi-ness. Despite his chiseled chin and expertly highlighted chestnut hair, he was too rough to be handsome—what might have been good looks were dampened by the downturned frown lines at the corner of his mouth. I could see his resemblance to Nick in his build and profile, but nowhere else. Whatever softness Nick possessed had turned hard in his brother.

He examined Trey with a sharp, reductive gaze. "It really is you."

Trey didn't say anything. He didn't even open his mouth, just stared, the words stuck in his throat.

I took the lead. "Quint Talbot?"

"Of course. Who else would I be?" He didn't ask my name, just walked back into the house, waving us in. "Let's get this over with, I have things to do."

Inside the house smelled stale and cold. It was empty of furniture—no drapes, no rugs, no art on the white walls—and Trey's footsteps echoed against cool marble tile. The metal staircase curved upward like a double helix to the second floor, its blond oak steps the only color in the room.

Trey stood at the foot of it. Quint stood opposite him, impatiently buttoning his cuffs.

"You look different," he said.

Trey thought about that. "I am different."

Quint's eyes flashed with surprise, then he laughed. "Touché." He pulled on a suit jacket. "You got questions, you better ask them. I—"

His phone rang. He glanced at it, narrowed his eyes, then silenced it with a tap of his finger, obviously annoyed. I wondered if it was Nick he was ignoring, or perhaps Portia, or perhaps the trio of investors he'd dodged. I'd spent five minutes with Quint Talbot, and I already knew he trailed pissed-off people like a wake.

He switched his gaze back to Trey. "You have five minutes."

Trey's hesitation vanished. "Your brother said you were here the night of the alleged shooting."

"Alleged?" Quint snorted. "Try imaginary."

"Could you elaborate?"

"I was in here, going over the staging paperwork. I—"

"Where exactly?"

"Right here." He moved his hands to indicate a rectangle. "There used to be a table, but the *Buckwild* people took it. Nicky was outside sucking down a cigarette. I'd told him I could bring the paperwork to his place, but he insisted on coming out here. Had some idea that it would help him process the trauma."

"Where was he standing?"

Quint pointed toward the bank of glass doors. "Over by the diving board. I took a call. Suddenly I hear this earsplitting scream, and I run to the door, but Nicky's already running back inside." He shrugged. "That's it. You want more detail than that, talk to Nicky."

I could see the backyard through the windows along the rear wall, terraced grasses and bedraggled flower beds surrounding a stamped concrete patio. A kidney-shaped pool shimmered with water as blue as a South Seas lagoon—unlike the landscaping, it was pristine. Freshly serviced, I decided. Thick stands of trees created a privacy screen between the backyard and the surrounding properties. Had I not just walked across one of the busiest streets in Atlanta, I would have sworn we were at the edge of a great wilderness.

Quint's phone rang again. He stuck his hand in his pocket and silenced it again, this time without even glancing at the screen.

"Who called you that night?" Trey said.

"The *Buckwild* showrunner, making arrangements to pick up the last of their crap. Which they did last night, only they also took my security cameras, every damn one. What good is a system without cameras?"

"None at all."

"Exactly right." He shot his sleeves, adjusted his tie. "Look, I told Finn I'd cooperate with Nicky's…whatever this is. But the situation's cut and dried. Nicky imagined everything. It never happened."

"How do you know?"

"I didn't hear a gun, for starters. But I searched for a bullet the next morning, just in case. Didn't find a thing. Nothing. Zippo." He fixed us with a look. "You do know about my brother's mental instability, right? Paranoid delusions. He's supposedly fine now, but I'm not so sure. He's been more unstable than usual."

"How?"

"His routine has gone to hell, for starters. He's insisting on being a part of the house sale, so he's meeting realtors etcetera etcetera etcetera. He's insisting on being at the press party this weekend, when I've told him over and over I have it under control. I blame Addison—that's his fiancée. She's currently petitioning to be his sole conservator, which makes her as crazy as he is, but is anybody listening to me? No. Nicky may be nuts, but he can be very persuasive when he's trying to make you think he's not. People don't understand that."

He said this as an accusation. As if we were also trapped in one of Nick Talbot's delusional webs.

Trey kept his expression professionally bland. "Does Ms. Canright agree with your assessment?"

"Addison makes sure he takes his meds, that's her contribution. Tracks his cholesterol, feeds him vitamins. Homeopathic bullshit. But she has no clue how seriously fucked up he is."

Trey had been watching Quint this entire time without registering a single lie. I could tell when he spotted one of those. It was like a hawk spying a squirrel. But he'd betrayed nothing.

"Am I understanding correctly," he said, "that you don't believe there was an attempt on your brother's life Friday night?"

"You understand perfectly." Quint buttoned his jacket. "The staging crew will be here in an hour. I want you two cleared out as soon as they arrive."

Trey nodded. "Of course."

"Good. The sooner we get this monster off our books, the better."

He left without a good-bye, trailing a wave of aftershave. But I noticed he'd used the same word Nick had to describe the house.

Monster.

Chapter Nineteen

Trey studied Quint Talbot as the door slammed shut, doubly loud in the cavernous space.

"Well?" I said. "Was he lying?"

Trey didn't look away from the door. "No. But he wasn't telling the truth either."

"Technically true but deliberately evasive?"

"No. There was no pretense. It seems as if…as if he knew the truth, but knew even more about not knowing the truth. Does that make any sense?"

"Not really."

He blew out a breath. "I was afraid of that."

He stood at the base of the stairs, the exact spot where he'd found the body of Jessica Talbot. Where he'd broken his training. Where he now stood making a concerted effort to not look at the floor.

I came up beside him. "Don't get trapped back there."

"Back where?"

"In the past. That's not why you're here."

He faced me, his expression a mix of annoyance and frustration. "I know. I made mistakes then. And I'm still making mistakes."

"What do you mean?"

"At the beginning. I couldn't ask him…I was trying, but…"

I felt a pang of sympathy. Most of the time Trey handled his brain trauma as disinterestedly as he handled the other artifacts of the accident—the titanium rods in his spine and knee, the scar tissue, the migraines. But now he looked like somebody had pulled the rug out from under him.

"You couldn't think of what to say?"

"Yes, but more than that. I was trying so hard not to say the wrong things—like anything from the files—that I couldn't say the right things."

"You got there eventually."

He shook his head. "Eventually is not good enough."

"Of course it is. You're in virgin territory. You didn't do investigations when you were a cop, and yet here you are in this crazy complex situation full of triggers and flashbacks and surprises. Maybe you weren't as quick with the words as you wanted to be this time. So you prepare differently for the next time."

"The next time?"

"Hypothetically speaking."

He took a deep breath, released it slowly. His gaze was fixed on the staircase. It curved upward, a graceful spiral of white iron and golden hardwood. I tried to picture that awful morning—the blood and confusion, the barking of orders and crackle of the radio. Normally Trey was brisk, precise, procedural. But today he stood where he'd once knelt beside the body of Jessica Talbot.

"So here you are now," I said. "Trey Seaver, premises liability and security agent. What do you do?"

He gave a start, as if I'd pulled him from a daydream. "Oh. You mean right now?"

"I do. Because if you're gonna give this place a going-over, you'd best get on it. The staging team will be here soon."

"Right. Of course."

He reached into his jacket and pulled out the mechanical pencil and notepad he kept in there. He flipped open to a clean page, clicked the pencil to get fresh lead, and started sketching. This was always his first step in any premises assessment. First, he stood in the middle of the room and turned in a slow circle, like a human compass. Then he walked the perimeter, viewing the scene in different lights and from different perspectives.

I stood to the side, out of his way. The room was disturbing in its emptiness, like a socket where a tooth should have been. Looking more closely, I could see the holes in the plaster where cameras had once been mounted, tangled wires still dangling. There were gouges in the floor where equipment had been dragged, scuff marks on the baseboards. The room's past permeated the walls and gave off something like a subconscious smell. It was nothing compared to Trey's memories, however. I was sure those burned so bright he could practically touch them.

Engrossed now in his sketch, he had regained his former efficiency, quick with the lines and angles as the living area took two-dimensional form on his notepad. I tried to imagine it as the set of *Buckwild*, crammed with bodies and noise and glare. Here the lights, there the cameras…

The cameras.

"Trey?"

He continued sketching. "Yes?"

"This place wasn't empty Friday night. When Quint and Nick were here. Quint said the production team cleared things out last night."

"Correct."

"Which means the reality show cameras were still here on Friday. You can see the marks where they were mounted. Like right there. And there." I pointed to the corners of the room. "Maybe not operational, but…what are you doing?"

He had his phone out before I could finish. "I'm texting Finn. She needs to find that equipment. If there's footage, she needs to preserve it." He looked up from his phone. "Thank you. That was an excellent point."

I shrugged off the compliment. "You know me. Queen of the Girl Detectives."

He narrowed his eyes at me in a puzzled way, but then he got right back to pacing off the living area. I searched for a chair, and seeing none, took to the floor. I couldn't bring myself to sit on the stairs. Watching Trey work was usually a visceral pleasure, but here, in this stark disturbing place, I couldn't ignore an alarm bell of concern. What was he doing? Where was this leading? He was a goal-driven individual, a carrot-and-stick man. Did he think he could figure out what had happened to Jessica Talbot if he could figure out what had happened—or not happened—to Nick?

He stopped at the windows and contemplated the back yard. "Quint said he looked for bullets and didn't find any."

"That's what he said." I joined Trey. "But then, he's not trained in looking, is he?"

Trey reached for the door handle. "No, he is not."

Chapter Twenty

The back lot showed both the ravages of the Buckhead Buckwildness and the efforts of a professional cleaning crew. The annuals in the flower beds had died and not been replaced, and the lawn was patchy brown in places. But in the center gleamed the turquoise pool set in concrete bleached as bright as a celebrity smile.

In the distance, I could see a stone wall running along the edge of the grounds, topped by wrought iron. Very pretty, but not difficult to climb over. This was Trey's peeviest peeve—security features that weren't actually secure. The property was lovely and yet empty, as soulless as the stark white house. First a homicide, then three seasons of commercial debauchery, and now a shooting. Well, an alleged shooting.

"Any initial impressions?" I said.

Trey didn't look up from his notebook. "Not yet."

As I watched, he walked the perimeter, downloading the blueprint into his brain. The grounds occupied about two acres, half of which were paved and turfed, the rest thick with slender trees.

"Be careful not to disturb anything," he said.

Of course things had already been disturbed—the film crew had tromped around collecting the last of their equipment and apparently every scrap of outdoor furniture—but Trey was working with what he had. He still had a sniper's eye for distance and didn't do any actual measuring. Beyond the border wall I could hear distant traffic, muffled and muted.

"Tai? Would you stand at the edge of the pool? Right beside the diving board?"

Where Nick had been standing when he'd heard the shot. I did as Trey asked. "Are you onto something?"

"Perhaps. Face south, please."

I turned. The sky glowed peachy warm over the trees in front of me, deepening to golden orange to my right. The barn-like guest house lay behind me, the patio to my left. I could see the interior of the living room where Quint had been that night, organizing the paperwork. I could imagine him in that room of glass, like a shark in a fishbowl. Trey turned in a slow circle, one full revolution, then walked behind the guest house where he disappeared from view.

My phone rang, startling me. And then I remembered. I closed my eyes. *Oh no.*

I answered it and started spilling apologies. "Oh God, Rico, I'm sorry. I completely...we were supposed to have drinks."

"I *am* having drinks. Where are you?"

He didn't sound annoyed, just disappointed. I was too. Back in high school, we'd been inseparable. Now he ran with a crowd of writers and actors and poets, mostly black like him, edgy and creative and fierce. Not a single one of them wanted anything to do with suburban Civil War reenactors Outside The Perimeter.

"You're not going to believe this," I said, "but I am in the *Buckwild in Buckhead* house pretending to be the target of an assassination attempt."

Silence. "Do I even want to know?"

"It's complicated."

"Your usual kind of complicated?"

"Yes and no."

Trey reappeared underneath a tree at the corner of the property, a fully leafed oak much older than the saplings around it, probably preserved during the original development. He knelt and examined the base, prodding the dead leaves and grasses underneath with his pencil.

Rico sighed. "A'right. Raincheck then." He delivered a calculated pause. "But Dante was looking forward to meeting you."

"Dante?"

"Yeah." Another pause. "My guy."

"You have a guy? You never tell me anything anymore."

"I was trying to! But you decided you'd rather be doing whatever you're doing."

Trey rose and took two steps in my direction and held an index finger in front of his face. Sighting the target. I could feel the imaginary crosshairs on me, and a delicate shudder ran up my backbone.

"I am so sorry. Tell Dante I owe him a drink."

"Yeah. And you tell Trey I'm sorry he's stuck keeping you out of trouble again."

I started to explain that wasn't exactly what was going on, but Rico had already hung up. I listened to the dead air for a second, then sat on the diving board, chin in hand.

"You finding anything out there?" I called.

Trey pointed to the tree. "This is the only concealment available that has a clear sightline to the patio. Any reasonably trained shooter would set up here."

"So you're standing on the shooter's location?"

"Alleged shooter. And I don't know. I didn't find shell casings or any other evidence that a shooting took place. But…"

"But?"

"If I were called here to target someone in that house, this is where I would set up."

I saw his reasoning. The other landscaping features and the guest house created a wall around the cloistered pool area. The shot wouldn't have been difficult distance-wise—even a handgun would have been adequate—but it would have required patience.

Trey started walking toward me. "At first I was puzzled why Talbot would have been targeted while he was still in shadow. But if the setup site was here, the shooter would have had to take the shot before Talbot reached the edge of the pool. The guest house would block the sight line before, the cabana after."

I could see what he was talking about. Nick had come out the French doors, cigarette still unlit. He would have been silhouetted against the bright living room, not yet illuminated in the watery blue glow of the pool lights. It would have been a tricky shot, but entirely possible the second he stopped walking.

"So they took one shot and missed," I said. "Why didn't they shoot again?"

Trey examined the pool. "I don't know."

I knew some things about single bullets. It was the sniper's creed: one shot, one kill. Only this shot hadn't killed, it had missed. And the shooter had not fired another one.

"The shooter was interrupted," I said. "Or spotted. Or in danger of being interrupted and or spotted."

"Possibly."

"Which would mean there's a witness somewhere, if that's the case."

Trey nodded in acknowledgment. He was listening, but his mind remained focused on his surroundings. "If the shooter was standing under the tree, and if Nick was standing beside the diving board, then the bullet had to go…there."

He pointed toward the bank of windows gleaming in the sunlight. Unbroken. Not a shard out of place.

"Your theory has a problem," I said.

He wasn't listening again. He pushed past me, making a beeline for the windows, his eyes on the ground. He stopped short at the edge of the patio, where the concrete met the grass.

He crouched and pointed. "Something was here."

I followed his finger to a circular patch of dead grass about two feet in diameter. The ground was dry, the blades crushed to a half-dead yellow.

"Something with a round base," I said. "Heavy and recently moved. You think whatever was here caught the bullet?"

"Alleged bullet. And it might have. If my calculations are correct."

I nudged the squashed grass with my toe. "You think the film crew took it?"

"Perhaps."

"But wouldn't they have noticed a bullet hole?"

"Perhaps. Perhaps not. It depends on a number of factors." He stood. "But if I am correct about the location of the alleged shooter, and if the other events of that night took place according to the statements we have, then according to my calculations, the alleged bullet is most likely not on the premises anymore because whatever caught it—whatever stood there—has been moved."

That was a lot of ifs and allegeds. Except for one part. Which I did not miss.

"You're saying it's entirely possible that somebody really did take a shot at Nick Talbot."

Trey exhaled. "Yes. That's what I'm saying."

Chapter Twenty-one

Back at the base camp, we made our way through the rabbit warren of trailers to where we'd left Nick. Now that the photo shoot had ceased, the set felt deserted, as did the mountain. There was a loneliness about it, pervasive and hollowed out.

Trey was about to knock on the trailer door when it flung open, and a woman gasped and tripped and would have pitched straight down the steps if he hadn't caught her. She righted herself and jerked away from him, breathing hard. Skinny, pale, black hair cut stick straight with razored bangs across her forehead. Like every other crew member on the set, she wore jeans and a tee, but hers seemed crisp as a uniform.

Her eyes widened behind her black-framed glasses. "You're not Nick."

Trey reached for his guest pass. "No, ma'am. I'm—"

"Who are you?" Her eyes flew to the keyring in his hand. "Why do you have Nick's keys? What's going on here?"

She had her walkie-talkie out before I could blink, index finger poised to call security. Trey looked my way, utterly helpless, and I remembered that no one knew about the attempted shooting except Nick and Quint, which meant we needed some extemporaneous falsehoods and needed them pronto. And that was my department.

I took the keys from Trey's hand and extended them like a peace offering. "We're with the staging team. Just returning these to Mr. Talbot."

She snatched them from me. "Nick didn't go to the house, did he?"

"No, we left him here."

The woman finally relaxed. I glanced at the ID card strung around her neck. Addison Canright, Nick's fiancée and partner in adultery. I'd pictured someone more femme fatale, less liberal arts grad student, but there was no accounting for taste. Who would have thought Trey would go for aggressive redneck?

Addison stared at Trey, her eyebrows knit in puzzlement. "Don't I know you?"

Trey wouldn't look her in the eye. Of course she knew him, from Nick's grand jury trial, only Trey had been wearing the Atlanta PD uniform at the time. He shook his head, but Addison wasn't letting go.

"Are you sure?" she said. "You look familiar."

He kept shaking his head. She kept staring. I broke out my hugest smile and tried to look wholesome and trustworthy. "You probably saw us poking around earlier. We're both big fans of the show."

She hiked an eyebrow. "Oh really?"

"Absolutely. You've got a real transgressive subtext going, intersectional feminism complicated by the power dynamics of self-othering."

Her head snapped back. "Yes! It's the through-line of the series. The matriarchal world of the canine versus the patriarchal realm of the human. Wild versus civilized, instinct versus rationality." She returned the smile, shaking her head in pleased astonishment. "God, I thought people only watched it for the were-sex."

I didn't tell her that I only watched it for the were-sex, which was hot and plentiful. Rico was the one who insisted that something more intellectual was going on. I guessed he was right. Gold star for the class valedictorian.

"Absolutely not," I said. "It's the smartest thing on TV."

"You have no idea how much I needed to hear that. This place can be so hostile." She put her hand on her chest. "Don't get me wrong, the South has charm. But just when I think I might want to go native, somebody has a big damn Confederate parade or some watermelon festival, and I die a little inside." She widened her eyes. "Not people like you, of course. I mean the other ones. You know the ones."

Yeah, I knew the ones. I made myself keep smiling, though. I could make myself smile at just about anything, a trick of the tour guide trade where tips made the difference between a night on the town and a six-pack of Bud Light in front of the TV.

Trey cleared his throat. "Ms. Canright?"

"Yes?"

"Have you been to the Buckhead house recently?"

She stiffened. "Nick and I don't set foot on that property, and we never will. Because I don't care what Quint tells you, Nick is not to be involved in any stage of the process. If you have any questions, talk to me. Leave Nick out of it."

Trey opened his mouth and closed it. She obviously had no clue Nick had even been out there Friday night, much less about the shooting. Trey was just as obviously itching to interrogate her further, but he knew he couldn't. And it was taking everything he had to keep those questions in his mouth.

I shook my head sadly. "Such a lovely home. A shame what happened to it. And now all that stuff missing."

She frowned. "Stuff?"

"Apparently the previous production company absconded with the security system. Among other things."

She gave a delicate snort. "Don't worry, Quint will sue. He'll end up making money off this, watch and see."

Her contempt for her future brother-in-law practically oozed from her pores. She examined us curiously, still blocking our way into the trailer. I was worried that any second her brain cells would collide and she'd figure out who Trey was. Or he'd blurt it out accidentally.

I heard footsteps behind us and turned to see Nick. Addison spotted him too. He favored her with a slow grin, nodded politely at us.

She put her hands on her hips. "It's past time for your meds."

"I was getting dinner before the craft table closed," he said mildly. "You should get over there yourself, the vegan Caesar's running low."

She glared at him. "Have you heard?"

"Heard what?"

"Your brother's really done it now. First he's all about speeding up production, now he's demanding the entire season of scripts up front. Just because a few investors are throwing their weight around."

"The ones who were at the photo shoot?"

"Yes. Those."

He sighed. "I suspected as much. Let's take this inside, okay?"

Addison stood aside reluctantly, and the three of us joined her in the trailer. She watched as Nick went to his makeup table, opened a drawer, and pulled out a pill box the size of a large steak. He popped open the compartment and washed down a handful of meds with the remains of his tea just as his phone started beeping. He tossed the pill box back in the drawer and closed it with his hip.

Her expression darkened. "That script schedule is insane. You have to do something."

"Like what? Quint's the EP. He can ask for whatever he wants."

"Talk to him."

Nick laughed. "Why? I'm not a producer anymore. I take orders like everybody else."

"But you're his brother. Surely—"

"We'll deal with this later, okay babe?"

He put his arm around her waist and steered her from the room. I heard their footsteps on the metal stairs, hushed conversation.

I dropped my voice. "Was she telling the truth?"

Trey thought about that. "She didn't read as lying."

"You do realize that if Nick is innocent, she's the one who had the most to gain from Jessica's death?"

"I do."

I wasn't sure he did. Except for Nick, Trey was having a hard time processing the Hollywood people. I wondered if their time in the land of make-believe had fuzzied up their sense of fact and fiction. Or maybe they existed in a world where things were true simply because they wanted them to be. Either way, Trey wasn't getting good traction.

Nick returned with a smear of lipstick on his lower lip and a big grin. "Thanks for keeping everything on the down low. Addison worries enough as it is."

She also keeps you under her thumb, I thought, but did not say this. She was petitioning to be his conservator. Being able to demonstrate that she had his physical care under wraps would go in her favor, even if from the outside, it looked a little overzealous.

"Has something happened?" I said.

He picked up his tea again. "Quint's asking for the whole of Season Two, thirteen scripts, before they start filming the first episode."

"That sounds like a lot of work."

"It is. It's also highly unusual. Usually we film maybe one or two scripts ahead of the writers, but apparently some investors want to see the whole thing upfront."

"Because of Portia's cliffhanger?"

Nick took a sip of tea, thought for a few seconds. "Maybe. I don't know. It's weird, that's all, and Addison is right to be unhappy. But I'm not sure what I can do about it. Like I keep saying, not a producer anymore." He plunked his mug on the counter and wiped his mouth with the back of his hand. "So. What did you find at the house?"

Trey stepped forward. "The evidence supports your version of events."

Nick's eyes widened. "Really?"

"You seemed surprised," I said.

"Well…yeah. I mean, I know how things went down, but I wasn't expecting there to be evidence. What kind of evidence?"

Trey pulled out his notebook. He explained in succinct terms. Nick sat in the stylist chair and listened until Trey finally snapped the notebook shut.

"The next step is recovering the security cameras and whatever object might have caught the bullet," he said. "Do you remember what was standing between you and the house?"

"No. It was dark, and I was focused on other things. Like not getting shot."

"Could you find out?"

He flashed a wan smile. "Why?"

"To recover the bullet. If possible."

"Why?"

Trey tried to remain patient. "For the crime scene techs."

Nick laughed. "Oh wait, I get it. You took me seriously about calling the police." He shook his head. "Sorry. I'm not doing that. I never was. That was a bluff to get you out here."

Trey's eyes narrowed. "Mr. Talbot—"

"I'll tell Quint what you told me, and he'll tell Finn. She'll do whatever it is she does and keep it off the official record. Because I am not—do you hear me?—not going to put myself at the mercy of the Atlanta PD ever again."

"You don't seem to understand the seriousness of what I'm telling you."

Nick took another swig of the now-cold tea. "When I was in high school, I read this story. 'Appointment in Samarra.' Do you know it?"

"This is no time for—"

Nick ignored him. "A man sees Death in the marketplace, so he runs. Gets on his camel or whatever and takes off. Gets to Samarra. Starts looking for a place to hide."

"Mr. Talbot—"

"And then, bam, there's Death again. The man gives up. Fine, he says. Take me. But first tell me what you were doing at the marketplace earlier. And Death says…"

Nick stopped talking, frowned. I heard it then too, footsteps pounding up the metal steps. Not Addison's. I spun around, just as the door flung open and a man burst into the room—dark tangles under a burglar hoodie, manic eyes, cell phone brandished like a blazing sword.

He pointed it at Nick. "Time to answer for your sins, you murdering son of a bitch!"

Chapter Twenty-two

I took one look at the guy and reached for the hot tea kettle, not my weapon of choice but good enough in a pinch. I needn't have bothered. Trey grabbed the guy's wrist, wrenched his arm behind his back, and twisted. The guy screamed. The phone hit the floor and went skittering my way.

Nick snatched out his walkie-talkie. "I need security at the makeup trailer, pronto. It's Martinez again."

I put one foot on the phone, kept my fingers wrapped around the kettle. Martinez lunged in my direction, and Trey angled into the hold, an elegantly simple maneuver that turned the guy's knees to jelly. He screamed again and scuffled, but Trey's voice was calm.

"Stop moving and it will stop hurting," he said.

The guy moved. It hurt. He stopped. With his single hoop earring and dark wash skinny jeans, he looked like an escapee from some pirate-themed boy band. And he was mad, spitting frothing mad. I bent to pick up his phone, and he started bellowing.

"Give me that!"

I held it out of reach. "Like hell."

The guy cursed and spat in my direction. Trey eased Martinez's arm up another inch, and he whimpered. I checked the phone. A video app was recording, so I smashed the stop button, turned to Nick.

"Martinez *again*?" I said.

Nick's mouth twisted in disgust. "Yeah. This isn't the first time he's snuck on set. We caught him months ago at the production studio. He showed up while we were filming at Stone Mountain too."

I didn't ask if they'd called the cops. Of course they hadn't.

I heard shoes on the metal steps, another crackle of radio static. Two burly guys in khaki uniforms burst through the door. Trey handed Martinez over to their care, and they each grabbed one arm and hauled him off. Now that he was out of the pain compliant wrist lock, he was feeling chatty again.

"She'll come back to me! She'll know what you are if it's the last thing I do!" He dragged his feet at the door, his voice strident. "The rest of you should be ashamed! Every dollar you take from that murderer makes you complicit! His sins are yours!"

He kept yelling as the security men hustled him out the door, a steady stream of insults and curses and paranoid, stream-of-consciousness blather that ended with him screaming Addison's name. Trey stepped forward and watched them leave, finally shutting the door. Nick went to his makeup table and rummaged in the drawer, hands trembling. Trey stayed at the door and watched as Nick once again pulled out his bottle of herbal relaxants.

"Who was that?" he said.

Nick raked his hands through his hair, loosing it from the ponytail holder. "That was Diego Martinez. He was at Iowa with Addison."

"Iowa?"

"Iowa Writer's MFA program. Very prestigious, hard to get into. She's talented, he's...well, maybe he was talented, but he's too fixated on Addison to use it. Developed a heavy crush on her. She thought she'd ditched him when she moved to Georgia, but then Jessica died, and we were in the news, and he found her again not long after the hearing. And he's determined to save her from me."

Trey folded his arms. "Does she have a restraining order?"

"Of course. And that worked for a while. But a few months ago, he decided to stalk me instead. We kick him out, but he finds the base camp, over and over again." He took a deep steadying breath. "God. Quint's gonna tear security a new one."

"He should. How long has the breach been happening?"

"Um, let me think. Right after we started location work, so…six months?"

"And you've informed the authorities?"

Nick shrugged. "You know how it goes. Keep everything under the radar. Quint doesn't like media complications."

"But he doesn't mind compromised security?"

"Martinez just wants to yell at me. He's never been armed. What I can't figure out is how he keeps finding me. We keep base camp locations secret."

I gave the phone a swipe and opened the menu. The Google app was still working, its helpful icon hovering right over our location. I checked the search boxes. Instead of an address, Martinez was using GPS coordinates.

"Not so secret," I said.

I turned the phone around so that Nick could see. Trey came closer and pointed to the text box.

"Redbird? What does that mean?"

Nick cursed under his breath. "That's our film code. It's the key to deciphering the correct location markers. Nobody outside of the team knows that."

"In that case," I said, "you have an informant on set."

Nick dropped into the chair, his hands visibly shaking now. "Yeah. I think you're right."

Trey's eyes were stern. "Mr. Talbot, your security is failing you."

"We'll bump it up. Quint likes bumping things up."

"Listen to me. You need to contact the authorities."

"I've already told you, that's not gonna happen." Nick smiled wearily. "So thank you for coming, but we're done here."

"I don't think—"

"And I can't believe I'm saying this, but I'm glad you came. I know it was only because I threatened to tell the cops that you took a shot at me, but still. No hard feelings, right?"

Trey stared. "What?"

"Because in a strange way, it's been good to see you. I never thought I would say that, but it's true. And now it's time to lay the past to rest. Move forward."

"Mr. Talbot, I am reasonably certain that someone tried to kill you."

Nick laughed, but it was half-hearted. "Not very hard."

Now Trey was really confused. "Mr. Talbot, I just told you—"

"Nick. For the love of God, call me Nick." He sighed. "Yes, I heard you. Someone tried to kill me. I already knew that. And really and truly, I think I wanted it to be you. I wanted to look you in the eye and see it. And then I wanted…oh hell, I don't know what I wanted. Maybe I wanted to confront you. Maybe I wanted to outsmart you. Maybe I just wanted to know…you know?"

Trey didn't reply right away. His eyes held a similar resigned determination. "I am very good at risk assessment. Please believe me when I tell you that you are in danger."

"So what do you want me to do, call the cops?"

"Yes."

"They'd haul you in. You'd be the number one suspect."

Trey took a deep breath. "I am prepared to deal with that."

"Well, I'm not. Your kind didn't treat me well last time. How much sympathy do you think I'd get this go round, huh?"

"Mr. Tal-"

"Nick."

Trey exhaled slowly and deliberately. "Nick. This is a serious situation."

"Don't I know it? And my brother will deal with it in some serious manner. Which is how things always happen and how they always will until I am once again my own man."

"What does that mean?"

"It means I'm trying hard to stay on the right track so that I don't need anybody acting as my conservator. Not my brother. Not Addison." He extended his hand. "Thank you for your time. I'm sorry I threatened you. The past is the past. Let's leave it there."

Trey took his hand, shook it gravely. He seemed to come to a decision and reached into his jacket. He pulled out a pen and a business card, wrote something on the back of the card and handed it to Nick.

Nick held it between two fingers. "What's this?"

"My personal cell number. If there are further incidents, please let me know."

Nick shook his head, puzzled. "You're offering to help me?"

"Yes."

"Okay. That's weird. But okay."

Trey straightened his spine. "It's not weird. I'm an ASIS-certified premises liability agent. I can—"

"No, I mean it's weird that you would want to help me." He examined Trey closely. "Why would you?"

"I don't know. But I do."

Nick slid the card into his back pocket. He looked astonished and grateful at the same time. "In that case...thank you."

"You're welcome." Trey started to leave, then turned back. "You and your fiancée have been stalked by Martinez for six months, and you put *me* at the top of your suspect list?"

Nick shrugged. "You seem like a man who carries a grudge."

Trey thought about that. "A valid point."

Chapter Twenty-three

To my surprise, Trey ended up at my place again. This was highly unusual, especially for a Monday night. Also unusual was that the second we got to the shop, he went straight upstairs to my apartment without breathing a single word. I listened for the shower. Nothing.

I switched off the lights, locked the doors, and re-engaged the security system. The shop descended into darkness and silence, broken only by the blinking red lights of the alarms and the hum of electronics. I climbed the stairs and found him lying on the bed in the dark, fully dressed, still wearing his shoes. He had his hands folded on his stomach, and he was staring at the ceiling.

Okay, I thought. *Plan B.* So I went to the pantry and poured a giant bowl of Lucky Charms. Then I got into bed and munched cereal until he finally spoke.

"Why did I do that?" he said.

I tossed one of the marshmallow pieces into my mouth. "Do what?"

"Give Nick Talbot my personal number."

"Oh. That."

"He won't call. It is clear that his brother makes the decisions, and his brother shows no inclination to deal with the problem outside of his own security team. Which is sub-par from what I've seen."

"Totally sub-par." I licked sticky crumbs from my fingers. "Is there any chance Marisa would let you take the case officially?"

He shook his head. "Not after what happened in the spring."

The spring. So many unfortunate happenings to choose from. Trey had pulled his gun on her. He'd disobeyed her direct order and followed me to Savannah. And then he'd gotten himself mixed up as a witness in multiple murders which had resulted in much news coverage, and as Marisa was fond of reminding us, in the corporate security business, there really was such a thing as bad publicity.

I scrounged around for the last marshmallow. "She would blame me for all of this, you know."

"Correct."

"Because she blames me for every complication in your life."

"Also correct." He slipped me a sideways look. "It's not an unfair assessment."

"Not unfair at all. Your life was rather boring when you met me."

He didn't argue. I put the bowl on the bedside table and lay down next to him. The only light came from the streetlamp in the back lot. It sliced across the studio apartment in an amber swath.

"Do you miss it?" I said.

"Miss what?"

"Your boring uncomplicated life."

"No. It was more structured. Less problematic. But it wasn't... you know." He rubbed his eyes. "Sometimes I try to think about what my life would be like if you hadn't complicated it. But I can't imagine my life without you in it."

He said it so matter-of-factly, like sharing the weather forecast. He caught me off guard this way again and again, delivering words that tangled my tongue and weakened my knees.

I took his hand and squeezed. "Same here."

"Good. I'm glad. Except that now...now I'm confused again."

"About me?"

"What? No." He rolled his head to the side. "Why would you say that?"

"Because we were talking about...never mind. Go on."

He ran his thumb over my knuckles, lightly. I felt a familiar tingle then, like a shot of whiskey.

"I'm confused about why I wanted to help Nick so much," he said. "Because I did. I still do."

"You're feeling guilty."

"No, I'm not."

"Yes, you are. You had an idea back in the day that this man was a murderer. You maintained that idea up until a few hours ago. But now you know better. And now you have to deal with the part you played in the awfulness than befell an innocent man."

Trey considered this turn of events. "Okay. Perhaps I am feeling somewhat guilty. But that's not the problem."

"What is it then?"

"As you said, he's innocent. And if he's innocent, the evidence has to be reinterpreted in that light. It still supports the theory that Jessica's murder was staged, but not that Nick was the person who staged it."

"Macklin?"

"No. He would have done a better job."

"Somebody else?"

"Yes. And I want to find out who. Whether Nick wants me to or not."

His voice was calm, deceptively so, but his eyes gave him away. Bright, even in the half-lit room. He wanted to investigate. He wanted it so much he didn't know what to do. He didn't want to want it—but want it, he did. And I knew why. Trey hadn't been able to save his relationship with Gabriella. Hadn't been able to save Jessica's life or see that her killer was brought to justice. But now, he had a chance to rectify one of those things.

"You don't need Nick's permission to look into this. Finn's either."

"That's not the problem. The problem is…there are many problems. I'm not making the best choices right now."

"What are you talking about?"

He exhaled in frustration. "I shouldn't have gotten the files. I shouldn't have agreed to the meeting. I shouldn't have gone to the Talbot house—"

"You shouldn't have taken that stalker guy's phone."

Trey's forehead wrinkled. "I didn't take his phone."

"Oh, wait." I smiled. "That was me."

And I pulled Martinez's phone from my pocket.

Trey stared. "How did you get that?"

"Security hauled him out the door without asking for it—they really are sub-par." I waggled it. "It's dead now, so it's also useless until we can get it recharged. Which means we'll probably have to crack the passcode."

Trey was shaking his head incredulously. "You just...took it. Just like that."

"Yep. Because I'll let you in on a secret." I leaned closer. "You're not the only one whose life has gotten boring."

He looked relieved to have the topic out in the open. "I know. I've been concerned. You haven't been...*you* lately. You've been very..."

"Boring?"

"Cautious. And you have reason to be, I understand, but cautious is not like you." The corner of his mouth quirked just the slightest. "Taking Martinez's phone, however, is exactly like you."

"And wanting to help an unexpectedly innocent man whose life is in danger is exactly like you."

He examined my face in the tawny light, curious now, letting his eyes roam from feature to feature as if memorizing or remembering or both. He rolled toward me, then took the phone and placed it next to the cereal bowl.

His hand moved to my hip. "I saw you."

"Saw me what?"

"Reach for the teapot when Martinez came in the door."

I slid my foot down his calf and hooked a toe in his shoe, sent it tumbling to the floor. "Guilty as charged. But then you put him in a rear wrist lock, and I didn't need to bash him after all."

His hand slid under my shirt, tracing a line up my spine. I arched into his touch, and he nuzzled the crook of my neck, pressing a kiss to the tender spot right above my clavicle.

His voice was soft in my ear. "Tai?"

"Yes?"

"I need to tell you something."

"Okay."

He raised his head and looked me right in the eye. "This afternoon. It was…multi-syllabic, starts with S."

"Surprising? Significant?"

"No, something more…" He licked his lips, shook his head. "More like…you know."

"Satisfying?"

"Yes. That's it. Immensely satisfying."

He said it as if he were divulging a particularly delicious fetish. He was burning to make things right, or—if that wasn't possible—to make things more sensible. To find the answers that perhaps changed nothing, but which at least rendered the void of understanding a little less empty.

"So keep investigating," I said.

"I want to." He brushed his thumb against my lower lip. "But I can't do it alone."

"Of course you can."

He shook his head. "No. I can't. My interactions today clearly demonstrated that. But you? You did very well."

"Trey—"

He kissed me. It was a kiss designed to shut me up, a trick he'd learned from me and utterly perfected. But as his fingers tangled deeper in my hair, he lost himself in it, so many wants meshing together. I kissed him back, drawing more response from him, echoing and redoubled, a feedback loop of pleasure and desire. His lips were warm and soft and expert, and his hands… oh, sweet mercy, his hands…and I wound my arms around his neck, his shoulders, feeling the shift of muscle along his back.

This was the Trey I knew, but he was also tantalizingly unknown, a familiar stranger rising from the ashes of his former self, cinders still sparking in his hair. There was no hesitation, no confusion, no uncertainty.

"Help me investigate," he said.

I stared at him. "Are you serious?"

"Of course I'm serious."

"But you hate it when I investigate. You say I ask too many questions, you tell me I antagonize people." I wrapped my leg around his hips and rolled him on top of me. "You complain about my methods all the time."

"Not all the time." His voice was a rough whisper against my neck. "Not all your methods."

I kissed him some more, deeper and hungrier, and I was dragging my shirt over my head when I felt the vibration against my hip. His phone buzzing. He didn't immediately reach for it—I kept him occupied for a good five seconds more—but eventually he untangled his fingers from my hair and slipped them into his pocket. He didn't untangle the rest of himself, though he did bring the phone to eye level and squint at it.

"Local number. Unknown."

I got a ping of excitement. "It's Nick."

"You don't know—"

"How many unknown numbers do you get on that phone? Zero. It's Nick."

He kept his thumb on the phone. His breath was ragged, but the question in his eyes was impossible to miss.

"Tai—"

"Yes, the answer's yes, of course I'll help." I kissed him quickly but thoroughly. "Whatever you need, partner. I'm all in."

He hit the button. "Seaver here."

Chapter Twenty-four

A very annoyed and scuffed-up Nick paced the driveway of the modest brick ranch house, a red Mazda headfirst in a bank of shrubbery. His shirt was covered in dirt and what appeared to be blood, one eye swollen shut, his hair a matted tangle. He looked like he'd gone three rounds with a mad bear.

Trey and I watched from my car. Finn had warned us to keep our distance, and we'd obliged. From what I could see, Nick had gone right past the garage, barely avoiding a pine tree before crashing into the hedge. Addison stood next to him. She looked a bit worse for wear too, her outfit covered in the fine powder of a detonated airbag.

"Addison was in the passenger side?" I said.

Trey looked up from his notebook. "It's her car. She's the reason the accident wasn't as severe as it could have been. When Nick lost consciousness, she took the wheel."

"He was driving?"

"Yes. She said that she normally drives, but that tonight she had a migraine."

It was chaos and disorder, all the things Trey hated. And yet he was staring at the scene with a kind of wistfulness. He put down his pencil when the back door opened and Finn climbed in. She wore a expertly tailored business suit and full makeup, hose and high heels, as if she'd been pulled from a corporate raider workshop.

She shut the door. "Clusterfuck. Utter and total."

"What happened?" Trey said.

"Nick took the entrance at speed. Plowed over the mailbox, then scraped that telephone pole before Addison managed to swerve them into the boxwoods instead of the brick wall."

Nick was in fine form. Every time Addison took his arm, he shook her off. He was unsteady on his feet, swaying and then lurching to catch his balance. A man in gray slacks tried to put a stethoscope against his chest, but he kept batting the man's hand away. A concierge physician, I guessed. The Talbots did everything privately, even their emergency care.

"Drunk?" I said.

"That's what I thought," Finn said, "but he blew zero point zero on the VIP doc's breathalyzer. Twice. He's slurring. Can't recite the alphabet. A blindfolded toddler has more balance. But he's not drunk."

Trey cocked his head, eyes on the scene. "Other symptoms?"

"Headache. Nausea. Confusion."

"Those are concussive symptoms."

Finn pointed a finger at him. "Right you are. Except that he was displaying these symptoms before he crashed, according to Addison. You're looking at the contributing presentation, not the concluding one."

"Is the physician aware of this?"

"Yes. Addison's convinced he had a stroke or something. Quint is yammering that he's relapsed and that it's all Addison's fault."

"Quint's here?"

"He's on the way. He insists we take Nick to the inpatient clinic for psychiatric evaluation. Nick insists that someone tampered with the car."

Trey made a soft scoffing noise, but he didn't dismiss her comment. Every drunk who crashed his car probably said the same thing. But Nick wasn't drunk.

"How cognizant is he of his own condition?" Trey said.

"He thinks he's fine and is therefore not going to the ER."

"He should go."

"That is what I explained to Addison, and what she is trying to explain to Nick. He's not listening. Of course they might still drag him in. Because he may not be drunk, but something's sure as hell wrong."

Nick had his finger in the doctor's face. Finn sighed loudly and shook her head.

"I would say he's high. Only thing is, Addison said he was right as rain when they got in the car. So unless he had a secret stash of coke or bath salts or whatever the kids are doing these days stashed in the glove compartment—"

"Was Addison with him the entire time?"

"Yes. She says he's clean and med compliant."

"Does she have a list of those meds?"

"You bet she does. Hard copy in Nick's wallet for the doc, digital for the rest of us. I figured you'd be asking, so I texted you a copy."

Trey checked his phone. I knew where his brain was going next. I could practically see it sending up signal flares.

He studied the list. "Could Quint be right? Could this be a recurrence of his mental illness?"

Finn shrugged. "I'm no expert, but my gut feeling is no. This isn't how paranoid delusional disorder normally manifests, plus, according to Addison's testimony last week at the conservatorship hearing, his condition is being managed with therapy and medication. His doctor and psychiatrist agree."

Trey continued to study the list of medications. I peered over his shoulder. The herbal relaxant Nick had been popping like breath mints was on the OTC list, along with a dozen other pharmaceuticals. The rest were a mash-up of prescription meds, some I recognized and some I had no clue about.

Finn kept one eye on the accident. "Quint is gonna be pissed as hell if he finds out you're here. Which may be one of the reasons Nick called you, who knows, but you should stay in the car regardless."

Younger sibling syndrome, I decided. I still displayed symptoms on occasion. No matter how sensible said older sibling's advice, the younger sibling often flouted it out of sheer spiteful stubbornness. Whatever Quint said, Nick would do the opposite.

"What are the chances the cops will get involved?" I said.

"It's not likely. This is a minor crash on his own property with no other persons involved. No serious injuries except perhaps some concussive damage, which—yes, Mr. Seaver, I see you shaking your head, and yes, I know that concussions can be deadly. So I've tried. But he's not budging. Neither is Quint. Addison is the only one of this trio with any sense." She frowned. "That's another strange thing. Usually Nick does what Addison tells him without fuss. He's balking now."

"Is he worried he'll get committed again if he goes to the hospital?"

"Probably. I don't actually blame him there. But still."

Trey had turned his attention to the crash site, especially the car. "Did you get photographs of the accident?"

Finn pulled a small digital camera from her bag. "Here. I've documented every angle that exists."

Trey swiped through them. "You said he reported that the brakes failed."

"He said everything failed—the brakes, the steering, the horn, the door. According to Nick, the whole car ceased functioning."

Trey looked up. "But that's not…that makes no sense."

"Of course it doesn't! You can't tamper with an entire car!"

There was something nibbling at Trey, but before he could get to it, a silver Jaguar pulled up crazily at the curb. A figure got out and marched toward Nick, leaving the headlights on.

Quint.

I pointed. "Uh oh. Irate brother at twelve o'clock."

Finn reached for the door handle. "Oh, bloody hell!"

She slammed the door behind her and jogged toward the scene. Quint had managed to get within six feet of Nick before Finn stopped him. She positioned herself between the two men, hands open and in front of her. Nick lunged at Quint, only to be restrained by Addison, who was stronger than she looked. Finn said something to Quint, who backed away, even though his face was roiling with anger. Addison put her hands on Nick's shoulders. He didn't shake loose. She moved closer, put her face next to his. He nodded once, let her lead him toward the front steps, where he finally sat. The doctor knelt in front of him. Nick didn't resist any further.

I sat back in the seat. "One problem down."

Trey's index finger was tapping against his thigh. He kept running down the list of medicines.

I pointed. "You take that one. That one too."

"Yes."

"Could he have overdosed himself by accident?"

"It's possible. This is a complicated medication schedule. According to every report, however, he's maintaining it."

"Thanks to Addison."

"Yes."

I remembered Nick's giant pill case, the nasty antioxidant tea. Addison took her role of caretaker very seriously. Trey's finger was still tapping.

"You think something else is going on, don't you?" I said.

"I do. And I think I know what it might be."

He swiped the med list closed and hit speed dial. I heard a male voice answer.

Trey spoke quickly. "I'm sorry, Jean Luc, this is Trey. I apologize for the late hour, but if you could please put Gabriella on… Yes, it's important. Thank you."

Jean Luc. Gabriella's current main squeeze. I thought about Saturday night at her place, the candles and wine and lingerie, and contemplated the weird dynamics of the situation—exes who weren't totally exed, boundary lines constantly being renegotiated. Or crossed.

I shook my head. "Don't bother her. She's—"

Trey held up a finger and returned to the conversation. "Gabriella, I…no, nothing's wrong. I'm fine. Tai's fine. We're fine. But I have a question. What did you have me taking for anxiety before the current formulation? The one you changed after the doctors started me on the cyclobenzaprine?" He scribbled some words in his notebook. "*Piper methysticum.* That's what I thought. Because of the synergistic CNS effect, correct? Is there a test to check those levels?" More scribbling, nodding. "How long? Okay. Thank you. No, I'm fine. Really. Apologize again to Jean Luc."

He hung up and stared at his notebook. Through the window, I could see Nick and Addison and the doctor in an official huddle, Quint on the outskirts, looking seismic.

"What's going on?" I said.

"Nick's manifesting the symptoms of a kavalactone overdose."

"A what?"

"Kava is a common ingredient in herbal anti-anxiety formulations. It's safe in proper dosages, but contraindicated for anyone taking drugs in the benzodiazepine class because the psychoactive effect is compounded. Liver failure and pulmonary compromise can also occur. The symptoms are exactly as Nick is presenting, especially the unusual disorientation."

"Do I want to know how you know this?"

He winced. "I once spent a very unpleasant twelve hours in the emergency room after combining the two. I remember feeling as if my environment wasn't responding properly, like Nick is describing. I couldn't even open my bedroom door."

"Coordination problems?"

"No. More like a lack of agency. At the time, it felt as if the door was wrong, not my ability to open the door. It's how Gabriella recognized what had happened."

"Gabriella screwed up your meds?"

He frowned. "Of course not. I screwed up. One time and never again, for that particular mistake anyway." He drummed his fingers faster. "Nick's chart shows both cyclobenzaprine and clonazepam. But his herbal relaxants don't have kava."

"Could someone have tampered with his meds?"

"Possibly. It would have to be someone who understood

herbal pharmacology. And had access to his medications. Kava has a very pungent smell, however. It's hard to disguise."

"Any other way to get it to him? Like in something he ate or drank?"

Trey shook his head. "It has a distinctive taste as well."

"Stronger than lapsang souchong?"

Trey blinked at me. "What?"

"That tea you drink, the one that tastes like turpentine and ashes. Nick drinks it too, and that taste could disguise anything."

"Not kava. Pu-erh might, but that's an uncommon—"

"What did you say?"

"Pu-erh. It's—"

I grabbed his knee. "Get Finn over here! Now!"

Chapter Twenty-five

Once I explained my hunch and Trey explained the pharmaceutical mechanics, Finn called one of her minions and put a lockdown on Nick's trailer at the Kennesaw base camp. She snagged his tea from the car herself. Trey watched her from the passenger side of the Camaro, itching to get out. But he stayed put.

"You did good," I said.

"I remembered the information. You provided the causal link."

"It was more than that. You connected your own past to somebody else's present. Theory of mind and peripheral processing."

He raised an eyebrow at me. "You've been reading my cognitive neuroscience books."

"*Psychology Today*, actually. My brother's article about a certain Subject J."

"Oh. That's me."

"So I gathered."

Trey returned his attention to the crash scene, even though only Finn and Quint stood there. The doctor had taken Nick inside, Addison right behind. Eventually, Finn sent Quint packing, and she came back to the car.

She grinned at Trey as she shut the door behind herself. "If I could give you a gold medal, I would. Nice work."

Trey tried to keep his expression blank, but the slight flush along his cheekbones betrayed his embarrassed pleasure. "When will you get the results back on the labs?"

"I have to find a place that can test for kavalactones first. That's not a standard test. Until I do, the doctor is running some liver enzyme levels and putting him on IV fluids, just in case."

"Did you ask Addison about it?"

"I did. She's familiar with the contraindications and insists she doesn't include kava in his daily regimen."

I didn't need to ask Finn if Nick was going to the hospital. He wasn't. He wasn't doing anything that might catch the attention of the cops, or the press, or end with him in the psychiatric institute.

Finn focused her attention on Trey. "I meant to ask…how did your interview with Nick go?"

Trey considered. "Very well. I think."

"Did he do it?"

"Do what?"

"Kill his wife. That's what you wanted to know, isn't it?"

Trey looked startled at her bluntness. "Well…yes. But no, I don't think he did it."

"And the alleged shooting?"

"I believe him on that as well."

She leaned back in the seat, assessing him. "When I got here, Nick said he'd called you. He said you went to the house today, and then intercepted a stalker, and then he showed me a business card that had your name and number on it. I assume you gave that of your own free will?"

"Yes."

"Why?"

"Because I realized he was correct. He was a target. And I wanted to help."

She tilted her head in a fetching manner. "Do you still?"

Trey got this wary look, like Finn had been digging through his diary. "What do you mean?"

"There will be a press party Friday night on location in Adairsville—the usual gossip mag writers, plus people with money to invest who want to feel Hollywood-important. Nick wants to be there, Addison too. Now I know I can't ask for you officially.

Marisa would never go for it. But if you're free, I'd love to have you onsite this weekend. So would Nick."

Trey went a shade paler. "I don't...I mean, that's..."

"Nothing official. Just keeping watch behind the scenes, like my own private Wizard of Oz. And, of course, Tai would be there too. Just as unofficially." She favored me with a knowing smile. "Which she's very good at."

Trey was not saying yes, even though he wanted to, very much. Investigating on his own was one thing. Investigating at Finn's behest quite another.

"What would you need from me?" he said.

"Information. Presence. Insight." Finn smoothed a lock of hair behind her ear. "I can hire close protection and security consultants out the wazoo, but you've got an insider perspective none of them can match."

She did know, I decided. All the complications of the case. Why it would be irresistible for Trey and invaluable for her. Trey sensed the deeper machinations too, though he couldn't quite pin them down.

"I'll be there," he said.

"Good to hear." She moved to get out of the car, fixed me with a look. "About Martinez...what did you do with his phone?"

I sighed inwardly. *Oh well*, I thought. *Time to be a team player.*

"It's back at my shop."

Annoyance flitted over her features. "Under lock and key, I hope?"

"Trey designed the shop's security plan. There isn't a more secure lock and key in the metro area."

"Good. Keep it safe tonight. I'll get it from you tomorrow."

She exited the car, smoothed her skirt. Her blouse remained unwrinkled, her pantyhose unmarred by even a single run. Tonight she was corporate professional. Who knew who she'd be tomorrow? Only one thing was certain.

I'd be seeing her.

• • ● • •

Trey gazed out the window all the way back to Kennesaw, letting the passing street lights and thrum of tires on pavement soothe him. Exhaustion had finally set in—I could see it in the set of his mouth, the bleariness in his eyes. He still sparked, though. Tiredness hadn't tamped that down.

I swung out to pass a puttering panel van. "You are going to be in a heap of trouble if Marisa finds out."

"Technically—"

"Marisa won't give a hot lick about technicalities. Your ass will be grass."

Trey's hands rested in his lap. "If she finds out."

"She's the freaking CEO of a corporate security firm. Of course she's going to find out. And then she's going to ask you, point blank, what the hell you're up to."

"And then I'll tell her."

"And then?"

"She will most likely get very angry. But I'm accustomed to that now." He turned to face me. "I understand this isn't a rational decision. But over the past year, I've grown more comfortable making emotional decisions that don't, on the surface, seem logical."

Like being with me, he didn't say. He didn't need to. I remembered the Trey I'd met a year and a half ago. The clipped responses, the hesitation, the thick and impenetrable wall around his emotional castle. For reasons I still didn't understand, he'd lowered the drawbridge and let me come galloping in.

"How are you going to do this without involving the police?"

That one flummoxed him. He had to think really hard. "If those are the parameters Finn needs, I can comply. I understand rules."

"Yes, but you're allowing Finn's rules, and the Talbots' rules, to override your rules."

"No, I'm not. I'm simply choosing between two conflicting protocols."

I didn't bother arguing with him. Trey had some blind spots, but he knew his own tricks as adeptly as any magician pulling rabbits out of a hat. He could keep one foot in reality and one in illusion and not lose his balance. He was doing it again, rewriting his own operating manual.

"Chances are good somebody tried to poison Nick Talbot," I said.

"Overdose him."

"Same difference. It's a matter for the police."

"I agree. And if there was an overdose, and if it was intentional and not accidental, then combined with the attempted shooting, it would provide enough anecdotal evidence to open an investigation. Without lab results, however, the evidence remains circumstantial." He frowned. "There is another problem with involving the authorities, however."

"And that is?"

"I spent my free time today reviewing the files, including the transcripts from Nick's interrogation. I compared them to my own notes, cross-referenced those with the OPS files." His frown deepened. "Nick invoked counsel, but the interrogator convinced him to resume questioning without legal consultation."

"But that's not legal."

"It is, as long as the continued questioning is approved by the suspect."

"Nick agreed?"

"He did. He was under duress, however. I recognized the symptoms. He was contradicting himself. Repeating questions. He became agitated. Belligerent."

I recognized those symptoms too. In Trey's case, exhaustion or mental stress usually brought it on. In Nick's? He'd lost his wife only to be blamed for her murder. I imagined myself in that room, alone, detectives at my throat, unable to contact the person I loved—the person who could alibi me—because our relationship was secret. I would have been megawatt belligerent. Like borderline homicidal.

"You think he was coerced."

Trey turned his face to the window. "I think I understand why he would not want the police involved again. After I reread the transcripts, reread Price's reports…" He took a long time getting to the next part. "I think I agree with him."

I tried not to sound as flabbergasted as I felt. "Really?"

"Really. Price's OPS investigation is ongoing because there are still…problems."

"Dirty cop problems. Even in the cops who are supposed to be watching the cops."

He opened his mouth, then closed it, shook his head. He couldn't even say the words. He'd been kidnapped and beaten by dirty cops. Those had been prosecuted. The ones Keesha was after still wore the badge. Knowing this ate at him like acid in the veins.

He released a deeply held breath. "What I am saying is this. This situation is more complicated now than it was three hours ago. So I understand if you can't."

"Can't what?"

"Continue to help me."

I remembered the way he'd kissed me, hard and hungry. I reached over and took his hand, rubbed my thumb across his knuckles, a reminder of where we'd left off. And then I adjusted my grip on the steering wheel, turning my wrist up to reveal the tattoo there—Trey's name. I'd inked it on my pulse point during one of the darkest times of my life to remind me of what truly mattered.

"Remember why I got this?" I said.

"Yes."

"Good. Don't ever forget." I kept my eyes on the road. "I told you once, and I'll tell you again—all in, partner. Always."

Chapter Twenty-six

I spent Tuesday back in business, which was brisker than usual in the square. The big magnolia had no flowers this time of year, but it gave good shade, making the spot attractive to visitors even if the benches sagged and the grass was patchy. The taqueria two lots down had started to draw some of the tourist crowd, who picked up contraband *Moonshine* tee shirts two for twenty. The proprietors had installed a life-size prop poster of Portia, which had prompted lots of photos hashtagged with #LongLiveLuna. The storefront next to me remained vacant, though Raymond Junior across the square said he'd seen a Korean church group touring the place the week before.

Finn had called not long before closing time—she had our paperwork ready for this weekend, she'd said, though I had no idea what that meant. We were meeting her at the gym where Trey taught his women's self-defense class. I hadn't been in a while. I'd had lots of excuses. It was time to drop them and get back into training.

But first…I had a phone to break into.

So I called Rico, who was grumpy because he was at his IT job. He became extra grumpy when I asked him to help me crack Martinez's passcode.

"Stop worrying," I said. "It's not technically illegal."

"Whose is it?"

"This trespasser stalker type."

"And why do you have it?"

"I confiscated it as per regulations."

Rico laughed. "Now you sound like Trey. Except that Trey would not be violating another person's privacy by snooping in a phone he wasn't supposed to have."

"You might be surprised."

"Whatever. You got this phone in front of you?"

"I do."

"Is it charged up and turned on?"

"Yep."

He took me through the steps, an uncomplicated if somewhat counterintuitive process. In less than sixty seconds, the phone flashed to life, glimmering illicitly in the palm of my hand.

"That's it?" I said.

"Yep."

"Wow." I swiped the screen and Martinez's email app opened. "Thank you."

"Don't mention it. And I mean that literally. I do not want to be involved in your shadiness."

He hung up on me before I could explain. I was contemplating what to explore first when the shop phone rang. I cradled it between my ear and shoulder. "Dexter's Guns and More."

"Hey Tai, it's Ray. I got a little situation over here."

I went to the front window. Ray's lunch crowd had petered out, though a few of the old-timers remained. It looked calm as a convent over there, but something had him spooked.

"There's a fellow here," he said. "Young, Mexican maybe. I mean Hispanic."

Bless Raymond, he was trying. "Okay."

"He's been sitting at the table a while, looking out your way. Betsy Ann said she ain't had no trouble out of him, except for him watching your place like a hawk. Said she's brought him four sweet tea refills and one rib platter and he paid with a nice tip. But he's still sitting there, nursing that drink."

"This guy, he got a little mustache, one earring, like maybe he wants to be a pirate?"

"That's him."

Diego Martinez. Expanding his stalking résumé to include me. I slid my fingers into the biometric gun safe under the counter, and the lock chirped, flashed green, and opened. I stuck the phone inside and locked it back.

"I think I know what's going on," I said. "You care if I come through the kitchen and take a look at things? He'll bolt if I come in the front door."

"Is it gonna get rough?"

"I doubt it."

He chewed on that. "A'ight. Come on, then. Betsy Ann will let you through. And I got some reinforcement under the counter, if you know what I mean."

"It's not gonna come to that."

But just in case I pulled my .38 from under the register and slipped it into my carry bag. Then I made one more phone call.

• • ● • •

My stomach growled as I pushed open the screen door. The kitchen smelled like dish soap, smoke, and a bubbling pot of Brunswick stew. Betsy Ann stopped picking the meat from a hog jowl to point into the restaurant area. I peeked through the door.

Yep. Diego Martinez in the flesh, eyes glued on my shop. He was still looking out the window, cleaning his teeth with a toothpick, when I slid into his booth opposite him. He whipped in my direction, eyes wide.

"Looking for me?" I said.

It took him a second to get his bearings. Then he tried to act all cool and nonchalant and menacing, which would have been more convincing if he hadn't had a smear of maroon sauce under his nose.

"You have something of mine," he said.

"The only way you'd know that—and know how to find me—is if you activated the tracking on it."

He didn't admit to anything. "It's mine. I want it back."

"Talbot Creative owned that phone the second you tried to take video with it. There were signs up warning you about that… if you'd come in the proper way." I glanced out the window. "Oh, look. The cops."

Diego blanched when he saw one of Cobb County's finest rolling through the square. Deputy Butch—who nurtured a slight crush on me and was happy to oblige my request for a drive-by—crawled his cruiser past the shop, his buttermilk complexion shining even through the tinted glass. Diego did not bolt. He seemed to want to, though, so I gave him points for steadiness.

I propped my elbows on the tabletop, steepled my fingers. "It's like this. I've got no skin in this game. But I do have access to everything you have on that phone. Pictures. Texts. If you've got tracking turned on—and you obviously do—I've got a guy who can tell me everywhere you've been over the last six months."

He wiped his mouth and tried to look nonchalant. He'd gnawed the ribs down to bone and gristle, practically licked his plate clean. My stomach growled again, and I cursed under my breath. So much for intimidating.

"You know how this works," I said. "You tell me what I want to know, I make sure you get your phone back. Eventually."

"Why should I trust you?"

"Because it's the only deal you're getting."

He came to his decision abruptly, leaned forward. "Addison's in trouble. She has no clue how bad Nick Talbot really is. He was in some workshop she led for people in recovery, activated her savior complex big-time. I warned her about that, but she didn't listen."

Betsy Ann sauntered by with a sweet tea and fries for me, raised a questioning eyebrow. I nodded and she left, dropping a heavy glare on Diego as she did.

I picked up one of the still-sizzling fries. "You and Addison met at the Iowa program?"

"Yeah. She graduated before I did and moved down here for an adjunct job, started volunteering at the rehab center. We tried the long distance thing, but it didn't work. We stayed friends, though, and swore if we ever got to L.A., we'd—"

"Wait, you and Addison were dating?"

"Dating? We were living together." His eyebrows lowered. "If Nick told you different, he's lying. Fucker lies about everything. Lying fucker."

I chewed another too-hot fry and tried to think fast. This did not jibe with my previous information. Which meant that either Diego was lying, or Addison had sold Nick a fairy tale. I watched as Diego rattled the ice around in his empty glass. He didn't look deranged today, just heartsick.

I reached for the ketchup. "Tell me how you found the base camp."

"There's this app. Star Track. It's real-time, location-based."

I knew the app. It claimed to supply notifications for specific celebrities, maps with directions to the location of said celebrities, links to every online gossip mag that existed, and an in-app search engine. It was a stalker's virtual Swiss army knife.

"I had to find her," he said. "Nick's brainwashed her, just like the others."

"The others?"

He looked frustrated. "Damn, you don't know shit. Nick has a following. When he was in jail, when he was on trial, women wrote him. They proposed. They offered…whatever. They wanna make a bad boy good, you know what I'm saying? There's literally hundreds of them in the Nick Talbot group."

"That's in Star Track?"

"Yeah. It's how I…you know. Found him."

So someone in the group had insider information. I made a mental note to myself: look up the Nick Talbot group. I unloaded too much ketchup on the fries and tried to still look serious. "Am I gonna find anything incriminating on that phone?"

He gave me a hangdog look. "I've got some pictures of Addison."

"Pictures you took?"

"Yeah. Nothing creepy, just…you know. Her."

"Did Addison know you were taking these pictures?"

"Some of them. I mean, we were together for almost a year."

"But she doesn't know about all of them."

"No." He looked at his lap, trying to tamp down the anger and humiliation, then raised his head. "You're not one of them, are you?"

"One of who?"

"Nick's people. You're not paid to look the other way, are you?"

"I'm not paid for anything."

He nodded, bit his bottom lip. "All right, so do what you have to do with the phone. But I had to try. Addison's in danger. And she won't talk to me anymore, so...I had to do something."

His eyes were pleading. Behind the counter, Betsy Ann dumped a flat of silverware in a plastic bin, creating a racket, letting me know she was there if I needed her.

"I'll do what I can about the phone," I said. "But you gotta stay the hell away from Addison and Nick in the meantime. I don't care what happens."

"Whatever. Just make her understand. Please."

My cell phone beeped, warning me that it was time to hit the road. I wrapped a napkin around my fries as the cruiser snaked through the square again. Deputy Butch, protecting and serving.

"I'll do what I can," I said.

Chapter Twenty-seven

The gym where Trey taught was old-school iron and sweat. I spotted Finn in the parking lot waiting next to her Jeep. She was back to what I was beginning to think of as her template look—jeans and tee, no makeup, hair sticking up in blondish points.

"Hey," I said. "How's Nick?"

"He's at home today, resting. The doc says he's fine."

"Any results on the tea?"

"That's gonna take a while." She looked at me over her sunglasses. "You said you had Diego's phone?"

"Yep."

"What did you find on it?"

She didn't say it as an accusation, just a point of information. I handed it to her.

"Several things. Diego admitted he'd been following Addison around, and there are tons of pictures to prove it. The usual obsessed former lover portfolio."

"Diego says he and Addison were lovers? That's not what she told Nick."

"No, it's not. But the photos on that phone back up his story—they were an item before Addison came to Georgia. But that's not the most interesting thing. The night someone took a shot at Nick? Addison said she was at home working. But Diego has pictures of her leaving the house an hour before. Time-stamped."

"Addison was lying about being home all night?"

"Yep."

"Deception in the information age. Not easy." Finn swiped through the images, shaking her head. "What else did you find?"

"Diego used this celebrity-sighting app to track down Nick, who became his target after Addison got a restraining order. Here. Let me show you."

I pulled up the app on my own phone, went into the Nick Talbot group. It had almost two hundred members. The sightings and shared photos had started right after he arrived in Atlanta, but changed dramatically after his stints in rehab. No more club shots, drunk shots, limo shots. Now it was Nick at Whole Foods, Nick chowing down on Mongolian barbecue, Nick jogging on the Greenway. Ordinary moments only. Yet he was still catnip to a certain kind of female, still gave off a whiff of danger.

"Diego is one of the few guys in there—the rest are female groupies."

"You think one of them is dropping inside information, like where the base camps are?"

"That would be my guess."

Finn pocketed the phone as a group of women in booty shorts and fitted tanks filed inside the gym, no doubt headed for Trey's class. Finn followed them. Inside, the speakers poured out a grinding nightclub noise punctuated by grunts and clanging weights. Behind the check-in desk, a corkboard featured photographs of the trainers and instructors, including Trey, an older photo from before I'd met him.

The owner looked up and grinned at me. He was short, bald, and heavily tanned, a semi-pro body builder. "Looking for Trey?"

"I am."

"Check the ab station."

I signed the check-in sheet, put Finn down as a guest. "Thanks, Mac."

"No problem."

He flashed a smile and went back to sorting protein bars. Finn followed me down the narrow corridors between the lat pull-down and the row machine. I spotted Trey in the corner, upside down on the core extension, knees locked on the pads, hands behind his head. When he spotted us, he curled himself up and off the equipment. Three women in the corner pretended not to watch, so I pretended not to see them when I kissed him hello.

He wrapped a towel around his neck. "We can talk in the classroom."

I followed him inside, Finn right behind. It was familiar territory to me now, this bare room with the padded floor and heavy bags and the smell of leather and sweat. Trey rubbed at his face with the towel and held out a hand. Finn handed a file to him, and one to me.

I opened the folder. "What are these?"

"Paperwork for your covers."

"Our what?"

"Covers. Nick wants the situation to remain under wraps. Only he and Quint and the Talbot Creative Board know why you two will be at the press party. And Addison. After I explained to Nick the danger she was in if he didn't tell her, he relented and spilled the beans. But those are the only people privy to why you're actually there. *Et voilà*...covers."

I opened my folder. It was a dossier as well-collected as any background profile. Photographs, résumés, news clippings, social media sites. She'd pulled my college transcripts. Multiple classes at multiple institutions, including two semesters in the archeology program, but no actual degree. All the shop's information was included as well.

I waved the file at her. "But this is still just me."

"Not quite. I had them do a pretty significant scrub."

"Them?"

"The ORM specialists. Online reputation management. Before they took a broom to your online presence, do you know what the number one autocomplete suggestion was for Tai Randolph?" She smiled. "Murder."

I swallowed hard. "The mess this spring."

"Oh, that's the most recent hit, yes. But lots others. No

longer." She smiled bigger. "Do you know what the number two suggestion was?"

"Let me guess. Reckless?"

Finn shook her head. Trey looked up from his folder.

"Me," he said.

Finn nodded. "Yep. The ORM specialist couldn't quite delete you, but he did pile a lot of stuff on top of you."

I was a little stunned. "That's it? You just erased Trey from my life?"

Finn scoffed. "Of course not. I wish it were that easy. No, anybody seriously looking will find the connection in an instant. We're just trying to discourage the casual "who the hell is she?" crowd. I had a good foundation—you did business with Talbot Creative when they first came to town, and I simply piggybacked on that. You'll be just another local with Hollywood in her eyes. They'll fall over themselves ignoring you."

"But they saw us at the set. Both of us. And then Trey put a takedown on Diego."

"Only the security team knows that. Otherwise Trey was a shadow that day. We just need to…" Finn wiggled her fingers at him. "You know. Blur him a little bit. That's why we're getting Mr. Seaver a new persona for the event."

Trey looked up from his folder. "You can't be serious."

She eyed him shrewdly. "I needed a background you had the skill set to inhabit. That meant killing people or being a valet. I chose the one where you parked cars. Until you got fired anyway. But I'm assuming that wasn't for lack of parking ability."

He glared at her. Her eyes sparkled. She was baiting him. He was rising to it.

He extended the folder back to her. "Absolutely not."

Finn ignored him. "Why not? Being at the valet station will work very well for this particular operation. You get to observe behind the scenes. Peek in the guests' cars as they arrive. Dig around in their consoles for illicit receipts."

He shook his head. Extended the folder more forcefully.

Finn sighed dramatically. "Okay fine, technically you're the security manager. Other people will be doing the actual grunt work of running and driving. But you'll have a nametag and a cheap suit. Everybody will look right through you, even with those cheekbones."

Another shake of the head. "I will not—"

"And with an assumed name and cover, there will be no evidence anyone at Phoenix Incorporated could use to prove you were ever there. Not even Marisa will be able to find you."

Trey didn't stop glaring, but I saw the wheels turning in his head. He tucked the folder under his arm and ceased arguing.

Finn looked satisfied. "It's only one night. And this way you're right in the thick of things if we need you. We being Tai. I won't be on premises."

I looked up from my paperwork. "What? Why not?"

"Because they know what I am. Everybody clams up when I'm around. Don't worry, I have covert protection in place, close protection for Nick. Plus the usual perimeter protocols and the resort's own security team."

Trey made a skeptical noise at that. Finn tapped his folder.

"I'm not talking about those studio rent-a-clowns Quint hired at the base camp. Look at your paperwork. I included the résumés of the team I have in place. You'll find them satisfactory, I am sure."

He took her up on it, opening the folder again and paging through it. "Where will Tai and I be staying?"

"You, Mr. Seaver, are in the staff cottage, which is connected to the check-in station, so you're at choke point for all entries and exits with video surveillance of the entire resort right in front of you. Tai is in one of the guest cottages because she's one of the guests." Trey opened his mouth to protest, but Finn didn't let him get one word out. "She's in the cottage right next to the station, don't even start."

I shook my head. "Why would somebody like me, a glorified prop person, get to stay in one of the fancy cottages?"

"Good question. I'm sure somebody will think of it."

"And then they'll come talk to me."

Finn tapped her temple. "See? Brains at work. Trust me, with you in the foreground and Trey in the background, we'll have the intelligence gathering covered."

Trey was still wary. "I refuse to be named Steve."

"Too late. Your name is already on the manifest. And your nametag."

He glared harder at her. She beamed at him and gave the heavy bag a shove, watched it swing.

"Go ahead, Mr. Seaver. Get acquainted with yourself. I'll check in later. In the meantime, you'll need to down market your wardrobe. Lose the Italian fanciness and get something off the rack."

He ignored that. "When do I need to be there?"

"Friday at four. Tai will come later, around seven, with the other guests."

And which point we had to pretend we didn't know each other. Trey did not like that. He didn't like a lot of the plan, but the professional part of him knew that Finn had done a bang-up job. He wasn't ready to admit it, however.

He handed me his folder. "Keep this, please. I need to get the attendance rolls from the front desk."

And then he left. I waited until he was out of earshot before I turned to Finn. "What in the devil was that about him getting fired?"

"I know, right?" Her eyes twinkled. "When he was twenty, he worked at the Ritz Carlton as a valet. Part-time evenings. I managed to dig up his employee record. Two great evaluations in a row. And then suddenly…boom. He's fired."

"Why?"

"I don't know. He was rehired a week later. I poked some more, but that part of his record is sealed, and I mean tight. Lawyer work. I recognize legal legerdemain when I see it. He's never mentioned this to you?"

I shook my head. When Trey was twenty, he was a college

junior with his sights set on the Atlanta Police Department and a good start on his criminal justice degree.

Finn frowned. "Huh. That's even stranger." She shrugged. "Oh well. An investigation for another time. I've got to run, but I'll meet you Friday, get you the final details."

She gave the weight bag one last punch and left. I remained behind, ravenously, ridiculously, deeply curious. Trey may have thought he could just walk out of that conversation, but there was something he and I had in common—once we caught the scent of interesting prey, we found it really hard to let it go.

He'd be letting go of this particular secret, though. I had ways of making him talk.

Chapter Twenty-eight

The class was scheduled to work on back choke, but I knew back choke so well I could do it in my sleep. Turn the head to relieve pressure on the windpipe. Drop the center of gravity to put your opponent off balance. Follow-up options abounded—thumb to the eye socket, elbow to the solar plexus, punch to the groin. So many ways to wreak havoc on the tender vulnerable parts of a no-goodnik.

Trey waited on the mat, barefoot. He didn't bow or make any other acknowledgment when I joined him. This was no martial art we were practicing—no forms, no katas, no ritual politeness. Just down and dirty self defense.

I pulled out my handwraps. "You're annoyed."

He narrowed his eyes at me, and I realized we were at the crucial juncture where the rubber hits the road. Or not. The rubber could also spin in place and smoke and scorch and go absolutely nowhere.

I stood face to face with him. "We're going to be separated. You didn't see that coming, but since this whole investigation is your idea, you know you can't back out of it. But you want to. Bad."

He didn't saying anything. I started wrapping my hand—three times around the wrist, five times around the palm, criss-cross between the fingers. Perfectly designed to distribute the force and protect the delicate metacarpals and phalanges.

"So yes," I said, "you get to be annoyed, but you don't get to—"

He snatched the wrap out of my hand without even breaking eye contact, then rolled it into a neat ball. "You're right. I'm annoyed. I did not foresee that Finn would want us working separately, and I don't like that. I should have expected she would, though—it's good strategy—and that's also annoying me. But mostly I'm annoyed that even though I thought I had progressed beyond this point, I have not. I still want to protect you. I can't help it. It overrides logical processing."

He moved even closer, toe to toe. I didn't back up. He stuffed the handwrap into my waistband, leaving a piece dangling over my right hip.

"Today the class is working on back choke," he said. "You, however, are working on close quarter weapons retention."

And then he reached for the wrap. I moved away before he could get his fingers on it, but I knew he hadn't really been trying. He was giving me a chance to get in gear. It wasn't a courtesy a criminal would extend, but Trey did, at least in the first phase. The zone of proximal learning, he called it.

"Fine." I adjusted my stance, opened my hands. "Let's do this."

No helmets. No shin guards. This wasn't going to be rough. It was going to be fast, though.

Trey dropped his shoulders and took one step backward. I lowered my hands to waist level, angled my hip away from him. He was going for the weapon, in this case a balled-up piece of elastic on my hip, right where I'd side carry. He had speed and expertise on his side. Also agility. I had grit and sheer meanness, plus a few other tricks up my sleeve.

"So you got fired from the Ritz Carlton," I said.

He flexed his fingers. "I did."

He moved quickly, a sidestep and snatch. I back-pedaled, almost tripping, but the wrap stayed on my hip.

I tsk-tsked as I circled him. "You said you didn't have any secrets."

"This isn't a secret."

"Then tell me about it."

He didn't answer. Instead, he lunged. I moved to block, but he fooled me with a feint, and I was off balance when he caught me from behind. He had me pinned before I could blink, both arms wrapped tight as a vise. I cursed under my breath. I hated it when I fell for an obvious trap.

I struggled to keep my feet planted. "Don't act like you've won. You have to move your hand to get to my hip."

"I know."

"And I'm breaking this hold when you do. Plus I'm being real sweet because you're not protected. Because if we were really training right now, I'd donkey kick you in the groin."

"And if that didn't work?

"That always works."

He tightened his grip. "If it didn't?"

"Fine. Just to make sure, I'd take out your knee." I tapped his kneecap lightly with the heel of my foot, then brought it down slowly. "I'd squash your instep next. Slam the back of my head into your nose for good measure."

I moved my head backward until I felt it touch the bridge of his nose. He didn't move to avoid me, but he didn't let go.

"All good options," he said. "But what if you're fighting an armored opponent?"

I swiveled my head and looked up at him. "Tell me why you got fired. I won't laugh."

He loosened his grip just the slightest. Not enough for me to break the hold, but enough to give me some leverage. That was how I knew it was another trap. He was wearing his bland innocent face. He fooled a lot of people with that.

"Do you really want to know?" he said.

"I really want to know."

He adjusted his stance, redistributing his weight. Something was coming, and I tensed for it before I remembered that I was supposed to stay flexible. There would be no tussling, so I needed to come up with a break, not an attack. I wanted to attack, though. Offensive maneuvers were my specialty.

Trey's mouth was warm against my ear. "Because if you really want to know, I'll tell you. If you ask the right way."

My heart did a backflip. I heard female conversation at the door, the first of the students. I could feel his chest rising and falling against my back.

I relaxed against him. "If I coax it out of you syllable by syllable, you mean."

"Yes. That is exactly what I mean."

I dropped my center of gravity. He almost moved to catch me, but caught himself. I hooked my foot around his ankle to throw him off balance, then hit the mat butt-first and pivoted, kicking both feet toward him. To get to me, he'd have to come through a flurry of heel strikes to the face.

"Ha!" I said. "What are you gonna do now?"

He put his hands on his hips, not even breathing hard. "Yield, I suppose."

The words were utterly satisfying. But I hadn't won yet, not entirely.

"Why couldn't Finn find a record of it?"

He shook his head. "If you want me to tell you—"

"Yeah, yeah, yeah. I remember how to get things out of you, don't worry." I hauled myself up, dusted off my backside. "But I can find out without resorting to a honey trap."

"You can?"

"I can. You think otherwise?"

"I didn't say that."

I gave him a thorough examination. He was calm, curious. Whatever he had hidden, it wasn't something dark and melodramatic. He was dangling it like bait, playing with me.

"Care to make a bet?" I said.

"What are you wagering?"

"When I find out—"

"If."

I tapped a finger on his chest. "*When* I find out, you have to come camping with me. In a tent. On the ground."

He flinched, tried to cover it. "And if you don't?"

"Then I will consent to getting the information the old-fashioned way. Word by word, straight from your lips. Even if it takes all night. Deal?"

He considered. "Deal."

I stuck out my hand, and he took it. I grinned at him. "You are in such trouble, boyfriend."

"I know." He tilted his head, and the spark in his eyes flared tender. "You're smiling again. I've missed that."

That pulled me up short. He was right, of course. I hadn't been feeling very smiley. But now...the light bill was still overdue. The DNA results were still in the drawer. The hornet's nest of complications still hung from my family tree, poisonous and tricky and dangerous as hell. And now I'd heaped a new mess of complications on my plate. But strangely enough, I felt energized instead of worn down. I wasn't sure what this said about me except that perhaps Eric was right—we all needed an outlet.

"In the meantime," I said, "we've still got a case to solve."

"Two cases," he corrected.

He was right about that too. The Talbots wove a tangled web spanning almost four years. But it was also the first time he'd called what we were doing a case.

"And you," I said, "need to buy a cheap suit."

"Apparently so." He looked toward the door as the rest of his class streamed in, then back at me. "Are you staying here tonight?"

Traffic from Buckhead to Kennesaw would be a nightmare in the morning. I'd have to get up stupid early. But the bed at Trey's place was bigger and softer and full of Trey. And once he went to sleep, I would have free run of his employment files. I decided rush hour was Tomorrow Tai's problem, not mine. She could deal with it in the morning.

"Of course I'm staying," I said.

Chapter Twenty-nine

Of course I regretted my decision to stay over once I was in the morning commute, relentless as usual. The weather was glorious as long as I kept the windows rolled up and pretended that the air quality index wasn't creeping into the red zone. I checked the traffic on my phone. Two accidents, a gas leak, and construction. I was going to be on the road a while.

Spending the night had been worth it, though, even if all we'd done was catalog the massive amounts of information we'd collected. I'd enjoyed watching Trey put it together, aligning this evidence with that circumstance. I hadn't asked him any further questions about the firing, and he hadn't offered any further information. At breakfast, he'd barely raised an eyebrow when he saw his employment folders sticking out of my tote bag, which told me two things: one, he was enjoying watching me scramble, and two, I wasn't going to find the answer in the paperwork.

Which reminded me.

"Call Ritz Carlton Buckhead," I said, and my phone dialed me through. I had to go through a receptionist, the bell captain, and a mid-level manager before I finally got to the assistant human resources supervisor. It took me thirty seconds to realize he was going to be of no help whatsoever.

"Can you at least verify the dates that Mr. Seaver worked for you?"

"No, ma'am. We are not authorized—"

"But—"

"Good day, ma'am."

The guy hung up politely but definitively. This was not surprising, but calling them had been a necessary first step. Now on to the second step…whatever that might be. I drummed my fingers on the dashboard. Traffic ground to a halt yet again, suddenly, illogically. I caught the reek of burning tires. It was going to be a long morning.

• ● ● ● •

At work, I sold ten boxes of shot cartridges to the same guy who bought them every week and who insisted every week that the government was rationing ammo. A reenactor client picked up his priming wire and blasting caps. Around lunchtime, I made another pot of coffee and jumped into an online auction on my computer, setting my sights on a left-handed officer's sword with a presentation inscription, an unusual bit of militaria.

My assistant Kenny watched the bidding with some interest. "That for Mr. Reynolds?"

"It is."

"That means you can bid as high as you want, right?"

I laughed. That was the fine thing about shopping for Reynolds, his wide-ranging tastes and generous wallet. Kenny put down the boxes he was unloading and peered over my shoulder.

"What is that mess you're watching on your phone?" he said.

"Season One of *Buckwild in Buckhead*. In fast forward. "

The show was as bad as I'd expected—pixilated nakedness, bleeped expletives, corn pone accents, and over-the-top theatrics in every way except for the fights. Those were honest-to-goodness redneck scrapping.

Kenny scratched his head. "Looks like a bunch of people who weren't raised right."

"Three seasons of it. Wanna grab some coffee and join me?"

"No, ma'am."

He picked up his load, and I went back to the show. Somehow the producers had managed to find the crassest collection of Southerners to ever walk the green earth. They poured champagne in the hot tub. They made out on the buffet table. There were slapfights aplenty, mostly between Daizie and Daiquiri over Braydon, a tanned roughneck with a three-drink-minimum leer and a bleached-blond ponytail.

I shook my head. "My people, my people."

I quickly discovered that the footage fell into four categories. The first two—confessional single-camera monologues and videos of the Buckwilders out on the town—were useless to me. There was also indoor video, courtesy of the cameras that Quint insisted the production team had stolen. I was interested in the fourth type, the outdoor scenes.

"Come on," I said. "Show me the corner behind the pool."

The camera operators were not cooperating. They trained their lenses on the parade of cleavage and ass, not the pool decor. Kenny brought in the last of the boxes.

"What's this show got to do with this weekend?" he said.

"Background investigations."

"Oh." He pushed his glasses higher on his nose. "I thought you said you were done messing with other people's problems."

"Trey's the one messing, and he has his reasons. I'm supporting him. That's all."

Kenny dusted off his hands. "Whatever you say, Miss Tai."

He headed for the storage room, whistling. He was such a cheerful presence, good-natured and smart, a member of the local historical society and a skilled reenactor, or as he preferred to be called, heritage interpreter. I didn't tell him that his extra hours had wiped out my bank account, that I was counting on the sword sale to Reynolds to fund our electricity for another month.

I put that thought out of my mind and got back to the Buckwildness.

The first season was a waste, with the field trip to the High Museum especially cringe-worthy. The second season managed to out-tasteless the first by hauling the Buckwilders to the

Cathedral of St. Philip, which they kept calling St. Phil on the Hill. The third season was promising more of the same until the tenth episode, a Cinco de Mayo pool party with massive sombreros, mustache stickers, a mariachi band, and, standing right between the pool and the sunroom windows...

A giant turquoise cactus.

I hit pause. The cactus was easily seven feet tall and was covered in shiny bits of mosaic tiles. I could never get a good look at the base, but I would have bet my last dollar it was circular with a diameter of approximately two feet. It also looked familiar. I went back to the episode list and pulled up the field trip to an art gallery in Little Five Points.

And there it was. The turquoise cactus. I hit pause. The name of the gallery was Expresso. I did a quick search, wrote the address on the back of my hand.

"Kenny!"

He stuck his head out. "Yes, ma'am?"

"You have the shop for the rest of the afternoon. Lock up on your way out, okay?"

• • ● • •

Little Five Points felt like hanging out with a slightly trashy best friend. It was the first place Rico had taken me when I'd visited him for the first time—we had mojitos and tacos at the Tijuana Garage and I bought a pair of go-go boots at the Junkman's Daughter. I could still do those things. L5P was still dreadlocked and funky. But with its geography sandwiching it between two affluent neighborhoods, prosperity was booming whether anyone liked it or not. The infamous Clairmont Lounge was slated to become a boutique hotel, and the now-defunct Murder Kroger was being torn down with a twelve-story office building to rise in its place.

The Expresso Gallery straddled the divide between gentrification and authentic homegrown weirdness. It sat at the corner of Euclid and Moreland, Atlanta's very own Haight-Ashbury, and even though it was open, it appeared deserted. The walls were freshly painted with primer, still wet in places.

"Hello?" I called.

"Yes?"

I turned around. A woman entered from a side door, her long brown hair held back with a bandanna. She wore overalls over a tube top, and buff paint smeared one cheek. A tattoo that said Goddess of Kush ran up the inside of her forearm.

I showed her the image of the cactus on my phone. "Do you recognize this piece?"

"Oh, yeah. Commercial. Derivative. Appropriative."

"Evidence."

She didn't even blink. "Really? What kind of crime?"

"A confidential one."

"Murder?"

"No."

She looked instantly bored. "Oh well. That thing was one of LaLa's."

"Can I speak to…her?"

The woman popped her gum. "Him. And he's gone."

"Gone?"

"Yeah, it's a rule. Loser doesn't pay the rent, loser has to hit the road. Or course some losers will then deface the walls with crypto-fascist manifestos, and I have to spend my afternoon repainting." She wiggled her nose like a rabbit, wiped her forehead with her forearm. "LaLa let the TV people borrow that piece, for the exposure. They returned it Saturday afternoon. I sold it to pay back rent."

"Can you tell me who bought it?"

"This chick headed out to Burning Man. It's going on her festival fire at the Playa and then the ashes will be scattered in the desert, symbolizing—"

"That sounds great, but…" I tried to keep my smile steady. "It really is evidence. It can't be burned."

The woman shrugged. "Outta my hands now."

"Can you give me the contact info for the person who has it?"

"You got a warrant?"

"No. I'm not a cop."

She folded her arms. "Then you're out of luck. If word got around I was selling my mailing list—"

"I don't need your list. Just one name."

She shook her head. "Sorry. No can do. Not without—"

"A warrant, right. I heard you." I tapped my foot, thought a little harder. "This chick. You know how to find her?"

The woman shrugged coyly. "Maybe."

"You think she'd be open to a resale?"

"Maybe."

"How much would she want? Including the commission for yourself, of course."

The woman's eyes turned cagey. How much could someone like me pay? She gave me the up and down, noting the khakis and plain white button-down, good leather boots worn all to hell, no jewelry except gold studs in my ears. Thank goodness she couldn't see my bra, which was a La Perla cross-back that had set Trey back five hundred dollars, or she would have upped the price considerably.

"It's a stalking case," I said.

She stopped evaluating me. "It is?"

"Yes. And I shouldn't be telling you this, but there's a life on the line."

I didn't tell her the life belonged to a rich white male. That turned out to be a good move. I watched her eyes get hard.

"Wait here," she said, and put down the roller brush.

An hour later I had a number, and a name, and an address. What I didn't have was a check for thirty-six hundred dollars. I waited until I got back in my car to call Trey. He didn't answer his cell, so I tried his work phone. To my surprise, I got a familiar female voice.

"Hello, Marisa," I said.

Her tone was annoyed. "Is this Tai?"

I tried to think of a better answer than yes. Failed miserably.

I sighed. "Yes. Could I please speak to—"

"Where's Trey?"

"What?"

"It says on his calendar that he's taking personal leave. I assumed that meant with you."

Oh crap, I thought. *Now she's suspicious.*

"He mentioned he had errands to run," I offered.

"Like what?"

"He didn't say."

"Really? And I thought you two were bound at the ankles, like some kind of two-person chain gang."

I couldn't tell if she was angry or just her usual ice queen sarcastic. I was the thorn in her side, after all, corrupting her famously reliable premises liability agent into someone who didn't always snap to at her command.

I forced a laugh. "Ha! Well, gotta run. Nice talking to you." Then it hit me. "If he's not there, what are you doing in his office?"

"Answering his phone," she said, and hung up.

So I tried Finn. That call went straight to voice mail. In desperation, I tried one more number. To my astonishment, Nick Talbot himself answered.

"Hello?"

I cleared my throat. "Mr. Talbot—I mean, Nick. It's Tai Randolph, Trey's partner. I need you to buy some art."

Chapter Thirty

Nick told me to meet him at the production studio, a warehouse-looking building in the middle of an industrial park. I pulled into a deserted parking strip, then followed the sidewalk past a row of crepe myrtles until I reached a gray metal door. A sign warned me not to enter if the red light was on. It wasn't. I knocked, and heard footsteps coming.

Nick opened up. "Hey. Come on in."

I followed him into a room the size of an aircraft hanger, echoing and dark. It smelled of dust and machine oil, with lighting grids like giant metal spider webs on the ceiling.

"Nothing going on today," he said. "All the action's up in Adairsville, getting ready for the press party, so I'm minding the store while the important people do important things."

He took me to a tiny office crammed with plywood furniture. Pale blue walls didn't match the brown carpet, which wasn't even a fancy brown. It reeked of closeout sale, as did the bargain-basement cabinets. The only decoration was a color-saturated poster for *Moonshine*, this one featuring Luna in profile against a red moon, a feral gleam in her eyes, the LeMat revolver on her hip. She looked lean and ruthless, dangerous as a lit fuse, a white-blond braid snaking over one shoulder.

Nick shut the door and sat behind a drawing table. He smiled crookedly. "Welcome to the heartbeat of Talbot Creative."

I sat opposite him. "Y'all didn't go for flashy, I see."

"Not even a little. We didn't expect to be here for very long, frankly. Now that *Moonshine's* taken off, we're expanding to the bigger facilities down the road. We'll get actual leather chairs then."

Except for a still-swollen eye, he looked well. Maybe a little paler than usual, but not sickly. He noticed my examination.

"IV fluids and a good night's sleep. Liver enzyme tests came back good."

"So…no overdose?"

"The doc says something went wrong, that was for sure, they just don't know what yet. Finn says those tests will take longer. Titrating out the something-something." He stifled a yawn, reached for his mug. "Addison now keeps all my food and beverages in her office. Locked. Even I can't get to them. She is not a happy camper. But enough…" He smiled again, blandly. "So I'm buying art today?"

"Yes, but not for artsy purposes. Trey's theory is that this particular piece of art caught the bullet meant for you."

"Really?"

"Yeah. Big turquoise cactus. With mirrors."

He looked startled. "Wow. That's uh…unmistakable."

"Did you notice it that night?"

"No. But it was dark. And I was in stealth mode, you know? In my bubble. Trying to keep out the negative energy."

I did know. Trey sometimes had difficulty with his bubble too. If Nick had been focused on just getting through the evening, his would have been pretty thick, almost impenetrable.

I shook my head. "Why did you go? You knew it would be hard."

He fiddled with a pencil, eyes down. "I wanted to bury that whole episode, finally and for good, and I thought it would be easier with Quint there. He's very no-nonsense, you know. So I told Addison I was running an errand here at the studio. I left her at our place steady working." He exhaled through pursed lips. "I came clean with her the night of the crash, told her everything. She was *so* mad. But mad as she was—at me and

Quint both—she agreed to keep the police out. She saw what happened last time the APD got their hooks in me."

I remembered Trey's analysis. I couldn't blame Nick for wanting to avoid another interrogation. I also couldn't tell him that Addison had lied to him as well, that she wasn't at their place the night of the shooting. Maybe he already knew. Maybe he was providing an alibi, protecting her the way she'd protected him when he was accused of Jessica's murder. Regardless…

"Does Addison work at home a lot?" I said.

"She's a writer. She's always working." He leaned back in his chair, hands behind his head. "Look, Addison can be overprotective, and Quint can be a downright ass. But it's because they care about me. So even if you find a bullet, and that bullet has fingerprints and a signature on it, we'll deal with the situation ourselves." He waved a hand in my direction. "Which means, according to Finn anyway, you and Trey. And you obviously have your own reasons for keeping things on the QT."

He didn't phrase it like a question. But it was.

I uncrossed my legs. "Can we talk? Person to person?"

"Sure."

"Trey was convinced you were a killer. Now he's convinced you're not. He's wracked with guilt over what happened to you, and he's trying his best to make it right again."

Nick looked discombobulated. "Okay. And?"

"And so he's on the justice trail. He has his own reasons to avoid getting the authorities involved, as do you. And your brother. And Finn. And me." I leaned forward, folded my arms on the table. "That means you need to be telling the truth, about everything."

"Are you accusing me of lying?"

"Not yet."

He studied me. Not aggressively. Surprisingly calm. I was dying to quiz him about Addison, Diego Martinez too, and the contradictions between their stories. Was Nick lying or lied to? Was this information best kept in pocket or deployed strategically?

A knock interrupted us. Nick turned around, and a man stuck his head through the crack in the door. He was short, stocky, with thick salt-and-pepper hair and a tailored dove gray suit. Like a hobbit who shopped at Brooks Brothers.

Nick held out his hand. "Thank you, Oliver."

The man hesitated. "If we could speak out here a second?"

Nick didn't budge. "Do you bring a check or not?"

"Nick—"

"Check or not? Simple question."

"Quint said no."

Nick's eyes simmered. "Does my brother understand that this is a piece of evidence in an investigation that he himself needs to keep quiet? That if this piece of evidence gets into the wrong hands, we'll have cops breathing down our necks *and* a PR tsunami?"

Oliver wasn't rolling over. "Quint said you need to come talk to him first."

Nick started shaking his head, his jaw clenched. Oliver looked concerned, but didn't say anything. Nick pulled out his wallet and handed me four crisp hundreds.

He shoved his chair back. "There. See if you can at least make a down payment. Can you find your way back out? I have to go yell at my brother now."

I stood too. "Absolutely."

Trey returned my call just as I reached the car. "I got your message," he said. "Did you say something about a giant cactus?"

I pulled out my keys. "The quick and dirty is this: can you buy a ridiculously expensive piece of ridiculous art and maybe or maybe not get reimbursed for it? Because if you can't, your missing bullet may be headed to Burning Man, where who knows—"

"Yes. I can."

"Cool. I just texted you the contact info."

Across the parking lot, I saw a female figure marching toward my car fast and angry, fists pumping like a really aggressive fitness walker. Addison. Her black hair swished as she pushed her sleeves up, and even from a distance, I could see the fury in her eyes.

I unlocked the door but didn't get inside. "Uh oh. Enraged fiancée headed my way."

"What's happened?"

"Stay on the line and find out."

I slipped the phone into my back pocket as Addison came around my car. "What in the hell did you say to him?" she said. "His pulse rate is through the roof."

"I suspect that has more to do with Quint than me."

Addison didn't seem to hear me. "You need to back the hell off. I know how your type operates, and I won't have it."

My type? I pushed up my sleeves too. "Listen. I am in no way putting the moves on Nick Talbot. I have zero interest. But you, you interest me a lot."

She looked startled. "What?"

"Oh yes, you are definitely a person of interest. Let's start with—"

My phone vibrated through my jeans. Insistently. I didn't have to look to know who was texting me. I closed my mouth and took a deep breath. *Don't say anything,* I told myself. *Do not mention her and Diego's actual relationship. Do not bring up that she lied about her whereabouts the night of Nick's attempted shooting. Do not explain that if those lab results show he was indeed overdosed, and that if we really do pull a bullet from that cactus, then she was going to be our prime suspect.*

I yanked open the car door. "Never mind."

She glared. "Upset him again and you're fired."

I got in the car. "Guess what, Buttercup? You didn't hire me, so you can't fire me."

"No. But I can make Nick do it."

"Probably. And then when the next shooter doesn't miss, you can explain to the prosecutor why ditching the people trying to protect him seemed like a great idea."

At the word "shooter," her cheeks flared crimson, and her eyes flashed behind the glasses. I thought for a second she was going to come at me, and some part of me went liquid and bright at the prospect.

Addison pulled out her radio. "Security. We have a situation in the front parking lot. Make sure the woman in the red hillbilly car leaves the property this instant."

And then she stomped back toward the production offices. I reached for the seatbelt, put the phone to my ear just as two security guys appeared, Addison pointing helpfully in my direction.

"Are you okay?" Trey said.

"I'm fine. But Addison's showing her true colors."

"Indeed."

I pulled out of the lot, tossed the security guys a little wave. "Thanks for the text."

"You're welcome."

"I was about to start running down the list of every piece of evidence we had on her just to watch her implode with fury."

"I guessed as much. That would have been counterproductive at this time."

The security guys watched me leave. Traffic was heavy, dusk falling. The sky had gone gunmetal gray, low cloud cover trapping the day's heat close to the ground.

"About the cactus," I said.

"I took care of it."

"You did?"

"Yes. I'll explain later tonight. Right now I have to go."

At the other end of the line, I heard traffic noise. Not Phoenix noises.

"Where are you?"

"Chastain Park. I'm attempting some reconnaissance."

"Is this more training?"

"No." A pause. "Would you like to join me?"

"Sure. Reconnaissance sounds fun." I pulled onto the highway. "You're not claiming this is your turn at date night, are you? Because if there's no making out, it's not date night. And reconnaissance does not sound conducive to making out."

"It's not. Will you come anyway?"

I thought about that. I did love stake-outs. There was something about the darkness and the hush, two people in a car, the danger and subterfuge.

"Who are we surveilling?"

"Not a *who*, a *what*. The Talbot estate. I'll text you the coordinates."

"I thought you said you were in the park?"

"I am. I'll explain when you get here."

And then he hung up.

Chapter Thirty-one

By the time I got to Chastain Park, the last smear of sunset was dying at the horizon. The coordinates Trey had dropped me put his location east of the Talbot home, across Powers Ferry at the edge of the park trail. I checked my phone again. Supposedly I was standing right beside him, but he was nowhere in sight.

I pushed down a ripple of panic and thumbed him a quick text. *Where are you?*

His reply came almost instantly. *Look up.* I tilted my head back and scrutinized the branches spreading above me. A flash of movement caught my eye, a blur of black and green about twenty feet up.

I moved closer to the trunk and craned my neck. "You've got to be kidding me."

Trey was sitting in the crook of a thick, almost horizontal branch, legs stretched out, booted feet crossed at the ankle. He had his hands folded on his stomach, his back against the trunk.

"What are you doing?" I said.

"Surveillance."

"How'd you get up there?"

"I climbed."

He played a flashlight beam around the base of the tree, where a tidy metal ladder ascended into the branches. It was sturdily mounted, designed to blend in with the bark. I grabbed a rung and hoisted myself into the dense canopy of leaves. When I reached the top, Trey extended a hand and steadied me onto the seat, a small rectangle painted the same dark green and gray pattern as his pants. It was built for two as long as the two didn't mind close company.

I eased myself down. "SWAT equipment?"

"Deer-hunting. Price let me borrow it."

I balanced my feet on the footrest. Trey handed me a bottle of water, readjusted himself. We were shoulder to shoulder, perched like strange birds while the traffic rushed beneath us.

"Marisa can't get you from behind your desk no matter how hard she tries, and yet here you are, literally up a tree." I unscrewed the water bottle and took a swig. "Speaking of. She's seriously pissed at you."

"I suspected as much based on the messages she left. Did you speak with her?"

"Briefly. Where were you this afternoon?"

"At the camera store."

He pointed to a case bungee-corded next to him. I saw a camera there, shiny new, with a long-distance lens already screwed in place. The binoculars around his neck were also new.

"Did you get the matter of the turquoise cactus taken care of?" I said.

"I extended my offer. We'll know tomorrow if it was accepted."

Once my eyes adjusted, I could see right into Nick Talbot's former backyard. Dark now, no outdoor lights except for the pool, just as it had been the night of the shooting. In the ice-white guest house, one room burned brightly, and though the shades were pulled, I could see a figure moving about inside.

"Who's that?"

"Quint. He appears to be residing in the guest house."

"Oh, really? Alone?"

"Presently, yes."

He raised the binoculars, trained them on the house. He'd told me once that the thing he enjoyed most about being a sniper was the recon. Peering through the scope of a Bergara BCR20 rifle, gathering intel, relaying his discoveries to the rest of the team.

"So there's marital unrest in the Talbot household," I said. "Is that why you're spying on him?"

"Not spying. Surveilling. And yes, it is. Finn's currently surveilling Portia." He handed me his phone without removing his eyes from the binoculars. "With interesting results."

I swiped through a series of photos featuring Portia in the darkened corner of some restaurant, her features illuminated by candlelight. A man sat opposite her—broad shoulders, iron-gray hair, square-rimmed glasses. In one frame, their heads were bent close. In another, Portia glanced furtively over her shoulder.

"Ah. Portia's having an affair."

"That's one theory. Finn has yet to verify it, nor has she identified the man in the photo."

Everything was theory with Trey. It would take photos of Portia and her dining companion naked and rolling around in satin sheets to make adultery a fact. But the two did look illicitly cozy.

I returned the phone to Trey's pocket. It felt good off the ground, the air filtered by shadows and leaves. The humidity could still choke a horse, but at least the breeze didn't smell like baked sidewalk.

"Is this legal?" I said.

"What, covert surveillance? Of course."

"Even up a tree in Chastain Park, which is city-owned, and as such, has a million restrictions about what people can and cannot do?"

"I have a permit."

He pointed to a card clipped to his sleeve. The same special permit that allowed him to hide in trees at Doll's Head Trail. I had to admit, he'd dotted his I's and crossed his T's. That part was classic Trey. But the rest of this…

I nodded down below. "Does Quint know you're out here being covert?"

"He knows we're investigating."

"So that's a no."

He shot me a pointed look. "It's called covert surveillance for a reason."

The leaves caught the edge of the first evening breeze, rising on thermals. Night birds flitted in the foliage, darting, otherwise silent. No squirrels, thank goodness.

I stretched my legs alongside Trey's. "You're using cop words, but you're behaving like a criminal."

"I am not."

"Yes, you are. All last weekend, you played bad guy while the trainees played good guy. And now here you are up a tree spying on people."

"Surveilling."

"Uh huh. How many trees did you ever climb as a cop?"

He kept the binoculars up. "I worked as an urban counter-sniper. Treetop hide sites were not appropriate for that work."

"So zero?"

He ignored me. I knew that Trey could alter his personality, his very brain waves, by changing his clothes. In an Armani suit behind a desk, he was polite and businesslike. In workout clothes on the mat, he was disciplined and relentless. And up a tree, in special ops camo, he was a SWAT guy again. Sort of.

I drank some more of the lukewarm water. "So what exactly does Quint's marital trouble have to do with Nick Talbot's assassination attempt? Or Jessica Talbot's murder?"

"I don't know."

"But you think they're connected?"

"I think we cannot afford to ignore any avenues of investigation."

"We being you and Finn?"

"We being you and I." He lowered the binoculars and handed them to me. "Finn is directing the investigation, but we're the team." He picked up the camera. "Also, I suspect I've missed something. Something I should be seeing, would be seeing if I could configure the evidence correctly."

"About Quint?"

"About the shooting. And Quint. And Nick. And the house. I—"

He aimed the camera down below, quickly firing off a series of shots. I adjusted the binoculars and scanned the backyard. A light bobbed in the living room, someone's cell phone flashlight coming through the darkened house. The visitor came out the back door onto the patio, then past the pool and straight to the guest house.

I pointed. "I know that guy! He was at the studio earlier and got caught in an argument between Nick and Quint. Oliver something."

"Oliver James. CFO of Talbot Creative, formerly Quint Talbot's personal accountant."

He took another flurry of photos. Down below, Oliver knocked on the door of the guest house. Quint opened it a sliver. The two men exchanged terse words. Then Quint slammed the door. Oliver didn't leave, though. He walked over to the pool, pulled out a pack of cigarettes, and lit one up. He took a long drag, blew smoke at the sky.

"What do we know about him?" I said.

"Four years at Stanford for his bachelor's, then two more for his master's. Opened his own accounting firm in Los Angeles, then sold that and joined Talbot Creative. He became the CFO five years ago, and then...wait. Look."

I refocused the binoculars. Quint came out of the guest house, fastening his shirt. He said something to Oliver, who turned around, anger blossoming on his face.

"Dude is not happy with Quint," I said.

"And Quint is not happy with him."

The argument continued. Quint was working himself into a fury, steaming and frothing. He stomped back into the guest house and slammed the door. Oliver dropped his cigarette on the etched concrete and ground it out with the toe of his fine leather loafer. He left in a huff. Quint watched him through the window. He glared at the cigarette like he was going to yell at Oliver to come back and get it. Instead, he went outside and picked up the butt, distaste flaring across his features. He carried it back into the guest house and slammed the door again.

"Has anyone interviewed Oliver?" I said.

Trey shook his head. "No. But I'll tell Finn and see what she decides."

I started to argue, and then bit back the response. This wasn't my call, it was Trey's, and he was much more adept at following a chain of command. I chafed at any chain. Or command.

I settled back against the tree trunk. In the guest house, the lights went out. A small lamp flickered on a few seconds later, followed by the blue glow of a computer screen. Quint had retired to the bedroom with his laptop.

Trey sat back too, camera in hand. "You should have known the Ritz Carlton wouldn't share my employment record. And that I would have the account flagged so that I would be alerted if an unauthorized person tried to access it."

I shrugged. "I suspected as much. But I had to cover all the bases."

"Of course." He nudged the toe of my boot with his. "Are you ready to give up yet?"

I nudged him back. "Not on your life."

Chapter Thirty-two

I spent Thursday morning getting the shop ready for Kenny. He didn't like modern firearms, but he was comfortable with the reenactment trade, so I locked the semi-autos and revolvers in the main safe, prepped the day box, ran the ATF paperwork... and then spent lunch rewatching the season finale of *Moonshine*. The last scene showed Portia's character Mad Luna as she'd been at the photo shoot—gore-spotted, blond hair in tangled fairy-locks, a gun in each hand. She stood alone, the ruins of her ancestral home crumbling behind her. Then a shotgun blast from offscreen, the heavy thud of a body dropping, a spatter of crimson on the mossy rocks. Fade to black.

I finished the last of my sandwich, rewound the final scene for another watch. No wonder Quint Talbot was desperate to keep the production schedule moving. *Moonshine* was as addictive as heroin with twice the merchandising potential. It was the hit he'd been waiting for his whole life.

My phone rang, and I hit pause, freeze-framing Portia's brazen, blood-smeared face.

It was Eric. "I got your message. What's wrong?"

"Why is that always your first question?"

"Experience." The sounds of cutlery and lunchtime conversation backgrounded his voice. "Seriously, what's up?"

"Has Trey ever mentioned anything about getting fired from the Ritz to you?"

Eric hesitated. Trey had long ago given my brother permission to share what would have otherwise been confidential information with me. He'd served as Trey's occupational psychologist after the accident, guiding him through the transition from cop to corporate security agent, and more importantly, through the maze of his own reconfigured brain. Eric was still tentative with his answers, though.

"He wasn't fired. He left of his own volition to enter the police academy."

"There's a firing in there somewhere. He's admitted as much. But I can't find a record of it."

"I'm not surprised. Employment records are not public."

"How could a PI find it then?"

"Those things sometimes float around in cyberspace, officially dead but showing up in certain searches, even if the record itself has been deleted." A pause. "It doesn't make any sense, though. Trey was admitted to the Ritz's Leadership Center for training. They wouldn't have let him in there with even a hint of termination on his record."

Eric was right. The Ritz ran a tight, picky ship. I reached under the cabinet and hauled up the stack of employment files I'll pilfered the day before. I paged through the folders until I found one marked with the Ritz's iconic lion head logo.

"You mean the Executive Culture and Experience program?"

"Yes, that. That was one of the reasons Marisa was so eager to hire him for Phoenix. She sends all her executive protection people to it."

"Marisa trains her bodyguards in etiquette?"

"Executive culture. And Phoenix isn't the only company that does so. It's an especially good transitional tool for former cops."

I flipped through the pages. Certificate of completion, signed and dated. A slick newsletter from the Buckhead Ritz headlined with an article about Trey and another employee graduating from the program. The photo on the front showed Trey and the other young man—stocky, suntanned, with blond curls and an exuberant grin—shaking hands with the hotel manager, everybody smiling.

My heart contracted. Trey was so young, baby-faced. His smile was hesitant. He didn't like the spotlight, even then. I started to close the folder, but the other guy's name caught my attention. John McDonald. I knew that name, but I couldn't place how. He didn't look familiar, but then, the photo was fifteen years old.

"Why aren't you asking Trey these questions?" Eric said.

I typed the name John McDonald into the search box. As expected, it returned almost a hundred hits in the metro area. Even narrowing the search down by age still gave me several dozen names.

I cursed under my breath. "We have a bet that I can't find out on my own."

"And?"

"I'm losing."

Eric laughed. "I suspected it was something like that. How is he doing?"

I hesitated. Should I tell him we were off chasing wild geese and perhaps a killer? My brother could be as lecture-y as Trey at times. Still, he was an expert on all things cognitive, especially the particular workings of Trey's mind.

I tapped my pen on the counter. "Do you remember the Jessica Talbot murder?"

"Of course. It was front-page news."

"Did you and Trey talk about his OPS investigation?"

"Some, yes. No charges filed. Trey was cleared. It all went on that other officer, what was his name?"

"Joe Macklin."

"Yes. Him. God, that was a big deal around here. My neighborhood got hit, did you know that? This couple returned from vacation and all the silver was gone. Old pieces too, Paul Revere stuff. Twenty thousand dollars' worth. The husband was angry about not being there at first, but after the murder, he thanked his lucky stars he wasn't home."

"You think Jessica's death was a robbery gone bad?"

"Makes sense. The break-ins stopped after that."

I remembered Garrity and Trey both saying that there was still a LINX alert for that crime, but that none of the hits had panned out. The Buckhead Burglar had either moved on to less patrolled pastures, given up stealing, or died.

"How did Trey seem when he talked about that case?" I said. "I mean, in your professional opinion?"

"The same way he seemed about everything at the time, utterly complacent."

"You didn't sense any obsessive angst?"

"No. Why? What's happened?"

Eric's voice was smooth, inviting. So I took a deep breath and told him the story—all I knew of it, anyway. Eric listened. He could listen like the desert soaking up rain.

"And how is all of this affecting you? Especially considering the other matter."

Eric knew about the DNA test, even if he didn't know the results were in my cash register. My brother looked like the man who'd raised me, who'd taught me to love the salt marshes, taught me how silence could be nurturing and how silence could cut like a rusty knife. Eric had hazel eyes, like most of the Randolphs. I had eyes that were mossy gray, eyes I'd always called hazel because there was no other word for that silver-boned green.

Not Bennett Randolph's eyes. Beauregard Forrest Boone's.

My hands started shaking. "That's a harder question."

Eric didn't reply. It was a psychologist's trick, I knew, as canny as any interrogator. Leave the space and people will talk to fill it. But I had no idea what could fill the space between us. How to even begin? He was a decade older than me, wiser in many ways. I'd grown up in his shadow, nursed our mother through her death in that same shadow, supported by his money but not his presence. And now, with that envelope in the drawer...

I started to say something, but at that moment, a sleek black sedan pulled to my door, taking up two of the empty spaces. I could see the driver, but the backseat occupant remained a mystery, hidden behind tinted glass. The driver looked in my direction, assessing.

"I have to go," I said.

"Okay. But listen, you know I'm here—"

"I know, I know. Gotta run. Thanks for your help."

I slid my phone into my back pocket as the driver came into the shop. He pushed open the door, bells jangling in his wake. Black slacks, white shirt, tiny earpiece with the lines snaking down inside his collar. He didn't take off his sunglasses, and he entered the shop the way Trey did—assessing, wary, noting blind spots and exits.

"Can I help you?" I said.

He didn't answer. He returned to the car and opened the back door. And Portia Ray unfolded herself from the backseat.

Chapter Thirty-three

She was far less Luna than she'd been at the photo shoot. Instead of bootlegger clothes, she wore yoga pants and a fitted running jacket, and instead of a machine gun, she carried a bright blue designer bag. With a baseball cap covering her ice-blond hair and sunglasses shielding her eyes, she looked exactly like an incognito celebrity. The driver opened the shop door for her, then posted himself outside, hands folded low across his groin, feet slightly splayed.

Once Portia was safely in the shop, she took off the cap and shook out her hair. She glowed even under fluorescent lights, her skin so perfect she seemed airbrushed.

She pulled off her sunglasses and smiled. "Tai Randolph."

I cursed inwardly, but returned the smile. "That's me. What can I do for you?"

"You came to see Nicky yesterday at the studio. And you were at the base camp on Monday. I saw your name on the security logs. Your name was also on the supplier contacts, so when I saw it again on the list for the press party, I decided you were a woman I needed to meet."

"Why?"

"Because I knew you could help me with this."

She rummaged in her bag and pulled out an antique revolver. I recognized it immediately—there was no mistaking that delicately spurred trigger guard and double barrels, the top a .42

caliber, the underbarrel a smoothbore sixteen-gauge. Notoriously inaccurate but deadly at close range, the LeMat was dear to the Confederate heart, the favorite of legends like General P. G. T. Beauregard and Jeb Stuart. This one had most of its original blued finish and an intact serial number, inching its price tag into five-digit territory.

"That's the LeMat I sold your technical director," I said.

"It is. He sold it to me yesterday. He said now that we have the replicas made, we don't need it anymore."

She slipped her finger in the trigger, closed one eye, and pointed the thing at my front door. I put a hand on the barrel and lowered the muzzle.

She clucked her tongue. "Don't worry, it's unloaded."

I kept my hand on it. "Every gun is loaded until you check."

She didn't look the least bit chastened, but nonetheless laid the gun on the counter. I rotated the cylinder and checked each chamber, gave the shotgun barrel a good examination too. Outside, her bodyguard/chauffeur scanned the sidewalk. Maybe he was expecting fans to rush out of nowhere like some Hollywood-dazzled flash flood, but unless the folks at the taqueria spotted Portia, he'd have no trouble today.

She watched me. "Do you have bullets for it?"

"It doesn't take bullets. You need lead balls and caps and wadding, black powder too." I sent the gun back her way. "And yes, I sell those. But a LeMat is a pain to load, and it will run a chain fire on you in a heartbeat."

"The TD said the same thing. But I haven't had any problems with it."

I was surprised. "You fired this on set?"

"Not this one, one of the replicas. They won't allow real weapons on set." She ran her index finger along the barrel. "It made a lot of noise, but that was it. Noise and smoke and nothing else. But this gun...this gun has history. I can sense it when I hold it in my hand."

I'd heard similar talk from my clients. Antiques supposedly soaked up the past like some kind of metaphysical battery.

Reenactors spoke of tapping that energy on the field, feeling it connect them to the long-dead soldiers who'd carried the relics into battle.

"I understand the appeal," I said, "but if this were my gun, I wouldn't be shooting it."

"Why not? Is it dangerous?"

"Probably not. This one's in solid shape. But shooting it could destroy its resale value."

"I won't be reselling it."

She took it in hand again, but didn't point it. Her expression was curious and cunning, very Mad Luna, but also analytical and shrewd. Very Portia Ray, I decided. Unlike my reenactment clients, she felt no stirring inside her, no connection to a larger purpose. It was a tool to her, as practical as a screwdriver.

"Regardless," I said, "if you plan to take it anywhere besides your car or home or place of business, you'll need a carry license."

"Can I get that from you? Ammunition too, the whole deal?"

"The license comes from the probate office, but I can supply the rest, including a nice carry bag. If you'd like to pick one out—"

"No, you do it. Send everything to me in care of the TD. Put it on the *Moonshine* tab."

"Of course. I'll have it delivered in the morning."

"Thank you." She returned the gun to her bag. "I'll admit, I'm not very good with guns and bullets and such. But if Luna and I are in it for the long haul, I need to learn."

I smiled. "Very admirable."

She smiled too, regarding me with frank appraisal. She was here for something that had nothing to do with the gun. I was about to quiz her when she got down to business.

"What were you really doing at the set, Tai Randolph?"

I blanked my expression. "What do you mean?"

"I mean Nicky said you were bringing props. But you weren't. I checked with the TD." She leaned forward in a just-between-us pose, propped her elbows on the counter. "Yours wasn't the only pass Nicky approved that day. He also approved one for this tall drink of water in an Italian suit, one Trey Seaver, currently of Phoenix Corporate Security, formerly of the Atlanta Police Department."

Dang it, I thought. *She's a better detective than I am.*

"And?" I said.

"And that means you're no ordinary gun supplier. Because I remember Trey Seaver. Very well." She tapped my countertop with her forefinger. "And you two left together. In a Ferrari."

Crap. She'd seen everything.

"Is that why you're here?" I said. "To quiz me about Trey?"

"I'm here because I want to know what's up. It's something with Nicky, isn't it? What is it this time? Drugs? Sex parties? He hasn't gone off the deep end again, has he?" Her cheeks flushed with sudden emotion. "Quint came out here because of him, did you know that? Nicky started using again, and Quint had to give everything up to take care of him. Has Nicky dearest explained that?"

I got a pang of empathy and reminded myself that she was an actress. This was her job, provoking a response in me. Was Quint really that caring a brother? I had a hard time believing it. From what I'd seen, he wanted to control Nick more than care for him. And if he and Portia were so cozy, why was he living in the guest house?

Portia shook her head. "Addison thinks she cured him. He was all cute and dangerous when she met him, a bad boy in need of a good girl. Nicky mumbling nonsense? Nicky not bathing? She won't want any part of that. Wait until she sees him in his underpants with breakfast still in his beard."

I remembered Addison the night of Nick's crash. She was getting a taste of the challenges, that was for sure. And stepping up to the plate, I had to admit, even if she carried a whiff of martyrdom about her. Like saving Nick Talbot was her ticket to heaven, and she was willing to mow down anyone in her path to do it.

Portia's eyes grew bright and wet, but her jaw was taut with anger, not sadness. "I'm sorry. I didn't mean to get personal. It's just that…" She exhaled in a burst, straightened her shoulders. "How much?"

"How much what?"

"How much would it take for you to get me the script for next season's premiere?"

I felt my jaw drop. "I'm sorry, what?"

"The script. Look, I know you're sniffing around for dirt. You'll find it, especially about Quint and me. I couldn't care less. But if you come across that script…"

She let the words trail off. I remembered her in the season finale, on her knees, her beautiful face bloodstained and defiant. *Moonshine* had made her a household name, and the second season promised to be even more lucrative.

"You want to know if you're coming back."

"Damn straight I do. Quint said the producers haven't approved the script, and just to prolong the agony, he's making the writers complete all of the Season Two scripts before we start filming. The investors want it, he says, but that's bullshit."

I remembered back at the Kennesaw base camp how Addison had been complaining about the same. Apparently she wasn't the only one pissed about Quint's handling of the script situation.

I shook my head. "I have no access to the scripts. And even if I did—"

"Oh, don't even try it." She laughed. "Former Special Patrol Officer Seaver? He's obviously got bigger people to answer to. But you? You make your own rules. I can tell." She lowered her voice, looked me in the eye. "Find that script, and I'll triple whatever Nicky's paying you."

"He's not paying me anything."

She examined my features, decided to play it cool. "Whatever you say. Just remember, if you need a friend, you've got one in me."

"How so?"

"I know things." She bit her lower lip, like she was deciding whether or not to trust me. "Take Addison, for example. Her interest in Nicky is pure, no doubt. But she's smart enough to understand that even true love can have a profit margin."

"What does that mean?"

"Talk to her and find out." Portia dropped her sunglasses on her face. "There are some smart moves to be made here. Getting me in your corner is one. And you can start by finding that script."

She smiled, shouldered her bag. And then she walked right out of my shop and into the dazzling high noon glare.

Chapter Thirty-four

Getting into Trey's apartment required two separate keys, a swipe card for the elevator, and a visual inspection by the concierge, who in a less fancy place would have been called the manager and who would've had better things to do than lurk in the lobby glaring at me. It was after seven when I finally stood at Trey's door, juggling my research and the take-out bag containing my dinner. I opened the door with my foot, switched on the light with my elbow…

And then I froze.

The turquoise cactus stood in the middle of his living room, its metallic plates and mirrored dongles reflecting the lamplight. The thing had all the subtlety of a disco ball, and there it was in Trey's black and white apartment. I was still standing there gawking when I heard the ding of the elevator and a familiar tread. I waited as Trey came up behind me.

"I had nothing to do with this," I said.

"With what?"

I stood aside. He stopped in the threshold, cocked his head. "It's here," he said. "Very good."

And then he went inside as if there wasn't a grotesque turquoise cactus next to his coffee table. I followed him, incredulous.

"You were expecting this?"

He placed his briefcase on his desk, unknotted his tie. "I told you I would take care of the situation."

"Yes, but I didn't expect you to have the situation delivered."

"It was the only way I could keep it secure."

He had a plastic bag over his arm from a place called Menswear Incorporated. He draped it over the sofa and circled the cactus with hawkish intensity. Suddenly he paused, then pointed.

"There."

I followed his finger and saw a ragged hole barely bigger than a pencil eraser. He pulled a penlight from his pocket and directed the beam around the marking. Then he marched right to his desk and rummaged around until he found a small ruler and a yellow notepad. He brought these back to the cactus, dropped into a crouch.

"Well?" I said.

"It's a bullet entry."

"No exit?"

"Highly improbable. This cactus appears to be solid wood, at least eighteen inches in diameter."

He slapped the ruler up next to the hole, measured it twice. Scribbled that into the notebook propped on his knee.

I peered closer. "What are you doing?"

"A field estimate on the angle of impact. Arcsine of width divided by length."

He was speaking in trigonometry again. I didn't bother asking for a translation because I understood the thing that mattered: we had before us the evidence that Nick Talbot was telling the truth, that he wasn't delusional, that on Friday night someone had stood at the edge of his property and fired a bullet at him. Up until this moment, criminal wrongdoing had been hypothetical. Now it was real, tangible, and evidential.

Trey went to his desk and retrieved the camera. He handed me the ruler. "Would you hold this next to the entry, not touching it?"

I did as he asked while he knelt at the base of the cactus and snapped a series of close-up photographs.

"The cops are not going to approve of your chain of evidence," I said.

"Since we're not law enforcement, chain of evidence won't officially start until the investigation moves to active status."

He moved in for a close-up while I held the ruler in place. That was when I finally noticed the rest of the apartment. A spanking new file cabinet stood next to his desk, which supported a mountain range of folders. On the wall above that was a giant whiteboard covered in circle maps and hierarchy trees, dry erase marker lines connecting theories and suspects. He'd mounted corkboards on both sides of that and stuck notes, photos, and newspaper clippings all over every square inch.

In the middle of the information overflow was a photograph of Jessica Talbot, her mouth open in laughter, her eyes mischievous. It was the same candid shot I'd seen in newspaper articles, nothing like the staged images from the magazine covers. I remembered Trey's crime scene sketch, her vivaciousness reduced to a two-dimensional outline. A body. But not here. Here she was the star she'd always wanted to be, the epicenter.

"Omigod," I said. "I spend one night away, and you create a lair."

Trey stayed focused on his math, his lips moving silently as he worked the equations. I was perplexed. We'd found a key piece of evidence. This was the moment when he typically planted his feet, folded his arms, and demanded that somebody call 911. But not now. Now he was the sole monarch of his very own investigative kingdom.

"What are you going to do if Finn drops the case? Because she doesn't serve justice, she serves the Talbots. And the Talbots serve themselves." I turned to face him. "Have you even told her about this one-man CSI operation you've got going on?"

He didn't look up from his notebook. "You can put down the ruler."

I stared. "This is your plan? Hide the evidence up here so that if Finn decides to sweep this investigation under the rug, you can move it forward despite her?"

He kept scribbling in the notebook. "Not hiding. Securing. And Finn knows I have this."

"So if she wants it, you'll hand it right over?"

He remained absorbed in his calculations.

"Right. Exactly what I suspected. And what about Keesha? She asked you to keep those files a secret."

He looked up at that. "I have. And I will. But I can use them as a starting point."

"For what?"

"For finding out who fired this bullet."

"And you're willing to break every rule to do that."

He stood. "Not every rule."

"Trey. Listen to me—"

"I am listening." He put his hands on his hips. "However, you are hardly one to criticize. You kept Martinez's phone, which you hacked. Then you downloaded all the data into your own personal computer."

I pointed. "You mean that data you have up on the corkboard? The data I don't recall giving you permission to access?"

He didn't even blink. "You left it on my desk."

"Near your desk. In my tote bag."

A light shrug. "Your open tote bag. On my desk."

"Barely touching your desk."

"In my apartment."

I crossed my arms. "So that's how you're going to play this?"

He crossed his too. "I assumed that since you told me the information was in there that I was free to access it. My apologies if that wasn't the case."

He was actually correct—I had intended that—but I wasn't about to admit that now. I exhaled, felt the breath run right out of me in a slow trickle. And then I took another breath, one that filled not only my lungs but a dark contracted space deep inside. The space that held the thing I was really worried about.

"Trey? You do remember what happened the last time you got over-invested?"

He winced, and his voice softened. "I remember. And I'm sorry. I know how difficult that was for you."

"You don't need to apologize. But you do need to be aware."

"I am. That's the difference between now and last time. I know the warning signs now and how to ameliorate any…"

"Complications?"

"No. It starts with a D."

"Decompensation."

Trey nodded, crisply. "Yes. That. I don't want to decompensate again. So I'm paying attention. And I have you to point out any warning signs I might miss." He gave me a serious look. "Not that you're responsible for maintaining my psychological stability. I'm responsible. Not you. That's not what I meant. I simply meant…you know."

I could feel the full force of his attention on me. It was one of his greatest tricks, this ability to envelope another person in his personal radar. In bed, it was positively intoxicating. But in other circumstances—say, an interrogation—it felt very much like being fried by a laser beam. He was doing the trick now. Everything around me was fading into the background, and I could feel his gaze, tactile.

"I know," I said. "And you're right, you do have me. One hundred percent."

He looked profoundly relieved. "Thank you."

He got back to work. While he continued his measurements, I examined his gathered evidence—Jessica's murder was the central crux of his concern. He had constructed timelines for every person of interest, including himself. His timeline was black with red cross-hatches, each marked by an alphanumeric identifier linking it to a piece of information on one of the many maps, also color coded, though I had no idea what the various shades signified. But Trey did. That info was humming through his brain along with every other data point in front of him.

The photo he'd chosen to represent himself was the one I'd seen at the gym, an older one that I would have bet my last dollar had been taken around the time of the murder. Trey was nothing if not chronological. I peered closer at the intricate lines radiating and connecting.

"You got lucky back then," I said. "Your dash cam and GPS alibied you for Jessica's murder. And you got lucky now because I can alibi you for the shooting Friday night. But you know who doesn't have an alibi for Friday?" I tapped another line, this one purple. "Addison."

"She has no motive either."

"We'll see about that. I had a very interesting conversation with Portia that implied otherwise."

"Portia? When did you talk to her?"

"She came to see me this afternoon. Waved an unloaded LeMat around, then tried to bribe me to hunt for next season's script."

Trey straightened. "Are you serious?"

"Dead serious. She implied that Addison's interest in Nick involved both love and money. Also, she's onto us. I'm not sure how quiet she'll keep things, but I suspect we can count on her discretion if we play nice with her."

"What does that mean?"

"It means…I don't know what it means. Portia is the wildest of the wild cards."

Trey nodded, thinking, thumb pressed against his lower lip. I looked at his photograph pinned to the corkboard, then back at the man himself, and something went ping in my brain. A connection I hadn't caught before.

I couldn't fight the grin. "In other news, I just got one step closer to figuring out why you got fired."

"You did?"

"I did."

"Interesting." He slipped me this look. "You could, of course, find out right now."

I bit my lip and shook my head. "Nope. Tempting though it is."

He smiled then, one of his real smiles, and I realized that I shouldn't have worried. He was in no danger of decompensation. He was thriving on this…whatever it was we were doing. He sighed extravagantly and headed for the bedroom, shrugging off his jacket as he did.

"Let me know if you change your mind," he said.

Chapter Thirty-five

It was still dark outside when I woke to the whirr of the treadmill, so I pulled the covers over my head and lazed back into sleep. Almost an hour later, I heard the sounds of packing, so I pushed back the duvet and squinted into the first dull light.

Trey stood at the foot of the bed. He was dressed in one of his Armani suits, the bargain basement coat and jacket still in their garment bag. He disappeared into the closet, and I heard the rustle of plastic, the scrape of hangers.

I dragged myself upright, yawned and stretched. "I guess I won't see you until around seven."

"Probably not."

"And then what?"

"Tonight is mainly investigative. Most of the information we gather will turn out to be unnecessary, but that's impossible to determine at the onset. So the challenge today will be getting as much intel as we can. And then tomorrow you and I meet with Finn and start finding the connections."

"What about the bullet?"

"What about it?"

"Doesn't that change the plan?"

"No. Not our part in it."

He sat at the foot of the bed and put on his black Brioni lace-ups. They were Italian calfskin leather, hand-stitched, with a dab of grip tape on the sole in case he had to sprint and a paper clip inside the heel in case he needed to pick a pair of handcuffs.

"Those are not down-market shoes," I said.

He tied the laces with a snap. "I know. But I didn't have time to break in a more appropriate pair."

I examined his new suit behind the plastic. The fabric was black and serviceable, but didn't have the drape and hang of his Italian couture. The tie on top of the precisely folded socks and underwear was also new, and polyester.

I reached for the one around his neck, a black silk Ermenegildo Zegna. "You have a clip-on tie in your suitcase."

He raised his chin and let me work, but he didn't say anything.

"You only wear those if there's a chance someone will try to strangle you." I cinched the knot, smoothed it flat. "You're expecting trouble, aren't you?

I held out my hand. He dropped his cuff links into my palm and extended one wrist.

"I'm preparing for any eventuality," he said. "As are you, I assume."

He said this with a flick of his eyes toward the gun safe. His weapon would be staying put, but mine would be coming with me.

I straightened his lapels, smoothed the front of his jacket. "Yes. I'll be prepared."

"Good." He held out his other wrist. "I am reasonably certain we won't need such preparations, however. Finn has both visible and covert agents working the event. I reviewed their dossiers. Their qualifications are impeccable. In addition, there is the resort's own security team."

"Which you pronounced sub-par."

"This is a different team. From Armstrong."

One of Phoenix's rivals. Trey had spoken of them in the past with respect. He'd explained to me once that there was no such thing as one hundred percent safe, that the best one could plan for was as safe as possible. I guessed that was the territory we were venturing into.

I followed him to the living room as he gathered the rest of his things, including a square black bag with a lightning bolt logo. He stopped at the threshold, his suit over his arm. "Finn said she'll have you hooked into the audio surveillance system."

"Yes. I'm meeting her at the shop later to pick up my equipment."

"Good. I'll have other precautions in place."

I pointed to the new bag. "Like whatever that is."

He gave me a tiny smile. "Yes."

I stood on tiptoe and kissed him, kissed him good, and was rewarded with his hands on my waist. He left them there longer than a simple good-bye warranted, his thumbs resting on my hips. Finally, he took a deep breath and pulled away.

"One more thing." He retrieved the keys to the Ferrari from his pocket. "Here. It doesn't fit my cover."

I took the keys, a little astounded but not about to argue, not one bit. "Are you gonna drive the Camaro?"

"No. I have a rental waiting. Something more in keeping with a security manager's salary."

I laughed. "You're getting into this."

He paused, thought about that. "Yes. I think I am."

I closed the door behind him, listened to his footsteps and then the ding of the elevator. He was on his way. I leaned back against the door and pressed my hands against my stomach, trying to still the butterflies there. Why was I nervous? Trey was competent and ridiculously organized. He was stretching out of his comfort zone, yes, but dealing with the situation as professionally and analytically as he did any assignment.

And I wasn't anxious about my own role in the case—sneaking around was second nature to me. I'd pretended to be twenty-one when I was sixteen, brazening my way into clubs with jacked-up cleavage and a bootleg ID, sending my parents into despair. My mother had been smooth as buffed ice, and my father—or the man I'd known as my father—had been gentle and quiet. I was none of those things. I was fire-tempered and rough around the edges. I was barely civilized.

The understanding came to me in a rush. It wasn't anxiety, it was anticipation, because despite my better judgment, I loved hazard, thrived on risk.

I was just like Boone.

I remembered him from when I was little, with his salt-calloused hands and fisherman's squint. When I was a teenager, he'd supplied me and my friends with illicit liquor, sheening me with a kind of outlaw celebrity. He was larger than life, practically mythical, and I could not begin to imagine him and my mother, my society-driven, manners-obsessed, proper Methodist mother…

The butterflies morphed into bats, and I took a deep breath, massaged my diaphragm. I had Eleanor Randolph's sturdy build and unruly hair, the parts of herself she'd tried hardest to change. Did we also share an attraction to the subversive and reckless? Had that been her gift to me, bequeathed in my blood and bones?

Yes. The answer was yes.

No wonder working this case felt as exhilarating as riding a wrecking ball. Every danger-loving gene in me was swinging wild and loose.

Chapter Thirty-six

That afternoon, Finn showed up at the shop in a flowered church dress, a matching handbag clutched in one hand and a backpack in the other. I could tell from the way she carried both that they were heavier than they ought to be, probably because they packed some firepower.

"I saw the Ferrari," she said. "Trey left it for you?"

I locked up the register. "He did."

"Smart move. That will definitely get them talking." She dropped the backpack on the floor and started rummaging in it. "Did you manage to peel him out of the Armani?"

I grinned. "That *is* one of my particular talents."

"Good." She grinned back and held up a shopping bag. "Mind if I change?"

I pointed to the storage room. She went inside but didn't close the door. Her voice was muffled. "Speaking of Trey, have you found out yet?"

"Found out what?"

"Why he got fired."

I poured the last of the coffee into my travel mug. "Nope."

"Damn. I was hoping you'd have done better than I did. Having some personal leverage and all."

I didn't tell her that I had one very promising avenue of investigation, once I remembered where I'd seen the name Jonathon McDonald. Right under my nose, it had been. But until

I heard what he had to say, I wouldn't be sharing those details with anyone, especially not Finn.

"Your new accoutrements are in the backpack," she called. "Give them a look-see."

I peered inside. "I have a new phone?"

Finn came back into the shop barefoot, now wearing leggings and a workout tee. "A burner. But it's got 4G LTE and a five-megapixel camera. Also audio recording capability—tap the microphone icon and whatever conversation you record will be sent wirelessly to a remote data storage center. Same with any photographs." She came over and rummaged in the handbag. "The wi-fi can be spotty up there, so wear this at all times."

She handed me a chunky bangle bracelet, gold plated with black lacquer. I slipped it over my wrist.

"What is it?"

"A hot-spot generator. Creates wi-fi wherever you are, which is necessary where we're going. Lots of dead zones."

I whistled. "Damn. That's James Bond stuff right there."

"I just got back from a trade show." She tossed her kitten heels into the backpack, pulled out a pair of Nikes and ankle socks. "It's a brave new world for spying, I tell you. No more tape rash or battery packs burning a hole in your bra. Just turn on the app, and everything being said around you will go real-time into the audio surveillance channel."

"And right into Trey's ear."

"That's the only way he'd consent to you two working separately." She hopped up on my counter and laced her shoes. "He still doesn't trust me, but that's okay. He's much more useful when he's suspicious."

She removed the barrette from her hair, and her bangs fell over her forehead in a stiff wave. She took a towelette from her bag and started wiping away her pastel eyeshadow and pink lipstick.

"And the end game?" I said.

"Now that it's become clear that someone actually is trying to kill Nicholas Talbot, my job is finding out the who and why of it." She ran her fingers through her hair. "The labs came back positive. He did have an elevated kavalactone level in his blood. The pu-erh tested positive as well, both the leaves and the tea itself."

"Which means the kava was added in the trailer."

"Yep."

"Time to alert the cops?"

"Not my call. But the lab I use is certified. The results will stand up in court, as will whatever ballistics tests we do on that cactus. I have a lab that can take care of that too."

I didn't tell her she'd have to pry it from Trey's hands, assuming she managed to infiltrate his den of investigation. I watched her finish her make-up—a slick of mascara, a daub of blush. She looked fresh from a Pilates class.

I leaned one hip against the counter. "Does Nick know you're using him as bait?"

Finn gave me a half-smile. "I wouldn't put it like that. But yes, he knows that whoever is trying to harm him will see this event as a prime opportunity. He insisted we proceed."

"Does Trey know this is the plan?"

"He knows a trap when he spots one. I'm sure he also knows it's the best move we have at this point, a move that cops can't make. Civilians in jeopardy and all that." She spritzed a cloud of body spray and walked into it. "I answer to the Talbot Creative board, no one else, certainly not the fine men and women of the law, though several have been sharpening their knives for Nick. That's why I need you."

I scoffed. "You mean Trey."

"No, I mean you." She shoved her dress in the backpack. "Look, Trey's great. He's a detail man, good with data. Clear-headed and excellent in an emergency. Plus he's got insider knowledge of the backstory here and quite possibly a vendetta. But he's a bonus. You're the one I wanted for this."

"Me? Why?"

"Because you're a damn fine investigator." She finished fluffing her hair. "Selling guns and rebel flags is never gonna satisfy you. But this? Girlfriend, this is what you were made for."

• • ● • •

She left soon after our conversation, said she'd check in with us later. I finished getting the shop ready for Kenny. I had my S&W secured and my carry bag prepped with extra speedloaders, with a change of clothes ready for pick-up at Gabriella's shop. I finished packing, locked the door behind myself. My phone rang before I was out of the parking space.

"Hey, Tai. It's Mac. The desk said you'd called?"

I could hear the noise of the gym at Mac's end. It was hard to imagine him as a slightly chubby twenty-something with surfer-blond curls, but then, that photo was fifteen years old. He'd lost the hair and gained some muscle, but he was the same Jonathon McDonald shaking hands with Trey in the Ritz's newsletter photo.

"Yeah, I just needed to ask you some questions about your time at the Ritz. Back when you and Trey were valets."

Mac didn't say anything. Lawyers and hotel HR managers were as close-lipped as spies, but Mac? Mac had no such limitations. He was still hesitatant.

"Man," he said, "that's been a while."

"You still remember, though, don't you? Why Trey got fired?"

No reply. I heard clanging iron, the boom of bass, laughter and conversation.

"He was railroaded," Mac said. "You gotta understand that."

I smiled. "I'm listening."

Chapter Thirty-seven

The trip from Kennesaw to Adairsville took less than an hour. A railroad terminus during the Civil War, the city had once delivered arms, munitions, and other supplies from the factories in Atlanta to the Confederate front line. Now it was bucolic, with twisty roads and rolling farmland. The Ferrari ate up every curve, and I had to keep a hard check on the throttle. It felt like chaining concrete blocks to a racehorse.

Beardsley Gardens lay well off the beaten path, past hills specked with solemn cows and fat oblivious sheep. I waited while the attendant checked off my name, then drove into the heart of the property. Instead of one main building, the developers had created a mini-village, with cobblestone streets and climbing rosebushes and English cottages in well-mannered rows. A quarter of the resort had been sectioned off solely for the movie crew, accessible through a second parking gate, this one valet-only.

I drove up to the gate, pulling to a stop behind a silver Jaguar. Except for the hornet-yellow mechanical arm in front, the security station looked as quaint as the other cottages. Behind it, I saw the parking area, a freshly-mowed square bordered by trees. It was only half-full, but I suspected it would be packed before the evening was over.

The door of the Jaguar opened, and Quint Talbot stepped out. A valet jogged up to him while another started unloading the trunk. Quint handed over the keys without looking at either of them; he was too busy checking out his reflection in the car window and smoothing down his hair. Portia exited the passenger side, sunglasses on her face, her mouth set in a straight line. They waited at the station until a club car zipped up, got loaded with their luggage, and then zipped them away just as efficiently. The first valet beckoned me forward, then laid a finger on his earpiece and stepped back.

Trey came out of the station. He said something to the valet, then approached the driver's side of the Ferrari. I had a sudden flashback to the teenage Trey, working his first job. Nervous. Eager. Nothing like the self-possessed man in front of me, whose suit didn't fit quite right and whose name tag said "Steve" and who still—still—made my pulse rev.

Trey opened my door, his expression blank and professional. "Ms. Randolph. Welcome."

He extended a hand. I let him pull me upright.

"Thank you." I gave him the keys. "I'd appreciate it if you'd see to my car personally. It needs a firm hand."

He inclined his head politely. "Of course."

He dropped the keys in his pocket—I knew that's where they would stay, not in the valet stand. I already had the tip folded between my fingers, one of the crisp new hundreds that Nick had given me as a down payment on the turquoise cactus. I held it out, not breaking eye contact.

"Something for your trouble."

Trey automatically slipped the bill into his pocket without looking at it, his Ritz training revealing itself. He'd find it later, and then we'd have a very interesting conversation. Before he could call for a club cart, one pulled up with a squeal and lurch. The cinnamon-haired runner from the Kennesaw set fidgeted behind the wheel.

"I have this one," she said. "Nick's orders."

Her name came to me in a rush. Bree. I eased into the seat, shot a look at Trey over my shoulder. He nodded, though his brow furrowed. His first test—letting me out of his sight. While he watched, Bree grabbed my overnight bag from the valet and tossed it into the cart. I barely had time to get my feet inside before she tore down the path at bat-out-of-hell speed.

She consulted a clipboard but didn't slow down. "You're in 1540? That's right around the corner."

"Is it?"

"You could've walked."

I clutched the seat. "I still can."

"Nope. Nick said you were to be personally delivered. So that's what I'm doing."

We rumbled past the ruins of the old manor house, moss-covered and twined with ivy. I knew it had been an Italianate villa from the early nineteenth-century, roofless now, a labyrinth of bricks maintained by the resort. Its saga was a particularly Gothic tale of the antebellum South, featuring war, murder, hauntings, cotton money, yellow fever, tornadoes, and curses, the perfect setting for a story like *Moonshine*. There was no filming going on this afternoon, though. Instead, a party team hauled tables and chairs under a cavernous white tent set up next to the crumbling villa.

"Those are the ruins of Luna's family home," I said.

Bree popped her gum. "Spoiler alert. It's not really in Ireland."

I remembered the episode, a dive into the past to explain the complicated backstory that brought Portia's grandmother from the mountains of Connemara to the Blue Ridge foothills of Atlanta. The ruins resembled images I'd seen of that raw country, the same place where Trey's ancestry ran.

"So I guess Luna makes it to next season?"

Bree popped her gum, jerked the wheel to avoid a chipmunk.

I lurched and grabbed the support bar. "Come on, surely you know if she lives or dies."

"Even if I did, I'd never tell." She slammed to a stop. "We're here."

My cottage nestled against the edge of the trees, a stone's throw from the security station. Like the others I'd passed on my way in, it was painted periwinkle blue and landscaped within an inch of its life. My map rendered the forest beyond my patio as a series of vague triangle shapes, pathless and devoid of amenities. The rest of the guest cottages lay like a necklace around a kidney-shaped lake that curved into the golf course.

Bree delivered her recitation in a bored voice. "The press party starts at eight. Breakfast begins at seven. You'll find your farm menu in your reservation packet."

"Farm menu?"

She didn't literally roll her eyes, but her contempt was clear. "Talk to Gabe at the barn. He's the animal wrangler. He can set you up with the chore of your choice in the morning."

In other words, work. Feeding pigs and mucking out stalls and wiping down sweaty horses. I shook my head. Rich people. So disconnected from normal life they thought chores were recreational.

"Well," I said. "Won't be doing that."

Bree did roll her eyes then. "I know, right? It was Addison's idea. And the guests are eating it up."

I could see said barn in the distance. It was red, of course, with a tin roof. Engineered quaint to be sure, but wholesome enough.

Bree started to grab my bag, but I waved her off. "I can get it."

"Suit yourself."

She barely waited for me to get out before she kicked the club cart into gear and sped down the lane. I unlocked my door using an old-fashioned metal key and surveyed my one-room surroundings—walnut writing desk, massive wrought-iron bed, dark green drapes. No animal heads or horn chandeliers, just an oil painting of an English fox hunt with galloping horses and baying hounds. Hunting lodge lite.

I inspected behind the curtains. No interlopers. I'd just knelt beside the bed and peeked underneath when Trey called.

"Do you find the cameras?" he said.

Right to business he went. Which meant he hadn't looked in his pocket.

I stood up and checked the bathroom. "You mean inside?"

"Yes."

I surveyed the bathroom. Double sinks, jetted tub, plush bathrobes. No lurkers.

I pulled aside the shower curtain. "Is that how you spent your last two hours, turning my quarters into the Big Brother special?"

"It took me forty-five minutes. Do you see them?"

The bathroom cleared, I did a slow three-sixty in the bedroom area. "There's the obvious one in the corner above the chest of drawers."

"And the covert?"

I did a quick assessment of the room's layout. "There's a blind spot next to the desk, which means the camera has to be...aha. Right above the TV. Nicely disguised by a grapevine trellis."

"There are also two outside, one at the back entrance on the patio and one on the front. The video feeds go to my phone, not the main security system."

"For your eyes only, huh?"

"Yes, assuming you've granted access. Just like in the shop. Of course you can access them as well, with your phone. Use the same log-in."

I pushed open the patio door and was greeted by the smell of pine. The sun set in a melt of blood orange and crimson, an autumn sunset despite the temperature. I couldn't hear even a hint of traffic, only the distant hum of a club cart, the delicate rubbing of leaf against leaf. I looked under the eaves and spotted the state-of-the art surveillance camera mounted in the corner.

"Also," Trey continued, "I've set up breach alarms on the doors and windows. I'm texting you the code so that you can use your phone as the keypad. I'm enabling that now."

My phone beeped with the incoming text. When I opened it, a link appeared. When I clicked it, a new app bloomed on the screen.

I went back inside. "Do I have any further instructions for tonight?"

"Nothing beyond the original plans. Did you get the clothes from Gabriella?"

"I did."

I tucked the phone between my shoulder and ear and unzipped my suitcase. I rummaged around until I found the tee shirt. I held it up for the camera. "See this? Two hundred and fifty dollars. For a plain white tee. She loaned me a suede vest too. Six hundred for that." I held up a necklace. "This is a rock on a skinny leather thong. A designer rock, though, so a thousand bucks. Hang on a second, I'm putting you on speaker."

I tossed the phone on the bed, pulled my old shirt over my head and slipped my arms into the new one. I had to admit, the fabric was lush and lovely, gliding like a whisper. I slipped on the vest, turned in the mirror. Trey still hadn't said anything.

"You there?"

"What?"

I grinned up at the camera. "I'm not distracting you, am I?"

A soft exhale at his end. "I have to get back out front. Check your mic before I go."

I pulled up the app on my phone. "One two, one two."

"Copy that. Let me make sure it recorded."

Another few seconds passed. A clock on the wall chimed eight. I turned my new bracelet in the light, admiring the way it shimmered.

Trey's voice again. "Everything worked at this end. As long as you have the bracelet, all you have to do is turn on the app, and the system will start recording and transmitting."

"And you can listen while it's doing that?"

"I can."

"From anywhere on the resort?"

"Correct. We can meet after the party and compare information."

I examined my reflection in the mirror. "Wait, you're not coming to the party?"

"Not unless you need me. I've got to manage the exit and entrance protocols until midnight." A hesitation. "Do you need me?"

I thought about it. I wanted him there, but only because I wanted to see him, talk to him, share what was beginning to feel like an actual investigation. A case. An adventure. I got tingle of excitement, and Finn's words popped into my head: *Girlfriend, this is what you were made for.*

"I'll be fine," I said.

"Okay. But if you need me...I mean, if you need assistance... or me. Or both. I'm not..." A frustrated exhale. "You know what I mean."

"I do. And I will. And if you need me, or assistance, or both, you know the drill."

"I do." I couldn't see him, but I could tell from his voice that he was smiling. "Seaver out."

Chapter Thirty-eight

The last glimmer of the setting sun mottled the party tent with a patchwork of light and shadow. No food yet, but the bar looked open, and most importantly, well-stocked—the liquors were top shelf, complemented with enough champagne to float a boat.

As Finn had promised, the other guests did indeed fall all over themselves ignoring me. They sat at their tables or mingled in corners—here a band of culture critics, there a sales team with smiles like sharks. I recognized the men from Monday's on-set photo shoot, the hotshot investors who'd demanded the ramped-up script schedule. They didn't mingle, preferring to scope out the crowd with mercenary intent. I felt their collective gaze settle on me. Was I worth knowing, worth courting?

They returned their attention to their drinks. Question answered.

I decided to take up position at the bar. Situated next to the entrance, it provided a clear view of the entire tent—tables draped in white linen, a parquet floor for dancing, a jazz band setting up in the corner. Soft white lights and ivory candles bathed everyone in a pearly glow. Even the bar gleamed golden, and I couldn't resist running a finger across the grain.

The bartender noticed my appreciation. She was short and square, briskly efficient, a russet bun at the nape of her neck. "It's a reclaimed door from the farmhouse that used to be here. Gorgeous, isn't it? They sure made them sturdy back in the day. Big too."

I knew why—it was a cooling board door. During the days of at-home wakes, it would have been brought down from its hinges, the body laid atop it for the duration of the funeral services, then afterward returned to its everyday position. I decided to keep this tidbit to myself.

"Lovely," I said.

"What can I get you?"

I started to ask for a beer and then remembered that somebody else was paying. "Maker's rocks, please."

While she fixed my drink, I gave the tent a closer examination, this time for security cameras. I spotted only one, unsubtle as a hay bale. When my whiskey arrived, I waited until the bartender wasn't looking, then hoisted it in a salute in that direction.

A familiar voice caught my attention. "You made it."

I turned. Portia smiled at me, diamonds dripping from her earlobes, looping like a constellation around her wrist. Even in elegant slacks and a saffron blouse, she looked like Mad Luna. Avaricious, possibly savage, with a charisma so powerful it was practically gravitational.

She dropped her voice. "Well?"

"Well what?"

"Did you find the script?"

I sipped my whiskey. "You get right to things, don't you?"

"I don't have time for small talk. Did you find it or not?"

"Sorry, no."

She turned her back on the bar and propped her elbows on it. "Have you at least found out who took a shot at Nicky?"

Damn it, I thought. *Portia knows everything.* She saw my surprised frustration and laughed.

"You're not the only spy on premises." She put her martini to her lips, but didn't actually take a drink. "So tell me. Is it true? Did somebody try to kill my brother-in-law?"

I shrugged. "Confidential. Sorry."

She looked across the tent to where Nick and Quint stood side by side. The investors had moved in on them, like a wolf pack closing a circle. Quint stayed silent, jaw clenched, heavily into his drink. Nick smiled, shook hands, his face open and animated, his hair tamed. No drink for him, only a sparkling water still in the bottle, no doubt from Addison's controlled stock. He bore little resemblance to the frenzied incoherent man he'd been Monday night. In fact, he seemed downright charming, and the investors were hanging on his every word.

Portia scrutinized him. "I never considered that the rumor might be true. How do you keep track?"

"Of what?"

"All the suspects. I bet there's a dozen people who'd love to see him dead."

"Like you, for example?"

"Yes," she agreed, then laughed again. "I probably shouldn't have said that, but sure. I was alone in my trailer that night, so no alibi. Plus we've never gotten along. Nicky's a giant sucking anchor in my life. Quint's too. Have you checked out Quint?" She pursed her lips, shook her head. "No, Quint's a terrible shot. But then, the bullet missed, didn't it? That part sounds just like Quint."

"Except that he was in the living room."

"His only claim to innocence. No way to get around back and pop off a round at his baby brother. Of course, if he really wanted to kill Nicky, he would have done it during the indictment hearing. That was when the little twit cost us the most money."

I let her talk. She acted as if all of this were a movie. As if the plot could be twisted and turned for the maximum bang.

"Oh!" Her eyes widened, and she put her hand on the inside of my elbow. "Is that why Trey is here? Because someone from the backstory is actually the villain? A long-lost sibling maybe? Assassin on the lam? And of course, there's the most obvious suspect."

I played my part. "Who would that be?"

"Well, aside from Trey—who I am assuming has an alibi, otherwise that case would be open and shut—don't cops look to the significant other first?"

"You think it was Addison?"

"It makes sense."

"How?"

She swirled her drink. "Let's ask her. Here she comes now."

I turned around and saw Addison making like an express train for our station. She'd pinned her hair up, and her pale skin gleamed against a scarlet slip dress, backless. She looked like a little girl playing dress up, but her face was so stiff with anger that her lips didn't seem to move

"That was low even for you," she hissed.

Portia regarded her over the martini. "I simply dropped a word to your prospective agent that there was no way you'd be legally allowed to sell that potboiler of yours. Talbot Creative owns your work product."

"Not if I wrote it before I signed that contract. Which I did."

Portia lowered the glass. "Too bad you don't have the money to argue that in court."

Addison was seething, but there was something else glowing about her besides anger. Something righteous. She wore the confidence of someone with a secret weapon in pocket, and I got a twist of apprehension.

She straightened her shoulders. "Congratulations on a great season. I hope you got everything out of it you wanted. And more."

"Meaning?"

Addison turned on her heel and left without saying a single word to me. Portia watched her walk over to Nick, who welcomed her with a grin and introduced her around. Quint threw back the rest of his drink, signaled a waiter for another.

"What was that about?" I said.

Portia's voice was laced with satisfaction. "Addison's shopping a screenplay about Jessica's murder. A bio-pic. It never got any traction before, but now, if somebody's trying to kill Nicky, it smells like a potential hit."

Across the tent, Addison slipped her arm around Nick's waist. He turned his face to her, and I was struck by the raw emotion I saw there. As if the two of them were in a room of their own.

Portia continued. "See, the story didn't have a proper ending before, but now there's a twist. Agents love a twist." She set her drink on the bar and pushed it away, untouched. "So there you go. Why would Addison want to kill Nicky? She wouldn't. But if somebody else is trying to murder him, that's a gravy train she can hook her little red wagon to." She shook her head. "Too bad the killer missed. A hit would have pumped the advance into seven digits."

"You said she wouldn't be able to sell it."

"Not outside of Talbot Creative. But Quint would pay her six figures for it, easy."

"So he could kill it?"

Portia gave me an amused simper. "Oh honey, hell no. He'd ride that puppy all the way to Sundance. Don't buy his act. He loves publicity. Just not the unprofitable kind." She waved to someone across the tent. "Speaking of acts, I have to go mingle. I suppose you do too, if you're going to find that script."

She waggled her fingers at me and disappeared into the crowd. The hum of conversation had grown louder, a buzz that filled the tent, packed now with bodies. I raised my glass to my lips...

And then I stopped short.

Rico sat at a table next to the band. He had a beard now, trimmed sharp as a scimitar, and his waist was smaller than I remembered, though he was still stocky in the chest, big boned and broad shouldered.

I pushed down a mild panic. Should I duck out? Hide? Call Trey? Before I could decide, he spotted me. He did a double take. And then he grinned and shoved his chair back. I grabbed my bag and met him halfway.

The grin widened. "I didn't expect—"

"Shhh!" I grabbed his elbow. "Come with me."

I dragged him toward the corner, shooting a look at the camera. My phone started buzzing instantly. Trey. I pulled Rico into a quiet spot behind the partition that disguised the sound system.

"You don't know me," I said.

He arched one magnificently studded eyebrow. "The hell I don't."

"I'm undercover."

"As in?"

"On a case."

Rico frowned. "Where's Trey? Does he know about this latest nonsense?"

"It's not nonsense, and yes, he knows. That's him texting. And he's listening to every word we say because I am wired, my friend. Like a double D bra." I moved closer. "Didn't you see him at the valet station?"

"We didn't come in that way. We had to use the employee entrance."

"We?"

"Dante and me. It's his gig. I'm tagging along." He pointed toward the band stand, where a slight black guy with a serious face and round glasses sat behind a cello. "I almost didn't come. I told Dante I wasn't going to any more weddings, but he said this one paid serious money, so—"

"Wait, what? Did you say wedding?"

"Shhh!" He leaned closer. "That part's confidential. But yeah, a surprise you-know-what. The newest white girl thing. Next he'll be playing gender reveal parties and flashmob prom-posals—"

"Are you sure?"

"Of course I'm sure."

At that moment, Nick went up to the band, hand in hand with Addison. As if on cue, the singer smiled at them and said, "Ladies and gentlemen, I'm gonna turn the mic over to my man Nick here for a second."

I felt my stomach drop. Suddenly I knew why Nick had been so insistent on attending this party, why Addison looked like she had a bomb behind her back.

"Aw hell, they're getting married!" I said.

Chapter Thirty-nine

Nick's smile was sheepish, but genuine. "Thank you all for coming to celebrate the first season of *Moonshine*."

The applause that followed was hearty. I snatched up my still-buzzing phone and called Trey. He started talking before I could get a word out.

"What is Rico doing—"

"Never mind," I said. "They're getting married, so you need to get down here!"

"Who's getting married?"

"Addison and Nick. Right now!"

"Now?"

"Yes, now! Get down here!"

Addison took the microphone. She was skittery and jazzed, her smile wide, eyes too bright. "But we have a confession—Nick and I are celebrating something a little more personal tonight."

The band struck up a jazzy arrangement of the wedding march as a guy in a white smock and an official-looking leather book came forward. At the other end of the tent, Quint elbowed his way to the edge of the crowd, his face the explosive red of nuclear meltdowns.

The guy with the book took his turn at the microphone. "Friends and family, as your official celebrant, I am pleased to—"

"Like hell!" Quint bellowed.

He threw his napkin on the ground and started pushing through the crowd, straight for Nick and Addison.

I grabbed Rico's shoulder. "Tell Dante to kill the mic!"

Rico didn't even ask what was going on. He waved a frantic hand at Dante and then drew his finger across his throat. I took off to intercept Quint just as Addison stepped in front of Nick, who then tried to step in front of Addison. They tangled up in their chivalry, which allowed Quint the chance to grab Nick's arm. Portia remained to the side, her face smooth and alert, a connoisseur of train wrecks. And Bree had her phone in front of her face, filming the unfolding drama with rabid glee.

Quint got right in Nick's face. He shoved the microphone away, but his words were loud enough for everyone to hear. "She's using you, you idiot!"

Nick didn't back down. "Shut up!"

"I get to say whatever the—"

"I said, shut up! I have had it with you!"

I shoved myself between the two men. "And that is enough of that."

Quint made a fist. I pressed my hand flat against the center of his chest.

"There are over a hundred cameras on you right now," I said. "So unless you want this to be how your name gets in the news this week, you need to calm your ass down."

Nick's voice rose. "Go ahead! Put it in the news! I don't care! I'm sick of you, sick of your rules, and sick of this fucking show!"

Addison took his arm. "Baby—"

"No!" He shook free. "I am goddamn tired of his shit!"

Quint's face was purple. "I don't care what you're tired of! I have hauled your ass out of jail, out of drunk tanks, out of whorehouses! I have paid for rehab after rehab after rehab, paid for doctors and more doctors and lawyers, so many fucking lawyers!"

"I never asked—"

"—so, no, you don't get to get married without my permission!"

Addison shouldered into the melee. "He doesn't need your permission because the judge granted me full conservatorship this morning!" She whipped out a piece of paper and waved it in his face. "Check your mailbox."

Quint put a finger in Nick's face. "I dragged myself all the way to the other goddamn side of the country for you!"

"The judge—"

"Fuck the judge! You ruined us once already with your astoundingly bad choice of a wife, and I'm not—"

Nick launched himself at Quint, who swung for him. I ducked as Addison yanked Nick back, but Quint kept on coming. He managed to get a blow to Nick's chin before I grabbed his arm and snatched it behind him.

He tried to twist out of my grip. "Let me go! I—"

I adjusted the angle of Quint's arm, and his knees almost gave out. His face squeezed, and he froze, panting in fury. I moved close behind him so that the audience couldn't see what was going on, so that only he could hear me.

"You struggle. You hurt. You decide."

Quint snapped his head around. "Let me go right now, or I will—"

I pulled his elbow up, and he cursed. I put my mouth right next to his ear. "You either calm down, or all of these people get to watch me calm you down. Your choice."

Quint relented. He nodded once, and I released him. I didn't move, though, stayed right on his ass in case he pulled some new nonsense. He didn't, but he remained red-cheeked and smoldering, pure volcano-about-to-spew furious.

"You will regret that," he said, and jerked his jacket straight.

He stomped out of the tent. Nobody moved, but I could still hear the clickety whirr of cell phone cameras. The room was a stew of confusion…except for the bartender. She'd come from around the bar and was standing in neutral position, her hands open, shoulders dropped.

Addison took off at a run, Nick right behind. They vanished through the tent flap into the night. Portia hoisted her second untouched martini in my direction, as if the scene were a private staging just for her entertainment. Rico motioned to Dante, who took up his cello. One quick confab with his group later, and some nerve-smoothing jazz filled the tent.

I heard footsteps coming fast, and Trey appeared in the doorway. He surveyed the tent, breathing hard, looking confused and alert and totally thwarted.

I jogged over to him. "Hey. Show's over. Did you hear everything?"

"I did. What did you do to Quint?"

"Rear wrist lock."

"Well done." He was breathing more regularly now. "Where did they go?"

"I don't know. Quint stomped off thataway, Nick and Addison the other way, and Portia's still here."

Trey pulled out his radio. When the station answered, he delivered a series of ten-code orders. Around us, the gathering moved back into drinking and gossiping mode.

"A wedding." He shook his head some more. "I did not predict that."

"I didn't either. But it explains why Nick wanted to be here—he wanted to get the deed done before Quint could wreck it."

"Then why not have it done civilly, at the courthouse. Why here? Why now?"

"Good questions."

Trey was still watching. He and the bartender exchanged a look of complicit understanding. She nodded toward one of the waiters, who put down his tray of champagne flutes and followed briskly behind Nick and Addison. I noticed the telltale bulge at his ribcage as he slipped out the side door. The bartender moved back behind the bar, eyes sharp for further disturbance.

"So now we know two of Finn's covert team."

"We do." Trey tilted his head, listening through the earpiece. "Nick and Addison have a man on them. The secondary operative says Quint is headed for the bar at the main resort. He'll stay under surveillance there."

A single couple moved to the middle of the dance floor, and that popped loose the awkwardness. A woman in a bronze halter dress started undulating, sequins catching the light. Bree the surly assistant still had her phone out, and she was staring with curiosity at Trey and me.

"Uh oh," I said. "We're getting looks. Quick, act like you're interrogating me."

Trey's forehead creased. "What?"

"Hands on hips. Frown meanly."

He did as I asked, although he looked more confused than mean. I flung my hands in the air and widened my eyes, tried to look like I was arguing.

"What are you doing?" he said.

"This is me telling you I didn't see anything, but you don't believe me, so shake your head."

He did. He also moved closer, right into my personal space. Suddenly, even in his discount suit, he exuded authority, and I fought the urge to take a step back. Or take a step forward. Command presence—it ratcheted his sex appeal into the stratosphere.

I shook it off. "Now take me by the elbow and march me behind that partition next to the band."

Trey did exactly as I asked. I put up a semblance of a protest, and as his fingers gripped my arm, I felt a warm melting at the base of my spine. I let him propel me behind the screen, my back against his chest, as the band moved into a reggae number.

He released my arm and faced me. "Was that okay?"

"Oh yeah. That was perfect."

"Good. Now what?"

I steadied myself, though I could still feel heat in my cheeks. "Now we address our next challenge. Because that Bree chick is taking pictures again."

Trey raised an eyebrow. "Again?"

"Yes. Of the fight, of Nick, of you and me. But you know what she hasn't done, not even once?"

"What?"

"Take a selfie."

Trey rolled that fact around in his head. "That's unusual?"

"For a twenty-something at a celebrity party? Highly unusual."

"Do you have a theory?"

"I do."

So I told him. His eyes narrowed.

"Interesting."

"Yep. So go talk to her."

"But—"

"You're the security guy, not me."

He shook his head vehemently. "But you have the better interrogation skills. You ask the right questions. You—"

"You do fine with a little advance prep." I chanced a peek around the edge of the screen. Bree was still standing beside the bar, texting her heart out. I ducked back before she spotted me. "So—"

"Hold on. That's my phone." He pulled it out and examined the readout, his expression becoming more concerned by the second. "It's Price. I have to take this. You go talk to Bree. I'll meet you outside."

"Trey—"

But he took off for the exit before I could say another word.

Chapter Forty

I ordered another bourbon and took it over to where Bree stood in the corner, texting. She ignored me until I cleared my throat, then raised her head and gave me a withering look. "Yeah?"

I gave her one back. "Did you even read those signs?"

"What signs?"

"The ones at the gate. At the production company office. At the Kennesaw base camp. They all say the same thing. Unauthorized photography and/or video strictly prohibited and punishable by fine and/or imprisonment."

"So?"

"So the resort security manager is getting ready to haul you down to the police station because the Talbots are going to press charges. He just told me so."

She blanched, and her mouth fell open a little. She was desperately holding onto the bravado, but I could see the tiny cracks in the facade.

"But everybody takes pictures!" she said.

"Yes, but not everybody posts them to a stalker app."

"It's not for stalkers, it's for fans!"

"No, sites that share celebrity locations in public are for fans. Like if you see George Clooney elbow-deep in fried chicken somewhere. Not sites that leak base camp locations. Do you realize how much danger you put everyone in?"

She paled even more. "Diego wasn't dangerous! Nick said so himself. And Nick was never in danger, I would never…"

She caught herself before the words came out, but the blush gave her away. Nick was wrong. She wasn't after some golden ticket to stardom. She was after him.

"You saw Diego's profile in the Nick Talbot group and started sharing confidential info with him, knowing he'd eventually snap." I shook my head, puzzled. "What I don't get is why. If you really care about Nick, why would you...?" And then I got it. "You wanted Diego to spill the beans about his relationship with Addison so that Nick would know Addison lied to him. You were trying to break them up."

She folded her arms and clammed up. Bull's eye.

I shook my head. "Wow. That's gonna add aiding and abetting to your rap sheet."

I saw the first tremble in her lips. She was about to cry. Part of me felt bad for continuing to press, but then I remembered Nick with his head in his hands, and poor dumb Diego, and the part of me that wanted to smack her took the reins again.

I made my voice stern. "Listen. I don't care if you leaked locations or took pictures. Talbot Creative might, but I don't. Lucky for you, I'm not the cops, and I don't answer to the Talbots."

"What about the security guy?"

I smiled. "He's not here right this second, now is he?"

Bree examined me warily. "Why are you telling me this? What do you want from me?"

"A little inside information, that's all. And who would you rather take a chance on, me or Mr. Law and Order?"

She blinked her eyes clear and talked quickly. "Nick told me about Diego a long time ago, so I knew who he was. I also knew he was harmless, just stupid in love with Addison." She practically spat the name out of her mouth. "I saw his profile on the Star Track app and dropped him a message. He told me the truth about Addison, that they were together—like serious—until she moved to Georgia."

"So you hoped that they'd get back together and leave Nick free for the taking?"

Her eyes flashed. "She doesn't care about Nick. He's just an interesting story she's trying to cash in on."

An echo of what Portia had said earlier. It would also explain the whole surprise wedding instead of a quick and tidy visit to the justice of the peace. The former made a better plot twist.

"How did you find this out?"

Bree hesitated and glanced toward the exit. Trey had pushed into the tent, his face a mask of consternation. He looked exactly like every TV cop on every network cop show, like he was about to chuck everyone into a police van and sort it all out downtown. He spotted us still talking, but didn't come over.

Bree dropped her voice. "I snooped in her trailer. But it wasn't my idea!"

"No. It was Portia's."

"Yes! She wants that script, bad. But I couldn't find it. I found sample pages from Addison's bio-pic, though. And a card from Hammershein Media."

"Who?"

She nodded toward a table in the corner. A man sat there, elegant and self-possessed. I recognized his wavy steel-gray hair and square chin—he was the man in the clandestine restaurant photos with Portia.

"Winston Hammershein. He's Portia's new agent. Nobody knows that yet, though, especially not her old agent. Especially not Addison." Bree looked left and right, so close now I could smell the gin on her breath. "I told Portia about the bio-pic, and she convinced Hammershein he should get Addison to submit it so that she could get a look at it. But she knows Addison can't sell it, not as long as she works for Talbot Creative. And she knows Quint can sue if she tries."

Pieces were starting to click into place. Vengeance moved in cycles as precise and orderly as a solar system. And at the center of those orbits, there was always a massive black hole of thwarted ego.

Bree wore a sheen of sweat across her forehead. "Look, I know this makes me look bad, but I've been trying to catch a break for years. Then one day Portia asked for me personally, to deliver her protein shakes. That's a big deal, you know. To get a personal request. Eventually she asked me if I'd...you know."

"Spy?"

"Yeah."

So it had been simple as that. Quid pro quo of the most rudimentary level.

"That's how you move up? By becoming somebody's favorite gofer?"

"It's one way." Bree was so close her chin almost touched mine. "Whatever the talent wants, we runners deliver. Vegan, gluten-free, low-carb. Portia wants her shakes with almond milk, no dairy, done up with some herbal concoction she gets from a doctor in China. Or India. I can't remember."

I got a prickle. "Kava perhaps?"

"I don't know. I never asked. She has bottles and bottles of the stuff in her trailer." She looked left and right, dropped her voice. "And sometimes I get her some special herbs, if you know what I mean."

She placed two fingers against her lips and mimicked a long deep inhale. I didn't need an explanation.

"That could get you in serious trouble."

"I told you, that's how it's done. I get her whatever she wants, she makes sure I keep a job." Bree shook her head, and her cinnamon hair swished. "You gotta understand, nobody sees people like me. We're equipment, like the dollies and the light boards. To get ahead, we gotta give the Portias what they want."

"What about Nick?"

Her eyes softened. "Nick's not like that. He pays attention to people."

So that was it. A crumb of human connection, and she'd decided she was in love.

"Have you ever told Nick how you feel?"

She looked at me like I was an idiot. "Of course not! Why would I do that?" Her face scrunched up pitifully. "Can I go now, before the security guy comes over here? Please? I told you everything I know."

"You can go. But keep this conversation to yourself. You don't want a conspiracy charge on top of everything else."

She scurried away. I watched to make sure she'd left, then ordered another bourbon. I took it outside. I waited for Trey behind the ruins, white Christmas lights illuminating the ruddy brick and twining ivy. The sun had fully set now, and the tent glowed ivory against a sky like wet indigo velvet.

Trey appeared out of the shadows and stood beside me. "They're shutting down the party early."

"Not the press Talbot Creative hoped to get?"

"Not at all. What happened with Bree?"

I filled him in. A crew of workers tied back the canvas panels at the entrance, and I could see inside the tent as the party broke up. Dante stepped from behind his cello. Rico tossed down the last of his drink. Portia took the arm of a strapping guy in a fitted black tee shirt and skinny jeans. She laughed, but her eyes searched the room. Quint was still nowhere to be seen.

"So to sum up," I said, "I told her not to leave the resort or you'd arrest her for conspiracy."

Trey looked aghast. "I can't do that."

"I know. But she needed some incentive to keep her mouth shut. That did it." I sipped the bourbon, let it warm my tongue and throat. "What did Keesha want?"

"Oh." He stopped assessing the tent and looked my way. "She said the Buckhead Burglar is in custody."

I almost spilled my drink. "What?"

"He was arrested in Tallahassee. A detective in major crimes spotted the LINX profile and called Price."

"Damn. Bad day to be him."

"Yes. But he swears he didn't kill Jessica Talbot."

"That surprises you?"

"No. What surprises me is that he has an alibi."

"God, doesn't everybody?"

"His alibi is backed up by a judge." He showed me an image on his phone, an official summons of some sort. "When Jessica Talbot was killed, he was contesting a speeding ticket in Waldo, Georgia."

"So he definitely didn't do it."

"He did not." Trey put his phone away. "Price is on her way there as we speak. She wants to interview him in person."

Of course she did. This was further fuel for the fire she'd built under Joe Macklin. And I understood. She needed an answer. Answers weren't closure, but they were something. Trey had looked Nick in the eye and seen one true thing—that he had not killed his wife. And now he needed to protect him, especially since Finn was perfectly happy to use Nick as bait. Trey may have been the only thing standing between Nick and the celebrity suite at the morgue.

"All right," I said. "What's next?"

Trey checked his watch. "I need to get back to the station. Nick has asked to speak to you before you go back to your cabin. He and Addison are in 1650. Once you're back inside your room, lock up and stay there."

"Are you sure? I—"

"Yes, I'm sure. And don't forget—"

"The security code. I won't."

There was electricity to him. I wanted to kiss him, good and thoroughly, but we weren't supposed to be fraternizing. He still hadn't looked in his pocket.

I hoisted my bag on my shoulder, reassured to feel the weight of my weapon in there. As I walked past Trey, I stopped shoulder to shoulder, our biceps barely touching. He was warm from his recent sprint, and I caught his scent, a potent mixture of starched cotton and evergreen aftershave and skin.

I dropped my voice to a whisper. "This is me not kissing you good-bye."

He leaned his head infinitesimally closer. "I know."

Chapter Forty-one

I didn't call for a club cart. Instead, I walked the winding path that led around the edge of the property, the pines slender and black against the sky. The woods thinned as I approached the back of the cabins, and the night opened up above me, wide and spangled with stars. It was cool here, fragrant with late honeysuckle and hay from the barn. I could smell the lake even if I couldn't see it, clean and mossy.

The break in the clearing led to a simple wrought iron gate, and beyond that, a cemetery. It was very small, with rows of granite markers that glowed in the moonlight. Modest as cemeteries went, it was nonetheless immaculately groomed. I didn't remember seeing it on the map.

My phone buzzed, and I put it to my ear. "Hey, partner."

"How did you find out?"

I laughed. "You finally looked in your pocket."

"How?"

"I'm not telling."

"You have to."

"No, I don't. That wasn't part of the deal. Camping was, though, so start deciding where you want to go. I heard Cloudland Canyon is nice this time of year. Well, except for the scorpions." I tested the latch, and the gate swung open noiselessly. "Hey, did you know there's a graveyard behind the ruins?"

"What are you doing out there?"

"It's on the way to Nick's."

"No, it's not. It's in the woods. There are things in the woods."

I laughed. "*Now* you sound like yourself again."

He was silent for a second. I waited for him to argue some more, but he didn't.

"This place isn't on the map," I said.

"Not the guest map. It is on the security map, however."

I knelt beside one monument, plain as such went, memorializing the family and the slaves who built and tended the plantation, all of them buried together, owner and property. I looked at the gathered dead and felt the familiar punch in my gut. I knew this land had once belonged to the Cherokee, before their treaty was violated and they were driven down the Trail of Tears. And I knew that each lovely brick of the villa had been laid by dark, enslaved hands, every single one. No wonder they lit up the ruins with year-round Christmas lights, desperate attempts to drive out the shadows.

I heard the crunch of footsteps and froze. A familiar smell wafted my way. Tobacco smoke. I turned slowly and saw a figure at the gate, illuminated by the burning tip of a cigarette. I lowered my voice and switched my phone to my left hand, dipped my right into my bag. I closed my fingers around the butt of the revolver.

"Trey?" I whispered. "There's someone here."

"Who?"

"I can't tell."

The figure moved forward into a patch of moonlight. A man, short and stocky. He raised the hand with the cigarette. "Sorry to startle you. I didn't realize I had company."

The Talbots' accountant, Oliver James. I removed my hand from the bag and walked over. "Hello again, Mr. James. We've met."

He peered closer. "Oh yes. Ms. Randolph. I'm sorry I was the bearer of bad tidings that day. Care for a smoke?"

He held out the pack of cigarettes to me. I took one, and he lit it with gentlemanly grace. I took a long, deep drag. Menthols, not my favorite, but that didn't matter. I could feel Trey's disapproval emanating from the phone.

I sighed. "My boyfriend detests cigarettes."

"Addison does not approve of them either," Oliver said. "She's designated every single square foot of this place a tobacco-free zone."

"But not the secret graveyard?"

He shrugged. "It's the safest spot for transgression. Nobody comes back here. One must actually ambulate and that's beyond the ken of these guests. They prefer the fake cemetery anyway, the stage-built one out behind the barn. This one here isn't grave-yardy enough."

I sucked up the sweet minty smoke. Typical Hollywood, and typical Atlanta. I'd gotten used to having the dead underfoot in Savannah—that entire city was built on graves. But Atlanta did not love its real ghosts, only its imaginary ones.

"You used to do cemetery tours, didn't you?" Oliver said.

I examined him through the haze of moonlight-laced smoke. His softness disguised a sharp cleverness.

He chuckled. "You can drop the pretense. Quint told me who you are and why you're here."

"I thought he wanted to keep this under wraps."

"Quint tells me everything. He takes care of the big picture necessities, and I grind out the details."

"Are you friends?"

He gave me a quizzical look. "Friends? No, not friends."

"You must be very talented then. You were an accountant one year, CFO the next. That's some career track you found. Lucrative enough to follow all the way to Atlanta."

He blew a stream of smoke over his shoulder. "My, you *have* done your homework. To no avail, unfortunately, because you're on a fool's errand."

"You don't think somebody's trying to kill Nick?"

"I say this with the utmost compassion, but he's crazy. As the proverbial bedbug. Have you ever heard of Munchhausen syndrome? Where people do terrible things to themselves to get attention?"

"I have."

He tapped his temple. "That's Nick."

"His diagnosis was paranoid delusional disorder."

He made a noise. "Pfft. That boy's got diagnosis on top of diagnosis. Crazy covers all the bases. I've been with this company for five years now. Nicky's dragged it through a swamp of failures. This boondoggle, that fiasco. Getting him started in make-up was cheap, just a few buckets of latex and some fake scabs."

I tapped out the ash on a nearly gatepost. "Why keep him in the business then?"

"You've met Quint. He is not the most charismatic of men. He's got looks, money, but not a single asset in the charm department. People adore Nicky, though. They throw their dollars at him. Hell, Addison liked him enough to fall in love with him and stay in love with him even when he was accused of murder."

He said the word "murder" with relish, hitting its notes like an opera singer. I imagined we made a very noir-ish scene, he and I—wreathed in smoke at the edge of a graveyard, moonlight cutting across our features in white ribbons.

Oliver jabbed the cigarette at me. "Now you, Ms. Randolph. You may be here strictly for professional reasons, but your friend, the tall, dark not-a-director-of-parking? He's got more of an ax to grind, I imagine. Considering his history with the Talbots."

I didn't bite. Oliver laughed.

"Yes, I know who he is too. This is my first time coming face to face with him, though." He leaned closer, his eyes alight with juicy malice. "He's gonna break Nicky's alibi for Jessica's murder, isn't he?"

"What if I told you Mr. Seaver was convinced of Nick's innocence?"

"I'd say Nicky's got him fooled too." He ground out the cigarette. "Look, I don't care what Addison says about him being clean. I don't care what Quint says about him being a harmless nut. Do yourself a favor and do as I do—stay the hell away from Nick Talbot. For your own good."

I kept my voice casual. "Is that what you and Quint were arguing about the other night? At the guest house?"

Oliver froze for a split second, then he smiled, but it was a plastic smile, as convincing as a toupée. "Well. You have finally managed to surprise me. I didn't know I was under surveillance."

I gave him a smile back, just as saccharine. "You didn't answer the question."

"No, I did not. Very astute of you to notice." He rubbed his hands together as if dusting them free of dirt. Still smiling, though. "Goodnight, Ms. Randolph. Be careful out here. You never know who you might meet in the dark."

Chapter Forty-two

I found Nick and Addison at their cabin, the waiter who was not a waiter posted up at the door. He checked my ID, but wouldn't let me enter. Behind the door, I heard Addison and Nick talking. Eventually Nick came out, shutting the door behind himself, cigarettes in hand. He gestured toward the back patio, and I followed.

"Addison hates it that I smoke," he says. "I have to sneak these."

He offered the pack, and I took one. My second transgression of the hour. He extended his lighter, and I lit up, deciding that at least my addiction was serving a larger purpose.

"I know the feeling," I said. "You two okay?"

"Sure. The wedding was a formality. We got married this morning nice and official." He held up his hand where a platinum band now gleamed. "We're leaving Talbot Creative. I've had an offer from Pinewood, and Addison has some nibbles from agents about her bio-pic. Many agents, many offers, not just the fake one from Hammershein."

I paused with the cigarette halfway to my mouth. "You know about that?"

He grinned at me. "Portia's machinations? Of course. But the screenplay will sell better if everybody thinks I don't, maybe even spawn a bidding war." He looked at me, his eyes burnished by the cigarette. "I know about all the things, Tai. About Addison's history with Diego. About Bree's spying. About the fact that

Addison wasn't at home the night I was shot. She was meeting with an even bigger agent than Hammershein." He put a finger to his lips. "Hush hush."

"Portia said Talbot Creative will sue if she moves forward with that."

"They won't. It's my story, I own it, not them, and they know it." He let smoke trickle out the side of his mouth, holding the cigarette at his hip. "Portia will be pissed as hell. She comes off terribly in the story, big surprise. But she'll have her hands full with Season Two, so—"

"Luna survives?"

"Of course. You think the board would put that cash cow out to pasture just because Hammershein promises her a big-studio movie back in L.A.? Hell no. She's stuck for the rest of her three years."

"You're saying Portia wanted to be killed?"

"Portia wanted out of her contract, she didn't care how. But that's not going to happen."

I finished my inhale, let the smoke linger in my mouth. Some exotic brand I didn't know, toasty and rich and brain-swimmingly potent. I'd pegged Nick as cute but dumb, a massive misjudgment on my part. He'd been playing everyone, Trey and me included. But then, we'd been playing him as well. I thought of Trey's apartment, now an evidence lab. He had his own motivations—he'd cobbled guilt and vengeance and maybe even justice into a machine capable of steamrolling right over Nick if necessary. We were none of us innocent. No, not one.

I blew the smoke toward the sky. "Story fodder. All of it. The secrets, the wedding, the drama. Getting Trey involved, and me. Plot points and narrative arcs."

He shrugged. "I used to be a producer, remember? I know what sells."

"And the shooting? And the accident?"

"Oh, those are very real. Sometimes stories get away from you. That's why I agreed to all the bodyguards." He stared at the burning tip of his cigarette. "I'd just put one of these between my lips when the shot rang out. Now I think about that every time I light up."

"As well you should."

He looked at me. "I know you think I'm being flippant about that, and the accident. Or maybe you think I'm crazy too. Or lying. But there's nothing like almost dying to remind you of how alive you are." He examined the cigarette again. "Probably why I smoke. Courting death with every inhale. I'll tell Addison that. She'll like the metaphor."

I couldn't help it. I laughed. "It's a good one."

"Yeah." He examined me through the smoke. "You believe me, don't you, about the important things? The accident, the shooting?" His face was somber. "Jessica."

"I do."

"Because Trey said so?"

"Yes. But I think I would have anyway."

He nodded solemnly. "They say it was that burglar. Now that you've seen the evidence, what do you say?"

I thought of Keesha driving south in the night, headed for the panhandle of Florida, just beyond the Georgia line. She wouldn't stop except to get gas. She'd drive straight through.

"I say you might be getting some closure there real soon."

"Really? That will be…I don't know what that will be. It wasn't as if Jessica and I were happy. And then I met Addison." He examined me seriously. "You ever been saved, Tai? I mean literally."

The memories came flooding in all at once. Gabriella at Trey's door with a pot of soup, Garrity in a blizzard with a helicopter. Rico telling me not to go with Jeremy Fuller the night he crashed his truck right into the Altamaha River and they didn't find it, or him, for weeks. My father—yes, he would always be my father no matter what that envelope revealed—pulling me to the surface after the riptide got me. And Trey holding me against his chest in the dark while sirens wailed in the distance.

"Yes," I said. "I've been saved. Many times."

Nick nodded. "Then you know what it is to owe your life to another person."

I could see that his eyes were bright, even in the dark. He believed what he'd just said. I thought hard about my next words, thought about myself, and Trey, all of us.

"I know this much. Nobody ever really saves you. They show up for you. They offer their hand. But in the end, you have to make the choice to take it. In the end, you always save yourself." I shrugged. "Or not."

He looked at me strangely. "Yeah. I guess." Then he sighed, a deep exhale that released a lot of pent-up energy. "Thanks for talking. I gotta get back to my wife now." He handed me the still-burning cigarette. "Ditch this for me? I don't want to spend my wedding night in the doghouse."

Chapter Forty-three

Once I got back to my cabin, I slipped my .38 into the bedside table drawer, still holstered. This was the out-of-town procedure—safe from accidental discharge but otherwise accessible. I undressed in the dark, the moon illuminating the space like a lamp. I stretched out the knots in my shoulders, leaving my clothes in a heap in the middle of the floor, then pulled on one of Trey's old tees. I'd barely gotten my head through the neck hole when my phone started screeching, the screen flaring red, strobing in time to the blaring security alarms.

I snatched it up. According to the interface, every single alarm had triggered simultaneously. Front and back door breaches, window breaches, maybe even a breach from above. That couldn't happen unless there was an army outside. I listened. No army. I reached into the drawer just as the alarm stopped.

I held my breath, phone in one hand, the other wrapped around the revolver, unholstered now but still in the drawer. All quiet. I knew that shouldn't have happened either. The alarm required a code to go all clear, and only two people had the code—Trey and me—and I had my finger poised on his speed dial when he called me first.

I spoke quickly. "Trey! There's something—"

"False alarm. My apologies."

"What?"

"Come onto the patio and I'll explain."

I let go of the gun and unlocked the back doors. A night breeze riffled the hem of the tee shirt and pulled my hair into my face. After a few seconds, I spotted Trey standing at the edge of the woods. He looked left and right, then came closer.

"I'm sorry about that," he said, his voice low. "I was making a final perimeter check, and I accidentally triggered…everything."

I folded my arms. "Making a final check on me, you mean."

He didn't argue. He'd given up on the suit jacket, which he had folded over his arm. His white shirt was the only thing that kept him from blending into the darkness.

"You could have used the front door," I said. "You know. Knocked."

"I was trying to be discreet."

"You were trying to be sneaky."

His voice rose. "I was trying…" He exhaled in frustration, pitched his voice lower. "I was trying to text you to tell you to switch off the system and let me in. But I had the access screen pulled up at the same time, and I triggered the live test simulation by mistake."

"I could have had the gun out. I could have shot you."

"You'd already put your gun away."

I flung a hand in the air. "So? I could have had it aimed your way in less than three seconds."

"Yes, but you're trained to aim only at an identifiable target with clear background, neither of which you had."

I was still annoyed. So was Trey. And he was something else too, though I couldn't quite put my finger on it.

"Let me get this straight," I said. "You show up outside my room at midnight—"

"Eleven-fifty."

"After coming over the river and through the woods—"

"Around the woods."

"—alone in the dark, without letting me know, just because you wanted to assess the security system?"

Another shrug, this one lightly tossed off, barely moving his shoulders. "Of course."

I examined his face, but the interplay of moonlight and shadow concealed his emotions. So I stood on tiptoe and looked him right in the eye. Up close I could catch it—the deliberately steady gaze, guileless and innocent. Trey rarely lied, but when he did, this was what it looked like.

I tilted my head. "Trey?"

"Yes?"

"How did you know I'd already put my gun away?"

He blinked at me, not saying a word. I stepped even closer, the grass cool under my bare feet, Trey warm in front of me.

"You stood there and watched me undress," I said.

He put his hands on his hips. "You left the curtain open. I've warned you many times—"

"About perverts lurking, yes, you have."

He narrowed his eyes at me, but didn't defend himself. I laughed, which earned me another sharp look. He put one finger to his lips, but that made me laugh harder.

"You gotta work on your peeping tom game," I said, and then utterly lost it. I laughed until I was weak in the knees, hic-cupping, tears in my eyes. Trey endured the spectacle without comment. Eventually, I pulled myself together and wiped my eyes on my sleeve.

Trey's voice was stern. "Are you finished?"

I swatted his arm. "Don't act prissy. It's not like anybody's still asleep after that unholy noise you unleashed."

"It was an accident. I was distracted. There's no reason for you to compound the...whatever."

I caught it in his voice then. Sheepish amusement. He still had his hands on his hips, but his mouth was kinked at the corner. I couldn't tell in the dark, but I knew he had to be blushing. He couldn't help it. He had an Irish complexion and an altar boy soul.

"Are you off duty now?" I said.

"Technically. I'm still on call, though, so I have to be back at the station in an hour."

I smiled. "That's okay. We can do a lot of debriefing in an hour."

He exhaled softly, let me take his hand to lead him inside. But then he stopped. "Tai?"

"Yes?"

"How *did* you find out?"

I looked up at him. The night was sweet with late summer, the moonlight clear and potent as liquor. In the dappled shadows, it was easy to forget that there was any world beyond the circle of us. Mayhem raged, some of it barely a hundred feet away. But with Trey, there was sanctuary. He created it as deftly as any defense system.

"Do you really want to know?" I said. "Because if you do, I'll tell you. If you ask the right way."

He didn't move for another fifteen seconds. Then he slipped his hand from mine, not breaking eye contact as he retrieved the radio from his pocket.

He pushed the call button. "Seaver here. I've completed the perimeter patrol."

A hiss of static, then a voice. "Got that, sir. You going ten-ten?"

"Affirmative. You have the radio for the next hour."

A voice crackled back. "Copy that, sir."

"Seaver out."

He slipped it back in his pocket, pulled off the earpiece and tucked it in his pocket too. He ran his gaze over my eyes and mouth, my throat, the rest of me. I didn't move, stood stock-still in the cool silvery light as he took my hand and turned it palm up, then pressed a kiss to the thrumming pulse point at the inside of my wrist. The breeze quickened as he snaked his other hand under the tee, from the small of my back up the curve of my spine, trailing goose bumps and shivers, and I literally—literally—got so dizzy with the blood rush I thought I might fall out on the patio.

I wrapped my arms around his neck. "That is definitely the right way to ask."

He laughed lightly, in the back of his throat. Laughter was new from him, rarer even than that dazzling roguish smile. And I felt a deeper thrill, one beyond sensation, one that came from the understanding that in the tangled web of his past, present, and future selves, Trey was simply Trey. And he was all mine.

I kissed the center of his chest, right above his heart. "You think sixty minutes is long enough to get all the details?"

"Most likely. Accounting for the typical variables." He canted his head. "But there's no rush, is there?"

I reached for his belt buckle. "There might be."

Chapter Forty-four

He dressed in the dark, sitting on the edge of the bed. I stayed naked under the sheets. I'd hoped to entice him to stay, but duty called. Or something like duty. Whatever it was pulling him back into the night.

He turned his head sideways. "How did you convince Mac to tell you the rest of the story?"

"He got the idea I was mad at you, and that worried him. So he explained. Everything."

Trey slipped into his shirt. "I'm waiting for your commentary."

"On what? That you got fired because you were offering gigolo services on the side?"

"I was not! That is exactly—"

I laughed. "Hush. I'm messing with you. Mac explained very clearly that that wasn't what happened."

Trey shot me a somewhat mollified look and continued dressing. The lawyer had been a regular at the hotel, Mac has said, a business traveler. If Trey was on duty, she'd ask for him, tipping him a hundred to personally care for her Porsche. And then one night, she'd written her room number on that hundred, and Trey—young and broke and one hundred percent heterosexual male—had gotten off work and gone up to that spectacular suite. And then he got fired the next day when one of the other valets accused him of being, in Mac's exact words, a rent boy. But Mac told the lawyer what had happened the next time she showed up, and she threatened the HR department with many nasty lawsuits. In the end, Trey's supervisor at the Ritz not only hired him back, he sent Trey and Mac both to executive training as a bonus/bribe/apology. And once Mac opened his gym, Trey ever after taught a weekly self-defense class there, gratis.

I wrapped my arms around my knees. "She must have been one helluva lawyer."

He nodded. "She was. After that, I never saw her again."

"So this wasn't a big romance?"

He shook his head. The story itself was longer than the story of how I'd found out, which I'd given up after approximately three minutes of "interrogation." Trey hadn't been surprised. He knew I didn't have a withholding bone in my body.

"Why hide it?" I said. "You didn't seriously think I'd be upset, did you?"

He continued buttoning his shirt. "No. And I wasn't hiding it. It's just that I'm still learning how to...reconnect? Is that the right word? When I'm talking about myself?"

I curled around the pillow. He was reconnecting his social network one person at a time, and reconnecting himself one story at a time—who he'd been before the accident, who he'd been after, and who he was now.

"Reconnect is the right word," I said.

"Good. Because the person in that story doesn't feel like me. But he was. I mean, I was. The same. And yet different. It's the same feeling I get reading the OPS transcripts of my testimony." Then he gave me a sidelong glance from under his lashes. "I *was* worried, you know."

"About what?"

"That you'd think badly of me. For being...I don't know."

"Scandalous?"

"Yes. Perhaps."

I propped my chin in my hand. "That's a valid worry. I've never done anything so shocking in my whole life."

Trey's eyes tracked my face from eyes to chin, concentrating a good five seconds on my mouth. Then he gave me an inscrutable

look and turned away, back to searching for his shoes. I smiled a
little. I knew he'd seen the lie, but for whatever reason, decided
not to engage. For the time being anyway.

"So now what?" I said.

"Now I go back to the check-in station."

"Of course. You don't wanna be derelict in your duty." I kissed
his bicep. "You especially don't want to get caught sneaking over
here for a booty call."

He narrowed his eyes at me, but he wasn't annoyed. He
started to put on his clip-on tie, but instead slipped it in his
pants pocket along with his earpiece.

"Have you heard from Keesha?" I said.

"I have. She has the suspect in custody. During the interrogation, he confessed to all the burglaries, and the judge in Waldo has
confirmed that he could not have been involved in the murder."

"Which strengthens her theory that it was Macklin."

Trey knelt beside the bed and stuck a hand underneath.
"Actually, no. She's decided that it was Nick Talbot."

"What?"

He straightened, one sock in hand. "She said I was right,
that no cop would have faked the scene so ineptly, not with a
criminal who had such a precisely documented MO. Her words.
The burglar agreed. He had, apparently, considered the Talbot
home as a target and rejected it. Too much unpredictability, he
said. Too many lovers coming and going at all hours, too much
crazy. His words. He thinks Nick is guilty too."

I took in this revelation. Trey continued patting around under
the bed for his other sock.

"Did you tell her you'd changed your mind about Nick?" I said.

"I did."

"And?"

"She hung up on me. Which is not surprising. I think I would
have hung up on me too."

Still shoeless, he sat once again at the foot of the bed. I finished buttoning his shirt. I took my time with it, knowing it
would be the last time I'd see him until morning.

"Are the rest of the Talbots behaving?" I said.

"Portia eventually went to the bar at the main resort with one of the tech crew. Quint went back to his cottage alone, where he spent an hour on the phone with Talbot Creative's legal counsel, who is meeting him here first thing in the morning. Nick and Addison have stayed in their cabin."

"No further attempts on Nick's life?"

"None." Trey raised his chin and let me straighten his collar. "Though Finn was right—I did discover something interesting while working the valet stand. For someone who doesn't believe anyone is trying to harm his brother, Quint came well-armed. He has a handgun in the glove compartment, a Ruger SR45. Loaded."

"And he left it in the car?"

"Yes."

"So he's not expecting to need it."

Trey leveled a look at me. "If he needs a weapon, he'll use the one he had hidden in his golf bag. A Sig Sauer .357."

I whistled low and long. "Whoa."

"Indeed. He's concerned about something."

"Yes, but whatever it is, it has nothing to do with keeping his brother alive. Which is utterly unsurprising. With Nick dead, all the money in the trust will be his to manage."

"At the moment, yes. But if the judge's ruling stands and Addison is indeed Nick's sole conservator—and if she and Nick are married, that is a likely outcome—then she controls everything."

"Which means Addison's motives to see him dead just doubled. Not only would she control his estate, the price of her screenplay would go through the roof."

Trey didn't argue. We'd both seen every motive under the sun—people killed for love, for fame, for money, for security, and for sheer unmitigated meanness. We were all born with a trigger. For some of us, it was as easily sprung as a rabbit trap.

"Oliver thinks Nick's a killer," I said. "Quint thinks he's insane. Addison wants to control every second of his life. And who knows what Portia thinks except that I suspect she'd throw anyone and anything under the bus to ditch *Moonshine* and head back to L.A. on the next plane."

Trey nodded. "Yes. That seems like a valid summary."

"And Nick thinks it's all fodder for the movie of the week that is his life. He is the only person *not* taking any of this seriously."

Trey frowned. "What do you mean?"

So I filled him in on my conversation with Nick, including the part where he'd been lying to us. Trey took it better than I expected. Just another collection of secret motives and secondary schemes to file in their proper places. I examined him in the dark. I wished that I wasn't sending him into the night unarmed. But then I remembered the look on his face when he'd pulled his weapon on Marissa, the cool predatory intent that had quickly morphed into shame at the realization of what he'd done. She'd been blasé. He'd been mortified.

Outside the window, I heard the rustle of leaves, the soft ripple of wind. No traffic, no horns, no jackhammers. Trey fetched his jacket, but instead of putting it on, he draped it over his arm.

"Suit not to your liking?" I said.

Trey frowned in distaste. "The sleeves are cut too high. And it doesn't hang properly."

I laughed. "You've gotten spoiled, boyfriend."

"I have not. I've simply developed certain…preferences."

"Which is the very definition of spoiled."

He didn't argue. Our hour was up. Time to send him back to his room at the station and hunker down in my own. Trey didn't move to leave, though. He sat on the edge of the bed, watching me in the dark.

I got to my knees and kissed him lightly. "Are you sure you have to—"

"Did you hear that?"

I listened. And then I heard it too. Definitely footsteps, definitely on my patio. Trey stood in one fluid motion, his hand dipping toward the holster that was not there as he moved toward the patio door. I scrambled for the drawer, letting the sheet fall away as I pulled out my gun.

Trey assessed the situation, then toed the door open. A loud bray echoed through the room, and he jumped back so quickly he smashed his elbow into the wall.

He sucked in a sharp breath. "What is…why is…that?"

The donkey nosed its way into the room and shook its shaggy head, sending dust motes and hay everywhere.

Chapter Forty-five

"That," I said, "is a donkey."

Trey gaped at it. "What is it doing here?"

"I have no clue."

I wrestled the tee shirt on, tried to remember where I'd left my jeans. The donkey sneezed. It was delicate and well-groomed, like something from a manger scene, with heavily lashed eyes, pert ears, and a slightly dazed manner. It bumped its forehead against the bedpost, and I reached over and scratched between its ears.

Trey had moved as far away from the animal as he could. "What do we do with it?"

"We get somebody to put it back. And before you ask, no, donkey wrangling is not my thing."

Trey absorbed this information. He still wasn't budging. The donkey got bored with me and shook my hand free. Then it ambled off toward the patio.

I spotted my jeans at the foot of the bed and wriggled into them. "Come on."

Trey still hadn't found his shoes, but he reluctantly followed me onto the patio. We watched as the donkey trotted toward a patch of sunflowers. Trey started to say something, but I held my finger over my lips. *Listen.* He cocked his head, caught what I had—other animal sounds in the night. Two goats also munched on the sunflowers. In the distance, I heard disgruntled chicken noises, flapping and clucking.

I stared. "What in the—"

A scream startled me, and I whirled around. Portia stood swaying at the edge of the clearing, her entire body wrapped around one of the more muscle-bound tech crew.

She pointed past me. "Was that a cow?"

"A donkey. What are you doing out here?"

She tucked the bottle of liquor behind her back. There were grass stains on her knees and her blouse was buttoned haphazardly.

"Nothing," she said. "What are *you* doing out here?"

"Trying to figure out why there's a donkey on the loose."

"Oh." She switched her examination to Trey. "Why aren't you wearing shoes?"

Trey started to say something, couldn't find anything, so he shut his mouth. He folded his arms and turned to me. I sighed and stepped forward.

"Why aren't you in your room?"

Portia shrugged. "I got lost. This guy found me." She laughed and leaned against him, her hand flat against his chest. "I take back everything I said about the South. You grow big, good men here."

The guy had the sense to be embarrassed and worried. Trey had one eye on the two of them and one eye on the periphery. I couldn't tell if he was most concerned about Quint, random bad guys, or more livestock erupting onto the scene.

"Did you see anyone or anything unusual while you were out?" I said.

Portia collected herself. "Like what?"

"Like perhaps somebody skulking around the barn?"

"We weren't anywhere near the barn. We were coming back from the lake." She smiled up at the guy. "Right?"

He nodded obediently. "Right."

Other cottage lights started flickering on, doors opening, curious heads peeking out. The goats and the donkey made contented munching sounds.

Trey finally composed himself. "Thank you for your cooperation, Ms. Ray. Now if you'll please go back to your quarters until we—"

"No."

Trey looked perplexed. "No?"

"No. As in you don't get to tell me what to do. None of you do." She threw her head back and raised her voice. "You hear me, Quint Talbot! I am through pretending our marriage is worth saving! I don't care what the investors think!"

She wobbled as she spoke, and her paramour of the moment caught her arm to steady her. Trey dropped his shoulders, hands loose and open. His expression was calm. I got a little shiver. *Uh oh.*

"Ms. Ray," he said. "I need you to return to your cabin. If you do not want to return to your cabin for whatever reason…" He sent a sharp look at the tech. "Then I need you to return to any cabin, and stay there. Do you understand?"

"I—"

"Do you understand?"

His voice echoed against the edge of the forest. Command presence. Working, once again, like a charm. Portia stopped talking. She kept one hand on the liquor bottle, her other arm wrapped around the guy. He seemed to be the only thing keeping her up. Trey pointed toward the cabins, and she sauntered in that direction, alone, taking her good sweet time. The tech looked a little stunned to be abandoned so abruptly.

Trey pointed toward the staff cabins. "You go too."

The guy went. I could see heads peeking out of other cabins. Trey ignored them. I did too. Something else had me concerned.

"Trey? I watched Portia all night. Not one drop of alcohol passed her lips. And that liquor bottle was almost full."

He looked puzzled. "What are you saying?"

"I'm saying maybe she's not drunk. Remember what Bree told us? About her overly enthusiastic use of herbals? There's a chance she's been overdosed too. According to Bree, she keeps tons of that stuff."

Trey exhaled in exhaustion and frustration and who knew what else. "I'll alert medical."

The second he finished radioing in the request, I heard a door slam. Then Quint came stomping toward the fire pit.

"What in the hell is going on?"

Trey explained. A nanny goat ambled over and snagged a wayward marshmallow. Quint raked a hand through his hair.

"One goddamn fiasco after another," he said.

Trey remained calm. "Mr. Talbot. Your wife—"

"I know. I'll take care of it."

"No, sir. She needs to be examined by a doctor. She could have been overdosed, like your brother was."

"I'll get our doc to check her out."

"I've already sent for the on-call physician."

"Then he can turn his ass around." Quint practically spat the words. "There was no overdose, it was Nicky trying to get attention. You had one job, to keep him from fucking everything up, and you couldn't even do that. Now there's yelling, drama, freaking animals running everywhere. It's got Nicky written all over it."

Trey didn't say anything, but I knew what he was thinking. There was an operative watching Nick and Addison. If either of them had left their room, we'd know about it soon enough. But Quint was just getting started.

"I'm going to bed. Here are your orders." He ticked off on his fingers. "Stay away from my wife. No doctor but our own. Get these people back inside." He stepped closer to Trey, dropped his voice. "And if my wife gets one mention in Buzzfeed or the *National Enquirer* or a single goddamn tweet, I am suing you, and Finn, and anybody else I can get my hands on."

And he stomped back to his cabin. Trey watched as Quint rounded the shrubbery. Soon we heard the slam of his cabin door, and the soft footsteps of his personal protection detail step into place. Other cabin doors stayed open, however. For the scandal-ravenous hordes, we were presenting a buffet of screaming, adultery, and livestock behaving badly.

Trey pulled out the radio. "Op one, body check on your targets, please."

A crackle and hiss. Then a voice. "Ten twenty-nine, sir."

"Both subjects?"

"Yes, sir."

"Thank you."

He kept the radio in hand, contemplating. Nick and Addison were in their cabin, safe. Quint too. Portia was still unaccounted for, however.

"Are you putting somebody on Portia?" I said.

"I don't have anybody. But I'll alert the resort's team. They can locate her, keep her monitored."

"So you think she might have been overdosed too?"

"I think it's a reasonable concern. In the meantime, I need to check the barn. And call for a…what was the phrase you used?"

"Donkey wrangler?"

"Yes. One of those."

I was impressed. The Trey of a year ago would have been so discombobulated at being caught barefoot and barely post-coital that he would have retreated behind the wall. But not this Trey. A moment's befuddlement, but now he was back in charge. His radio chirped, and he pressed the call button.

"Seaver here."

The voice was scratchy. "Sir, there's been a…complication."

"What kind of complication?"

"You'd better come see for yourself. It's…complicated."

Trey sighed. "Copy that. Responding."

He stared at the radio. His eyes were tight, probably from the first throb of a headache. It was going to be a long night.

"You handle the complication," I said. "I'll go check the barn."

"That's not—"

"You need my help. You said so yourself. And I know you had ideas about what that might look like, but kiss 'em good-bye. Take some headache meds, get your shoes, then go to the check-in station. I'll find out what happened at the barn."

He shook his head. "Not alone. And before you argue, that is not an overprotective concern, it's a tactical one."

At that moment, the door to one of the other cabins opened, and a bedraggled Rico peered out. He spotted me, shot me a quizzical look.

I patted Trey's shoulder. "Don't worry. I won't be alone."

Chapter Forty-six

Rico fiddled with his flashlight until it finally lit up. "I remember now why I don't hang out with you more often."

"Sorry. It's an emergency."

"Old MacDonald run amok is not an emergency."

We'd taken one of the club carts. He'd made me drive. Dante had offered us coffee to go, as if we were setting out on an all-night mission, but I assured him we were just going to check on the animals. That was all. No need to treat this like a wagon trail over the Donner Pass.

Rico splayed the beam ahead of us while I sent mine around the periphery. I was hoping to spot runaway livestock, but it also seemed a good idea to make sure we weren't walking into a trap. Though I wondered what kind of trap involved setting loose a bunch of farm animals. Rico had ideas.

"Abandoned barn," he muttered. "At night. This has slasher movie written all over it."

"Chill, dude."

"Wait and see. Some maniac wearing a mask is gonna come out from behind a tractor and then swack!"

Rico mimicked an ax slicing into the side of his neck. He'd never had a high opinion of my ability to stay out of trouble.

"Why the hell are you and Trey messing around out here?" he said. "Is this one of his corporate security assignments?"

"No."

"Because if it is, he and I are going to have a serious talk about letting you—"

"I said, it's not." I sent the beam into the treetops. "And Trey doesn't *let* me do anything. That's some sexist bullshit right there."

My flashlight caught a squat brown shape in a pine tree. I thought it was a chicken at first, but then it took off in silent swooping flight.

"Owl," I said.

Rico muttered something under his breath about white chicks and nature specials. He was grumpy, but that was par for the course. I'd gotten used to his grumpy. It was reassuring, like the tides.

"Gabe the animal wrangler says he's on the way," I assured him. "He says he'll get the donkey and the goats, if the goats cooperate. He said the chickens will have to wait until morning. That they've…something. Whatever chickens do at night."

"Gone to roost?"

"Yeah. That." I spotted the path leading to the barn and hooked a left. "Look at you, with your farm boy vocabulary."

This got him to laugh. "I haven't been to a farm since our mothers made us take riding lessons in middle school. Do you remember that?"

I laughed too. "Of course. They thought it would make us upright and presentable."

"Major fail."

We both laughed some more. Horses. In my ten-year-old opinion, they'd been mad-eyed and foam-mouthed, intent on stamping my tender girlflesh into hamburger. It had been an adventure, though, one of the first I'd shared with Rico. As we drove a modified golf cart through a faux English countryside, I was grateful to know that it hadn't been the last.

Rico held his flashlight steady. "So what *are* you and Trey doing here?"

"The truth? We're here because someone may or may not be trying to kill Nicholas Talbot, but you didn't hear that from me."

"For real?"

"For real."

"What does that have to do with all the animals?"

"I don't know. But I am going to find out."

The club cart hummed us off the paved path onto the grassy field surrounding the barn. Out here it was even darker, the sky black behind the fat full moon.

"Do you remember the Buckhead Burglar?" I said.

"Oh, hell yes. Prime example of rich people panic. Kids getting shot to death in Bankhead, big deal. Some Betties get their heirloom spoons stolen, and the entire city loses its collective grip." He shook his head. "And then the murder happened, and my ex's mama acted like it was the Fall of Saigon. The rabble coming for her kind, all that. That was when I stopped dating white boys."

It wasn't, but I didn't remind him of that. Trey wasn't the only one trying to reconnect. Rico and I were too, despite our limited demographic overlap. That hadn't bothered us in high school, where we were both outsiders. We'd bonded in the margins. But the gap between was harder to bridge now.

We reached the barn, looming against the trees. There was no lighting out here, but even from a distance, I could see the door was open wide.

Rico cursed. "Yep. We're in a horror movie. This is where it gets horrible."

"Wait here."

"Like I'm gonna do anything else."

I left him in the cart and aimed my flashlight inside the barn. The space was dark and empty, cavernous. It smelled like sweet hay and manure and…something else. I took a tentative step inside, ran a hand along the wall until I found the switch. I popped it on, and a fluorescent light sputtered to life, revealing bales of hay, a tractor, some riding tack on the wall. The pervasive chemical stench was heavy and unnerving and also strangely familiar. And then I saw it—a puddle on the floor, the candle on its side in the center. Trails of liquid stretched out in four directions, one to each corner of the barn.

I breathed down the panic. "Oh hell."

"What?"

"Somebody tried to rig up a fire."

Rico didn't move. "Tried?"

"Yeah. Tried and failed."

I dropped into a crouch. Up close, the acrid liquid was eye-watering. Not gasoline. Not kerosene. I closed my eyes and let the memories form, but all I could get was...

"Sleepovers?" I said.

"What?"

"Nothing. I'm free associating." And then I stood up abruptly. "Sleepovers. Of course. It's acetone. Like in nail polish remover."

Rico sniffed. He still didn't come inside, though. I knew I was supposed to leave everything untouched for the cops, and the cops were absolutely coming now, no way around it, no matter what the Talbots wanted. But I also knew that the candle could still have fire at the wick, and that a tiny spark could flare into an inferno at any second. So I plucked it from the acetone. Just a regular old paraffin candle, cold and crushed, the wick slightly charred.

"Looks like something heavy and hoofed stepped on it. Snuffed out the flame."

Rico gestured for me to put it down. "Leave it alone and call Trey."

It was good advice. As I pulled my phone out, I detected another smell at the barn door. It was so faint than only another addict like me could have noticed it. Tobacco. I looked down. Several cigarette butts lay crushed just outside the door. I bent close. The cigarettes were dark and unusual, but familiar. Nick's brand.

My phone vibrated in my hand. Trey calling.

"Hey you," I said, "we've got a very big problem here."

"Here too."

"My problem is attempted arson."

There was a long exhale. "My problem is auto theft with aggravated assault and a missing person."

"Oh fuck."

Another exhale. "Yes. Exactly."

Chapter Forty-seven

Rico insisted on accompanying me to the check-in station, and I did not argue with him. Puttering down the curving lanes in the dark, it was easy for Rico and me to be together. I wished that we had time to talk—about Dante, about the letter in my cash register, about life. But time was not a resource for me this night.

I eased up on the accelerator as we hit a patch of gravel. "It's strange. You're like some weird comet that only comes around every seventy years."

Rico shook his head. "That is a dumb ass metaphor."

"I don't have literary tastes."

"No, you got dangerous tastes."

I wanted to argue, but I couldn't, not really. I was leaving behind an arson attempt, on route to even greater possible felonies. I carried a gun with me more often than I didn't. Even Trey, as sweet and kind and good as he was, was about as safe as a grenade with the pin half-pulled. I thought about these things as I stopped the cart outside the station. A yellow light glowed in the back room along with the flicker of video monitors.

I climbed out. "You take the cart back."

Rico slid over behind the wheel. "What about you?"

"Trey will make sure I get back to my cabin. But listen to me—I want you to leave, tonight. You and Dante both. Things are going down here, bad things, and I...I..."

"Yeah?"

I leaned over and hugged him. And he hugged me back. A real hug, the kind that crushed a little. It reminded me that I was a flesh-and-blood body, dependent and contingent and destined for dust, but at that precise singular moment, alive and loved.

"Dante and I are out of here," he said.

I straightened. "Good. Talk soon?"

"That's a bet." He jabbed his chin toward the station. "Go detect shit."

And then he puttered away. Just as he did, the back door opened, and Trey stood there, silhouetted against the amber light.

I stepped forward. "What's up?"

He opened the door wider. "Come in and I'll show you."

The first thing I noticed was the security array—four screens, each one broken into four quadrants showing real-time video feed. Each quadrant was linked to a single camera, which meant sixteen cameras overall. That left exploitable dark places aplenty. The second thing I noticed was the man standing in the corner. He was tall and well-built, with dark hair and solemn earnest eyes and feet splayed, hands folded right below his belt buckle. Cop stance.

Trey gestured in his direction. "Jonathon Davis, former MP. He's one of Finn's."

"Tai Randolph," I said. "I'm one of hers too."

The guard nodded. "Yes, ma'am. Mr. Seaver told me, ma'am."

I didn't tell him to drop the "ma'ams." Cops loved to "ma'am" and "sir," and military police got a double dose of it.

Trey motioned for me to sit at the monitor where he had a separate screen set up. It was dark, but he tapped at the keyboard, and it flickered to life. The images showed the feed from the parking area, the valet-only section. The time stamp let me know it was recorded footage.

The video began with stillness, broken by movement twenty seconds in. A club cart drove up, and Oliver James got out. He looked nervous, furtive. He pulled a keyring from his pocket and abandoned the cart on the path and climbed in a Mercedes. He threw a small overnight bag into the backseat.

Trey pointed to the time stamp. "As you see, at approximately midnight Mr. James got into his car using a spare set of keys he had on his person, not the set he turned over when he had the car parked. He left those behind in the valet podium."

"Which is locked, I assume?"

"Yes."

"So Oliver decided to leave quickly and deliberately without telling anyone?"

"Correct." Trey held down the space bar. "Now watch this next part."

Another car pulled into the lot, barreling right through the gate arm. Oliver took one look and ran into the woods. Two men got out of the backseat, one climbing into Oliver's car and the other heading straight for Quint's Jaguar, which he had cranked and ready to go in less than sixty seconds. Before they could pull out of the lot, Jonathon approached. Immediately, the man in the Jaguar peeled out of the lot while the man in Oliver's car pulled a long-barreled handgun and started firing. Jonathon took cover, and both cars hurtled out of the lot behind the first one.

I looked up. "Jonathon! Are you okay?"

"Yes, ma'am." He looked at Trey. "But I'm not sure what to do now."

Trey was absolutely sure. "We call the authorities."

"My orders were to run all such decisions through Ms. Hudson."

"Yes, she will want to know. But this decision is beyond her preferences. Or mine. Do you understand?"

Jonathon relaxed a little. He was caught between two protocols, not sure which to use. Trey had no such divided loyalties.

I was still confused. "They walked right by the Ferrari and headed straight for Quint's Jaguar. Why would a car thief pass up a Ferrari?"

Trey tapped at the keyboard to rewind the video. "Ferraris are easily recognized and tracked. They're complicated as stolen goods go, too complicated to sell or send to a chop shop."

"So these weren't professionals?"

"They were professionals, just not that kind of professional."

"A repo team?"

He shook his head. "Legitimate repo teams don't shoot at security. Or use suppressors."

Of course. No wonder the guns had looked enormous. "So nasty professionals?"

"Yes."

I sat in the desk chair and rolled it closer to the screen. Yes, that was definitely Oliver. And yes, he looked terrified as he bolted into the woods.

"Where's Oliver now?"

"I don't know. I've alerted security, but he hasn't been spotted."

"Hiding? Fled?"

"I don't know." Trey took a seat beside me. "You mentioned attempted arson."

"Oh, yeah. That. Should I explain before we call the cops?"

"I've already called them. So yes, please explain."

Which I did.

I gave the same rundown to Finn when she called thirty minutes later, with all the extras added in—the quickie wedding, the injunction, and the legal team headed up at the crack of dawn. I also described the barn burning that hadn't happened and the parking lot robbery that definitely had. I made sure to include angry Quint, conniving Nick, scheming Addison, sneaky Bree, and possibly drunken but certainly adulterous Portia. Also the fact that Oliver was onto us.

Finn sighed. "Okay. Keep everybody in their cabins until dawn's early light. I'll be there as soon as I get finished with this situation in Florida."

"You heard about the Buckhead Burglar too?"

She didn't speak for a second. "So much for filling you in on that. Can you two hold down the fort until tomorrow morning?"

"Of course."

"You've got Jonathon. Sybil and Mickey too. That makes five of y'all on the team, plus the regular resort staff. That's enough to keep all hell from breaking loose, correct?"

"I surely hope so."

"Good. I'll see you around nine AM. Give the cops my contact information. Prepare for this to blow up any second, but work it until it does. Shut the place down when it's done and get everybody back to the city." She muttered a curse. "Godforsaken wilderness."

Trey and Finn had their own confab before Finn hung up, and then he pulled me into his "suite" at the station. A place for on-call security to grab a breather or even a quick nap, it was a spare room with a twin bed and tiny bathroom, rough-hewn and utilitarian. A nondescript closet door and one heavily curtained window and four wood-paneled walls. That was it.

"Go back to your cabin," he said. "Lock the doors. I'll check in once I've dealt with the authorities."

"I'd rather stay here."

He shook his head. "The situation has become complicated beyond its original parameters. I never expected—"

"For things to get this crazy, yes, I know. How many times have I said that same thing to you? And how many times have you still shown up for me?"

He put his hands on his hips and looked at me, hard. I let him look, let him get a good eyeful of what I was about to say.

"The answer is, every single time. And so here I am. Ms. Reciprocation." I smiled at him. "You asked me to help. Let me help."

He hesitated for barely a second before handing me a radio and one of the earpieces. "Channel six is regular communication. Channel four emergencies. Keep the barn secure until the authorities arrive. As soon as they do, I'll send an officer your way. Jonathon and I will handle the situation here. Do you have your cell phone?"

I held it up. "Also my weapon. Just in case."

He nodded. "Good. Run the app if you decide I need to be aware of whatever is happening. I'll meet you back here as soon as the police have cleared the scene."

"Yes, sir. Anything else?"

The corner of his mouth twitched in a weary, almost-smile. "No, ma'am. Just be careful. Please."

Chapter Forty-eight

The next few hours passed in a blur. I met the officer at the barn and walked her through the attempted arson. I pointed out the cigarettes first, and then the candle and acetone set-up. She left me waiting outside for an hour while she investigated. Afterward, she quizzed me a second time to see if my story stuck together, and when it did, she strung up police tape around the barn and sent me back to the check-in station.

Trey had a similar report. He looked exhausted, his last reserves burned clean. He insisted on updating his information anyway, and had his timeline spread on top of an empty desk in the corner of the video monitoring room.

"How did Quint react to his car being stolen?" I said.

Trey pulled the rubber band off a stack of index cards. "Not well. He threatened to sue."

"Big surprise. What about Portia?"

"She's back in her cabin. Their physician determined that she was not overdosed."

"So she was drunk."

"I don't know. She refused to have her BAC tested and locked herself in her room."

"Entirely unsurprising."

"Entirely." Trey examined his layout, tapped his pencil against the tabletop. "While I was there, however, I took the opportunity to...inspect their quarters."

"You snooped."

"Inspected." He circled a word on one of the cards, then placed it on the table. "The supplement she uses in her shakes does have kava."

Portia's name now had a red asterisk beside it. Trey had moved her to the "suspect" category along with Quint and Addison.

"You think she poisoned Nick?"

"Overdosed. And I don't know. I merely found the means by which she could have."

"And she handed me motive on a silver platter. Opportunity?"

Trey pointed to a section of his timeline. "According to the showrunner's notes, she was in the makeup trailer right before we arrived on Monday."

"I figured as much. Of course, so was Addison. And Quint. Nick's trailer was Grand Central Station that afternoon."

Trey nodded. The security cabin was quiet this time of night, silent except for the hum of electronics. No footsteps, no cars, no conversation. Softly lit and spare, it felt like an outpost on the very edge of civilization.

"What about tonight? Do they suspect her of arson?"

"Attempted arson. And I don't know."

"Whoever did it knew there were no cameras out there. And they knew enough about Nick to frame him for the deed. They left his cigarettes on the ground. Used acetone as an accelerant, just like he keeps in his make-up kit." I sat on the edge of the desk and pointed to a different card. "My money's on Oliver. Why else would he be making a break for it at midnight?"

"I agree that his behavior is suspicious. But I can't think of a motive."

"Do the cops have any ideas?"

Trey put his hand to the back of his neck, rubbed out a knot. "If they do, they are withholding them from me. There's a BOLO out for him regardless." He kept his tone mild. "Quint, however, suggested that you and I might be responsible."

I stared at him. "You and me? Seriously?"

"Yes. He suggested we're working together to sabotage… something. He wasn't very clear about that, only that everyone was working against him—"

"—and he was going to sue, right." I shook my head. "Quint is suing us, and Nick's been playing us. The Talbot brothers have been one complication after another."

Trey didn't contradict me. He continued placing his index cards on the desk in rows and columns, a portable version of the wall of his apartment. Means, motives, and opportunities, suspects and victims, like a crime and punishment bingo card. Trey stared at the data as if some answer might bubble up. I looked over his shoulder, following the various lines and annotations…

And something did bubble up.

Something I had never considered.

I pointed to Nick's suspect card. "You were there when he said Addison was at home the night of the shooting. Remember? During our second visit to the makeup trailer?"

"Yes? And?"

"You didn't catch it."

"Catch what?"

"The lie." I got a light untethered feeling in my chest. "He lied to your face and you didn't catch it." And then I remembered. "I lied too."

His forehead wrinkled. "You did?"

"Yes, earlier, when I made the joke about my shocking past. You didn't catch it. It's been happening a lot."

"It has?"

"Yes! I just thought you were deciding not to call me on it. I mean, nothing serious, just jokes really, but still…"

Now he was really confused. "What? When? I—"

"Look at me." I blanked my expression, which never worked, not on Trey. "I have seven dollars in my wallet. True or false?"

He watched my mouth the entire time I spoke. Lies lay heavy on the mouth, I'd discovered. I could make my eyes sparkle as needed, my mannerisms as smoothly deceptive as required, but my mouth always gave me away.

He blinked at me. "Say it again."

I did. He shook his head, but didn't say anything.

I got lightheaded. "My wallet is empty, Trey. Utterly empty."

"Oh." He frowned, nodded slowly. "Okay."

"Okay? I just told you—"

"I know what you told me." He got to his feet, but didn't start pacing. He simply stood there, eyes cast to the side, arms folded. Seemingly calm, except that his respiration was becoming shallow. "I've always told you I wasn't infallible."

"This is different. You've been off your game with everyone."

"It's not a game. It's not on or off. It's…not that."

"And not just me. Finn—"

"I've never been able to read Finn."

"No, but we assumed she was an aberration. What if she's not? What if you haven't been able to read any of them?"

He still wouldn't look at me. "I don't know."

"We're here because you looked Nick Talbot in the eye and said he wasn't a murderer."

"He's not."

"You don't know that!"

I saw the first flare of panic in his eyes. He smothered it as I watched, replaced it with the cold impenetrable withdrawal. I could feel the invisible wall coming up between us, and when I reached for his hand, he snatched away as my fingers brushed his wrist.

He ran both hands through his hair, let them rest on the back of his neck. "I'm very tired. I can't think clearly. I need to get some rest and then we'll reevaluate."

"Trey—"

"Not now. I can't. I need to rest. Can you take the cameras until Jonathon returns?" He gestured toward the bank of video monitors. "Two hours. I only need two hours."

He needed more, much more, but he'd have what I could get him.

"Of course," I said.

• • ● • •

Trey closed the door behind himself, and I sat down at the array. Jonathon had brewed up coffee—strong and sweet, his secret to the night shift, he said—and I poured a cup. Wished I'd had whiskey to put in it. Wished I still had Nick's half-smoked cigarette.

I could see his cabin on one of the screens, guarded now by the woman who'd pretended to be the bartender. No more pretense from her, although everybody else was still spinning webs of deceit. We thought we'd been cleaning house of such, but we hadn't. That had been a pretense too.

I leaned back in the chair. Our entire justification for taking the case—that Nick was telling the truth when he said that he hadn't killed his wife—could be wrong. We'd been trying to keep a murderer out, and chances were good that a murderer was penned up with us. All the people we'd cleared of this misdeed or that—Nick, Addison, Portia, Quint—were suddenly suspicious again.

The resort lay quiet and still around us. A deer picked its way along the perimeter, a big eight-point buck. It wasn't yet the rutting season, so it was calm, interested in feeding not fighting. The wrangler had found the other animals and corralled them for the night, far away from the reeking barn.

Eventually Jonathon returned and took over the monitoring duties. I stepped into the night and called my brother. "I know it's two a.m., but it's kind of an emergency," I said.

"What's happened?"

I told him. Clouds had moved in, and now the moon shone behind a gauzy veil. Eric listened while I explained.

"Are you sure?" he finally said. "He really can't tell?"

"I'm sure."

Eric's voice vibrated with excitement. "This is amazing, exactly what I hypothesized!" I could hear him rummaging through paperwork. "The research has been clear, that this particular ability is linked to verbal expression, or the lack thereof, to be exact. Aphasia. Which Trey had, right after the accident. But since then, he's recovered much of his verbal ability. I know you've noticed."

I had. Over the year and a half that I'd known him, he'd grown quicker with words, more expansive in his vocabulary. He still hadn't lost the clipped cadence or the monotone delivery. But his sentences were more fluid now, often laced with a dry sense of humor, deft and self-aware.

"But what does that have to do with whether or not he can detect lies?"

"Nobody knows. Researchers have noticed the correlation, but that's as far as science has gotten." He paused. "I know this puts you in a challenging situation now—"

"No kidding."

"—but it's a good thing, really. It's healing. It's progress. And he's worked hard for it."

"Yes, but—"

"I know, I know. He's gotten used to being able to judge people pretty instantly. He's going to have to use his instincts now, just like the rest of us. But it means he's got a filter now. It means he's capable of interacting with people and environments, even stimuli-rich ones, without shutting down." Another pause. "You're responsible for that, you know."

"Me?"

"Yes. He's adapting to being with you. You totally over-whelmed him at first, but he persevered. Because you matter." A hesitation. "Because he loves you."

I remembered everything at once. Trey tending my wounds. Trey with the list of why he was with me. Trey handing me the keys to the Ferrari even though his heart had been thrashing around in terror.

My voice cracked. "Why me?"

"I could theorize—neurological completion, say, or the attraction of complementary personalities. Gabriella says it was destiny, that you two were meant for each other." Eric's voice was soft. "Does it matter?"

I tried to speak and couldn't. Trey had taken a massive blow, but was still trying, so hard, to do right by truth and justice. He believed in those things. And in me.

"You okay, sis?"

I wiped a tear from my eye. "Yeah."

"I know it sounds rough, but he can do this. He'll have to rely on his judgment now."

"But he doesn't have any! That's why he won't wear his gun, because he doesn't have the judgment to—"

"But that *is* judgment, don't you see? He trusts his own instincts. That is *huge* progress, Tai, huge."

It was. I knew it was. But all this progress was coming at a damned inconvenient time. I tilted my head back and stared at the shifting cloud-hazed sky.

"I'd better get back inside," I said. "Thanks for talking to me."

"Don't mention it. Just…can you get him back in my office when you're done with whatever it is you're doing? I'm dying to arrange some further testing."

I assured him I would try and hung up. Then I squared my shoulders. We had a mission. And we were going to finish it come hell or high water. I eased myself into Trey's room and lay down next to him on the narrow cot. He shifted to accommodate me, not waking, and I stretched out against his back, my face pressed into the nape of his neck. He was in the valley of deep sleep, his breathing steady and regular.

I closed my eyes and tried to join him there.

Chapter Forty-nine

I woke to an empty bed. This was no surprise, but it took me a second to get my bearings in the dusky gray light. Trey had left me a note— checking the perimeter, it said, back at eight. I pulled on my shoes, ran my fingers through my hair. I needed a bath, clean clothes, a toothbrush. I tried to lick my lips and my tongue stuck to the roof of my mouth. Definitely a toothbrush.

Jonathon still sat at the video monitors. He looked up when he heard me. "Good morning, ma'am. Would you like some more coffee?"

"That would be a lifesaver. Thank you."

I poured myself a giant cup, letting the first hot swallow burn my mouth. Jonathon looked as on point and professional as when I'd last seen him, his posture military straight, dark eyes clear and observant.

"Had any visitors?" I said.

"No, ma'am. Once the detectives left, it's been quiet."

"The main resort too?"

"Yes, ma'am."

The grounds looked calm on the monitors. The gardeners raked straw in the front flower beds, and a pair of runners loped along the nature trail. Otherwise few guests stirred, none at our end of the resort. Rolling mists and a low gray sky warned of rains to come.

"If Mr. Seaver gets back before I do, tell him I went to get a shower."

Jonathon nodded, his eyes glued once again to the monitors. "Yes, ma'am. Will do, ma'am."

I closed the door behind myself, feeling the first wet drops against my forehead. The walk was short, a hop and skip from the check-in station, and I'd pulled out my phone to punch in the security code when I heard a leafy rustle. A quick scan of the shrubbery revealed a figure hunched beneath a crepe myrtle.

I peered closer. "Oliver?"

Oliver held both hands in front of him. "Please don't scream! I won't hurt you! You gotta help me!"

He was still in his natty suit, but it was torn and dirty, his face a welter of scratches and mosquito bites. His voice was graveled, quavery, barely above a whisper.

I stepped closer. "What in the hell are you doing?"

"We need to talk."

"So talk."

"Not here. Inside."

I looked up at the security camera in the corner. Approximately twenty seconds had passed since I'd stopped. Either Jonathon or Trey could already be on the way. Or not. Depending. I didn't have my app turned on, so my phone wasn't recording the audio, which meant that Trey couldn't hear our conversation. But his personal video feed was functioning, and if he looked at his phone and saw Oliver on camera, if he thought I was being threatened...

I made my voice stern but calm. "I want you to listen to me very carefully, Oliver. You know who Trey is, so you know his background. You know he can blow your medulla oblongata out the back of your skull from half a mile away. You won't even draw a last breath, you'll just drop like a puppet with the strings cut."

Oliver was breathing heavy, his hair matted on his forehead. "I know."

"So tell me the truth, for your own good. You don't have a weapon, do you?"

He choked on a sob. "No."

I punched in the security code, and the light blinked clear, simultaneously dismantling the alarms and turning on the interior audio and video systems. I also turned on the recording app. If Trey had his earpiece in, he would hear everything Oliver and I were saying.

I held the door open. "Get in."

Oliver scurried inside, eyes skittering all around. As he passed me, he left an odoriferous wake of stale sweat and old cigarettes. He made straight for the armchair in the corner and sank into it, pulled a pack of menthols from his pocket.

"Where have you been?" I said.

"In the woods. Hiding." He lit up with trembling hands, the cigarette shaking as he held it to his mouth. "I want immunity. I want to go into Witness Protection."

"Why?"

"I'm not talking until I get into the program. Trey has the connections to make it happen, I know he does."

I didn't tell him he was wrong, that Trey didn't have the power to get anybody into anything. He did have connections, though, and if what Oliver had to say was important enough, he could work them. Regardless, I needed to keep Oliver talking, which he only seemed inclined to do if he had protection.

I sat opposite him. "I'll do what I can. If you tell me what's going on."

He glared at me, his bravado coming back. I was about to explain things more clearly for him when the shadow appeared on the patio, cool and smooth and noiseless. I had a moment of panic, but then the shadow knocked. Oliver jumped, and I exhaled in relief.

"That's Trey," I said. "And if he's knocking, he's coming in peace. So you sit very still while I let him in, and we'll see what he has to say."

$$\bullet \ \bullet \ \bullet \ \bullet \ \bullet$$

Trey was remarkably calm, considering. He'd given up on the cheap jacket and had his white shirt unbuttoned at the throat, no tie. Sleep had restored his cognitive capacity, and even if his temper remained prickly, he was willing to hear Oliver out. I knew this was only because every word of the conversation was being recorded, but still.

He put his back to the wall and faced Oliver. "What happened last night?"

Oliver shook his head. "I'm not talking until I get WITSEC."

Trey's jaw tightened. "I told you, I cannot—"

"Then you get nothing. And the bad guys keep on being bad."

"Mr. James—"

"Mr. Seaver. I know my rights. WITSEC or nothing." He smiled behind the wreath of smoke. "Tick tock."

Trey started to reply, but I held up my hand. He inclined his head, shifting the lead my way.

I smiled at Oliver. "In that case, it's nothing. You know why? Because we don't need you or your testimony. We already know everything we need to know, and we learned it from the Buckhead Burglar himself, who knew more about this mess than anyone imagined, and who is now in the custody of the Atlanta Police Department. You can check yourself, if you wish. But while you waste your time verifying things, the bad guys are, as you explained, out there cooking up badness. And while you do have some leverage, it's got an expiration date." I smiled wider. "So tick tock yourself, Oliver."

Out of the corner of my eye, I saw Trey fold his arms. He said not one word, knowing better than most how to work a silence.

Oliver closed his eyes and sighed. "The men who stole the cars work for the men who run the underground poker game we go to."

"We?"

"Quint and me." He sucked at the cigarette. "Quint's deep in the red, and not for the first time. Last year, he decided to cook the Talbot Creative books to relieve some of the heat. A series of fake vendors, one of the older tricks in the book. I spotted the ruse instantly."

"And you blackmailed him?"

He looked stunned. "What? No! I never blackmailed anybody! I did, however, let him bribe me to keep quiet. And I taught him how to work the numbers with more finesse."

"What about your own debts?"

"I played for fun, cut my losses. Quint? He chased it like heroin, right down the rabbit hole. Atlantic City, Reno, Vegas. Atlanta hit him hardest. Six figures."

This was a common occurrence, and not just in Atlanta. Big city rollers came down South thinking the tables were run by hayseeds. They figured it would be easy pickings, maybe a little low-rent, but profitable. They usually got their asses handed to them.

Oliver continued. "So Quint made a deal. He offered the gamerunners corporate shares in *Moonshine* as collateral."

"He can do that?"

"He's an executive producer. He can do whatever he wants. With the proper tools, of course." Oliver waved the cigarette. "Have you ever seen a studio contract? It's a maze, a tangle of legalese and loopholes. You can make money appear and disappear at will, depending on how you define your terms. Back end deals. Gross versus net. Shares versus stock."

"Can you prove this?"

"Of course. You met them at the party. The three men at Quint's elbow all night. Well, until the unfortunate surprise nuptials cut the event short."

I remembered them from the photo shoot too. Three men, well-groomed. Important investors, Bree had said, especially interested in Portia. Especially keen on talking to Quint.

"Racketeers take movie studio shares as collateral?"

"They'll take anything of value, hence the vanishing of Quint's Jaguar. And my own vehicle, the sons of bitches." The cigarette shook between his fingers. "But the shares are legit, a very solid investment. They know that. They also know that without Portia, the series will tank. So they want guarantees that she's staying."

"Which Quint can't provide."

"Of course he can. Portia's still under contract, so if she ever wants to work in Hollywood again, she's not going anywhere unless Quint lets her go. Which he is most decidedly not doing."

"Is that why he ramped up the script schedule? To assure his investors that Mad Luna Malone remained a part of the series?"

"Yes." Oliver put the cigarette to his lips and spoke around it. "Quint's tapped out. He's emptied his own savings, emptied the company. Emptied Nicky's accounts too. It's quicksand, and as soon as Addison gets access—which will be any day, now that they're married—the whole shebang comes crashing down." Oliver shook his head. "Quint's destroyed Talbot Creative, and he knows it. All the embezzlement, all the laundering—"

"That you helped him do."

"I never said I was innocent. But these people coming after us are stone cold killers. They murdered Jessica, then they tried to kill Nicky, and—"

I waved a hand at him. "Wait wait wait…what did you just say?"

Chapter Fifty

Oliver let the smoke trickle out the corner of his mouth. "You heard me. They killed Jessica. What, you think this is the first time Quint's gone into arrears? Please."

Trey stared. He was calmer than I'd expected, but I could see the turmoil in his face, sharpened by that irresistible need to know, to understand, and to punish. He was close, and he could taste it.

He stepped forward. "Why Jessica? She was Nick's wife, not Quint's."

Oliver stubbed out his first cigarette in a wine glass, pulled the crumpled pack from his pocket. "They were having an affair. Quint and Jessica."

It took me a second to get my bearings after that revelation. There had been rumors of affairs, but not with Quint.

Oliver smiled wryly. "Don't look surprised. Jessica got around, everybody knows that. And Quint hates Portia. Everybody knows that too. He can't divorce her, though, or she'll find out how much he's ransacked their savings. And she can't divorce him because that pre-nup she signed puts her on the streets wearing a paper bag, so they're stuck with each other. Some days I think the only reason they get up in the morning is so they can hate each other even more." He fished another cigarette from the pack with trembling fingers. "But killing Jessica got Quint's attention, let me tell you. He straightened up and flew right after that. For a while."

Outside I heard the lawnmower approaching. Oliver jerked, almost dropping his cigarette. He was on edge. So was Trey. But Trey was handling the interview, edging it closer to interrogation with every question out of his mouth. The mystery of who killed Jessica Talbot was being revealed right in front of him, piece by dirty piece. The emotional wallop must have been seismic.

"Did Nick know about the affair?" he said.

"No. I doubt he would have cared regardless. He was obsessed with Addison, still is. But if he knew *why* Jessica was killed…I don't know what he would do. I wasn't joking about his mental instability." Oliver fired up his lighter, cupped his hands around the fresh cigarette. "Quint didn't want Nicky to know that the same people who killed Jessica were also responsible for the bullet that almost killed him."

Trey glared. "That's why Quint has refused to go the authorities."

"The police would have discovered everything. Quint decided the best place for Nicky was the institution. No one could get him there."

I felt a flare of anger, and the words spilled out before I could stop them. "The missing cameras. Quint took them, not the *Buckwild* people. He needed to discredit Nick's story, but those cameras proved that there really was a shot."

Oliver stared at the burning tip of the cigarette. "Yes. So he hauled them to my place and bashed them to rubble with a baseball bat. Then he left the mess for me to clean up, the detestable bastard."

"Is that what you and Quint were arguing about that night? At the Talbot house?"

"That was one thing. I was also very unhappy about Nick's accident." He looked down at his hands. "Quint used one of Portia's herbal concoctions to drug Nicky. I'd told him this was a terrible idea, but—"

"He tried to kill his own brother?"

"Kill him?" Oliver looked at me in horror. "Of course not! He didn't know Nicky would be driving that night. Addison always drove. No, he only wanted Nicky back in the institution, where he'd be safe."

"He let his own brother think he was crazy—"

"Nicky is crazy! He needs to be institutionalized!"

"Which would conveniently allow Quint to retain control of his brother's assets."

Oliver shook his head. "There aren't any assets, not anymore. But it *would* prevent anyone from discovering that unfortunate fact. All we had to do was postpone the conservatorship transfer and keep Portia through next season, and *Moonshine* would have filled the coffers and nobody would have been the wiser." His eyes hardened. "Can we move to the part where I get protection now?"

I ignored his question. "What about the barn? Another scheme to make Nick look crazy?"

Oliver didn't deny it. "Yes."

"You left his cigarette butts to implicate him."

"Quint's idea. The acetone too. I was supposed to say that I saw Nicky hanging around there, but..." He closed his eyes. "I'd decided I'd had enough. I was leaving this fiasco and heading back to the city and then...hell, who knows what. I'm not constitutionally suited to go on the lam. But then those criminals came rolling up, and I had to shelter in the goddamn woods."

"You left the barn door open. Why?"

"So the animals could escape. Why else?" He gave a rueful smile. "Remember that when there comes a recitation of my crimes and sins. I may have burned down a barn, but I couldn't incinerate an innocent pony."

I didn't tell him his attempt had failed. Trey didn't either. Instead, he motioned for me to follow him into the bathroom out of Oliver's earshot. I did, positioning myself so that I could keep an eye on Oliver. He had resigned himself to our custody, it seemed. He sat on the edge of the armchair, legs crossed, staring out a window that had all the blinds drawn.

Trey got Jonathon on the radio. "Get Quint and Portia and put them in the check-in station. Keep them separate and do not let them leave until the authorities arrive. There have been developments. Restrain them if you must. Also, there is a group of men, three investors—"

"They're gone, sir. They left last night, right before the altercation in the parking lot."

Trey closed his eyes and rubbed his temple. "Unsurprising. How many guests remain?"

"Very few, sir."

"Good. Lock the valet podium in the office. If anyone else wants to leave, hand deliver the keys and check IDs. But first, find Quint and Portia. They are your priority, and may be targets themselves, so adjust the protocol accordingly."

Jonathon replied in the affirmative and signed off. Trey stood still, brow furrowed. Even if he didn't have his cranial lie detector, he had an instinct for truth. And Oliver's story was adding up in some places, but jarring in others.

"You're thinking the same thing I'm thinking," I said. "That bullet wasn't meant for Nick, it was meant for Quint. And Quint knows it."

"It's a valid theory. The shot was fired as Nick approached the pool. He was in darkness until that moment, but the shooter didn't wait for clear ID because there wasn't supposed to be anyone else at the house."

"Because the shooter knew Quint was there, but not Nick."

"Correct. In the shadows, they looked alike."

"Which explains why there wasn't a second shot. Once the shooter knew it wasn't Quint, he backed off." I shook my head. "That sick son of a bitch. First, he convinces Nick he's in danger. Then he overdoses him. Then he plans to blame him for arson. All of it so that Nick will get put back in the institution and Quint can keep control of his finances, not that there are any. He's a twisted—"

"Yes, he is. But something is not making sense."

"What?"

"Underground poker gamerunners don't murder, not even those connected to organized crime. Garrity worked major crimes for ten years, and saw only one assault due to unpaid debt. There are better ways to coerce people into paying."

"But you saw the video in the valet lot. Those car thieves came out guns blazing."

"And hitting no one, not even Oliver, who did not present a difficult target. They weren't interested in hurting people. They were interested in stealing cars, nothing more."

I looked back at Oliver. Still nervous, chewing his lip now, his foot jostling as he stared at the window with the blinds drawn. He'd been a sitting duck and had managed against all odds, through zero skill on his part, to still be alive. He'd bought Quint's story about the homicidal loan sharks, believed it with his whole devious heart. But the pieces weren't adding up. I started to go back into the room, but Trey put his hand on my elbow.

"No. We've asked enough questions for now. We have to wait for the authorities. Everything he says to us is hearsay and not admissible in court. He needs to be Mirandized and properly processed."

I cursed under my breath, but I knew Trey was right. Oliver was a valuable witness, and considering what had gone down at the previous grand jury trial, every bit of evidence and testimony needed to be as pristine as possible. But damn did I ache to interrogate him.

Trey's radio crackled. It was the valet, the real valet, not one of the covert operatives. He was breathing hard, practically panting. "Quint Talbot is gone. His wife too."

Trey pushed past me into the bedroom. "They weren't in the cabin?"

"Jonathon went to get them, but it was too late, and then they showed up here five minutes ago and stole a car and took off. He's sending me your way right now. He said to tell you it's a possible hostage situation, that he needs you back up front."

Trey yanked open the front door. "Which way did they go?"

"Toward the golf course."

Beyond the golf course was the main road—they were making a run for it. The valet hit the porch at a dead run, radio clutched in hand. He was young, barely out of his teens, wholly out of his element.

His eyes were wide. "Jonathon said I'm supposed to watch Mr. James while you handle the station. He said—"

"Were both of them in the car?"

"Yes, sir."

"Who was driving?"

"I don't know." He was getting his breath back, but his nerves remained shot. "Jonathon's alerted the authorities. They've scrambled State Patrol on I-75." And then the valet looked at me. "I'm sorry, ma'am, but…it was your Ferrari they took."

Trey's eyes flashed fire. "*What?*"

Chapter Fifty-one

The valet's eyes widened. "Their Jaguar was stolen, sir. So they took Ms. Randolph's car."

Trey reached for keys in a pocket that wasn't there because his jacket wasn't there. He took a deep breath and let it out. The valet took a step back, but he didn't drop his eyes.

"All the other keys were locked up, sir. But you left your jacket on the chair when you went to intercept Mr. James, and they tried to get into the key podium, but couldn't, and then they must have seen your jacket on the chair and—"

"Yes, I understand." Trey's expression was unnaturally calm. "Thank you."

The valet sent a look my way. No dummy, this guy. He'd figured out we were sitting on a powder keg, and not just because Quint and Portia were making like the Adairsville version of Bonnie and Clyde. Trey was dealing with a mess of his own making. He'd come running to my cabin in knight-in-shining-armor mode. Of course he'd left the jacket behind. He hated the jacket. Of course he had the keys to the Ferrari in his pocket. That was where he always kept them.

And now he was...I wasn't sure.

I examined his features. He turned away and addressed the valet.

"Is the resort on lockdown?"

"Yes, sir."

"Good. Stay here with Mr. James, locks and alarms engaged. Do not answer the door under any circumstance until I have called in the all-clear, understood?"

"Yes, sir, but—"

Trey took off at a run for the check-in station. I cursed and took off after him. To my astonishment, it felt good to be running. I could feel the stress hormones feeding exertion instead of anxiety, my heart pumping fresh blood, my lungs pumping fresh air. I picked up the pace, surprised at how easily my body moved into the next gear. I felt animal. Alive. Ready for anything.

I hit the station door. He'd left it wide open, which meant he knew I was on his heels.

"Trey?"

"In here."

I followed his voice. He stood at the bank of security monitors, scanning them. He handed me his phone without taking his eyes off the monitors.

"The Ferrari is still on the property. I activated the tracking signal."

The red dot that was the Ferrari moved across the screen very slowly and erratically, two states I never associated with it.

"They're definitely headed for the golf course," I said.

"Yes, but they can't get off the property that way. Two creeks and the lake border that end of the course. Their only exit point is through here."

He pointed to the map of the resort. The ruins. They looked impenetrable, but beyond them lay the barn and the stables. A cut between those would take Quint and Portia through a flimsy picket fence and onto the road leading back to the interstate. And once they hit the interstate, they would vanish like lightning.

"So let's grab the utility cart," I said. "It's sturdy and fast and—"

"Not yet. I need to know if we're dealing with two suspects, or a suspect and a hostage."

He had a point. Those were very different scenarios.

"Which do you think it is?"

He shook his head, agitated. "The answer's right there. I've seen the answer. But I haven't been able to put it together."

I knew what he was feeling. Somewhere in the maze of motive and machinations, media and money, there was the thread of a solution. Unfortunately, the security camera footage was grainy and unhelpful. It showed Portia and Quint approaching the Ferrari, its lights flashing as it unlocked for them. Trey's jaw clenched. I understood. It was like watching a faithful dog lick the hand of an enemy.

He hit the freeze frame, pointed. "Quint has a gun."

I peered at the image. Definitely a gun, most likely the .357 Trey had spotted in the golf clubs. But once the car was unlocked, neither he nor Portia hesitated. Quint threw himself in the driver's seat and Portia climbed in the other side...exactly unlike a hostage. I noticed something else—she had her new carry bag with her, the one I'd picked out.

"Two suspects," I said. "Portia probably has a gun in that bag, probably a LeMat."

"Does she know how to shoot one?"

"I am sure she does. She pretended otherwise in my shop, but that was an act. Which I fell for, because the next day I sent black powder and caps and—what are you doing?"

Trey abandoned the array for the closet in the corner of his suite. I hadn't noticed it before, but now I saw the keypad and the industrial lock, and I knew that nondescript closet for what it was—a weapons locker. He punched in the code and the door unlocked with a beep. He reached inside and snatched up two handguns, plus two mags filled with red and black projectiles, each one the size of a marble.

"Paintballs?"

He shook his head. "PAVA tens. Capsaicin powder. Like we used in the simulation, only not inert."

Damn straight capsaicin wasn't inert. A hit with one of those would guarantee hours of tears and mucus and hellfire. And Trey was loading up two handguns and a carbine rifle and shoving back-up mags in his pocket.

"Same specs as in the training," he said. "Pneumatic. Semi-auto. Target accurate to sixty feet, area saturation up to one hundred and fifty, so don't use it in an enclosed space."

He snapped the magazine on the side of the rifle. The thing was ninja black and had laser sights. It looked as deadly as an AK-47, which was deterrent in itself.

He handed me one of the handguns. "Do you have your .38?"

"Yes."

"Good."

He started to move past me, and I grabbed his arm. "Don't you think you should have something with some real bullets in it too?"

"No. But even if I did, there's nothing to have here. It's all less-than-lethal."

"But—"

"We don't have time to argue about this."

He shook free and headed for the door. He didn't wait for me, and I didn't give him a chance to. He grabbed the keys to the utility cart and his radio. "Jonathon, do you read?"

"Yes, sir. I'm headed your way. Local PD responding with a ETA of eight minutes, GSP scrambling a roadblock and clear-ing 75."

"Affirmative. I'm in pursuit."

"Sir? Did you say…?"

"Seaver out."

Trey shut the door and jogged toward the cart parked next to a stack of firewood. He threw me the keys and got into the passenger seat. "You drive. I'll track the Ferrari and monitor the radio. You—"

"Trey!"

He stopped talking. "What?"

"Look at me."

He exhaled, looked me straight in the eye. He was bleary-eyed, taut like razor wire, but he was in there. I could see him clearly. And he wasn't hesitating about having me along at all.

I hopped in and cranked up the cart. "Hold on tight."

Chapter Fifty-two

Trey might have had lousy mantracking skills, but even he could follow the Ferrari. It left huge scrapes in the manicured grass, like the rake of giant fingernails. The kick-up of white grit revealed where it had almost gotten stuck in the sand trap. After that, the tracks took a sharp turn to the right and ran parallel to the edge of thickly wooded rough, disappearing in the distance. From the looks of the untrimmed kudzu, there was no way even a four-wheel utility cart was getting through.

Trey waved his hand at me. "Stop!"

I slammed the brakes. "What?"

"Do you hear the engine?"

I listened. The Ferrari was audible from half a mile, but now I heard nothing. No engine, no sirens, no traffic. Only the light hiss of the rain and our own breathing.

Trey checked his phone. "The signal is gone."

"How? I've got a hotspot on my wrist."

"The navigational system has blackout areas up here. This could be one. Regardless, it's not tracking the car any longer." He pointed off to the right, to where the tracks disappeared. "They found a path around, somewhere down there."

"We could follow. Or we could cut through on foot."

Trey got out of the cart. "Through. And then head left toward the ruins."

He started off into the trees. I followed. Camouflaged by the shifting fog and thick foliage, we moved silently, our footsteps dampened by wet pine straw. I had my .38 in one hand, the pepperball-loaded pistol in the other. And my brain kept pummeling me with one thought: *what in the hell are you doing, Tai Randolph?*

I knew what Trey was doing. He was showing up. It was what he did. The call came, and he went, his entire mindset condensed to that one Pavlovian reaction. But why was I out here? And why did it feel as natural as breathing?

We threaded through the tangled green kudzu, briars catching on my jeans. These woods felt ominous, like the forests children were warned to avoid in fairy tales. The dread intensified when I spotted the crumbling walls of the ruins looming rust-gray through the trees.

Trey stopped, held up a hand. I stopped too. I heard voices then, muffled but close. Quint and Portia.

"—but bringing them to the set wasn't enough," she said, "oh no, you had to bring them here too!"

"I didn't have a choice! They wanted—"

"I don't care what they want! They're lowlife scum! And there you were prancing around, kowtowing to them like they were royalty!"

"Listen, just put down the gun—"

"Shut up!"

We were at the edge of the woods, the stone-paved garden path leading to the rear entrance of the ruins, each step slick with wet moss. The rain had grown harder, a steady patter. Trey didn't seem to notice. Every ounce of his attention was directed beyond the brick walls to where Portia and Quint were arguing.

"Let me fix this," Quint pleaded. "I fixed it last time, didn't I?"

"You didn't fix a damn thing. Nicky didn't go to jail, did he?"

"That was Macklin's fault, not mine!"

"No, it's never your fault, is it? Whose fault is it that you started gambling again, you want to explain that one?"

"If you'd just listen—"

"Now we're back where we were four years ago—with me scrambling to clean up your mess."

I got a chill. Up ahead, Trey shot me a questioning look over his shoulder, brow furrowed. I nodded to let him know I'd heard. Yes, Quint had "fixed" things. And I knew what that meant, knew it as surely as the sun was rising. Trey knew it too. I watched him drop his shoulders, face forward again.

"Things are different this time!" Quint's voice was insistent. "Addison can be eliminated. There isn't a jury in the world that would let Nicky go after a second wife kicks the bucket. Everybody thinks he relapsed—hearing gunshots, overdosing himself, trying to set a barn on fire. And then I could retain control of his estate and—"

"What about Oliver?"

"He won't talk—his fingerprints are all over the financials, and he knows it." Quint's voice turned desperate. "Look, I learned my lesson. You want a divorce? Done. You want off the show? Fine. I'll rip up your contract. Just don't do this." His voice softened. "We're a team."

"We *were* a team. Then you started screwing Jessica instead of working her!"

"That *was* working her!"

"No, that was you being you. And I'm tired of you."

"Babe, listen to me, put down the gun and—"

"Get up."

Trey moved forward. I fell in behind. The argument grew more intense—Portia threatening, Quint trying to talk her down—and I knew the protocol humming in Trey's head: save the hostage. He'd do it even if the hostage was someone as despicable as Quint Talbot. It obliterated even his reflexive need to control and protect me. He'd smothered that back at the check-in station, when he'd handed me weapons and keys. And yet there was something predatory about him now—rain soaked, rifle in hand, eyes narrow and focused.

Once we reached the bottom of the steps, we took cover behind the rose arbor. Through the leaves, I could see Quint on his knees, Portia with her LeMat aimed at him. She was panting and dirty and wet, her hair wild about her face, but she held the gun as steadily as Luna did, with the same merciless resolve. I remembered her pretend ineptness in the shop and cursed silently. She'd been planning to take him down even then. I could almost hear her defense: *It wasn't premeditated! I only had the gun because I was doing character research! I never planned to kill anybody!*

A red blotch bloomed on Quint's forehead, a fresh wound, and he had to keep blinking the blood and rain from his eyes. He raised his hands, palms out. "Killing me won't stop them! They'll come for you next!"

She laughed. "No, they won't."

"They will! You think that was Nicky they were gunning for at the house? No. They were there for me! And if I don't—"

"That was me, you fucking dimwit! I'm the one who tried to kill you!"

Quint's response was an incoherent noise of disbelief. Portia laughed again.

"With your own gun too, the Sig Sauer. Poetic justice, I decided, a lovely bit of thematic retrofitting. But killing you with Luna's gun…well, that's almost as beautiful. Now get back on your feet and get back to the car."

Quint was slow on the uptake. "You were the one who shot at me?"

"Yes, babe. I was. And I'm going to do it again, this time point blank."

"But why?"

"Because it is the only way to get out of that goddamned contract!"

Quint seemed flabbergasted. "That wasn't my fault! They wouldn't let me release you!"

"You should have tried harder to convince them." She tightened her hands around the revolver. "Get up. Now!"

"And what are you going to do after you shoot me, run?" Quint's voice grew bitter. "You couldn't stand it. You have to be seen and heard and loved and adored. You couldn't hide if your life depended on it."

"I won't need to run. I'll claim self defense. You already killed once, and you were going to kill again, sadistic fuck that you are."

"Nobody will buy it."

"Oh, they'll buy it. Because I'll wrap it pretty as Christmas morning."

Quint dropped his voice, begging now, but Portia wasn't relenting. Trey pointed to the arched opening to their left, a good spot providing both cover and concealment. I nodded, and he held up three fingers, dropped to two, then one. He crossed the grass soundlessly, and I followed as he moved left of the arch. I took position on the opposite side, peered through the cracks in the brickwork at the drama playing itself out within.

Portia shook her hair from her face. She was soaking wet, her pants slathered in mud. "Get up."

Quint's reply was garbled. Portia cursed, her chest heaving. She obviously didn't want to shoot him in the ruins. She had a different scenario playing out, one that involved him back at the Ferrari, but he wasn't budging. And she was recalculating.

I glanced at Trey, who caught the question in my eyes. He nodded, positioned his weapon at low ready. I stuck the pepperball gun in the back of my jeans, wrapped both hands around the .38. I waited for the nervousness to spike, for my hands to start shaking. But my grip remained steady, and not a single shadow darkened my vision.

Trey's voice cut through the damp air like a whipsaw. "Put the gun down, Ms. Ray!"

Chapter Fifty-three

Portia raised her voice. "Is that you, Trey? Behind the wall there? Tai too, I suspect." She exhaled theatrically. "I was wondering when you two would show up."

"The police are on the way, Ms. Ray. Put down your weapon."

"Oh, I don't think so. I still have to shoot my maggot of a husband."

"You don't have to—"

"Hurt him?" She spat blood and barked a laugh. "No. I don't *have* to. But I want to."

Quint's voice was hoarse. "She tried to kill me! She admitted it! She pretended to be drunk last night and let everybody see her making out with the prop guy! She wants it to look like I had reason to hurt her! She's been planning this—"

"Shut up, Quint." Portia's voice remained mild even as she got louder, an actor's trick. "You there, Trey? You listening? Because I'm about to make your day."

"Ms. Ray—"

"Quint killed Jessica."

Quint sputtered. "I did not!"

"And he tried to blame Nicky for it. Because with Jessica dead and Nicky locked up somewhere—jail, institution, it didn't matter where—my darling husband would control his entire estate."

"She's lying!"

"And it worked. For a while. He did get control of Nicky's money. But it's all gone. And I'm through covering for him now."

"Shut up, Patsy! It was all your idea!"

Her voice went shrill. "Don't call me Patsy!"

Quint had moved from desperation to fury—he'd take Portia down even if he went down with her. Trey absorbed the information, but he already knew the truth. Not Macklin. Not Nick. Not nameless syndicate thugs. Quint. He flexed his fingers around the handle of his weapon.

Portia raised her voice. "Did you not hear me, Trey? Quint's the killer you've been looking for all these years, and I have him on the ground in front of me with a gun at his forehead. But he has lawyers, a whole team of them. They'll get him off on some technicality. Some other cop will make a tiny mistake, and he'll walk free. You know how that goes."

Trey's expression wasn't calm anymore. His eyes were narrowed, his jaw clenched. I chanced a quick look through the bricks. Quint was on his knees, Portia in front of him, the antique revolver aimed at his forehead. I couldn't tell which barrel she had primed and ready to go, but it didn't matter—Quint wouldn't walk away from either.

Portia was on a roll. "You're not a cop anymore, Trey. You don't have to save the day. You can walk away, and we can all wash our hands of this lying, thieving, murdering—"

"Stop talking," Trey said.

"I'll claim self defense. You saw the video. He had a gun. He was desperate, crazy with jealousy. His scheme falling apart around him. I was lucky to get away, lucky to survive." Her voice was gentle, cajoling, a siren's song. "Remember the day Jessica died? Remember how it felt to watch her mother sobbing in the courtroom?"

"I said, stop talking!"

Trey's breathing had gone shallow. He tilted his head back against the bricks, and I knew the inside of his skull was a neurochemical traffic jam, vengeance and justice and rules seething and colliding. And I understood, I really did. I remembered his crime scene sketches, remembered my own dark nights, every time I'd ever felt helpless or hopeless or betrayed...

I readjusted my grip on the .38. Unlike the pepperballs, it could execute. Neatly and precisely.

"Trey?" I whispered.

He shook his head. "I don't know what to do."

"Yes, you do."

"No. It's all…and I can't think…I can't…"

"Yes, you can. Look at me."

He turned his face in my direction, and he let me see all the way in, to the deep well of anger. Grief and pain burned there too, helpless before the wild howling unfairness of it all. Yes, he wanted Quint dead. He wanted to do it himself, but letting Portia take the shot would be satisfying enough. Quint would be dead either way. She was right—he was not a cop anymore. He had no rulebook now, no guiding protocol. He was on his own.

Except that he wasn't.

"We came out here to stop this," I said.

"I know."

"So let's stop it. The right way. You and me. Okay?"

He didn't reply. But he did take a deep breath in, let it trickle halfway out. He peered through the brickwork for a final assessment of the situation. Then he pulled his rifle into ready position, muzzle down, finger alongside the barrel. I did the same. The adrenaline narrowed my vision and dampened the ambient noise, but I wasn't afraid. There was only the moment, simple and clean. Only the response.

I heard a familiar sound in the distance. Sirens. Portia heard too, and her arms straightened and locked as she extended the gun.

And that was all it took.

Trey whirled around the corner and fired three rounds, then flattened himself against the wall again. Portia screamed. Quint bellowed. I heard the sounds of scuffling as a shot rang out, then the clatter of the LeMat hitting the bricks.

Trey moved into the open archway. I trained my sights on the tangled couple rolling around on the grass, coughing and gagging as the pepper overwhelmed them. Trey covered his mouth with his sleeve and ran toward them, just close enough to kick the gun in my direction. I scooped it up fast, the sting of the capsaicin making my eyes water even from a distance. The wail of sirens intensified, and I spotted the strobe of blue lights as three cruisers ripped across the lawn and slid to a stop.

Trey still had the rifle out. He had it aimed straight at Portia, on her knees, moaning and choking. Quint hunkered behind her, retching violently.

"Where's my Ferrari?" he said.

Portia told him.

And then he emptied the entire magazine into them.

Chapter Fifty-four

The wrecker arrived right before noon. I stood next to Trey as it rumbled down the grassy lane. I left him just long enough to get an update from Finn, who'd arrived on the premises with a flurry of paperwork. Trey never took his eyes off the wrecker, though. He was still watching it when I returned.

"What happened?" he said.

I took a deep breath. "It's hard to piece together with Quint and Portia throwing blame all over each other, but here's how I understand things. When the Jaguar was stolen, Portia panicked. She told Quint they had to make a run for it, and he agreed. But neither of them planned on taking the other with them. They both saw this getaway as a solo act. That's why they both came armed."

"Quint killed Jessica."

"Yes. That much is clear."

Trey had his arms folded, eyes on the wrecker. "How did Macklin get involved?"

"Macklin and Quint went to the same underground poker game."

"Of course. Macklin had a history of gambling."

"And prostitutes. Expensive hobbies. He and Quint got into similar problems with the same people, and they decided to work together and split Nick's money once Quint managed to get control of it. They came up with the idea that Macklin would smuggle Quint onto the property during his first check that day."

"How?"

"In the trunk of his cruiser. Then Quint killed Jessica, left for the production company—"

"Through the backyard and into Chastain Park."

"Yes, just like you suspected Nick had done. Portia was waiting for him there with a car."

Trey didn't react. "And Macklin?"

"He drove around until the deed was done, then went back for his second 'gut check' and pretended to catch the killer in the act. That way both he and Quint would have an alibi. And Nick wouldn't, or so Quint thought. He thought Nick was off golfing by himself. He didn't know Nick was having an affair with Addison, that she would alibi him. And nobody predicted that you'd show up too quickly for Macklin to properly stage the scene. He did a pretty good job, though, of making it look like Nick had done a bad job with it. But then he had to clock himself in the head and pretend to chase the pretend assailant, which wasn't exactly part of the plan."

"Quint admitted this?"

"No. Portia did. She's flipping on him so fast it's hard to keep up."

Trey nodded again, still not looking my way. He'd already been interviewed. I had too. The rain had lifted to reveal bright sunshine, sudden and clear. It felt suspicious somehow, too cheerful, as if someone had delivered the wrong morning. Beyond the police tape, the wrecker crew and the cops were coordinating their efforts.

"Has someone told Price?" he said.

"Yes. She said the poor burglar guy is actually relieved. He's been living under a murder warrant for four years. Now he can stop looking over his shoulder. She also said to tell you that as soon as she gets him squared away, she's finding you."

"But I have no information. The detective in charge—"

"She's not coming as a cop. She's coming as your friend."

"Oh. Right." Trey kept his eyes on the gathered crowd and the wrecker crew. "What happened with Quint and Portia? In the Ferrari?"

"Apparently, Portia tried to grab Quint's gun, he lost control of the car, and the gun went flying. He managed to get out of the car before it sank and took off running. She caught up with him at the ruins."

Trey winced at the word "sank." The cops had yelled at him a little for his overenthusiastic use of peppershot. But they understood, they'd said. "Good on ya," they'd said, ending the situation with no loss of life. I suppressed my annoyance. If I'd smothered two people in capsaicin powder ballistics, the cops would have sequestered me in a corner and lectured me until my ears bled. But Trey was still one of them. He got a pass. I didn't bother telling them that it was the car he'd been pissed off about.

The car.

The wrecking crew had it winched now and was pulling it out of the lake one painful centimeter at a time. Branches snagged on the fender, mud sucked at the tires. My cousin Billie was a mechanic, and she always said she could fix a lot of things, but a car that had been submerged was a total loss.

I examined Trey out of the corner of my eye. His eyes were a little unfocused, his mouth in a straight line. He looked perplexed more than anything. He blinked, tilted his head. Blinked again.

"Portia knew everything," he said.

"Yeah. Quint's throwing massive blame her way. She'll definitely go down as a co-conspirator. Thanks to you, they'll both be behind bars tonight. The racketeering gamerunners will be answering some hard questions. The Buckhead Burglar is working a plea deal. And Nick Talbot will finally be exonerated." I poked his shoulder. "You made all that happen."

"No. We did."

I felt a warm pleasantness spread in my chest. "Nick sends his thanks, by the way. He had a little bit of a nervous breakdown at all the news, but Addison leapt into action like a high-strung Florence Nightingale."

"Is he okay?"

"He will be. And you will be too."

He took a deep breath. "Yes. I will."

Dozens of cop cars choked the pristine resort. The ambulance had arrived hot on their heels. The paramedics wore hazmat gear to deal with Quint and Portia, rinsing them in cold water and flushing their noses and eyes with saline drips before packing them off to the ER like drowned cats.

"You're right," I said. "About not carrying a gun anymore."

"I know."

"I don't think I should either, to tell the truth." I hesitated, then kept going. "I'm angry. All the time. And it's so easy to channel that into...you understand."

"I do."

We stood very close in the rain-washed, late summer light. It felt like the first day of the turning season. There were shouts in the distance, arms waving. Slowly the winch creaked.

"Did it help you?" I said.

"Did what help?"

"Therapy."

He nodded. "It did."

I laughed a little. "It's weird. I'm not afraid of murderers with guns, but I am terrified of sitting in a room with somebody like my brother and spilling my guts. That's just..."

I shuddered. Trey almost put his arm around me, but reconsidered, perhaps to avoid cranking the emotional intensity of the moment any higher. I could feel the intention, though, in the non-accidental touch of his fingers against the small of my back. He dropped his hand to his side, and I decided that things were perfect the way they were, the two of us shoulder to shoulder, facing the same direction, fingertips brushing.

"Was that Marisa on the phone earlier?"

He nodded.

"And?"

"I'm suspended again, this time indefinitely pending psychiatric evaluation and a hearing with the board."

"Oh. I'm sorry."

He shrugged. "It's fair. Generous even. She could have fired me outright."

The car broke the surface of the water. Trey flinched as they pulled it out of the lake, moss and mud and slime dripping from the wheels. Water gushed out the open driver's side door, and I saw a fish flop in surprise and plop into the lake. I remembered my first days in that car, learning about Trey as I watched him drive. I also remembered the first time I'd driven it myself, the crystalline realization that this was his identity I held in my hands, one of the most true and vulnerable parts of him.

The understanding came to me in a rush. "You knew Marisa would find out about this case, didn't you?"

Another shrug. "Perhaps."

"Perhaps nothing. You engineered it. Completely pulled the rug out from under old Trey so that new Trey could have a clean slate."

He considered. "I'm not sure what happened. Right now I am having a hard time reconciling what I know I know with what I don't know I know."

The car caught on a submerged branch, and the fender ripped free. Trey looked nauseated. Of course he hadn't reckoned on losing the Ferrari. We watched it get hauled onto the back of the wrecker, a sad and soggy hunk of metal. Beginnings and endings, we were always moving toward one or the other. Cycles and circles.

And I realized that I was okay too. Despite the craziness and the mayhem, the crises and cross purposes. Better than okay, thriving, and so was Trey. There was very little the world could throw at us that we couldn't handle. Downright formidable, we were. Partners in every sense of the word.

And I saw the next beginning and end coming at the same time. It was a Before and After moment, like when I'd made the U-turn that had taken me back to Trey's apartment. The Tai before that moment hadn't known how to love and be loved so fiercely and completely. A new understanding blossomed, and I got lightheaded with the rightness of it.

I took a deep breath. "Trey?"

"Yes?"

"Can I tell you something?"

"Of course."

"I don't want to run a gun shop." I thought hard about the words coming out of my mouth. "I want to be a private detective."

He nodded, his eyes on the distant tragedy. "Okay. I want a new Ferrari."

I wrapped my arm around his waist and cinched him close. "Okay."

Chapter Fifty-five

The drive from Adairsville to Alpharetta was a quiet one. Trey sat silently in the passenger seat of his rental car, holding his mother's rosary in his lap. It was the one item he'd salvaged from the water-logged carcass of the F430, and he ticked off the marble beads with practiced fingers, though he offered no prayers or words of penance.

The Ferrari manager had agreed to meet us at the dealership even though it was almost closing time. He was very gracious about it, made the appropriate noises of horror and sympathy at our story of the previous car's demise.

"Would you like to come into the office?" he said. "We can begin the paperwork there."

I shook my head. "No. He needs to get in a car right now."

"Now?"

"Yes. Right now."

The manager was a shade nonplussed. "But last time Mr. Seaver had very specific requirements."

"Yes, but now is different." I patted his shoulder. "Go ahead and get the financing in order. We'll be back in a second."

I watched while Trey made the rounds of the showroom like a visitor to some automotive petting zoo. Several of the display models were fresh from the factory. Others were secondhand, returned by unsuccessful drug dealers and suddenly broke dot-com millionaires. They all had one thing in common—six-figure price tags.

In a showroom of canary yellows and flame reds, Trey stood next to the only black car available, a California T. I joined him beside it. Just like his previous vehicle, it had a black-on-black interior with buttery, hand-stitched leather and polished chrome.

But Trey was shaking his head. "It won't work."

"Why not?"

"It's a convertible. I need a coupe."

I started to argue, then realized that would be pointless. He was still looking backward. He needed to be looking forward.

I opened the driver's side door. "Get in."

"I—"

"Just do it."

He complied, slipping the rosary beads into his pocket. I shut the door behind him and got in on the other side. The T felt friendlier than his old car, still low to the ground and styled for speed, but lighter, more playful than the deadly serious F430.

I read from the tag. "It's got a V8 twin turbo engine. Five-sixty horsepower with a top speed of one-ninety-six. Double clutch gearbox. And look! A fuel economy mode!"

He wrapped his fingers around the steering wheel. I could feel him simultaneously quickening and shutting down, excited and then restrained. He was trying to remember who he was. The Trey of danger zones and full throttle? Or the Trey of speed limits and stop signs?

He shook his head. "It doesn't feel safe."

"It's not. But you don't need safe anymore." I pointed at the button on the console. "Put the top down."

He shook his head more emphatically.

I turned to face him. "Listen to me. The rest of the stuff in your life, the black and white wardrobe, the apartment? Those are containers. Interesting, yes, and useful, but you can let them go whenever you feel like it. This car, though? This car is you, boyfriend, pure you." I leaned closer. "Trust me. This car has been waiting for you its whole life."

He ran his hand along the dash. "You've already opened the envelope."

I caught my breath. To an eavesdropper, that comment would have been a non sequitur.

"Yes," I said. "The second it came."

"So you know."

"I've always known. I wasn't waiting on the test results. I was waiting until I was ready to deal with them."

"And are you?"

The front door opened, and the sounds of the city hustled inside the showroom. And then the door shut, and we were once again in our sanctum, separate and air conditioned and orderly. But the outside was still there, surging and chaotic. One big dice game.

"Yes," I said. "As of this very second, I am dealing with the fact that I am the daughter of Beauregard Forrest Boone. And I am ready to find out exactly how that unthinkable thing happened."

Trey watched me say the words. "Okay."

He extended his hand toward the button. His finger hovered there. And it was like our first time, the tender skin underneath his armor, which he'd taken off for me piece by piece. He was unarmored now, as open as I'd ever seen him. I placed my own hand lightly on top of his, and we pushed the button together.

A soft whirring began as the roof opened above us, folding behind like origami, and Trey entangled his fingers with mine. Fresh sunshine spilled into the car, lemonade sweet, and the showroom ceiling came into view, with its champagne-colored lights and soft gold trim.

Trey tilted his head back and looked up. I let my head fall back too, resting it on his shoulder. All I could see was the showroom ceiling, that arching gilded boundary. And it was safe, that ceiling. But beyond it lay the whole of the expanding universe.

Author's Note

Tai and Trey's Atlanta is a place of bustle and leisure, nature and steel, tradition and edge, just like the real Atlanta. These two Atlantas co-exist easily in my imagination, but any native to the area will recognize some differences between my fictional version and the actual one (the most obvious being that in Trey and Tai's Atlanta, nobody spends nearly enough time waiting in traffic).

Tai's gun shop resides in my imagination; the city of Kennesaw is real, however. You'll find it slightly northwest of Atlanta, and it really does have a city ordinance requiring every head of household to maintain a firearm and ammunition. It also has a store specializing in Confederate memorabilia—Wildman's Civil War Surplus (although any resemblance between Tai's shop and this one is purely coincidental).

Trey's Buckhead neighborhood also exists, and includes high rise condominium buildings like his, chic bungalows like Gabriella's, and ultra-contemporary mansions like the Talbots'. Beardsley Gardens is a stand-in for the popular Barnsley Gardens; I tampered with enough of the resort's geography that I thought it best to give my imaginary construct a new name, though you will find the quaint English cottages and the ruins of the Italianate villa almost exactly as I described them. Most of the other places I mention—Little Five Points, Westview, Chastain Park, Adairsville, and the Kennesaw Mountain Battlefield National Park—are real, as are the histories and complicated geographies that Tai shares.

The film industry is alive and well in the Peach State—as of this writing, more feature films were made in Georgia than any other place in the world, including California (sorry, Hollywood!). Celebrity spottings are routine in the Atlanta area, as are the yellow directional markers that indicate base camps and on-location sets.

If you're interested in learning more about the research that went into this book, you can check out my *Necessary Ends* Pinterest board, plus my other series boards: *Civil War*—devoted to the War Between the States, especially Georgia's part in it; *Criminal Behavior*, which explores villains and scams and nefarious wrongdoings, *Trey and Tai's Accessories*, a collection of my protagonists' clothing, automobiles, and weaponry; and *Trey and Tai's Atlanta*, which includes the metro Atlanta landmarks that have cameo appearances in the series. You can find these, and my other writerly and readerly boards, at *www.pinterest.com/tinawh*.